For Nathan.
When we were too young to know better
we hitched our wagon to each other's star.
I always teasingly told you
that I modeled my villains after you.
But babe, you are
always my hero.

D0037058

Prologue

From the Journal of Jack Dodger

When I was five years old, my mum sold me. I never held it against her; even at such a tender age I understood that hunger and fear could make a person do things he thought he'd never do. In my new circumstance, I quickly learned the devil wore gentlemen's clothing, and I ran away, convinced I'd be better off on the streets than in an elegant house where fancy gents pretended respectability.

I was not long on my own when I fell in with a notorious den of child thieves, managed by a crafty old blighter who went by the name of Feagan. Under his tutelage I learned anything could be stolen—given the proper preparation. My own skills, my determination to succeed and thus to survive, were unmatched, and I soon rose in his esteem. He affectionately called me Dodger, and by the time I was eight, I found myself spending the better part of my evenings sitting in front of a coal fire with Feagan, smoking my clay pipe, drinking gin, and soaking in the rare bits of wisdom he shared with only a respected few.

But my palm constantly itched to hold more coins. One day a proper-looking gent offered me sixpence to lure a highborn family of three into an alley. I did it with false tears and the claim that my mum was dying. The man and his wife were promptly killed, but the boy escaped. Terrified by what I'd been party to, I was quick to chase after the lad, fearing the same fate as had befallen his parents awaited us. I followed him to another alley, where he collapsed, huddled, and cried. We didn't have time for such nonsense. To my relief, he didn't recognize me. The shock of it all, I supposed. I mucked up his clothes, his person, and convinced him I possessed the wherewithal to save him.

The boy's name was Lucian, but that sounded too swell, so I introduced him as Luke. Feagan handed me threepence for bringing in a new recruit. Not a bad tally for the day, even if it meant I didn't sleep well that night.

To my everlasting irritation, although I was only two years older, I felt responsible for the lad. When he was caught stealing, I stupidly thought to rescue him. We spent three months in prison. The prison brand that marked us served to strengthen our friendship, and we became inseparable.

Until the night he killed a man.

He was fourteen, awaiting trial, when the Earl of Claybourne declared Luke was his long-lost grandson. He was released into the old gent's care. Luke's good fortune quickly became mine. The old gent took me in as well. We were constantly at odds. He worked diligently to transform me into a gentleman, but I preferred to remain a scoundrel. It seemed a more honest way to go.

When I was nineteen, a solicitor informed me that I had an anonymous benefactor who had grand expectations where I was concerned and wished to bestow upon me ten thousand pounds so my future might be assured. I never questioned who my benefactor was, because I had no doubt he was Luke's grandfather—seeking to rid himself of me without disappointing his grandson. I had lived on the streets long enough to know money was to be made investing in vice. I purchased a building and transformed it into an exclusive gentlemen's club.

And so it was that I became a man of means, far exceeding what I was certain my benefactor—or anyone else, for that matter—had expected of me. But no matter how much money I earned, it was never enough. I was always hungry for the next coin. I would do anything, anything at all, to possess it.

Chapter 1

London
1851

The devil had come to call. Sitting beside him in her library, Olivia Stanford, the Duchess of Lovingdon, didn't know whether to be appalled or fascinated. He was an interesting creature, and while she'd heard many of the sordid tales regarding him, she'd never actually set eyes on him before that night.

His black, unruly hair, curling teasingly across his broad shoulders, spoke of a desire to rebel against societal constraints. The harsh lines of his face had been carved by a life of decadence, misbehavior, and excess. Yet, he was beautiful in a rugged sort of way, like the manner in which a jagged coastline at dawn could steal one's breath with its magnificence.

She lowered her gaze from a profile that had held her enthralled from the moment she'd walked into her library and met the deliciously wicked Jack Dodger.

His gambling den provided entertainment for many men of the aristocracy. Sisters, wives, mothers heard slurred references to the debauchery that occurred within Jack Dodger's domain when their brothers, husbands, sons returned home in the early hours, three sheets in the wind. The women, of course, discreetly exchanged stories over tea, and so Dodger's reputation, as well as that of his establishment, had grown among proper ladies who weren't supposed to know about such improper things. Women detested his existence and the opportunity he provided for the men in their lives to stray from all that was good and respectable, yet none could deny their ceaseless fascination with a man so devoted to sin.

Sitting near him, Olivia became increasingly aware of the raw sexuality emanating from him. She imagined women followed him into his bedchamber without a single word being uttered. She could smell the tobacco and whiskey fragrance that permeated him and, to her everlasting shame, found herself relishing the darkly masculine scent. Everything about him spoke of forbidden indulgences.

He was truly the work of the devil.

He even carried the devil's mark. The brand was clearly visible on the inside of his right thumb, because he didn't possess the good manners to wear gloves and his long fingers were splayed across the arm of the chair. While marking criminals was no longer a practice, Olivia knew what the *T* burned into his flesh signified: he'd spent time in prison for thievery. She had little tolerance for those who took what did not rightfully belong to them.

In spite of his questionable past and occupation, she could not fault the quality of his attire. It had obviously been sewn by the finest tailor in London, but the red brocade waistcoat beneath his black jacket was entirely inappropriate for this somber occasion: the reading of her late husband's will.

Why Lovingdon had insisted the notorious Jack Dodger be in attendance was beyond the pale. How did he even know the blackguard? As far as she knew he'd never visited Dodger's Drawing Room. However, her brother, the late Duke of Avendale, had frequented it quite often, providing her with the enviable opportunity to add greatly to the repertoire of scandalous tales circulated amongst the ladies.

But Lovingdon had been as pious as they came. The man hadn't even kept liquor in the house, and to her knowledge, wine had never touched his lips. She knew the same could not be said of Jack Dodger's. He had the fullest set of lips she'd ever seen on a man, a dark, dark red, as though they'd been soaked in fine wine, and she had little doubt they were accustomed to tasting all pleasures. His mouth was designed to lure the most virtuous of women toward forbidden passion. Why else would she find herself inappropriately wondering what it might be like to have him kiss her? She'd long ago stopped pondering the delight of kisses—perhaps because Lovingdon had been so dead-set against them. Yet there she was, imagining those lips playing over hers, enticing her in ways that Lovingdon never had.

Again she wondered why he had wanted Jack Dodger at the reading of his will.

Yet Mr. Beckwith, the duke's solicitor, positioning his papers at the desk across from her, had insisted it was not only so, but that Olivia was to be in attendance as well. So there she was, as always, honoring her responsibilities, no matter how distasteful they might be. From the moment she was born, a devotion to duty had governed her life. It was the reason that, at nineteen, she'd married a man more than twenty-five years her senior—because her father had arranged the marriage, and a respectful daughter did not go against her father's wishes, regardless of her own passionate yearnings.

Lovingdon had been honest from the beginning. Getting up in years, he was in dire need of an heir, and while marriage to him had not been all she'd hoped for, it was not as bad as it might have been. She'd earned his respect and had supreme reign over his household. And he'd given her a precious son, even if he'd been unable to give her his heart.

She was quite confident that Henry, as the legitimate heir, would inherit everything of importance. She had hopes the will would stipulate that the London residence was to become the dower house, because she loved it so. But it was rather grand, and usually the dower house was a smaller residence. Lovingdon, however, had never purchased any other London homes. If this residence was not left to her, then the decision regarding where she would reside in later years would rest with her son—when he was old enough to care about such things. But at present he was five and cared only that she read him a story before he went to sleep.

The solicitor finally folded his hands on top of the papers and lifted his gaze to his audience of two. His dark hair was peppered with silver. His blue eyes seemed larger because of his spectacles, and he gave the impression they allowed him to see a great deal more than the average man. "Mr. Dodger, I want to thank you for finding time in your busy schedule to be with us this evening," he said solemnly, as befit the occasion.

"Let's get on with it, shall we? I've a business to get back to." Jack Dodger's voice was rough, as though he spent a good deal of his time screaming until his throat was raw. Yet, it also reverberated with a pleasing quality Olivia couldn't quite explain. She could imagine him whispering near a lady's ear, tempting her toward disgraceful behavior.

"Yes, of course," Mr. Beckwith said. He picked up a long sheaf of parchment. "The will contains quite a bit of legal terminology which, with your permission, I shall not bother to read."

"Just tell me why the bloody hell I'm here, so I can go."

Olivia gasped. Jack Dodger gave her a disdainful look, the first time he'd bothered to give her any attention at all since they'd been introduced and taken their seats.

"Good God, don't look so appalled."

Considering the manner in which he was suddenly studying her, Olivia had a strange desire to check her buttons and make certain they were all properly done up. "I must insist vulgar language not be used in my home. I can't remain if you're going to be blasphemous."

"I don't give a damn if you remain or not."

"Mr. Dodger," Mr. Beckwith interrupted emphatically, an edge to his voice indicating he, too, might have reservations about the present company, "the duke insisted you both be in attendance. I shall get to the matter at hand, posthaste, before your patience deteriorates any further." He cleared his throat and began to read: "I, Sidney Augustus Stanford, Duke of Lovingdon, Marquess of Ashleigh, and Earl of Wyndmere, being of sound mind and body, do bequeath to my legitimate son and heir to my titles, Henry Sidney Stanford, all my entailed properties, as well as the assets and income derived from them."

Olivia nodded with satisfaction. She'd expected as much. It was only a bit of formality to state so in the will.

"To my devoted wife, Olivia Grace Stanford, Duchess of Lovingdon, mother of my heir—"

Blinking back the tears stinging her eyes, she wished Jack Dodger wasn't present to witness this portion of the reading. Her husband's last words regarding her were private and personal.

"—I bequeath a trust that if properly managed should provide her with two thousand pounds per annum as long as she lives. To Mr. Jack Dodger—"

Olivia barely had time to acknowledge the disappointment he'd not left her the residence, before her attention was snagged by the fact that at long last, the reason for the ridiculous summons of Jack Dodger would come to light.

"—I bequeath the remainder of my worldly assets, save one item, on the condition he serve as guardian and protector of my heir until the child reaches his majority or my widow marries and her husband assumes the role. When either of the stated conditions are met, Mr. Dodger will receive the final item—its value immeasurable."

From a seemingly great distance, Olivia became aware of a rushing sound between her ears, like the

beating wings of a thousand ravens fleeing the tower
of London and signaling Great Britain's downfall. She
was vaguely aware of paper crackling, as Mr. Beckwith
laid down the will. She couldn't have possibly heard
correctly. Her temples had begun to throb the moment
her husband had tumbled down the stairs and taken
a mortal blow to the head. The grief she was experiencing at the unexpected loss was playing havoc with
her mind, causing words to jumble and lose their true
meaning. As she tried to comprehend how that could
be, how she could force them back into signifying
what they were supposed to, Mr. Beckwith picked up a
black leather-bound book and extended it toward Jack
Dodger. "This ledger contains a listing of all the non-
entailed assets which will become—"

While Olivia watched in stunned horror, Jack Dodger
snatched the book from Mr. Beckwith's grasp before
he'd finished speaking, opened it, and began quickly
scouring the pages, each turn of the page a rasp against
her brittle nerves. Mr. Beckwith lifted another ledger
and extended it toward Olivia. "For your review, a listing of the entailed assets which go to your son."

Olivia shook her head. "I must beg your forgiveness,
but I don't quite understand the meaning of all this."

"From the moment the titles passed to him, your
husband kept precise records indicating which properties and assets were part of the entailments—"

"No, no. I'm referring to the will; you misread it. You
indicated that Mr. Dodger is to serve as guardian."

"Yes, that was the duke's wish."

"No, Henry is *my* son. *I* am his guardian."

"The law recognizes only the father as guardian. Upon

the father's death, if the child has not yet obtained the age of one and twenty, the father must appoint the guardian in his will." With no emotion whatsoever expressed, Mr. Beckwith sounded as though he were reading from a parliamentary document. "I'm sorry, Your Grace, but your husband's decision cannot be challenged."

"Not be challenged?" Olivia came to her feet in such a rush that she almost lost her balance. Mr. Beckwith also rose, while Jack Dodger remained seated, hungrily devouring the contents of the ledger. Obviously the man hadn't a clue regarding proper behavior when in the presence of a lady, but then she suspected the women who normally provided him with company would hardly be considered ladies. "Have you lost your mind? Somehow you managed to misunderstand my husband's intent. He can't possibly have meant to let this scoundrel—"

"It says here this residence and everything within it is mine," Jack Dodger suddenly announced, and Olivia's composure came almost completely unhinged. Not this residence, not the one place she had worked so hard to make a home.

Jack Dodger unfolded his long, lean body, dropped the ledger on the desk with a loud thump, and leaned ominously toward Mr. Beckwith. "Is this some sort of prank?"

Mr. Beckwith, to his credit, stood valiant against the devil's advance. "I assure you, Mr. Dodger, this is no prank."

"You're telling me a man I barely knew is leaving me" —he jabbed the ledger with a blunt-tipped finger— "all of this?"

"You knew my husband?" Olivia asked, stunned by the revelation.

He had the audacity to wave his hand at her as though she were insignificant, to be dismissed with no more thought than one might give a beggar pleading for coins.

"Yes, Mr. Dodger, it appears that is in fact the case," Mr. Beckwith said.

"And what of his debts?" he asked caustically. "I suppose I inherit them as well."

"There are no debts. The duke didn't believe in credit. He paid as he went."

That seemed to give Mr. Dodger pause, before he splayed his long, slender fingers over the ledger. "And the final item is more valuable than all of this?"

"As indicated in the will, its value cannot be measured."

"Do you know what it is?"

"I do. It's to remain in my possession until such time as it's to be handed over."

"He trusted you with something of immeasurable worth?"

"He trusted me with everything, Mr. Dodger."

Mr. Dodger seemed to consider that. "An item the value of which cannot be measured could be worth nothing."

"If I had to measure its worth, I would declare it the most valuable item the duke ever had the pleasure to possess."

"Bloody hell," Mr. Dodger said quietly in that raspy voice he possessed. "I need a drink."

In spite of the ludicrousness of the entire situation, Olivia felt all her appropriate upbringing and her need to be the perfect hostess shoot to the fore. "Shall I have a servant bring you a cup of tea? Or some lemonade perhaps?"

Mr. Dodger glared at her with eyes as black as his unredeemed soul. "I was thinking whiskey, gin, rum. All three if you have them."

"We don't keep spirits in the residence," Olivia said sharply, her indignation suddenly very much alive.

"Of course you don't."

"I don't appreciate your tone, sir."

"As though I give a damn what you appreciate."

Oh, the man was infuriating. Then he did the strangest thing. He slowly prowled the room, hungrily glancing around as if about to pluck and tuck everything into his pockets. Although now he no longer had a need to pilfer anything. It had all been handed to him on a silver platter.

After several long moments, he returned to the desk and stared intently at Mr. Beckwith. "*Everything within this residence is mine?*"

"Everything," Mr. Beckwith said somberly, as though he felt the weight of that single word on Olivia's heart. "On the condition that you—"

"Yes, yes, serve as the heir's guardian. Unlike the duchess, I have no difficulty comprehending the simplest of terms when they're laid out for me."

She couldn't let the insult pass, but for the life of her, she could think of no retort that might effectively put him in his place. She did feel like a dimwit. How could Lovingdon do this to her? More important—do this to their son? Did he care not at all what sort of man he would become?

Jack Dodger turned around slowly, looking at everything once more, as though he were feasting his eyes on a magnificent creation. "Was the duke a raving lunatic?"

The crack of Olivia's palm hitting Jack Dodger's cheek echoed through the room. Since she'd never in her life struck anyone, she hadn't realized how much her palm would sting. It took everything within her not to yelp or give any indication that she'd probably hurt herself more than she'd harmed him. "My husband was only recently laid to rest and you speak of him with such disrespect. How dare you, sir!"

Jack Dodger presented her with a slow, calculating smile that caused her stomach to plummet clear down to her toes. "The duchess has spunk. Who'd have thought?"

She wanted to toss him out of the house, back into the streets from whence he'd come. She turned to Mr. Beckwith. "His language is vulgar, his manners are atrocious. I simply will not allow this man to be responsible for the upbringing of my son."

"That's easy enough to remedy, Duchess," Jack Dodger drawled. "Find yourself another husband."

"It seems to have failed your notice that I'm in mourning. I can't accept suitors."

"Then you don't want me out of your life badly enough, Duchess. Trust me. There isn't anything a person won't do if he wants something badly enough."

Every time the word *Duchess* slithered mockingly off his tongue, the fine hairs on the nape of her neck prickled and her palm itched to slap him again. Before she followed through on the barbaric urge, she forced herself to address the solicitor. "Mr. Beckwith—"

"I'm sorry, Your Grace, but there is no prospect for negotiation on this matter if Mr. Dodger agrees to serve as guardian."

"Can you explain to me my husband's thinking?"

"I have served the duke for many years, Your Grace. It has never been my place to question his decisions. He seldom revealed his reasoning, and I cannot know everything that influenced him, but I'm certain in this matter he did what he deemed best."

If she'd not been raised to be a lady, she would shriek at the unfairness of it all.

"And if I don't agree to the guardianship part?" Mr. Dodger asked.

A momentary spark of relief gave Olivia renewed hope that this hellish nightmare would come to a satisfactory end. Apparently the man had the good sense to have misgivings about accepting the responsibilities thrust upon him.

"The first will shall be nullified and a second shall come into play," Mr. Beckwith said.

Olivia dared not ask, but she had to know. It seemed unlikely her husband could have made a worse choice than Jack Dodger, but if he was her husband's first who would serve as his second? The devil himself? "Who is appointed as my son's guardian in that will?"

"I am not at liberty to say," Mr. Beckwith stated calmly. "Mr. Dodger's decision must be made without any influence."

"Without any influence? What do you call giving him *everything*? If that's not influence, I daresay I don't know what is."

"I merely meant that your husband did not wish

who would serve as guardian to influence Mr. Dodger's decision."

"But surely it is someone more appropriate, someone familiar with the strictures of society. What does Mr. Dodger know of the nobility, our duties and responsibilities?"

"I know a good deal, Duchess," Mr. Dodger said. "After all, I am a longtime friend of the Earl of Claybourne."

She spun around at the mention of Lucian Langdon. "Another criminal? A man who committed murder? How in God's name is that supposed to reassure me? You can't possibly believe you are qualified to guide my son along the proper path to manhood."

"The proper path is often determined by where you're standing."

"What the devil does that mean? Yours is a world of decadence, Mr. Dodger. You—"

The words abruptly died in her throat. He was suddenly near, so very near, a heat burning in his eyes that could only have been ignited within the depths of hell, a heat that caused unwanted warmth to swirl through her core, that made her knees weaken, her palms dampen, and her mouth go dry.

"You should visit sometime," he said darkly, his warm, whiskey-scented breath wafting over her cheek.

"Pardon?"

"Visit my world of depravity. I would do all in my power to welcome you properly. You might even find it to your liking."

His voice was as powerful as a caress, stirring her to imagine that his welcome would involve his mouth, his hands—

It was evident in his eyes, the wicked things he would do to her, things she'd never imagined with Lovingdon. She should slap him again, she knew she should, but all she seemed capable of doing was trembling with something akin to . . . God help her . . . Was she feeling desire? It wasn't possible. It was only that it had been so very long since she'd felt a man's touch. Once he had his heir, Lovingdon had made it plain he didn't hold with the notion a spare was needed. One son was all he required. In that regard, she and Lovingdon had been well matched. They both put duty above all else. Regretfully, she'd come to discover that duty was a lonely taskmaster.

"Have you ever sinned, Duchess?" Jack Dodger asked in that strangely rough voice that hinted at passion barely tethered.

Only in my dreams hovered on the tip of her tongue. She wondered if Jack Dodger had fulfilled other women's fantasies. She had no doubt he was fully capable—

A harsh clearing of a throat caused them both to jump. She saw irritation flash across Jack Dodger's face as he moved back and slid his uncompromising gaze toward Mr. Beckwith. For a heartbeat, it appeared the solicitor was fighting not to retreat. He cleared his throat again, as though his courage resided in the deep rumble. "I believe, Mr. Dodger, your behavior toward the duchess is not at all warranted and certainly not what the duke envisioned when he named you in his will."

"I didn't think you knew what he *envisioned*."

"I know he respected his wife, sir, and he would be very disappointed if you didn't do the same."

"The man is dead. I suspect he's not likely to be disappointed in anything anymore."

"You, sir, are despicable," Olivia snapped before Mr. Beckwith could give him a proper tongue-lashing. "Have you no respect for my late husband?"

He turned toward her and she suddenly wished she'd kept silent. She truly didn't want to spar with him. She couldn't determine how to attain the high ground. Where he was concerned, she suspected it was impossible. He would always somehow manage to drag those around him into the gutter with him.

"I respect only those who have earned my respect. And they are few in number."

"I can well imagine what a person must do in order to earn your respect."

Some unidentifiable emotion—remorse?—shifted in his eyes. "Actually, Duchess, I suspect you can't." He turned on his heel and strode toward the door.

Dare she hope he was taking his leave, and in so doing, turning his back on this ridiculous first will?

"Where are you going?" Olivia called out.

"I want to have a look around, determine what all I'll gain by suffering through your presence." He stormed from the room without a backward glance.

With a gasp of indignation, Olivia hurried after him. This house was hers—*hers*—until he agreed to the terms of the will. Whatever she could do to dissuade him from consenting, she would do. She'd show him who was willing to do anything.

Although she did have to give him credit for being correct about one thing: somehow, without her noticing, her husband had gone stark, raving mad.

* * *

Considering Mr. Dodger's reputation, Charles Beckwith was inclined to follow the couple, but the duke had left specific instructions that he was not to interfere as they settled their differences. Only a fool would have expected the duchess to serenely accept so ludicrous a choice for guardian, and the duke had not been known for being a fool.

With a sigh, Beckwith leaned back in his chair to await their return and began to mentally prepare himself for the next round with Jack Dodger. He knew it had the potential to be challenging. He had to carry out the duke's wishes without compromising his own integrity.

He was not in the habit of questioning those who paid so handsomely for his services, but he did wonder if the duke had truly understood the ramifications of his actions. To Charles Beckwith, they seemed to serve but one purpose: to pave the way for disaster.

Chapter 2

I gnoring the widow following at a rapid clip, Jack Dodger strode briskly through the hallways and rooms, searching for anything familiar, anything that might signal he'd been in this residence before. He'd learned long ago nothing came easy, and this entire situation seemed far too easy. Well, except for dealing with the widow. She was the very definition of the type of woman he avoided at all costs. Judging him through a kaleidoscope of righteous indignation, she was so damned passionate about his being so damned unworthy. It didn't matter that she was right. Her belief in his unsuitability irritated the devil out of him, and he preferred holding the devil close. It was the only way to ensure he was never again taken advantage of, never again hurt, never again left to live with regrets.

The duchess had certainly not taken well to the news delivered by the solicitor. The fire of anger burning in her eyes had hit him like a punch to the gut, and he'd wanted to nurture it into a blaze of passion—

Damnation.

He knew better than to lash out at women, knew better than to reveal anything at all about his thoughts or feelings. Somehow the widow had forced him to throw caution to the wind. He'd begun to lose the upper hand in this game of . . . what? What in God's name was going on here?

So he'd stormed from the room because he'd learned that sometimes retreat could lead to victory. Sometimes effective strategy required a restocking of the arsenal or a bit of breathing room so a man could think clearly and make sense of things.

What sort of lunatic was Lovingdon to appoint Jack guardian of anything? The nobles were so protective of their heirs. It was ludicrous to place the lad in Jack's keeping. Still, it angered him that the widow was so appalled by the notion. He should accept the terms of the will simply to irritate her further. But he'd never been one to base his decisions on immediate reactions. He'd always thought out his strategy, always looked at things from every angle. Although in this situation the angle of inheritance was looming enticingly large and threatening to overshadow his common sense. While Jack had accumulated quite a bit of wealth over the years, his coffers weren't yet to the point that he wanted to spend his money on a palace such as this. It was monstrously huge and overflowing with statuettes, figurines, artwork, handsome handcrafted furniture, and everything else imaginable.

In his mind, he heard Feagan cackling. "Ye finally made it, boy. A fancy place in St. James. Who'd a thought?"

Certainly not Jack.

He had a practiced eye when it came to identifying valuables and the good duke had accumulated a fortune's worth. It was also evident that the family, from the first duke to the last, thought highly of themselves. Why else have all the portraits painted of various stages in their lives, from birth to old age? God, the nobility was an amazing lot—to think anyone would care what they looked like. On the other hand, judging by the number of portraits hanging on the walls throughout, someone obviously did care. Maybe he'd sell them to the heir for a pretty penny.

As though reading his thoughts, the duchess said, "I'm certain when Mr. Beckwith said 'everything' he didn't mean *every*thing. The portraits are obviously part of the entailment."

"How did you come to that conclusion, Duchess?"

"They are portraits of the dukes and their families, my son's ancestors. There can be no doubt they are part of his inheritance."

"We'll see." She made a reasonable argument, but he planned to study the ledger more closely, to memorize and account for every item. He'd not let her take anything that had been designated as his—not without paying a fair price for it. He had no intention of taking advantage of her, but neither was it in his nature to be charitable.

"I wonder what funds were used to purchase your clothing," he murmured.

"I beg your pardon?"

He came to a stop outside the third dining room he'd passed, and she almost rammed into him. Her fragrance did, teasing his nostrils now just as it had in the library. Sitting there, he'd wanted to lean toward her and inhale it more fully. Her scent was a subtle lavender, not the cloyingly harsh musk that prostitutes used to cover the odor of their business and other men.

Her face was set in a worried frown that drew her brows together over unusual amber eyes. From the start, their shade—almost gold, just like the color of the coins he favored—had caught his attention.

The top of the widow's head barely came to his shoulder. She was terribly young for a widow. She had to have been a child when the duke married her. With their difference in age, he would have been an old man to her. Had she loved him? Or had she simply wanted the title and everything that came with it?

"I was just wondering if your clothing was part of the entailment," he drawled.

Anger flashed over her features. "My clothing, sir, is mine. You'll not take it from me."

"Don't challenge me, Duchess, or I might be tempted to prove I could remove those widow's weeds before you could stammer an objection."

"Oh, you blackguard."

Turning away from her, he tried not to take delight in pricking her temper. Not very gentlemanly on his part, but then he'd never claimed to be a gentleman. He had yet to meet one who wasn't a hypocrite. Better to admit to being a scoundrel, more honesty in that. He didn't pretend to be what he wasn't.

Impatient, he headed back the way he'd come. He had to give the duke credit: he'd spent his money wisely.

Beneath his breath, he cursed a man he'd barely known, a man who had obviously judged Jack very well. Everything Jack saw, he wanted. He wanted to look at it and know that he owned it. He wanted to tear down the brick walls, replace them with glass, and let the world catch a glimpse of what Jack Dodger possessed. He wanted to gloat. He, the son of a whore, had not been trampled down by society. He'd risen above his beginnings. He'd conquered London.

By God, that was how it felt, walking through these magnificent hallways with their gilded trim and their painted ceilings. It could all be his for a very small price.

How much trouble could it be to serve as guardian of one boy? Of course, the real question was: how irritating would it be to deal with the merry widow? She was the type of woman he abhorred. Self-righteous, judgmental, thinking she was so much better than others. He'd like nothing more than to take her down a peg or two. Maybe that was the reason he'd brought up the subject of her clothing—certainly not because he'd been considering what it might be like to divest her of it.

Her black dress had far too many buttons to be of interest to him. They ran from waist to chin, from wrist to elbow. He imagined when she was out of mourning her clothes were just as boring. She struck him as someone who would think temptation ultimately led to hell, and that path was not to be traveled at any cost. Her dull brown hair was pinned up, a widow's cap covering most of it, leaving him to wonder how long it might be. Then he cursed himself for wondering anything at all about her personal intimacies.

She was a duchess, probably related to the queen in some form or fashion. Weren't they all? They certainly acted like they were. Even in his club, on occasion, they tried to order him about—but he'd created a world where he was king, where his word was law. They paid a yearly stipend to be admitted because he provided entertainment and never judged them for indulging. Unlike the woman following behind him. He'd seen the judgment in her eyes the moment they'd been introduced, the conviction he was beneath her. He'd felt her gaze remain on him after they'd taken their seats, had been keenly aware of her studying him as though he were some curiosity that should be on display at the Great Exhibition. He'd deliberately avoided looking at her, instead concentrating on studying the room while the solicitor had taken his time preparing things.

Jack emerged from a grand hallway into the foyer. Crossing quickly, he started up the black marble stairs.

"Where are you going?" she asked from behind him.

"I told you, Duchess, I want to see everything."

"But only bedchambers are up there."

"To a man such as me, as I'm sure you might have guessed, no room is more important."

He fought not to grin as he heard her growl behind him. God, whatever had the duke seen in her? From what he'd been able to deduce, she didn't know the meaning of humor. She was as rigid as a fireplace poker. Although he did have to admire her valiant fight to retain what she considered hers. A willowy wisp of a woman, she'd certainly turned into a lioness with the thought of her cub being turned over to Jack's care. If his own mother had only been so inclined, his youth might have been less harsh.

At the top of the stairs, he turned to his left and jerked open the first door he came to. He strode into the room and his gaze fell on the massive four-poster bed. The canopy was covered in heavy purple velvet. He heard the duchess breathing harshly as she came to a stop behind him, and he wondered briefly if she'd gasped for breath in that richly appointed bed. He shook his head to clear it of its wandering thoughts. What did he care if she'd found satisfaction there?

"The duke's bedchamber?" he asked, surprised by the hoarseness of his voice.

"Yes."

A book rested on the bedside table, a ribbon sticking out of it as though the duke had expected to return to it. It made Jack uncomfortable to think about that. He'd barely known the man, certainly not well enough to truly mourn his passing, and yet sorrow nudged him. He wondered what else the duke may have left unfinished.

Shaking off his morose musings, he glanced to the side, toward another closed door, beyond the sitting area. "And is yours through there?"

He heard her swallow. "Yes."

So the duke kept her near. Jack didn't know why that knowledge bothered him, but it did. He faced her. "What is it with the aristocracy and this insane notion they have that husband and wife should sleep in separate bedchambers?"

He wasn't certain he'd ever seen a woman as pale as she was, but suddenly a rose hue blossomed over her cheeks, and he found himself wondering if that blush had visited her in the duke's bed. Why did he keep having visions of her in that blasted bed?

"I suppose they do it because they can," he said laconically, not really expecting her to answer. She probably went to bed covered head to toe in something resembling a shroud. He took a step toward the sitting area—

"Please don't go into my bedchamber," she ordered softly.

The faintness of her voice shimmied through him, disconcerting him. All night she'd been demanding, angry, hurt, and upset. It seemed at odds she would choose now to be submissive. Perhaps she'd deduced that abrasiveness didn't influence his temper. Hitching up a corner of his mouth, he turned back toward her. "What's the matter, Duchess? Have all sorts of machines designed to give you sexual pleasure hidden away in there?"

"I don't know what you're on about."

He studied her for a moment, her black attire, the proper way she held herself . . . "Sadly, you probably don't."

Innocence had never appealed to him. He walked out of the room and continued down the long hallway.

"All the bedchambers are the same," she said from behind him. "I don't see why you need to—"

He reached for another door.

"I forbid you to go into that room," she stated emphatically.

Looking over his shoulder, he winked at her. "Never forbid me, Duchess. It'll only make me do it."

He barged into the room. A young brown-haired, brown-eyed woman, obviously a servant, gasped and came out of the chair she was sitting in beside the bed. A young boy abruptly sat up, the covers falling to his waist, his blond hair tousled, his golden eyes wide.

The duchess brushed past Jack, sat on the bed, and took the boy protectively into her arms. It irritated the devil out of Jack that she assumed the boy needed protecting from him, that she expected him to hurt the lad.

"The heir?" Jack asked flatly.

The duchess nodded. "Yes."

"Henry, right?"

"Yes."

"How old are you, lad?"

"He's five," the duchess said.

"Is he mute?"

"No, of course not."

"Then why didn't you let him speak? I asked the question of him."

"You're terrifying him."

"Am I?" He studied the boy. He was as slightly built as his mother, as pale. His eyes were huge and round, but Jack saw more curiosity within them than fear. "Are you afraid of me, lad?"

The boy peered up at his mother.

"Don't look to your mother for the answer, lad. Look to yourself."

"Do not take that tone with him," the duchess commanded. "You are not yet his guardian."

Jack didn't know whether to envy the boy for the protectiveness of his mother—a protectiveness he wished his own mother had bestowed on him—or to pity him because she was raising him to be a milksop. By the age of six, Jack could survive the streets by cunning, cleverness, and nimble fingers. He'd not been afraid to take chances. He'd learned how to dodge those who wanted to catch him. He'd been quick on his feet, but even quicker with his mind.

"Skill will get ye only so far, boy, but thinkin' will be wot keeps ye alive," Feagan had told him.

Learning the tricks of the trade had given him confidence, which had led to success, which had made him daring and fearless. He'd gotten where he was because he'd survived. He wasn't convinced this lad could wipe his own nose. Was that the reason the duke was turning his care over to Jack?

Jack had first met Lovingdon on a spring day in the Earl of Claybourne's garden. Jack had been left with the impression that the duke was a sad man. Years later, the duke had visited Jack's club a number of times, but nothing memorable had come of the occasions. At least nothing memorable from Jack's point of view. Had the duke noticed something in Jack's demeanor that indicated he had the wherewithal to be an effective guardian over this lad who was obviously mollycoddled? But even then, to give Jack everything he owned that wasn't entailed? Jack was suspicious by nature, and his mind was screaming out warnings, insisting something was amiss. He just couldn't figure out what, precisely.

Jack turned on his heel and headed toward the stairs.

"Where are you going?" the duchess asked, her shoes tapping rapidly behind him.

Lord, she was quick to follow. If his legs weren't so long, he didn't think he'd be able to outdistance her. "Not that it's any of your concern, but I want to speak with Beckwith."

Why was he bothering to explain himself? He explained himself to no one. He hadn't since he'd decided to make the streets his home.

He hurried down the stairs, the duchess nipping at his heels like a rapacious dog. He strode through the hallway that displayed possessions that had no doubt been gathered for generations. The liveried footman opened the door to the library. Jack walked inside and quickly spun around to face the duchess, barring her entry.

She stumbled to an abrupt, jerky halt, her breathing labored, her golden eyes wide, her luscious lips parted. When her mouth wasn't puckered up as though she spent her spare time sucking lemons, she had a damned kissable-looking mouth. It irritated him that he noticed, irritated him even more that he wondered what kissing her would be like.

"In private," he said and slammed the door on her. Her infuriated shriek penetrated the thickness of the wood, bringing him a small sense of victory. Not trusting her to do as he bade, he turned the key in the lock. Fortunate that the duke had kept it handy. He was no doubt accustomed to dealing with his wife's disagreeable moods and this room probably served as his sanctuary for solitude.

Jack sauntered toward Beckwith, who seemed innocently unaware of the turmoil roiling through Jack. The man was either a fool or as skilled at playing cards as Jack was. "It's been a little more than fourteen years since you approached me with the news I had an anonymous benefactor. That's the only reason I bothered to make an appearance tonight. Was my benefactor the Duke of Lovingdon?"

While it made absolutely no sense, that explanation was the only one Jack could come up with to explain this lunacy.

"I serve at the pleasure of many lords and gentlemen of considerable wealth, Mr. Dodger. Your benefactor wished to remain anonymous, and so he shall."

"Are you saying he wasn't Lovingdon?"

"I'm saying until your benefactor gives me leave to reveal his wishes, I will hold his confidence to the best of my ability."

"What if I beat you to a bloody pulp? I suspect you'd find your ability isn't what you think it is."

Beckwith had the audacity to grin as though he were slightly amused. Jack didn't like being made sport of, or worse, having his bluffs called. Swearing beneath his breath, he swept his hand over the will and ledgers. "This makes no sense."

"Is it important that it does?"

"It's important I understand why a man I spoke to on only a few occasions deemed it appropriate to give me so much for doing so little."

"Being guardian of a lord of the realm is a grave, serious, and important task, Mr. Dodger. Don't underestimate the power of your influence or the amount of work required to ensure the young lord becomes a man who can reach his potential."

Jack laughed harshly. "Blast it all, man, that's my point exactly. The duchess is correct. I am the last person who should serve as guardian and protector of her son. I abhor the aristocracy."

"That's unfortunate, especially as they are largely responsible for your unprecedented success. The duke felt differently regarding your qualifications for guiding his son into manhood. However, he also understood you cannot be forced to do that which you have no desire to do. You have twenty-four hours to give me your decision. At the end of that time, if you have not agreed to the terms and conditions of the will as presented to you this evening, your opportunity to gain all of this—and the final item—will have passed and the second will shall be brought into play."

"You speak as though this is an elaborate game."

Beckwith smiled knowingly. "Who am I to judge?"

Jack glanced around the room. He'd only ever seen more books in Claybourne's library. If he read one book every day for as long as he lived, he'd never get to them all. The leather-bound books alone were worth a fortune.

Jack returned his attention to the man sitting calmly at the desk. Nothing seemed to unsettle him. He was a man who took his power from those he served. "In the second will, what does he leave to the widow?"

"I'm not at liberty to say."

"Damn it, man, at least tell me if it favors her more than the first." Which Jack had thought were pitiful leavings to a wife, truth be told. Even for the hoyden who'd been traipsing along behind him.

"What does it matter?" Beckwith asked.

Jack rubbed his thumb along the line of his jaw. He'd not let the keys to a kingdom far grander than anything he presently owned slip through his fingers. He picked up the leather-bound ledger that Beckwith had given him earlier and bestowed upon the man the infamous cocky grin for which Jack was so well known.

"How do I signify that I accept the terms of the will?"

Chapter 3

With the fog swirling around him, Jack walked along the quiet street. He'd taken a hansom cab to the duke's residence. He could find another to take back to his place, only he no longer needed it. He had a carriage and horses. He had a residence and servants and doubts. With misgivings, he'd signed the document Beckwith had laid before him. In spite of his attempts to question and convince himself otherwise, he'd known from the moment Beckwith read the terms of the will that he'd not walk away from everything he'd been given.

He'd not expected the duchess to be gracious when told the news he'd accepted the terms. Surprising him, she'd simply nodded at Mr. Beckwith and said, "The servants will need to be informed."

She'd called them into the foyer. With Jack standing at the bottom of the stairs, she stood partway up, with all the regal bearing of a queen. He thought he now knew what a warrior looked like at the end of the day when the hard-fought battle had not gone his way, when he had to look into the eyes of those he'd sent onto the battlefield and convince them that honor was to be found in simply surviving. She'd been elegant and eloquent as she explained the residence was now Jack's and that they all served at his pleasure.

Not one word had been uttered by the staff. Jack imagined they'd have questions aplenty once the shock wore off. But he'd been content to leave them and the duchess while he adjusted to his change in fortune in solitude.

While he admitted that he didn't consider himself the best choice to serve as guardian to her beloved and overprotected son, he could certainly think of worse. Perhaps the duke himself had fallen into that category.

Jack often walked along streets with grand houses, trying to remember what he'd thought he'd never forget. The first fancy house in which he'd lived—he'd been five. The man had promised his mother he'd take good care of Jack. She'd seemed to know him and trust him. Maybe he'd been one of her customers.

All Jack remembered was that the man had fed him and bathed him and put him to bed. Crawled beneath the covers with him . . . done things. . .

Jack quickened his steps as though he were five again, running away.

The man had wept afterward, said he was sorry, promised to never do it again . . .

Jack detoured by a towering elm and pounded his fist into the trunk, relished the bite of the hard bark, and felt the pain ricochet up his arm. He didn't want to go there again, didn't want to return to being frightened and hurting. And ashamed.

Although he'd run away, a terrified cadence to his steps, he'd thought he'd always remember where that house had been. But London had changed in twenty-eight years. Jack couldn't even remember what the man looked like. He hadn't thought about him in ages, but now he wondered . . .

What would guilt cause a man to do? Would he seek out and leave everything to a boy he'd abused? Was Lovingdon the man who'd bought him? What did it matter now? He was dead. He'd left Jack a fortune. What did it matter if it was a fortune steeped in guilt and regret? Jack had only ever cared about accumulating the coins that ensured no one would ever buy him again. Now, no one ever would.

"Tell me what you know of the Duke of Lovingdon," Jack demanded. He'd been desperate for the taste of whiskey on his tongue, and since he was in the neighborhood, he'd stopped at Luke's residence. It had been only a week since Luke's hastily arranged marriage, and the couple did not seem inclined to take a wedding trip.

Sitting across from Jack, near the window that looked out on an impressive garden when it wasn't draped in darkness, Luke took a sip of whiskey. He'd dispensed with his jacket, and his shirt was unbuttoned at his throat. His dark hair appeared to have been fingered recently, and Jack suspected it wasn't Luke who'd done the fingering. Yet, in spite of his dishevelment, he had the look of a man in control, a man who knew his place in the world and was finally comfortable with it. Jack didn't like to admit it, but Lucian Langdon wore the title of earl well.

"He was well respected in the House of Lords," Luke said solemnly. "When he spoke, people listened. His passing leaves shoes that will be difficult to fill."

"So you thought he was a decent-enough chap?"

Luke shrugged. "Seemed to be. I only spoke to him on a few occasions. Politics mostly. Advised me that I always needed to know *why* I felt the way I did about certain issues. He was prone to asking *why* of the younger lords. Insisted we not be sheep."

"What of his wife?"

Luke shook his head. "We should probably ask Catherine. She's much more familiar with the ladies of the aristocracy than I am. Until recently, I didn't walk in their circles."

Catherine, his wife, was the daughter of the Duke of Greystone. He'd passed away recently, and her brother—who had been absent during her father's long illness—had returned to London and inherited the titles. It seemed of late the lords were dropping like flies. Jack wondered if Catherine's father would have approved of her marrying the "Devil Earl."

"Catherine doesn't fancy me. She won't help," Jack said.

"Catherine has a generous heart. She'll always help someone in need." Luke leaned forward. "What's going on, Jack? From the moment you left at nineteen, you've always avoided coming to my residence unless absolutely necessary—as though you feared you'd catch the pox—and yet here you are, just as I was retiring for the evening."

Reaching for the decanter on the table between them, Jack poured more whiskey into his glass. He downed the contents in one long swallow, relishing the burning sensation along his throat that eventually swirled through his blood. The problem with erecting walls was that climbing over them when he needed help was so difficult. "Lovingdon left all his non-entailed properties and assets to me."

Luke stared at him as though he'd stood and removed his clothing.

"My reaction was quite similar," Jack said laconically. If the widow hadn't turned to stone as well at the news, he might have thought he'd misunderstood the conditions of the will.

"Why would he do that?"

Jack shook his head. "That seems to be the question of the evening, and I haven't the foggiest idea as to the answer."

"Did you even know the man?"

"Barely. I met him once in the garden here. I think he was visiting your grandfather. He came into the club a time or two."

"Did he owe you a gambling debt?"

Jack poured more whiskey, took another long swallow. "As far as I know, he never gambled, drank, or whored. He simply observed. Some people are like that: voyeurs of sin. I never thought anything of it."

Luke held up his hands. "Just like that, he left you everything?"

"Well, he did include one minor stipulation, hardly worth mentioning. I'm to serve as guardian of his five-year-old son."

Luke's eyes widened as he dropped back in the chair. "Why in God's name would he entrust the care of his son to you?"

"I appreciate the faith. Sorry to have delayed your retiring for the evening." Jack came to his feet. His and

Luke's friendship had been strained of late. Where once they'd trusted each other with their very lives, now distance brought on by regret and secrets revealed separated them. He shouldn't have bothered to come, but the streets had made them brothers. As loath as Jack was to admit he needed anyone, he was suddenly desperate to have someone believe in him.

"No, you misunderstood. I have every confidence you would serve as a fine guardian. Lord knows, when we were boys, you saved my arse often enough. But why would Lovingdon leave the care of his son to a man he doesn't know other than in passing?"

Jack slowly shook his head. "I'm as baffled as you are."

"How did his widow take the news?"

He rubbed his cheek, remembering the sting of her slap. "Not well, not well at all, I'm afraid." He heard a light footfall and turned toward the door.

Catherine stood inside the doorway. "I'm sorry. I didn't mean to intrude. I didn't realize you had company. I was simply wondering what was keeping you."

From my bed were the words Jack thought were left unspoken. Catherine Langdon, Countess of Claybourne, was a beautiful woman. Her hair, the color of moonbeams, had already been let down for the night. For some reason, it made him wonder what the widow's hair looked like when it was loosened, what it might feel like to comb his fingers through it.

"Please join us," Luke said now. "Jack has some questions he'd like to ask you."

No, I don't, Jack thought irritatingly. *You have some questions you want me to ask her.*

But he stayed as he was because to leave would give the impression he was unsettled by her, and while that assessment might be true, he had no desire for her to realize it. She had too much influence over Luke as it was. No reason to give her leave to think she could control another man.

Jack watched as she floated gracefully into the room and sat in the chair Luke had vacated. Luke perched himself on its arm, his fingers immediately going to Catherine's tresses as though he couldn't be near her without touching her. It had been a strange thing to watch his friend fall under her spell. Luke would do anything for her—kill if need be. Jack couldn't imagine loving a woman that much, couldn't imagine loving a woman at all. Love made a person vulnerable, and he had no intention of ever being placed in a position such as that again.

"Jack has encountered an unusual situation here," Luke began. "It seems Lovingdon has bequeathed to him all his non-entailed properties, in exchange for which Jack is to serve as guardian of his son."

To her credit, the countess did little more than look up at her husband, a frown between her delicate arched brows, before turning her attention to Jack. "How might I help?"

Taking his seat again at her unexpected offer, Jack cleared his throat, hardly knowing where to begin. In dealing with the young widow, the more he knew about her, the more advantage he would have during any future encounters. His interest was as simple as that. Nothing more. "I was wondering what you could tell me about his wife."

"Olivia?"

"Has he another?"

"No, of course not. I don't know her well. Her father was the Duke of Avendale. I believe she was nineteen when she married Lovingdon. To be blunt, I think we were all a bit surprised that she'd marry someone considerably older. I don't believe she was wanting for suitors. I suspect the marriage had more to do with her father's wishes than hers." She affectionately patted her husband's thigh. "We're not all fortunate to love the one we marry." She tilted her head thoughtfully. "Are you going to serve as the lad's guardian?"

"Of course."

"He can offer you nothing you can possibly need," Luke said.

"Need has nothing to do with my decision. As you're well aware, I never turn my back on the opportunity to be wealthier than I am. Besides, now we'll be neighbors. I've inherited his London residence."

"But serving as guardian is a great deal of responsibility, Mr. Dodger," Catherine said.

"I don't think it'll be as bad as all that. Besides, I'm only obligated until the widow marries and then the duty will fall to her new husband."

"I know the duchess well enough to recognize she places duty above all else and adheres to the strictures of society religiously. She'll honor her husband for the full two-year mourning period."

"Then in two years and one day, I'll have a bloke waiting for her on bended knee."

"You're going to arrange a marriage for her?" Catherine looked positively aghast by the notion.

Jack shrugged, knowing no matter what he did, Catherine would find fault with his plans. "I don't see any reason not to. I'm not in mourning."

Besides, how difficult could it be to find the duchess a new husband? And money could purchase a good many things, including forgiveness for violating the rules of etiquette. Society might require that a widow mourn for two years, but Jack didn't see the need for her to mourn for more than a couple of weeks, if that.

A quiet ceremony and off to the country the happy little family could go. And Jack would have his lovely new residence all to himself.

"Wake up, darling," Olivia whispered softly.

Henry blinked his eyes open. He'd taken his fair complexion, his blond hair from his father, but his eyes favored hers. He was such a curious lad, always studying the world around him, trying to discern how things worked. Lovingdon had spared his son little time, but then few fathers did. It was the way of things for fathers to leave their sons' upbringing to others. Perhaps Lovingdon's lack of involvement had convinced him that little thought needed to be given to the selection of a guardian—but even then, Olivia couldn't justify his choice.

Pressing a kiss to Henry's head, she inhaled the sweet, milky fragrance of the child. She could not possibly allow a criminal to raise him. The best way to avoid that was to get him as far away from Jack Dodger as possible.

"I need you to get up and get dressed. We're going to the family estate in the country," Olivia told him.

The country estate was part of the entailment. It belonged to Henry and would put him beyond the reach of his appointed guardian. Once she was away from this madness, Olivia would be able to think more clearly and find a way to ensure Mr. Dodger had no influence over Henry. He seemed to be a man fond of coins. Perhaps she could turn the funds from her trust over to him. She would do whatever was necessary—do without, make sacrifices—to ensure Henry had the proper guidance. Nothing was more important to her than her son.

She turned to his nanny. "Helen, please pack a few things for Henry and yourself. I'm having a coach brought 'round to the front. We dare not tarry."

She could hardly believe the desperate measures to which Lovingdon's death had brought her. He'd been only fifty-one. When she'd married him six years ago, he'd seemed so frightfully mature, but in death he'd suddenly seemed so terribly young, taken before his time. She'd hardly had a spare moment to think about him, about what life would be like without him. And if she had, she'd have certainly never envisioned it taking the turn it had tonight. Still, she had responsibilities and she would see to them as best she could. Duty did not have the luxury of taking time to mourn.

Once everything was ready and Henry was properly attired, Olivia took his hand and led him down the stairs. Her lady's maid was waiting for her in the foyer.

"The footmen have loaded our things into the boot of the coach," Maggie told Olivia.

They'd packed very little because a hasty retreat was required in order to gain an effective escape. Escape. Not a word she'd ever thought to associate with her life, but there she was, fleeing into the night as though she were a thief. If she weren't so tired, perhaps she could think of another strategy, but at that moment she wanted only to be away from the madness. "Good. Let's be off."

With a footman carrying a lantern and leading the way, and another carrying her son, Olivia dashed out into the night. Down the grand steps that led up to the home she'd fallen in love with. Scurrying off into the darkness of night left a crushing ache in her chest. If she were a weaker woman, she thought she'd succumb to tears, but they wouldn't change her circumstance. She had to remain strong for Henry. She had to protect him at all costs. She knew Jack Dodger's sort. He wanted everything easily, without effort. Once they were gone, he'd not bother to come after them. He would have the residence and its contents, which she was convinced was all he truly wanted.

She hurried across the cobblestone drive, aware of the thick fog absorbing and muting the echo of her footsteps. This night seemed perfectly designed for stealing away.

A liveried footman opened the door to the waiting coach and assisted her inside. As she settled onto the plush bench, she became aware of a familiar scent—

"Going somewhere, Duchess?"

She released a blood-curdling scream at the unexpected smoky voice reverberating from the shadowy corner of the coach. She might have continued to scream if not for the infuriatingly dark chuckle that quickly followed. She now knew the echo of Satan's laughter, and it was not a sound that invited others to join in the merriment.

"Your Grace?" one of the footmen questioned.

"She's fine," Jack Dodger said as he grabbed the lantern from the footman and hung it from an inside hook, the lantern's golden glow illuminating the confines of the coach, illuminating him. He somehow managed to look amused and irritated at the same time. And so very, very dangerous.

Just inside the doorway, still held by the other footman, Henry had yelled when she'd screamed and now he was crying forcefully. Reaching out, she took him and pressed her trembling child to her quaking bosom. "Shh. Henry, it's all right. Mummy just had a fright, that's all. But this man will not harm you, darling. I promise you that."

As though reassured by her words, Henry stopped his crying and began to noisily suck his thumb. It was a habit of which Olivia wasn't particularly fond, but neither she nor his nanny had encountered any success in breaking it. At that particular moment, it didn't seem worth the bother of worrying over. She had much larger concerns to address.

If she were prone to using obscenities, Olivia thought, now would be a good time to spew a few. Jack Dodger appeared larger than before, and more ominous. She liked him even less and decided she'd had quite enough of him for the evening.

"What are you doing here?" Olivia demanded, in her most officious voice, the one she used when she caught servants slacking at their duties.

"The question, Duchess, is what are you doing? According to this book" —he tapped the ledger he held up as though its contents were gospel— "this coach is my property. Are you seeking to steal it from me?"

"How can it be your property? It bears the ducal crest."

"I suppose you make a valid point. I should have the crest removed posthaste as it does create confusion."

"It was the duke's coach."

"But unfortunately for you, it was purchased with non-entailed funds."

"You read that in the dark?"

"No, I read it in the library. I have an astonishingly good memory. I have but to read something once and it is as though a picture is drawn in my mind. But I doubt you truly have any real interest in my talent, so let us return to my original question. Are you seeking to steal from me? Do I need to send 'round for a constable?"

"Don't be ridiculous. I was just taking Henry to the countryside."

"In the dead of night?" Mr. Dodger asked.

"It's a cooler time to travel, and Henry is prone to sleeping when we travel at night. As I don't then have to keep him entertained, it makes for a much more pleasant journey for all involved, and I'm not sure why I'm explaining myself to you."

"I've found people usually go to the bother of explaining when they realize they're at fault."

"I've done nothing wrong." But her words sounded defensive and weak even to her own ears.

"Here's the problem as I see it. I'm Henry's guardian. If he's in the country then I cannot effectively guard him."

She could have sworn she heard humor laced through his voice. Did he think this was all some grand joke, that tonight's revelations had been designed for his amusement? She bit back harsh words that would gain her nothing except his anger. "As guardian, you don't have to actually *guard* him. You simply oversee his welfare, and you can do that by entrusting him to my care and letting me take him to the country."

"I'm not certain that's in his best interest."

"How can it not be?"

"You're raising a pansy. He screamed louder than you did."

"I resent that implication. You frightened us, lurking about in the shadows where you weren't expected—like some miscreant. Why weren't you standing outside the coach, as any decent person would? I think you deliberately sought to unsettle me."

"I think you're well aware that I'm hardly *decent*." He had the audacity to smile, all the while tapping that blasted ledger.

"You find this situation amusing?" she snapped.

"I find it vastly challenging."

Challenging was an understatement. "You and I can compromise. Take everything. Say you are his guardian. Let Henry and I leave."

"Unfortunately for you, Duchess, I'm a man of my word. I promised to see to the care and upbringing of the child, and so I shall. And I will do it here in London as that is where my business interests lie. Now, you are correct. Compromises need to be made and matters between us settled. I suggest we retire to the residence, where we may discuss them in more comfort."

"It's almost ten o'clock, long past a decent hour for visiting. Surely you're not implying that you intend to stay in the residence."

"It's my residence. The child is my ward. So, yes, I will be moving in."

He spoke so casually about something that was completely inappropriate. She had little doubt that he'd grown up accustomed to sleeping amongst strangers. "This is ludicrous. You and I are not related. We can't live in the same residence."

"You're a widow, not a maiden. No chaperone is mandatory. Although I assume you have female servants who see to your numerous needs. Let them watch over you if you fear you'll be tempted to come to my bed."

Olivia gasped with indignation. "You pompous beast! I would never come to your bed."

"And as I have no interest in coming to yours, I fail to see the problem. Besides, most of my business ventures require my attention at night, so more often than not I'll be at my club. Nothing untoward will happen."

Olivia refused to acknowledge the sting of rejection she'd felt when he admitted he had no interest in her. She didn't want to appeal to him. Still, it was painful to realize a man who no doubt was in the habit of chasing many a skirt had no plans to chase hers. It had wounded her terribly when Lovingdon had never returned to her bed once she was with child. Perhaps men found her unappealing. She supposed she should take comfort in knowing she was safe from Jack Dodger. Instead she felt an overwhelming need to weep.

"I beg of you, for the love of God, let us go."

He studied her thoughtfully, and she snatched onto her last remnant of hope that this ordeal would end in her favor. If he possessed only a shred of decency, it could be enough—

"I'm afraid I can't do that."

"Why ever not?"

"I grow weary of repeating myself. Leaving is not in the boy's best interest and I am his guardian. Now, you may either return to the residence like a proper lady—by walking—or over my shoulder. The choice is yours. But the time is now."

"Toss me over your shoulder? As though I was a common doxy? You wouldn't dare."

"I've told you before, challenging me will only make me do it." He reached for her—

She released a tiny screech, held Henry close, and pushed so hard against the back of the coach she was surprised she didn't break it and find herself tumbling into the boot. "Enough. You've made your point. You're a tyrant. I'm perfectly capable of taking myself to the house."

"A pity." He shifted on the seat. "I'll carry the boy."

"I'd rather you didn't."

For the briefest of moments, it appeared she'd hurt his feelings. She didn't know how that could even be possible when nothing except animosity existed between them.

"As you wish, Duchess," he said, his mocking tone reverberating around them.

"Will you please quit calling me that?"

"It's appropriate is it not?"

"Not the way you say it."

"Perhaps you can teach me to say it properly and in exchange I can share with you some improper things," he said in a low voice that caused her to tingle in places she'd never tingled. "We'll discuss the possibilities in the library."

"I have to read to Henry first. He can't go to sleep without my reading to him."

"That sounds like a ploy to put off the inevitable."

"I'm offended you doubt my words. Still, ask any of the staff. They'll confirm that I read to him every night. Not that I should need the staff's confirmation."

"I suppose you're right. I should treat you as an equal."

"An equal? You're a commoner."

"I was referring to the fact that we're both thieves. Although I must admit to being more successful at it. I'd have not gotten caught."

"I daresay you overestimate your abilities. At some point you did get caught. I noticed the mark upon your hand."

"Yes, rather unfortunate business that. Lucky for you, they no longer brand criminals."

She didn't see the point in telling him once again that she was not a thief. How was she to have known he'd inherited the coach? She needed to take a look at his ledger or study her son's more closely. "You're incredibly irritating, Mr. Dodger."

"It's part of my charm. Meet me in the library when you're finished reading to my ward."

With that he leaped out of the coach, causing it to rock with his movements, and announced to the servants who were still standing about, "The duchess has decided to cancel her journey to the country. Please see that everything is put back where it belongs."

Then he strode off into the darkness, leaving her on a spiraling descent into hell.

Chapter 4

Lounging on a couch in the library, Jack drank his whiskey, grateful he'd had the foresight to bring a couple of bottles from Luke's. He'd planned to return to his new residence to discuss the arrangements with the widow, and he'd decided they'd both need a good shot of the devil's brew to fortify themselves for what was certain to be an arduous process of working out the particulars regarding the care of her son. He didn't expect her to agree with anything he suggested.

He'd been quite surprised when he'd arrived and discovered the coach being readied for the duchess's hasty retreat. It had been a long time since the devil had possessed him, and he was not in the habit of frightening women, but he'd not been able to refrain from settling himself in the coach and awaiting her arrival. Unfortunately, he'd not taken into account that she'd have her son with her. Irritating her was one thing. Terrorizing the child was another matter entirely. He didn't hold with the notion of harming children. They lost their innocence all too soon as it was.

Damnation, he *should* just let her take the lad to the country. Simply pretend he was the guardian. He'd spent a good deal of his youth pretending one thing or another in order to swindle someone out of something. When he picked pockets, he'd often dressed in fancy stolen clothes so when he walked among wealthy folks he appeared to belong with them—someone's child just meandering about. All of Feagan's children were skilled at mimicking their surroundings, appearing to fit in, even when they didn't.

Was Beckwith going to check up on him, make sure he saw to his duties? Not bloody likely. He'd survived the delivering of his message, seen that the proper forms were signed. He'd earned his coin. Jack certainly had no plans to give him any more. He was out of their lives. At least until the time came for him to hand over the final item. *Its value immeasurable.* The words echoed through Jack's mind as though sung by a chorus of angels. All of this and then something more.

He glanced at the clock on the mantel, and then shifted his attention to a table where an assortment of clocks was arranged. The duchess had been reading to her son for almost an hour. What in the hell was she reading? One of Dickens's novels?

Then a horrid thought took hold. She was a clever wench, as she'd proven by sizing him up rightly enough. He'd cut off one avenue of escape. Perhaps she'd found another.

"Damnation!" he rasped as he surged to his feet, spilling good whiskey on his favorite waistcoat. He cursed the waste, and then downed the remaining contents of the glass before storming out of the library.

A footman lounging against the wall in the hallway came to attention, fear of reprisal over his lack of discipline evident in his expression. Jack cared little about how straight a man could stand. He cared only that a man furnished results and was there when needed.

"Have you seen the duchess since she went upstairs?" Jack demanded.

"No, sir."

He cursed again. Escape was definitely a possibility. Jack remembered seeing enormous trees near the house. She could open a window, leap across to one, and shimmy down it with no trouble at all. Jack had done that often enough when he'd lived at Claybourne's. The old gent had forbidden them to visit with Feagan if they slept beneath his roof. Jack had always assumed what the old gent didn't know wouldn't hurt him. And he'd refused to totally abandon Feagan. So he'd straddled both worlds. In many ways, he still did.

He rushed up the stairs, taking them two at a time. No other servants were about. He strode to the nursery, opened the door, and paused. . .

She had escaped—they both had, she and her son—into slumber. Jack's stomach knotted as the vague memory of sleeping nestled against his mother fought to become more vivid. He didn't want to think about her tonight, didn't want to consider everything a mother might sacrifice for her child, didn't want to wonder about what the duchess might sacrifice. Her devotion to her son had taken him by surprise. He'd somehow always assumed the aristocracy was above emotion. It wasn't often he misjudged a situation or people. But in this instance, he may have.

He glanced quickly around the room. The nanny was asleep on a small bed on the far side. He didn't know if that was common practice or just another example of the overprotective nature of the boy's mother. He wasn't familiar with a great deal concerning the particulars of a household. Lovingdon had set him a daunting task. He was baffled by his determination to see it through. He gave his attention back to the duchess.

She was sitting up on the bed, her head at an awkward angle, the open book on her lap. The boy was curled on his side, sucking on his thumb, snoring softly. One of his mother's hands rested on his head, her fingers lost in his blond curls, as though she could protect him with so simple a touch.

Yes, he should let them go. What did he know about boys? Oh, he'd protected a few in his time and had the scars to show for it, not all of them visible. But he was accustomed to teaching boys how to survive when they had no one to protect them. Several boys worked at his club: running errands, fetching drinks for gentlemen, carrying their chips for them. Jack wondered if Lovingdon had observed the confidence growing in the lads he hired. They were always fearful, not trusting their good fortune, suspicious of his motives when he first took them in. But in time they came around: began to walk with a swagger, speak without hesitating, understood their worth. Was that the reason Lovingdon had come to the club and not partaken of its offerings—to watch, to learn, to decide who could best prepare his son for the world?

A scoundrel like Jack Dodger?

If the boy were a street urchin, perhaps. But the son of a lord? Jack hardly knew where to begin. So why had he not accepted the easy way out of his dilemma when the duchess had offered it to him? Take everything and let them go. It made no sense to force them to stay, and yet he was reluctant to release them.

Jack shifted his attention back to the lady in question. In repose she possessed an unexpected, ethereal beauty, as all her worries faded away while she drifted into dreams. He wondered briefly what it was like to dream. He never did. Possibly because he so seldom slept. He was obsessed with obtaining all the wealth he could, burning the midnight oil as often as possible. He knew the true value of money. It protected a person from having to do things he didn't want to do.

Usually. He didn't particularly want to serve as the lad's guardian, and if the boy wasn't sucking his thumb, if he hadn't screamed louder than his mother, Jack might not have questioned the need for him to remain. A boy shouldn't be that frightened. No one should. What had caused him to have fears? And how did Jack begin to give him the confidence he required to honor his title? With late night talks before a coal fire, while gin warmed his belly and a pipe warmed his lungs? He didn't think the duchess would approve of that—which made the idea worth considering. Pricking her temper could become his latest vice. She irritated him for reasons he didn't understand. He was aware of her in ways he'd never been with other women.

The duchess was crammed into the small child's bed, her shoes resting nearby. Although she wore stockings, he could see that she had small, delicate feet. They made her seem vulnerable, and he had a sudden irrational urge to protect her. He could well imagine she'd object to that notion. She'd probably purposely remained there until she fell asleep, hoping to avoid another encounter with Jack. Silly woman. Eventually everyone had to face the devil and give him his due.

Tomorrow she'd learn that lesson; for tonight, he'd let her rest in innocence—but not in this bed. Waking up after an uncomfortable night would only serve to keep her out of sorts and make her more difficult to deal with, and she was difficult enough. He doubted they'd ever agree on anything.

With care he slid his arms beneath her, one at her shoulders and the other at her knees. His back would no doubt protest the abuse, but when he lifted her, he discovered she was as light as his own touch when he slipped his hand into another man's pocket in order to relieve him of his possessions. She made a little mewling sound as her head rolled into the nook of his shoulder. A scent wafted up that he recognized: laudanum. Maybe she slept no easier at night than he did.

Jack looked back at the boy, who was staring up at him. He mustered a smile, winked, and said in a low voice, "Go back to sleep. I'll hold the monsters at bay tonight."

The boy closed his eyes. Jack walked from the room and down the hallway to the door that led into the duchess's bedchamber.

Please don't go into my bedchamber.

He released a rough curse. What did he care about her wants and desires? What was she hiding in there? Her not wanting him to see it made him want to all the more. And why shouldn't he? The residence was his, which meant that legally her room was his. He had every right to open that door—

He cursed again and walked to the door that led into the master's bedchamber, a room that had once belonged to her husband and now belonged to Jack.

Bending his knees slightly, he managed to reach the knob, turn it, and shove open the door. The room was cast in shadows. The light from the lamps in the hallway and coming in through the window—from the gas lamps that lined the front drive—provided him with enough illumination to make out the silhouette of the large bed. He walked over to it and very gently laid her down.

She whimpered and mumbled, "I'm sorry. Forgive me."

Jack crouched down. "For what, Duchess?"

Her response was only a soft breathing. One hand rested near her hip, the other curled on the pillow. She'd removed her widow's cap—a silly bit of frippery—and he had a clearer idea regarding her hair. It was not as brown as he'd originally deduced but more a shade of auburn. A bit of the devil visited him again. Using deft fingers and the light touch of a pickpocket, he located a hairpin. Very gingerly, he pulled it out. Then found another and another and another, until her hair was free of its constraints, thick and heavy in his hand. Soft and silken. He rubbed several strands between his fingers. He didn't know why he felt this overwhelming compulsion to know the texture of her hair.

And to know something more.

He lowered his face to the curve of her neck and slowly inhaled the heady fragrance of her perfume. The scent was stronger there, as though a secret spot rested just behind her ear. Where else might she seek to tease a man? For she would tease—of that, Jack had no doubt.

Unfolding his body, he stared down on her. He wondered how many nights she might have lain in this bed, replete and sated. Had the duke held her afterward? The women Jack had bedded didn't require any special care, but he thought it would be different with a woman who wasn't bought. She'd expect more when coins didn't fill her palm. She'd require courtesies that filled her heart.

He backed up a step. There was something very pleasing about the sight of a woman in bed, especially when it was now *his* bed. For all the women he'd pleasured and been pleasured by, he'd never watched one sleep. Even in slumber, a woman was seductive and alluring.

He spun on his heel and headed for the door, refusing to be seduced, even by one as lovely as the Duchess of Lovingdon.

Jack strode into his gentlemen's club and relished the sights, smells, and sounds. The well-dressed men at the gambling tables. The rich aroma of good whiskey and expensive cigars. The clack of dice and the click of wooden chips. Piano music wafted from another room, where his girls danced with the gents, sometimes ushering them off to a corner for an enticing kiss, sometimes leaving the room for something a bit more illicit. Jack paid the girls well for entertaining the gents with dance and conversation within that room. Anything they earned on the other side of those doors was theirs and theirs alone. He didn't provide whores, but neither did he judge if a girl wanted more—as long as it was her choice. Everyone knew Jack Dodger didn't look the other way if his employees were mistreated.

He walked around the perimeter, studying the tables, the players, how the games seemed to be progressing. He noted the volume of noise. Rowdy men tended to spend more freely. He passed by one of the card tables where a game of brag was being played. A time existed when Luke spent a good deal of his evening there—not only because he was a partner but because he enjoyed a good game of cards. Since he was married, however, he was spending his nights with his wife. Not that Jack could blame him for that. She was quite a delectable piece.

As Jack passed by the cage where chips were bought, the man inside gave him a nod and quick grin, which meant business was good. He neared the room where women offered solace to the gentlemen who'd not been so lucky at the tables—or perhaps a woman was their choice of sin for the night. Standing in the doorway, he gave his eyes a moment to adjust. The room was dimly lit on purpose, to offer the illusion of secrecy. But no true secrets resided there. If Jack was of a mind, he could blackmail every man within these walls—but his business acumen was sharper than that. He provided a safe haven for men to indulge their whims. He'd learned at an early age that a person would pay almost anything for a safe haven.

A woman sitting on a gentleman's lap caught his eye. Prudence had been with him the longest. Youth was beginning to fade from her features, but a good deal could be said for experience. She whispered to the man, then unfurled her lithe body and sauntered enticingly over to Jack. She wore her blond hair loose and flowing down her back. Having always lacked modesty, she wore little more than silk draped over her body.

"'ello, love." She greeted him saucily. "Lookin' fer me?"

Jack gave her a long look mixed with appreciation for what she offered physically as well as regret. It was always a good idea not to let a woman know that he didn't desire her. Let her think it was something else that turned him away. "Not tonight, Pru."

She frowned. "It's been a while, Jack. 'aven't found someone else, 'ave ye?"

"No, just distracted. How are things going with the other girls?"

Prudence oversaw the girls who worked here, made certain they understood the rules, stayed clean, weren't abused. "Things are good, but I think yer goin' to lose Annie. One of the lords offered to set 'er up as 'is mistress."

"Does she want it?"

She nodded. "'e's a good bloke."

"Make sure she understands he'll never marry her."

"She knows, Jack. 'ell, we all know what we are."

"What you are, Pru, is a bit of wickedness. Every now and then a man needs that."

She winked at him. "Well, let me know when you need some. I'm still yer girl."

With a flourish, she returned to where her gentleman waited for her. Lately Pru was the only working girl Jack availed himself of. He didn't need jealousy among his girls. He paid Pru very, very well—not because she was particularly good, but because she never expected more from him than he was capable of giving.

He turned away from the room where men enjoyed the company of women.

Strolling back through the gaming room, he acknowledged a few of the gents. It was long after midnight, but still the room was crowded and spirits were high. Sin possessed no timepiece, which suited Jack well as he required little sleep.

He shoved open the door that led to the back rooms where his business was managed. He stopped by an open doorway, leaned against the doorjamb, and watched as Frannie Darling made precise notations in his ledgers. She'd been one of Feagan's children as well—the only one whose skillful hands had matched Jack's. No one had ever brought in as much booty as the two of them had.

Her red hair was pulled back into a bun, but it didn't seem to draw the skin tautly across her cheeks the way the duchess's had. Like the duchess, she also wore black, not because she was in mourning, but because she didn't wish to draw attention to herself. Jack had once bought her a dress of emerald green. He preferred bold colors and had thought she'd look beautiful in it. She'd blushed and thanked him profusely, but as far as he knew, she'd never worn it. She didn't like for gents to notice her, but notice her they did. Jack didn't think a single one of Feagan's lads hadn't fallen in love with her at one time or another. Even he wasn't immune to her charms.

Looking up, Frannie gave him the impish, shy smile that had won many a lad's heart. "There you are. You were gone a rather long time."

"The meeting turned out to be far more complicated than I expected."

"Did you want to talk about it?"

"Not particularly, but you need to be aware of some changes that are likely to occur."

"I'm not certain I like the sound of that."

Stepping inside, he glanced around. Unlike the residence he'd just left, this room was sparsely furnished with a desk and three chairs. The walls were plain. One set of small shelves held the ledgers that provided a history of his business. Against another wall was a couch. He wasn't certain what she used it for. She certainly didn't sleep there. Her bed was in an apartment accessed through an alley and stairs at the back of the building. He had his own apartment there as well, as did most of his employees. Cost him a bloody fortune, but a happy worker didn't take from the till.

"Why don't you sit down?" Frannie said.

Shaking his head, Jack took a step nearer and folded his hands around the top of the leather chair in front of her desk. "I spent too much of the night sitting." He jerked his head toward the open books spread across her desk. Frannie was a genius when it came to ciphering. Perhaps because Feagan would sit her on his lap and let her count the handkerchiefs and coins that the others collected through the day. He might not have realized it, but he'd given her a skill that served them all very well. "Did we have a profitable night?"

"We always have a profitable night. You're going to die a wealthy man, Jack."

Her voice contained a sadness that he didn't miss. He knew she objected to the importance he placed on money. He grinned. "Wealthier than I'd anticipated. The Duke of Lovingdon left me a fortune."

Her green eyes widened. "Why?"

"Bloody hell if I know." His fingers dug into the leather of the chair. "Did you ever speak to him?"

"Why would I?"

"He visited here on occasion."

"You know I avoid the gaming area as much as possible." Fine liquor made their customers friendlier than they might have been otherwise and caused them to misjudge their own appeal. The gaming area was not the place for a lady who wished to avoid the advances of men.

"He was also an acquaintance of Luke's grandfather. I vaguely remember meeting him at the Claybourne residence, showing him the locket."

"What locket?"

The locket contained a miniature of his mother. The night she'd sold him, she'd given it to him with the admonishment, "Never forget that I loved you, Jack."

Loved. He'd never known what he'd done to lose her love. In time, he'd stopped trying to figure it out. He'd put all his mental abilities toward surviving.

The day he'd met Lovingdon, he'd been in Claybourne's garden, studying his mother's features as drawn on the miniature, trying to determine if she would be disappointed in him if he didn't take advantage of all that the earl was offering him. He'd hated being in that fancy house. It had reminded him of another . . .

Jack shook his head. "It's not important. I thought perhaps you'd spoken with him at Claybourne's."

"Not that I recall."

"I don't suppose it matters. What's important is for

you to know I agreed to serve as guardian of his heir, so I may not be around as much as usual."

"Why you?"

"That seems to be the question everyone's asking, and again, I haven't a bloody clue."

"I think you'll make a remarkable guardian."

Jack laughed. In spite of being raised on the streets, Frannie possessed a bit of innocence when it came to Feagan's lads. She always believed some goodness resided in them, even when it was buried so deeply they couldn't find it themselves.

"Are you going to tell Luke about your change in fortune?" Frannie asked.

"I already did. I saw him earlier." He squinted. "I don't think he's quite forgiven me for my part in his parents' death." It had been only two months since Luke had learned the truth of that fateful day twenty-five years ago, a day that had changed all their lives.

"It's not your fault. You were only a child. You didn't know what the man had planned when he paid you to lure the family into the alley."

That's what Jack had claimed, and it wasn't entirely a lie. He hadn't known specifics, but he knew evil when it stared at him. He'd ignored his suspicions because he'd wanted the sixpence. He lived with the regret every day. He hoped the same wouldn't be true of the bargain he'd struck tonight. He slapped the top of the chair. "I'd best get to my business, make sure all matters have been taken care of so I'm free in the morning to oversee arrangements regarding my new possessions."

"I suppose congratulations are in order," Frannie said softly.

Jack couldn't shake off an ominous sense of fore-
boding. "Condolences, most like." He winked at her.
"'Night, Frannie."

He strode down the hallway, stopped in his office
to gather up his tobacco and pipe, and continued on
to the door that led outside. He stepped into the night.
The fog had grown thicker, hampering visibility. He
wondered if he'd find fog in the country. He might have
to eventually look over his ward's estates. Might prove
interesting. London was all he knew, but he knew it
very well.

Leaning against the wall, he stuffed his clay pipe,
struck a match, lit the tobacco, and began puffing until
the tantalizing aroma was swirling through him. It was
a much richer blend than he'd had as a lad. Still, it took
him back to a time when life had been simple, reduced
to collecting a certain number of handkerchiefs per
day. Jack hadn't been content with the silk. He'd preferred watches, jewelry, and other sparkly items that
brought a fair price from fences. He didn't always take
his stash to Feagan. He developed his own contacts. If
Luke's grandfather hadn't taken him in, he had little
doubt he'd have become a kidsman with his own den of
thieves that would have eventually rivaled Feagan's for
notoriety. That had been his goal, anyway. To become
the most famous, to be the one about whom ballads
were sung and stories were written.

He'd planned to teach boys in the artful ways of
thievery. And now he was supposed to train a lad to be
honest and upstanding, to sit in the House of Lords and
help to govern a nation.

Chapter 5

Henry Sidney Stanford, the seventh Duke of Lovingdon, knew his porridge was growing cold—and he detested cold porridge because it became all slimy going down his throat—but he was afraid if he tried to eat he might choke and die.

Of late, he was very much concerned with dying.

He didn't really understand it. He knew only that his father had died so they'd put him in a nice box, like his nanny did the toys he no longer played with. And he hadn't seen his father since. But his nanny had warned him that if he ate too quickly, he could choke and die.

He wasn't going to eat quickly, but he was very nervous and it felt like he had swallowed the ball his father would sometimes toss to him. It was because of the man. The man who had been in the coach. The man who had come for his mother last night. He was in the nursery now, walking around, looking at things. Every once in a while he would peer over at Henry, and when he did, the ball lodged in Henry's throat would grow larger.

"How long have you been his nanny?" the man asked.

"Since shortly after he was born, milord, I mean . . . sir," Henry's nanny answered, with a quick curtsy.

Henry's mother called her Helen; Henry was supposed to call her Miss Tuppin. But he always stammered when he tried to say her name, and she would rap his knuckles with a little stick she carried in her skirt pocket, so he never called her by name unless he absolutely had to.

She only whacked him when no one was around. He knew it was because she cared about him, and the fact that he wasn't a good boy was their secret. She didn't want to smack him, but he left her no choice. He didn't understand that, either. He knew only that he didn't want his mother to know he did things that earned him a smack. She thought he was a good boy, and even though it was a lie, he wanted her to keep thinking it so she would love him.

"So this is the day nursery?" the man asked.

"Yes, sir."

"And where he was sleeping last night?"

"The night nursery, sir."

"When does Lord Henry move to a proper bedroom?"

"He's not Lord Henry, sir. Never was actually. He was Lord Ashleigh. Of course, now he's the duke. His Grace."

"Quite right. And when does His Grace move to a proper bedroom?"

"When he's eight."

"There are rules even for childhood, I see."

"Yes, sir." Miss Tuppin looked over at Henry. "We don't always like them, but we must follow them."

"Do you like rules, Henry?" the man asked.

Henry dropped his gaze to his nanny's skirt pocket, the one where she kept the stick that he was to tell no one about, and shook his head.

The man laughed. "Good lad. I think we'll get along."

The man was tall, like Henry's father had been. They were all supposed to wear black now that Henry's father had died, but the man was wearing a dark purple waistcoat. Henry wondered if he should tell the man about that rule.

The man pulled out a chair, turned it around, and straddled the seat, folding his arms over the backrest. Henry had never seen anyone sit like that. He was certain it was the wrong way to sit, but Miss Tuppin didn't whack the man. Maybe she was afraid of him.

"Do you know who I am, Henry?"

Henry nodded, then shook his head. He sort of knew. The man upset his mother, but he'd also lifted Henry's mother into his arms with a great deal of care. And he'd looked at her as though he liked her as much as Henry did.

"My name is Jack Dodger. You may call me Jack."

"Sir, I don't mean to interfere, but that's not proper and he'll develop bad habits," Miss Tuppin said. "He should call you 'Mr. Dodger.' And if I might be so bold, you should call him 'Your Grace.'"

"You'll find, sweets, I'm not one for rules and have quite a few bad habits of my own." He looked at Henry the entire time he spoke. "You and I have that in common. I don't like rules either. Your father asked me to serve as your guardian. Do you know what a guardian is?"

Henry shook his head.

"It's the person who protects you. If anyone ever hurts you, all you have to do is tell me and I will see to it that the person never harms you again."

Henry shifted his gaze to Miss Tuppin. Her mouth was set in the hard line it always was when she whacked him. He looked back at Jack.

"I'm sorry your father died," Jack said.

"Is your f-father dead?"

"Probably. The truth is, Henry, I never knew my father. So, you see, we have something else in common. Neither of us has a father."

"Will he c-come back?"

Jack arched a brow. "Who? Your father?"

Henry nodded.

Jack suddenly looked sad. "No, lad, he won't. But he's asked me to take care of you, so if there's anything you need—" He started to rise.

"A puppy!" Henry blurted.

The man stopped. "You need a puppy?"

Henry nodded quickly.

Jack winked at him. "We'll see about that."

He walked out of the room. Henry looked at Miss Tuppin. Her gaze was on the door, and she was chewing her bottom lip like she was thinking about something very hard.

"Eat your porridge, Henry."

Even though the porridge was slimy, he did as he was told, because her hand had slipped into her pocket.

Olivia stretched beneath the covers. She still had a headache, her throat had become raw, and her eyes felt gritty. The laudanum had helped her sleep, but it had failed to relieve her of the symptoms of mourning. She wondered how long they would linger.

Then the lethargy wore off and she remembered the horror of discovering the terms of her husband's will. She sat up abruptly and held her aching head. Her hair tumbled around her. When had she loosened it? Had she gone to bed without braiding it? Then her gaze fell on her hairpins, lined up neatly on the bedside table.

Only, it wasn't her bedside table. God help her, it wasn't her bed.

With mounting horror, she glanced around the room. Her husband's bedchamber.

Before last night, she'd only ever come in here once, a silly attempt to seduce her husband when he'd failed to come to her bed for more than a year after Henry had been born. She'd thought perhaps he wasn't aware she was fully recovered from birthing and could return to her wifely duties. Instead, she'd discovered he'd not wanted her any longer. He had his heir. He'd looked at her with pity. She feared she'd looked at him with desperation. She wasn't even certain why she'd gathered her courage to go to him. It wasn't as though he'd been affectionate in bed. Perhaps because a brief touch was better than no touch at all. He'd not been a passionate man.

He'd been nothing like Jack Dodger.

That thought caused her heart to thunder. The manner in which he'd looked at her—as though he knew all her secret desires and was capable of satisfying them. The heat in his eyes made her shiver, not from cold, but from the longing to have a man gaze at her as though she were desirable. She'd always been the good daughter, the good wife, the good mother, the good woman. Duty above all else. But suddenly, too much was being asked of her. What was Lovingdon's purpose in bringing Jack Dodger into her life?

And how had she come to be in this bed?

Dear God, perhaps it wasn't her husband who had gone mad, but her. She didn't remember coming here. She was still fully clothed, save for her shoes. She remembered taking a small amount of laudanum to help relieve her headache, then reading to Henry. Afterward she was supposed to meet with Mr. Dodger—to convince him that letting them travel to the country was in the best interest of all. She'd simply wanted to take a moment to gather her strength before facing him. She'd closed her eyes . . .

And now she was here.

Had Jack Dodger sought her out? Had he brought her to his bed? Had he had his way with her? She didn't feel as though she'd been touched. She felt no tenderness between her legs. Surely after nearly six years of not lying with a man, she would be aware if one had bedded her. There would be some indication. As there was none, she could only deduce that, if Mr. Dodger had brought her to this bed, nothing untoward had occurred. He'd kept his word. Imagine that.

She didn't know whether to be relieved or disappointed. What sort of wantonness was taking possession of her?

Drawing up her legs, she rested her forehead against her knees. She didn't want to face the day. She wanted to run away. To the country. To a field of green grass and yellow flowers. She wanted to take off her shoes and dance barefoot. She wanted to laugh. She couldn't remember the last time she'd laughed. She was all of five and twenty, but of late she felt as though she was nearer to a hundred.

She wanted to crawl back under the covers, go to sleep, and wake up to discover that the reading of the will had been a dream. But duty called.

And Henry. Dear Lord, what if Mr. Dodger had decided to take his responsibilities seriously and seek out Henry? She had to check on her child. She scrambled out of bed and scurried to the door. Opening it, she peered out. No sign of the dreadful Mr. Dodger.

She slipped into the hallway and hurried to the nursery. To her immense relief, Henry was sitting at the short table eating his morning porridge. "Is everything all right, darling?" she asked.

He nodded. "The m-man said I c-could have a p-puppy."

"The man? What man? A puppy?"

"Mr. Dodger, Your Grace," Helen said. "He spent a few moments with the young duke this morning."

Olivia's heart fairly stopped. "Did you leave them alone?"

"No, Your Grace. As a matter of fact, Mr. Dodger insisted I stay in attendance so I could report firsthand anything you wished to know about his visit."

"Oh. Well." Her heart returned to its rhythmic beating. "That was rather considerate and unexpected of him."

"He's very different from what I expected."

"What do you mean?"

"Well, I don't think there's anyone who hasn't heard of Jack Dodger. He's rather notorious in some parts of London. But he seemed right nice this morning."

"Did he use profanity?"

"No, he just asked if the young duke needed any-thing." She smiled. "And of course, he said, 'a puppy,' because he's been on about that for months now. Mr. Dodger said he would see about it."

Cursing the man's ambiguity, she walked into the room and knelt beside her son. "Darling, that doesn't mean he's going to get you a puppy."

"B-but he said."

"His words meant that he might, but he probably won't, because they're such a lot of bother."

"I-I'd take g-good care of it."

"I know you would." She sighed. "I'll talk to him about it."

Henry gave her a sweet smile. She hugged him tightly. He was so precious. How he would change under Mr. Dodger's tutelage. "Now I need to get ready for the day."

She went to her room and tugged on the bellpull to summon Maggie. Her maid had already put away the things she'd packed for their hasty departure last night. Olivia spotted the leather ledger on her secretary. She had tucked it into her satchel because she'd wanted to study it when they reached the country estate. She walked to her desk and turned back the leather cover. Everything was so meticulously written out, with de-tailed descriptions—

Her breath caught. She reread the words written on the first page. She released a furious screech just as Maggie walked into the room.

"Your Grace—"

"Where's Mr. Dodger?" she asked succinctly.

"He's in the breakfast dining room."

"Help me to get ready quickly. I have a few choice words for him."

"The coach is my son's!"

Jack looked up from the page he'd been reading in his ledger while enjoying a leisurely breakfast. The duchess had arrived and she was furious. And in her fury she was breathtakingly beautiful. How had he failed to miss that last night? Or was it simply that a good night's rest had brought color to her cheeks and washed away her weariness? Mentally shaking himself free of her spell, he came to his feet. "Good morning, Olivia. Did you sleep well?"

"Don't take that tone with me."

"What? Cordiality? I'd have thought you'd appreciate it."

"Innocence. Do not pretend to be innocent." She marched toward him, tapping her ledger as she came. "You accused me of trying to steal from you, yet you knew good and well that the coach belonged to my son."

"I fear I did not. It's listed in my ledger."

"Show me."

He narrowed his eyes at her. "I don't believe I will."

"It's listed on page one of this ledger. If you don't show me yours, I shall assume you purposely lied and I shall so inform Mr. Beckwith who will no doubt reconsider whether or not to honor the first will."

Jack would take her to court before he'd have the first will set aside now. "Show me yours . . . and I'll show you mine," he challenged in a low voice.

She studied him for a moment as though she should read something else into his words, and for the life of him, he wasn't certain if she should or not. He wasn't accustomed to flirting with women in order to lure them into his bed. He paid for the women he wanted. Nothing else was required of him except parting with his coins. With the duchess, he had the uncomfortable feeling something more was going on between them and that it could lead him down a path he didn't wish to take.

As though making up her mind, she slapped the ledger on the table, turned back the cover, and placed her finger on the page. "There."

Slowly he lowered his gaze from her triumphant expression to the words written so neatly. "Black coach with ducal crest. Ah, I see."

"What precisely do you see?"

"A mistake, obviously. The duke put the conveyance in both ledgers."

"Knowing my husband as I did, I think that entirely unlikely. Lovingdon was meticulous and precise when it came to all aspects of his life."

"Including bedding his wife?"

Even as she glared at him, a rosy blush spread over her cheeks. Was she embarrassed by the question posed or the accuracy of his deduction?

"You provoke me on purpose to distract me. Any decent man wouldn't ask such a question of a woman."

"As we've already determined, I find 'decent' boring."

He heard her foot tapping the floor and had the feeling she'd like to slap him again. Truth be told, he wished she would. He deserved it. Whatever had possessed him to pose such an intimate question? What did it matter how Lovingdon had treated his wife in bed? If Jack didn't know better, he'd think he was feeling a spark of envy.

Her foot ceased its tapping. "I have shown you mine, now show me yours."

"My ledger?" he asked.

"Of course, you dolt. What else would we be discussing?"

"I don't know, Olivia, but I can think of more interesting things to show each other than our ledgers."

"You duped me last night, sir. I would know the reason for it."

With a sigh, he turned back the pages in his book and pointed. "There. Honest mistake."

She glanced down. "Black brougham? How do you confuse a brougham with a coach? The brougham is smaller, seats only two—"

"I didn't realize. I thought they were the same thing."

"I don't believe you're that misinformed, but be that as it may, now that I know the coach is Henry's, I can use it at any time without fear of being arrested for thievery."

"Actually, you can't. As Henry's guardian, I am also guardian of all his possessions."

"But Mr. Beckwith gave me the ledger," she pointed out.

"So you'll know what your son can expect to receive when he turns twenty-one, not because care of those items has been entrusted to you."

He didn't relish the defeat that caused her to sag. In truth, he knew she'd be a far better guardian over her son than he would. She'd fight to the death to protect him, while Jack would only fight until he was bloodied. His finances, however, were another matter entirely. Jack doubted she was well equipped to handle those. "You can't win. I hold all the power."

It seemed his words renewed her determination to best him. She squared her shoulders and lifted her chin. "You are the most irritating man I've ever had the misfortune to meet."

"Then obviously you've not met many, Olivia."

"I did not give you leave to address me with such familiarity."

"Did you not? You instructed me not to address you by your title, which leaves only your name."

"Mr. Dodger—"

"If I'd had a father, he'd be Mr. Dodger. As I didn't, there is no Mr. Dodger. You may call me Jack."

Olivia couldn't, she absolutely couldn't pretend such familiarity with this man. And she didn't believe for one second that he had truly believed a coach bearing the ducal crest was his property. He was extremely skilled at unsettling her. Snatching up her ledger, she spun on her heel and walked to the other end of the table, where she set down the book that was certain to drive her insane before Henry reached his majority. The notion of thumbing her nose at etiquette and marrying posthaste was becoming more appealing by the moment.

Needing to gather her wits about her before the next skirmish, she went to the sideboard and filled a plate with poached eggs, toast, and ham—even as she did so, disturbingly aware of Dodger's gaze following her movements. Her stomach tightened into knots with the thought of spending her morning in his presence. Her headache returned with a vengeance, and it was all she could do to remain standing. She nodded at the footman standing near the sideboard before walking to the table, where a second footman pulled out the chair for her while the butler stood observing everything. Normally the servants' presence didn't bother her because she and her husband had seldom engaged in any discourse that didn't concern the weather.

She feared the same would not be true of any subjects Mr. Dodger would introduce. Perhaps she would insist that all conversations focus on Henry and Henry alone.

Mr. Dodger took his seat with lithe movements that reminded her of a predator settling in to wait for the next opportunity to pounce on its prey. She was left with the impression that, while he'd turned his attention casually back to his ledger, nothing about him was as relaxed as it seemed. He was acutely aware of every aspect of his surroundings. It was common knowledge he'd survived a life on the streets. She imagined his survival had depended on acute senses. Lovingdon had always given the impression he was distracted while reading his newspaper. She had a feeling distractions were as foreign to Jack Dodger as the notion of adhering to society's rules.

She took a sip of warm tea, gathering her resolve for the next confrontation. She didn't particularly want it, but for the sake of her son, she had to make sure his guardian understood that children couldn't be toyed with as adults were. "Mr. Dodger."

"*Please*, Duchess. Jack."

His mocking tone left the unmistakable impression he held no respect whatsoever for her title.

"If you insist on my using your first name, then I shall refrain from calling you anything at all. Perhaps you could offer me the same courtesy," she suggested blandly.

"But I enjoy calling you something. Although I must confess you don't strike me as an Olivia. Have you a pet name?" he asked.

"No. And speaking of pets, you promised my son a dog."

He cocked his head, not bothering to hide his amusement. "Are you scolding me?"

"You didn't discuss the matter with me."

"I'm his guardian. I don't have to discuss anything concerning your son with you."

Oh, she bristled at his smugness. "Have you any concept at all regarding the amount of work required to see after a dog?"

"I've been to rat fights."

Olivia thought she'd have been in danger of bringing up her breakfast if she'd eaten any of it. "Other than that topic being inappropriate for the breakfast table, what has it to do with dogs?"

"Dogs fight the rats. I've seen the care and attention the owners give their dogs. They treat them like royalty, so I have a good idea of what is involved in caring for the creatures."

"And when it dies, how will my son deal with his broken heart?"

"I'll get him another one."

She released a deep sigh. "When you love something and lose it, it cannot be so easily replaced."

She felt the weight of his gaze as he tapped the open page of that blasted ledger. "Is that how you feel about your husband?"

"I will not discuss my feelings with a man who will use them against me." She held up her hands in order to cease this turn in the discussion. She would never reveal to him her feelings about anything. "You promised my son a dog. But you don't know him. He's an extremely sensitive child. I must insist in the future that you discuss with me any decisions you intend to make regarding Henry, before you discuss them with him."

He studied her, and she was left with the uncomfortable sensation that he could easily discern her feelings without her having to voice them, that he was as skilled at plucking out a person's emotions as he was at picking their pockets. "I hadn't realized it would upset you. I won't get him a dog."

He returned his attention to the ledger, as though the matter were settled simply because he had deemed it so.

Olivia didn't know whether to feel relief that there would be no dog or anger because he could so easily dismiss a promise he'd made to her son. When she'd brought up the matter, she wasn't certain what she'd wanted the outcome to be—his acknowledging he didn't know the first thing about taking care of her son, she supposed. Unlike most mothers, she didn't want to be a bystander in her son's life. She and Lovingdon had actually argued over the hiring of a nanny. While she understood that all children of the aristocracy were cared for by nannies, she didn't quite agree with the notion. She wanted a more active role, and this man was threatening to remove her completely from Henry's life. "Last night you said you were a man of your word."

Looking up, he gave her a cocky grin. "I am when it suits me."

She wanted to scream at the word games he played. She was accustomed to dealing with gentlemen, not scoundrels who changed their tune when the music no longer suited them. "You can't break your promise to him."

"Make up your mind. Do you want him to have the dog or not?"

"I don't want him to have the dog, but it would be far worse if you were to break your promise to him. Trust is a fragile thing, and you would teach him that a promise means nothing."

"Usually it doesn't."

"Perhaps in your world, Mr. Dodger, but not in ours."

"Jack."

The man was missing the point entirely. Why was she even wasting her breath arguing with him? Like all men, he would do what he had determined he wanted to do. "May we move on?"

"By all means. To what precisely did you have in mind?"

"I was supposed to meet you in the library last night—"

"So you were. You promised."

"I did not *promise*," she snapped.

"You said you would. In *my* world, when a person says something, the promise is implied."

Oh, her head was throbbing and she had a strong need

to return to bed and bury herself beneath the covers. "You've made your point. I fell asleep. I apologize."

"Do you always take laudanum before bed?"

"How did you know I did?"

"I smelled it on your breath."

Cold dread raced through her veins with the implication of that statement. "This morning I awoke in, well, not in my bed and I don't remember how I got there. Did you—" Squirming, she glanced around at the servants. While they didn't appear to be paying attention, she knew none of them were deaf. She leaned forward with the hope of Dodger hearing her while she spoke in a low voice, but the table was so incredibly long. Why did they even need a table this long in this particular room? It wasn't as though they often had guests.

"Did I . . . ?" he prompted.

She glanced around again. "May we dismiss the servants?"

"I don't believe there's a need. As I understand it, they are forbidden by some sort of servant code to discuss our matters, even amongst themselves."

"Yes, well—" She looked around again.

"When you failed to show as *promised*, I went searching for you."

"I see. I assume you found me."

He gave her a slow grin. "I did. You asked me not to go into your bedchamber. I saw no choice except to take you into mine."

He said it as though he'd done something for which he should be admired. She had little doubt carrying women into his bedchamber was an everyday—every *night*—occurrence.

"Did you take liberties?" she snapped.

"Trust me, Duchess: if I had, you'd remember."

The sudden intensity of his gaze was unnerving and gave her the distinct impression that he was envisioning himself in her bed, doing things with her body that would be far more memorable than anything she'd ever experienced with Lovingdon. It was unsettling enough to think of Jack Dodger holding her in his arms, against his chest, laying her on his bed, removing the hairpins—because now she had little doubt he was the culprit responsible for her loosened hair—but to contemplate his crawling between the sheets with her. . .

She dropped her gaze to the food on her plate to hide her shame that she longed to know what his deft fingers might accomplish.

"After depositing you on the bed, I went to my club. Ask Brittles. He had my coach, or what I thought was my coach, readied for me."

She looked over at the butler. Even though he was not supposed to be eavesdropping on the conversation, he gave her a curt nod. She forced herself to meet Dodger's gaze. "It really wasn't necessary to take me to a bed."

"The one you were in was quite cramped. I know many a woman who would have been grateful for my considerations."

"I've no doubt you do," she snapped. "I'm not one of them." She rubbed her brow. "I apologize. I'm not normally quite so difficult." She didn't consider herself difficult at all, but she doubted he'd believe that statement. "The past few days have been incredibly trying, Mr.—"

"Jack."

She swallowed. She didn't want to accept the familiarity that he was offering, but she was so weary of battling him. "Jack."

"There. Now, that wasn't so difficult was it?" He came to his feet. "As the past few days have been so trying, I suggest you enjoy a leisurely breakfast, and when you're done, come to the library and we'll discuss this unusual situation that your deceased husband has placed us in."

She watched in astonishment as he picked up his black book and walked out of the room. She could hardly fathom that a part of her actually regretted his leaving, but it was only because she was now alone, with nothing but her own thoughts for company.

And what strange thoughts they were. For a moment, when she'd walked in, it was almost as though she'd seen her late husband there, greeting her. It was a trick of the morning light, pouring in through the windows. She wasn't accustomed to so much light in this room. Lovingdon had always preferred to keep the world out. From what she'd been able to discern, before he'd married her, he'd never allowed a single drapery to be parted or a shade to be lifted. It had been a somber house, reflecting its owner's melancholy mood. He'd even asked her to restrict her desire for allowing in the sunshine to rooms he didn't frequent.

She'd have thought Jack—no, she couldn't think of him as Jack—would have preferred the shadows as well.

Chapter 6

Jack stood at the window in his library, gazing out on his well-manicured garden. *His* garden, viewed through *his* window from *his* library. He'd planned to study his ledger further, but he'd been unable to concentrate.

He'd been unprepared for the way the sound of his name rolling off the widow's tongue had made him feel. He'd wanted to ask her to say it again. He'd wanted to move closer to her and talk in hushed tones so the servants couldn't hear. He wanted to know why she truly objected to a dog. He wanted to ask what she knew of broken hearts.

Mesmerized by the play of sunlight dancing over the red in her brown hair, he'd remembered the way it had felt unfurling in his hand. He welcomed her disdain because it kept his own desires leashed.

He pressed his shoulder against the sharp corner of the window casement, ignoring the cutting bite. She'd bristled at his mocking use of *Duchess*, but her tone was no different. He heard the censure in her voice every time she called him *Mr. Dodger*. She knew what he was as well as *he* did: the bastard son of a whore, his father unknown to him, probably a stranger to his mother.

He heard the door open, but he stayed where he was. Her light footsteps grew louder as she neared, until he smelled her wispy fragrance. He didn't want to consider the joy that might be found in discovering the other secret spots where she applied it. She came to stand across from him, the damnable sunlight again catching her hair in ways that made him want to touch it, plow his fingers into it, and not be nearly as careful as he'd been the night before when removing the pins.

"Do you really not know who your father is?" she asked quietly.

That discussion was conversations ago, and he saw no reason to return to it, although it did occur to him that she might have been thinking about him as much as he'd been thinking about her since leaving the breakfast room. He suspected, however, that her thoughts focused on his faults, while he was reluctantly beginning to recognize her merits.

"I think we would do best to stick with the business at hand. What do you know of the nanny?"

Her golden eyes widened slightly in surprise. "Helen? She comes highly recommended. Both the duke and I have been incredibly pleased with her service. Why do you ask?"

"The boy seems far too quiet."

"Children are supposed to be quiet and well mannered—"

He laughed softly at the memories of his own childhood. "Not the children I knew."

"You grew up in the streets, Mr. Dodger. My son grows up in a home."

"Yet he is fearful, while I was not."

"He is simply reserved, as his father was."

Jack bit back the need to ask if he'd held on to that reserve when he'd taken her to his bed. Why was he so curious about the intimate details of their lives?

She looked out the window. "Last night you said that you barely knew Lovingdon. How was it that you knew him at all? Did he go to your club?"

"On occasion. What do you know of my club?"

"That it's a place well suited to scoundrels."

He hitched up a corner of his mouth. "You say that as though I force people to partake in scandalous behavior. I don't."

"You provide them with the opportunity."

"You see? There again, your tone implies it's a bad thing. Those who enjoy being wicked can't be stopped. They will go into the darkest alleys to find a gambling den, or liquor, or women. If it's a dishonest game, even if they win, everything will be taken from them, possibly even their lives. When they purchase a bottle, they don't know what's in it. Sometimes it's nothing more than piss." He held up his hand to stop the protest at his language that he was certain she was about to issue. "And the ladies: from the ladies they can get all sorts of ailments, some that will make them go blind or rob them of their sanity.

"And so, yes, I provide gentlemen with a safe haven, where the games are honest, the liquor is the best to be made, and the ladies are clean."

"I'm left with the impression you somehow consider your actions noble."

"As I said, you can't stop someone who is determined to enjoy wickedness. Why should I not profit from others' weaknesses? I've become very wealthy, and whom have I harmed?" Damn it all. Why was he standing there explaining his life, his choices, his actions? He'd always known others found fault with his endeavors, but he didn't, and that was all that mattered to him. He'd never cared for others' opinions.

"I suspect you harm without realizing it," she said.

That was the problem when arguing with the righteous: they didn't listen to the merits of the argument. "Be that as it may, I have no intention of harming your son."

She glanced over to the corner where yesterday a table had been covered with an assortment of clocks as though the duke had been trying to collect time. Now a variety of bottles and decanters were beautifully arranged and within easy reach of his desk.

"You've already brought spirits into the house," she said, and he heard the censure in her voice.

"But I won't force you to drink them."

"I never would."

"No doubt."

"What did you do with my husband's clocks?" she asked tartly.

For some reason, he preferred it when she was brisk with him. Maybe it was the spunk that he liked or the relief that it indicated she favored him not at all. It could prove unfortunate if an easy camaraderie developed between them. While she was no doubt aware they were not equals on one level, he was acutely aware they were not equals on many.

"They are *my* clocks. They are listed on page seven

of my ledger. I told the servants to distribute them all over the house, however they wished."

"A collection cannot be a collection if it's spread hither and yon."

"I don't give a damn about the bloody clocks. I care about my damned whiskey! Besides, their infernal ticking was driving me mad." Maybe they'd done the same thing to the duke, only they'd succeeded where he was concerned.

Jack inhaled a deep breath to rein in his temper, but it failed to work because it only served to bring her fragrance forward so he could smell it more deeply. He didn't want her enticing him. He wanted her married.

"Let's get to business, shall we?" He strode over to *his* desk and sat in *his* chair.

She hesitated before squaring her shoulders and marching over to take a chair opposite him. If he were a lesser man, her glare would have been intimidating. She certainly was determined to hold her own against him. He had to give her credit for that— that and the fact she cared so much for her son.

"Let me be honest—" he began.

"Are you implying you've not been up to this point? In my world, Mr. Dodger, a person is assumed to be speaking honestly, so his words need no clarification."

"Duchess, you do try my patience," he ground out.

"Then send me and my son to the country."

He wasn't half tempted. "Not on your life."

"It would make things easier all the way around."

"I find 'easy' boring. Therefore, back to the matter at hand. At my club, I have more than two dozen people in my employ. I manage them and my business without a great deal of bother. As a matter of fact, my business is run quite effectively and efficiently. Unfortunately, I know nothing at all about managing a household."

He watched as a subtle shifting in her expression took place, and he realized he may have given too much away and in so doing, granted her power he was not willing to relinquish.

"Whereas I," she stated with a calm reserve that caused everything within him to tighten, "know *everything* about managing a household."

"I thought you might. Therefore, I'll leave the management of the household to your discretion."

She smiled and it was the most mesmerizing thing he'd ever seen. It transformed her into someone who was young and carefree. It made him want to skim his thumb over her mouth. It made him want to get up, circle the desk, and take her in his arms.

"Not. On. Your. Life."

The want and desire crashed around him. Had she somehow managed to read his thoughts? "I beg your pardon?"

She rose with all the confidence of a woman who had just inherited an empire. "I will not manage the household."

She turned on her heel and headed for the door.

"Then you're welcome to warm my bed."

Even as Jack threw out the challenge, he wasn't certain what had possessed him to offer that alternative, although it certainly had appeal. If she brought half as much fire to his bed as she brought to her words, he thought they might have an incredible and unforgettable night.

Very slowly, she turned around. "You can't be serious."

"I'm not a man with a charitable bent. Today, you have a roof over your head, clothes on your person, and food in your belly. The roof and the food are mine, the clothes are still questionable as I've yet to locate them in my ledger. You're taking from me, Duchess, without giving anything in return. To let it continue is a poor business practice. If you wish to remain in residence, you must earn your keep."

"Earn my keep? As though I'm a servant or, worse, your whore?" She felt the fury shimmering through her. "You are a bastard."

"According to the law, yes."

"How can you be so callous? I've just lost my husband, my home, and, for all legal purposes, my son. Have you no kindness in you at all?"

"There is no profit to be made in kindness."

"Is that all you care about? Your gains?"

Jack cursed harshly beneath his breath. Why was she making this so damned difficult?

She'd angled her head accusingly as though she could intimidate him into changing his stance. Her hair was a rich brown with just enough red in it to make it interesting. He wondered what she'd look like dressed in red. Black made her appear too pale. But red, or purple, a deep purple—like royalty. . .

He shook his head. He never envisioned women in clothes—imagined them out of them but not in them. What was wrong with him?

The door clicked open to reveal the butler. Because the library was large, with several sitting areas arranged between the door and the desk, it took a few seconds for Brittles to cross the expanse, his footsteps eerily silent. It made Jack suspicious, the way the servants moved around so quietly. It wasn't natural unless a person intended to rob someone.

Brittles stood at attention until Jack looked at him, then he bowed slightly. "I'm sorry to disturb you, sir, but an Inspector Swindler from Scotland Yard wishes to speak with you. Are you home?"

"Of course, I'm home, man. I'm sitting right here."

Before Brittles could respond, the duchess cleared her throat and stepped into the fray. "Saying you're not at home is a polite way to inform someone you don't wish to see him."

"Didn't think they *lied* in your polite world."

"They're not rude in my world."

Jack wanted to argue further, but he didn't want to keep Swindler waiting. He'd take the matter up with the duchess later. He suspected they were going to spend a good deal of their time arguing about what each of them considered proper. He gave his attention back to the butler. "Of course, I'll see him."

As soon as the butler had left the room, the duchess advanced. "What have you done?"

"I chose not to lie and tell him I wasn't home. I thought you'd applaud my honesty."

"No, I mean, why is an inspector from Scotland Yard here? Did you rob someone? Kill someone?" She took another step nearer. "What have you done that would require Scotland Yard to come to this household? If you're arrested—"

Before she could finish delivering what Jack was

certain was going to be a dire threat that involved her running off to tell Beckwith, the door was once again opened. This time James Swindler strode into the room. It had always irritated Jack that Swindler had the uncanny knack to give the impression he belonged, regardless of the surroundings. He'd probably look comfortable strolling through Buckingham Palace.

He wore a beige wool jacket, cream-colored waistcoat, and a dark green cravat that brought out the green hue of his eyes, causing them to become his most striking feature. He often dressed plainly in order not to be noticed. Today wasn't one of those occasions.

Olivia was studying Swindler as though trying to decide if he was the lesser of the two evils presently occupying the library. Because he knew Swindler would demonstrate impeccable manners, Jack brought himself to his feet, suddenly not in the mood to be found lacking. "Duchess, allow me the honor of introducing James Swindler, from Scotland Yard."

"Inspector."

"Swindler," Jack said, "allow me to introduce the Duchess of Lovingdon. Recent widow." *And royal pain in my backside*.

Swindler bowed, no doubt impressing the widow with his courtly graces. It was surprising that a man as tall and broad wasn't clumsy. He had an inch or two on Jack in height as well as in the width of his shoulders. "Your Grace," he greeted her formally, irritating Jack in the process, for reasons he failed to understand. What did he care if the widow was charmed?

Swindler turned his razor-sharp green gaze to Jack. "Your missive said it was urgent."

"You sent for him?" the duchess asked.

Jack took a great deal of satisfaction in her shocked expression. "Sorry, Duchess. You'll be disappointed to learn he's not going to cart me away. And now that the formalities are over with, Swindler, do you want whiskey or gin?" He walked to the table where he'd had his lovely bottles of indulgences set up. No ticking.

"It's not even noon yet, Jack," Swindler said.

"For a man who doesn't live his life by a timepiece, there is never an inappropriate time for indulging," Jack said, pouring whiskey into a glass for himself.

"Unlike you, I do sleep," Swindler said. "I'll pass."

"Suit yourself." He strode back to his desk. "You can leave us now, Duchess."

He was halfway into his chair when she said, "As I oversee your household, I believe it imperative that I remain."

Her words stilled him, left him hovering over the chair. Not because they stunned him, but because she looked so incredibly pleased with herself, as though she thought she'd achieved some measure of victory over him. As much as it pained him to admit it, he rather liked it when she appeared pleased—not that he had any plans to work toward keeping her in that particular state. He dropped into his chair and took a slow sip of his whiskey. "Am I to assume you chose managing my household over—"

"Yes, quite," she responded quickly before giving her attention to Swindler. It grated that she dismissed Jack so readily, and it occurred to him she wanted to stay because Swindler interested her. He wondered how she'd feel about marrying a commoner.

"Perhaps you'd care for some tea, Inspector," she said.

"That'd be lovely, thank you."

She glided elegantly to the far door, and Jack realized he'd not given nearly enough time to studying her backside. She had a narrow back. He wondered how much of the flare of her hips he could attribute to petticoats. Why didn't women wear clothing that gave a truer sense of their form?

"Tea," Jack muttered irritably, knowing Olivia ws too far away to hear. "When did you start drinking tea?"

"It's a distraction when I have to question ladies who'd rather not be questioned."

"I wouldn't think you'd want to be distracted."

"Not me. Them. They get comfortable serving their tea and tell me things they might not otherwise."

His tactic made a great deal of sense. Little wonder that even with Scotland Yard's less than sterling reputation, Swindler was known for getting the job done. Jack was certain the man could make a good deal more money if he went into business for himself investigating private matters. But unlike Jack, Swindler seemed to have little interest in wealth.

"The tea will be here shortly," the duchess said as she returned to their area of the library and sat in a nearby chair. "I shall work not to be intrusive."

She suddenly looked like a young girl, sitting on the edge of her seat, thinking she might learn that Jack was in some sort of trouble. He had little doubt she'd like to see him dragged away in irons. He'd lived through that experience once. He'd rather die than go through it again. He indicated a chair across from him, and Swindler sat.

Jack leaned forward. "This residence belonged to the Duke of Lovingdon. He left it to me in his will. I want to know why."

Swindler shifted his gaze to the duchess, studied her for a long moment, and then looked back at Jack. "Does she not know?"

"She was more stunned than I. I think the solicitor, a Mr. Beckwith, may know the reason, but he claims he's not at *liberty* to tell me. I want you to go to his residence at midnight, kidnap him, take him someplace dark and dangerous, hang him up by his toes, and beat him until he decides he *is* at liberty to tell me."

The duchess gasped and shot to her feet, righteous indignation shimmering off of her in undulating waves. "You can't be serious. That's barbaric. I won't allow you to—"

"Your Grace." To Jack's disappointment Swindler interrupted her magnificent tirade. "Indeed he's *not* serious."

She released a tiny screech that was abruptly cut off as though she'd only just remembered she was a lady of quality. "You are despicable, sir."

"Come now, Olivia, where's your sense of humor?" Jack asked.

"It made a hasty departure when you entered my life."

Jack couldn't stop himself from grinning at the shot she'd fired. Damn, but he was beginning to enjoy her. She resumed sitting. How did she manage to sit so straight and stiff for so long?

"You see what she thinks of me?" Jack asked Swindler. "When you were announced, she thought you'd arrived to arrest me for some crime."

"Can hardly blame her for that. You do have a reputation for, well, for not always having the respect for the law that you should." Swindler held up his hand before Jack could protest. "But I'm short on time, so let's get back to the matter at hand. Were you even acquainted with Lovingdon?"

"He came to the club on occasion." Jack rubbed his thumb along his jaw. "But we hardly spoke."

"When you get right down to it, what does the reason matter?" Swindler asked. "You never before cared where your fortunes came from. Why now?"

Jack slid his gaze to the duchess. Based on her stern features, she'd obviously not yet forgiven him for his earlier prank. In truth, he'd hoped to infuriate her enough that she'd leave. "Shouldn't you be seeing to the tea?"

"I have every confidence it will be delivered as soon as it's prepared."

Damnation, he hadn't expected her to be present while he spoke with Swindler. He considered insisting she leave, but that would only increase her suspicions of him. Besides, perhaps she needed to hear this. "All right then." He tapped the desk, hoping he didn't sound like an alarmist. "I'm to serve as guardian of his heir. I want to make sure this situation isn't similar to Luke's."

Jack saw in Swindler's eyes that he immediately caught the connection. Luke's father had been murdered by Luke's uncle in an attempt to gain the earldom. It was Luke's uncle who had paid Jack sixpence to lure a family—Luke's family—into an alley. He'd hired men to ambush them there. His actions had irrevocably changed all their lives.

"Have you reason to suspect—"

"The duke had no surviving brothers. However, Beckwith told me of two cousins" —Jack handed him a slip of paper— "the first is next in line, the other follows. I need you to find out everything you can about them."

With a curt nod, Swindler tucked the paper inside his jacket.

The duchess again came to her feet. Could she not speak while sitting? "You're going to investigate my husband's family?"

"Something is amiss here, Duchess," Jack told her honestly. "The duke said I was to protect Henry. Protect him from what? An overzealous mother? I hardly think that likely."

She looked at him as though she thought he should take up residence at Bethlem Royal Hospital for the mentally ill. "So you think my husband's cousins would murder my son to gain the title? Is that what you're suggesting? My dear sir, that is the stuff of novels, not reality."

"Tell that to the Earl of Claybourne."

"I'd heard—" Blinking, she sat back down as though her knees had given out on her. "I thought it was only gossip. You know how people are. You don't truly think Henry is in danger . . . ?"

"I don't know what else to think, Olivia."

She was too distressed to notice the familiarity he'd used, or perhaps she no longer thought it important enough to warrant her wrath. Swindler, damn him, did notice and rubbed the side of his nose with his forefinger, a signal he'd developed in their youth to indicate when someone was giving too much of himself away. Swindler had been one of Feagan's lads, the best at ferreting out information.

"Well," Jack snapped, irritated that Swindler might mistakenly believe he cared more for the widow than he did. "What are you waiting for? You know what I need."

Like all of Feagan's lads, Swindler was accustomed to Jack issuing the orders, so he took no offense. He got up, walked to Olivia, and crouched before her. "Duchess, were you aware of any threats?"

The man sounded so nauseatingly sympathetic, so irritatingly caring. He'd never been one to shy away from revealing his feelings if he thought doing so would gain him an advantage. Olivia would no doubt think he was bloody wonderful. Good. She could marry him and Jack could turn this whole mess over to Swindler. If trouble was afoot, he'd no doubt be the best at discovering what it was and properly dealing with it.

Olivia slowly shook her head as though she could hardly believe the matter had come to this. "No, I, no, not that I'm aware."

"How did your husband die?"

"He slipped on the stairs and struck his head."

"Was he prone to being clumsy?"

"Of course not."

"Were there any witnesses to the mishap?"

"I saw what happened."

"Did anyone else see him slip?"

She hesitated, and Jack could see she was running various scenarios through her mind, weighing how best to answer. She'd seen him fall, possibly the only one, so if her word were brought into question—

"Swindler, he slipped," Jack said. "The stairs are marble, treacherous as ice. I almost lost my footing last night. I don't think you'll learn anything by pursuing that avenue."

"Quite right." Swindler unfolded his body. "I'll see what I can find."

A light rap sounded on the door. The footman opened the door and a female servant carried in a tray holding a tea service.

"Oh," Olivia said, coming to her feet somewhat unsteadily. If last night had been a shock for her, Jack could only imagine what the past few minutes had been. Yet still she remained gracious. "Your tea, Inspector."

"Thank you, but I really must be off. Another day, perhaps."

"I'll see you out," Jack said, grateful Olivia seemed too unsettled to join them. He followed Swindler into the hallway and, once they were beyond the hearing of the footman, asked in a low voice, "You're not thinking she tripped him up."

"No. She was worried about me thinking that, though. He couldn't have been very old."

"He was quite old, actually. In his early fifties, I'd say."

"Twenty years from now, you won't think fifty is so old. Why do you think she married him?" Swindler asked.

"I don't know. Do I need to find out?"

Swindler shrugged. "Probably not important unless we begin to suspect he was murdered."

"I can't see her murdering anyone."

"Know her well, do you?"

"I know her hardly at all," Jack admitted reluctantly. "Doesn't mean my assessment doesn't have merit. There was a reason I was very skilled at determining which pockets were worth the trouble to pick."

"And there's a reason you've asked me to investigate the matter for you."

"You're quite right, but I also want you to look into another issue." They walked from the hallway into the foyer, which was absent of servants. "Make some inquiries and see if you can discover if the duke engaged in any perversions."

"Perversions?"

"With young boys, specifically."

Swindler came to a halt, his gaze discerning. He was very clever, perhaps the cleverest of Feagan's lads. Jack knew by setting Swindler on this trail that Swindler would eventually figure out the aspects of Jack's past that he'd always wanted to remain secret, but it was a risk he was willing to take in order to discover the truth. While he suspected Lovingdon was *not* the man who'd bought and abused him, he needed confirmation to put any lingering doubts to rest.

Jack cleared his throat. "I know I was never your favorite among Feagan's lads, but do this favor for me, will you? Find out if her son is in danger."

"I'll make some inquiries, but I won't do it for you. I'll do it because Frannie would want me to."

"You love her, don't you?"

"Go to hell."

Jack laughed. "You're too late with that command, mate. I've been there since I was born."

Still chuckling, he strode back down the hallway. For a man who was suddenly saddled with unwanted responsibilities, his mood was improving. Olivia would see to the affairs of his household, leaving him free to take care of the matters that were important to him. Entering the library, he was surprised to see Olivia sitting at his desk, looking through his ledger. He snatched it from her and closed it smartly. "You're still here?"

She rose, her eyes narrowing as though she'd discovered the pages in his book were all blank. "I don't believe he was truly an inspector from Scotland Yard."

Jack arched a brow. "You don't? Then who was he?"

"Obviously someone of your acquaintance. You gave it away by offering him some spirits. But I don't believe for one moment you'd be friends with an inspector. I think all this was just an elaborate ruse to make me think my son is in danger, to make you appear more important than you are."

"To what purpose?"

She seemed to hesitate, then thought better of it. "I haven't determined what you wish to gain. Perhaps my leaving you in peace."

"That would certainly be worth obtaining."

She opened her mouth—

"No, you may not take your son to the country."

"To my sister-in-law's then. For a couple of hours."

"No."

"You can't hold us prisoner."

"Until I'm assured you're safe, I can."

"Why do you even care?"

"Damned if I know," he growled and walked to the window. "Take two footmen with you. They're to watch you and the boy at all times."

He heard her sigh of annoyance.

"My world is much more civilized than yours. I assure you, we're in no danger," she said, her voice filled with certainty.

"Then why me?" He spun around to discover she'd approached silently. She staggered back, while he fought not to. Devil take her. Who'd have thought she had the skills of a burglar? "Why me?" he repeated, not bothering to hide his anger, hoping she wouldn't realize how her proximity rattled him. Why did she have to smell so incredibly enticing? She was in mourning, for God's sake. Shouldn't she smell like death delivered? "I'm intimately familiar with the dark side of London. Why did your husband think your son needed a guardian with that knowledge? The one thing I'm good at is surviving. I've lived alone on the streets since I was five. I know danger when I sense it and I can read men with uncanny accuracy. If there is no danger, then why me?"

Her delicate brow pleated, and he forced his hands behind his back, holding them tightly to prevent himself from reaching up to smooth away the worry.

"You said he came to your club. Was it for the women?" Her voice had caught at the end as though she'd had to push the word out from the soles of her feet.

"He had you, why would he seek comfort elsewhere?" The words of reassurance felt strange on his tongue, but not as strange as the tightening in his gut with the thought of Lovingdon having her in his bed, at his dining table, in his library, at his side.

"Perhaps I was not enough," she said softly.

Devil take her. All Jack knew for certain was that Lovingdon hadn't gambled. He kept records of who purchased chips and in what quantities. "It wasn't the women."

She gave him a sad smile. "I'd have thought you'd be skilled at lying."

Why should he care if she was unhappy? But for some incomprehensible reason, he did. "I never saw him with one of my girls. That's the truth of it. He didn't gamble and I never saw him drink."

"Then why was he there?"

"He watched." It sounded perverted, even to his ears.

"What did he watch?"

He didn't want to say it, didn't want to admit that Lovingdon had been watching him. Whenever he spied the man, Lovingdon had been studying Jack as though he was some sort of mystifying creature. Perhaps this was all some sort of experiment. Move a man up in the world and see if it caused him to become a better man. The irony, of course, was that since he was dead, Lovingdon would never know the results. "He just watched all the goings on. Some people are like that."

"For what purpose?"

"Because they haven't the guts to do anything. They fear moral judgments. How the hell should I know? Go to your sister-in-law's and leave me in peace. But don't give one moment's thought to going to the country. If I have to come after the boy, I'll make your life miserable."

"I daresay, Mr. Dodger, that I'd hardly be able to tell the difference since you make it miserable now."

With fury equal to his, she spun on her heel and marched to the door. Watching the lovely sway of that backside as she made her exit, he decided he'd have to say things to force her to leave more often.

Chapter 7

Olivia conceded that going to see the Duchess of Avendale had been a mistake, because now Henry had a rabid curiosity about the Great Exhibition, after his cousin told him about all the wondrous things he'd seen. To make the situation worse, she returned home to discover she had a caller waiting in the parlor. While Helen took a very tired Henry up to the nursery for an afternoon nap, Olivia removed her black veiled hat, placed it on a table in the foyer, and replaced it with the widow's cap she'd left there before leaving. She felt as though she'd gotten caught doing something she wasn't supposed to and might be on the receiving end of a scolding.

Edmund Stanford, Viscount Briarwood, had chosen an inopportune moment to visit. Her husband's cousin had kindly handled the matter of the funeral and had overseen Lovingdon's final journey to the family crypt at the ancestral estate. He'd provided her with a strong shoulder to lean on. The notion that he would murder Henry and usurp the titles was ludicrous.

After patting a few final stray strands back into place, she strolled into the parlor.

"Lord Briarwood, how kind of you to call. I do hope you've not been waiting long."

Briarwood bowed. She could see the family resemblance in the cut of his squared chin. He was only a few years younger than Lovingdon had been, but already his wheat-colored hair was fading to white. He'd not inherited the family's tendency toward tallness. But what he lacked in height, he made up for in width, a shape that gave him a rather intimidating mien.

"Only a moment or two, Duchess. Quite honestly, I was surprised to discover you were making the rounds."

Olivia felt the warmth flush her cheeks at the chastisement in his voice. "I merely visited my sister-in-law. She's only recently widowed herself, and I thought she could offer me some advice on dealing with the wretched sorrow."

"Of course, forgive me for my presumption. I can only imagine how difficult all of this has been for you—"

I suspect you truly have no idea.

"—and allow me to again offer my condolences on your loss. Your husband is now at rest in the family crypt."

"I appreciate all you've done. I can think of no way to repay you your kindness."

"Think nothing of it. I promised Lovingdon I'd keep an eye on you, don't you know?"

Olivia couldn't prevent a fissure of unease from traveling through her. It was a woman's lot in life to answer to her husband, and suddenly she had far too many men hovering around her, making demands, and voicing expectations.

A maid brought in the tea service. Once she left, Olivia and Briarwood took their chairs in a small sitting area with a narrow table between them. Briarwood was not as lean as her husband had been, and the chair groaned beneath his bulk.

"When did Lovingdon ask you to look after me?" Olivia asked quietly as she poured them tea.

"I can't remember exactly. You know how it is. Men ask each other for favors all the time, never really expecting they'll be collected. I came here as soon as I returned to London. I wanted to make certain everything was in order. The will was read last night, was it not?"

Olivia's hand jerked and the cup rattled on the saucer as her gaze jumped to his. She could see her husband in his expressive green eyes. Lovingdon's eyes had been the same pale green, carried the same look of regret. When Lovingdon smiled, the joy never lit his eyes. It was almost as though he'd lived his life in mourning. She wished he'd confided in her, but like so many in the aristocracy, theirs was not a marriage of the hearts.

She waited until Lord Briarwood had taken the cup from her to speak. "Yes, yes, it was."

"Who did he name as guardian?"

She lifted her own cup, took a quick sip. "Who would you have thought?"

He grinned as though they'd been sharing a secret and could now tell the world. "I'd have thought he'd name me. We never spoke about the specifics, but I seem the most logical, being family and all—and the next in line. I want you to know that I consider it an honor to watch over both the young duke and you."

His presumption left her with a foul taste she couldn't explain. She was certain he had no ill will toward Henry, and yet she was bothered by his audacity—to assume so much. She was letting Dodger influence her. She'd have never been suspicious if he hadn't planted the seeds of doubt in her mind. "My lord, I truly appreciate your sentiments, more than you realize. Unfortunately, my husband named Jack Dodger as guardian."

Briarwood looked as though she'd jabbed him with a fireplace poker. "*The* Jack Dodger?"

"Yes, quite."

Clearly baffled by the turn of events, he stared at her as though she'd been responsible for them. "What would compel Dodger to give a care about a lord's son?"

"I'm afraid I can't even begin to guess, but Lovingdon secured his interest by leaving him all his non-entailed possessions." Because Briarwood was next in line, she thought he had a right to know. If he'd not been seeing to her husband's remains, she was fairly certain he'd have been in attendance last night.

Shaking his head, he studied his teacup as though trying to memorize the pattern of the flowers that surrounded the delicate bone china. Then he lifted his gaze to hers. "Dodger must have blackmailed him."

"Blackmailed him? Whatever are you talking about?"

"He must have threatened Lovingdon with exposing him for some misbehavior or some such."

Olivia pondered the possibilities. She couldn't imagine Lovingdon misbehaving. Considering Dodger's outburst earlier, it was obvious he was as perplexed as anyone regarding the conditions of the will.

"We'll contest the will," Briarwood suddenly announced emphatically, as though no other conclusion could be drawn and she'd agree with him. "It might create a scandal, but I can't see that we have any other choice. Having Dodger as guardian is taking a quick route to disaster. I daresay, your son will be tainted, his respectability questioned."

"Mr. Beckwith said the will couldn't be challenged."

"Of course he said that. Less work for him that way."

"And less expense for you," a deep voice rumbled.

Olivia screeched, jumped, and upset her teacup, pouring hot tea over her skirts. Fortunately, she had enough petticoats that she was saved from any serious injury. She set her saucer and cup aside, grabbed a linen napkin, and began blotting the tea and wiping it from her hands. The man had the infuriating habit of appearing where he wasn't expected. "I don't recall inviting you into the parlor, Mr. Dodger."

He held out his hands in the irritating manner that she was coming to recognize preceded irritating words. "I don't require an invitation as it's now *my* parlor. Afternoon, milord."

Briarwood had come to his feet, his eyes narrowed as though he trusted Dodger as little as Olivia did. "Dodger," he finally said.

"You're acquainted?" Olivia asked, stopping her frantic patting.

Dodger grinned with a touch of malice. "I told you, Duchess, I'm familiar with the aristocracy." He sat in a nearby chair, slouching back slightly, placing his ankle on his knee. She'd never seen a man sit in such an impolite manner. "Have a seat, Briarwood. We can discuss all the reasons why we don't want to do as you suggest."

To her surprise, her husband's cousin did sit. But his back was straight, his posture excellent. Breeding was so important. She could only begin to fathom the difficulties Henry would face if he was taught behavior by Dodger. His peers would laugh at him, insult him, and afford him no respect.

"Now, as I see it," Dodger drawled, "we have three reasons not to take this matter to the courts: the expense, because you will have to hire a solicitor; the terrible scandal that will be created, because something of this nature is certain to incite gossip; and the fact that the matter can be easily rectified if you but marry the duchess."

"M-marry her?" Briarwood stammered, clearly shocked by the notion.

"Yes, did she not mention that? I forfeit guardianship when she marries a man willing to take over the role. So, you see? You merely have to wed her—"

"I'm in mourning, Mr. Dodger," she repeated for what seemed like the thousandth time, through clenched teeth. How was it that the man failed to grasp so simple a concept?

"The ceremony itself could be handled very discreetly with a special license. Just as Lord Claybourne arranged his marriage while his new bride was mourning the loss of her father. Then off to the country you go. In two years, you return to London with tales of your insatiable love, and all is forgiven. Ladies excuse all manner of indiscretion when love is at its core."

"I'm not going off to the country—"

"I thought that's what you wanted."

"I want to be rid of *you*."

"Marriage achieves that end."

"I have no desire to marry Lord Briarwood." She jerked her gaze to Briarwood. "My apologies, my lord. I'm certain you were not considering marriage, but I am only newly widowed." And if she ever married again, she hoped duty wouldn't be involved. On the other hand, Dodger was correct. Marriage would effectively get him out of her life. She cleared her throat. "I hope I didn't offend you if you were consider—"

"No, I-I'd not entertained the notion. That's not to say I wouldn't, only that I hadn't considered it up until this moment." He shifted his gaze to Dodger. "I believe you've effectively distracted us with this marriage nonsense. How did you manage to convince my cousin to name you guardian?"

"I can take no credit for convincing him of anything. As to the reason he named me guardian, I haven't a clue. However, I have an inspector from Scotland Yard making inquiries. Do you know of any threats that might have been made?"

Briarwood seemed more shocked by that news than by the notion of marrying her. "Threats? What sort of threats?"

"Threats to kill the lad."

"Why would anyone kill him?"

"To acquire his titles."

"As I'm first in line for the titles, I suppose that puts me first in line as your suspect. Has it failed your notice that I already have a title?"

"Viscount. Hardly the highest of ranks. And it is but one, while young Henry has three."

"Mine is a higher rank than you possess. And one is sufficient for me."

"I'd have thought you a man of more ambition."

Briarwood leaped to his feet, none too agilely. "I resent the implication, sir, that I would greedily clamor for more and use illicit means to take that which does not rightfully belong to me. I shall be on my way." He bowed slightly toward Olivia. "Good day, Your Grace. If you have need of me, please do not hesitate to send word."

She rose to her feet. "My lord, I apologize for Mr. Dodger—"

"Don't be daft, Olivia," Dodger rudely interrupted. "You can't apologize for something that's not your doing. Besides, my behavior requires no apology."

"We're certain to disagree on that matter. And I may apologize if I wish," but Lord Briarwood was already heading for the door.

Jack Dodger twisted around in his chair and called out, "By the by, Briarwood—"

Lord Briarwood stopped and looked back, his eyes fairly fuming.

"—you are correct," Dodger continued. "If any misfortune befalls young Henry, you will be the first one Scotland Yard interrogates."

"Then I have no worries. The lad is safe from me. I'm not certain I can assure you that you're safe from me. I've never liked you."

Dodger had the audacity to smile. "Then do be sure to bring money with you tonight. You'll find your credit at Dodger's has been canceled."

Briarwood's face grew a blotchy red and his eyes fairly bugged out of his head. "Devil take you."

Dodger laughed in a velvety soft manner that seemed to hint he was as amused with himself as with Briarwood. "He did that long ago, so he's no longer a threat to me. And I suspect you aren't either."

Briarwood swore harshly and stormed from the room.

Olivia was shaking with outrage. "You provoked him on purpose."

Jack Dodger was still sprawled in the chair. With his thumb, he rubbed the underside of his jaw. "Why would he want to be guardian? That is the reason he came to see you, is it not? To find out who had been given the great honor of overseeing your son's journey into manhood?"

She swallowed back her need to lash out at him. "He thought it would be he."

"He thought, or he hoped?"

"What difference does it make?"

"What would he have gained?"

"Not everyone is like you, Mr. Dodger. They do things because they are the right things to do, not because something personal is to be gained."

He slowly unfolded his body and in his movements, she saw power leashed. He prowled toward her, his face set in an unreadable mask. She desperately wanted to decipher his thoughts, his intentions. She didn't want to retreat, but suddenly weak legs gave her no choice. She sank into the chair, pressing back as she had last night in the coach. He placed his hands on both arms of the chair and leaned in, effectively trapping her.

It was an odd time to realize he had the longest eye-lashes she'd ever seen on a man. Thick and spiky without an ounce of delicateness to them, but still so incredibly alluring. She wondered if they tickled a woman's face when he kissed her.

"Are you aware he is in considerable debt? Not only to me. If he were guardian, he'd not only be responsible for the welfare of your son but his estates as well. A very desperate man might think nothing of using those estates for his own gain."

"A man such as yourself?" she threw at him, her breathing labored, as though she'd just finished playing a game of tag with Henry.

"I'm not desperate, Duchess. Yes, I'm greedy. Yes, I want to die smothered in gold coins. Yes" —he held up his hand so she could see the horrid brand— "I have stolen in the past. But I've found a man can gain more wealth through legitimate means, and he never has to look over his shoulder while doing it. And perhaps your husband's choice of guardian was as simple as that. If you need someone to guard the coffers, you want some-one who doesn't *need* what the coffers hold."

Abruptly he pushed back and started walking toward the door.

"Do you truly think that's the reason he chose you?" she called out after him.

He stopped and faced her. "No. I just know that's the reason he *didn't* choose Briarwood."

"Your assumption only works if Lovingdon placed as high a regard on money as you do."

"In the end, Duchess, the only thing anyone cares about is money."

Watching him leave with a confident swagger, she fought to squelch the tremors that his nearness had wrought. For one insane moment, she'd thought he was going to lower those fascinating lips to hers.

For one shameful moment, she'd hoped he would.

"What the devil was Lovingdon thinking?"

Rupert Stanford watched as his cousin agitatedly paced his library. As he was prone to do, Edmund had arrived without announcement or invitation. He had the unfortunate habit of releasing flying spittle when speaking with such forcefulness. Rupert did wish Edmund would sit so his maid-of-all-work would have more success at cleaning things up when his cousin left. Rupert had an aversion to filth.

"Jack Dodger, you say?"

Edmund came to an abrupt halt. "Yes, Jack Dodger. *The* Jack Dodger."

"I'm not familiar with him."

"How can you not be? He owns a gambling establishment, Dodger's Drawing Room. He refers to it as an exclusive gentlemen's club, but everyone knows what goes on inside."

Rupert sipped his brandy, fighting off the urge to go wash his hands. The presence of his cousin always made him feel as though he needed a good scrubbing. "Gambling is not my vice. I've never been there."

"Now *I* might never be able to go back. He's canceling my credit, blast him, simply because I let my temper get the better of me. How else was I to react, I ask you? I couldn't let the insult go unanswered. He insinuated we'd kill the boy to acquire the titles."

"It's not the titles you want."

"No, dammit." Edmund finally dropped into a chair. "I was depending on Lovingdon appointing me to serve as guardian, to oversee . . ." His voice trailed off as though he was reluctant to admit what he coveted.

"His finances," Rupert finished for him. "So some of his wealth could miraculously, perhaps accidentally, become yours."

Edmund glared at him. They might have nothing in common, might possess different addictions, but they knew each other well. Or at least *Rupert* knew Edmund as well as any man, but he'd taken great care to ensure Edmund didn't know everything about him. Edmund enjoyed living above his station. Rupert preferred living below it.

"I'd not have stolen from him—merely borrowed," Edmund said glumly.

"You've been playing that game for so long, I think you've forgotten that to borrow means you must return it at some point."

Edmund tossed back his brandy in a single gulp. What a waste of fine liquor—on several levels.

"How old is Henry now?" Rupert asked, maintaining an air of boredom. "I've not kept in touch with the family."

"Five. And you didn't even bother to attend the funeral. That seemed rather odd, even from you."

"I fear I was not Lovingdon's favorite cousin. That honor fell to you."

"Which is the very reason I thought he'd appoint me guardian. What was Lovingdon thinking?" he repeated. "Jack Dodger is likely to have the lad working in his establishment."

"When he's older? I can't see that happening."

"Because you're blind, man. You live in this little world of yours and don't look beyond it. The man employs lads to take care of things for him. They gather our chips or fetch us a drink. Then he has his boot-boys. I've heard he has a pair of boots for every day of the week and has a lad for each pair."

"That seems a strange thing to do—to have that many boys around. Doesn't seem natural."

"There's nothing natural about Jack Dodger, I tell you. But now that I think on it, he does seem to have a peculiar interest in boys. Of course, this isn't the sort of thing you talk to a lady about. I suppose I should have a word with the solicitor."

"Have you evidence that Dodger has wronged any of these lads?"

Edmund held his tongue, but Rupert could see all the calculations going through his little mind. Edmund tended to bully people. Rupert's strength rested in persuasion. He possessed the devil's own tongue.

"I'd be careful of starting a rumor you cannot prove," he warned softly.

Edmund leaned forward. "Ah, but you see, there's the beauty. Perhaps I can't prove it, but then he can't disprove it. And in the court of rumors, who is going to be believed? A titled gentleman or a purveyor of sin?"

Chapter 8

He'd wanted to take possession of her mouth with a fierceness that astounded him. Leaning over her in the parlor, Jack had momentarily forgotten why he'd gotten up and gone over to her to begin with. Briarwood had completely slipped his mind, and all he'd been able to do was absorb her fragrance, lose himself in the gold of her eyes, ponder what it would take to make her rapid breaths come more quickly, and anticipate knowing the taste of her when he ravaged her mouth. But acting on his desires would have given her expectations he wasn't prepared to meet. He suspected the prim and proper duchess was not a woman who dallied with a man she had an aversion to marrying.

So he'd delivered his conclusions and walked away.

But she'd haunted him for the remainder of the afternoon while he sat in the library and met with the different men who were responsible for overseeing various properties: entailed and not. They handed over their books with grim expressions. He assured each that his services would be retained unless Jack discovered flaws in the recordkeeping.

By the time the evening shadows crept into the room, his head ached, his neck and shoulders were stiff, and his stomach was grumbling. He was anticipating opening his finest bottle of claret and sitting down to a well-prepared meal. If breakfast had been any indication, the duke had hired an excellent cook.

The door opened and Brittles walked in on his irritatingly silent feet. "Dinner is served, sir."

"Excellent."

He followed the butler to what he assumed was the family dining room. When they arrived, Jack discovered two footmen standing at the ready, but the table set for only one. He didn't like to admit the disappointment that slammed into him with the realization he'd be dining alone. "Isn't the duchess eating?"

"She's dining with the young duke in the nursery, sir."

"I see." He took his seat, watched as wine was poured and a dish was set before him. He took a sip of his wine. "Does the young duke always dine at this time of night?"

"No, sir," Brittles said, standing nearby. "He usually dines earlier."

The duchess had no doubt wanted to make certain she was otherwise occupied during Jack's dinner hour. Jack was growing weary of these games. He stood up, grabbed his wineglass and bottle, and headed for the doorway.

"Is dinner not to your satisfaction, sir?"

"It's fine," Jack called back. The company, however, was not. He stumbled to a stop. Company? When had he ever required company during his meals? Then again, when was the last time he'd eaten at a table? He usually took his meals at his desk. A slab of meat, a potato, enough to stave off the hunger while he plotted ways to increase his revenue. But he couldn't return to the table now without looking like a madman. Besides, he and the duchess needed to discuss a few things. Might as well do it in the nursery.

He took the stairs two at a time. The wine sloshed over the rim of the glass. He stopped momentarily to drain the contents, then continued up. He strode down the hallway and opened the door to the day nursery.

Everyone gaped as though Satan had unexpectedly arrived. Jack had always relished his tarnished reputation, but suddenly it was becoming quite bothersome.

"I didn't realize we were dining upstairs," he said laconically. "I would have been here sooner."

The young duke sat at the head of the table, his mother beside him. His nanny, who gave Jack a coquettish smile, sat at the other end.

"*We're* dining here," the duchess said. "You're not. Your dinner is being served in the dining room."

"It seemed a bit rude to deny you my company," he said as he took a seat at the table more suited to children than adults. His knees knocked up against it. He poured more wine into his glass, then looked at the nanny. "Be a good girl and fetch me a plate."

She stood up and curtsied. "Of course, sir, with pleasure."

She left him with the impression she'd be agreeable to far more than that if he required it. But he had no interest in her or any woman who expected more than coins from him.

Once the chicken and vegetables were set before him, he dug in with relish. "There are some matters we need to discuss."

"Must we discuss them here and now?" the duchess asked.

He took a bite of chicken, chewed thoughtfully. "By discussing matters now, I make the most use of my time. I eat while getting business taken care of."

"I fear any discourse with you will greatly upset my digestion."

"And you think I care about your digestion?"

"Truly, I think you care about nothing save yourself."

"I'll give you ten minutes."

"Ten minutes?"

"To eat without conversation. Then your digestion be damned."

"You are completely barbaric."

"Nine minutes."

She released a little growl and glared at him. He supposed he might need to take care in the future that she didn't poison his food. He was pushing her, and devil take him, he couldn't determine why.

"D-did it hurt?"

Jack shifted his attention to the boy, who was staring at his hand, no doubt the discolored skin on the inside of his thumb. It was quite hideous but Jack had always viewed being branded a thief as a badge of honor. His past had made him the man he was. He wasn't ashamed of it. "Like the very devil."

The boy's eyes widened. They were the same golden hue as his mother's. His light-colored hair, from what Jack remembered of Lovingdon, he'd taken from his father.

Suddenly Jack did feel ashamed of his past, for reasons he couldn't fathom. "But it was a long time ago."

The boy dropped his gaze to his plate, then hesitantly peered up at Jack.

"What is it, lad?"

"H-have you been to the Cr-crystal P-palace?"

"I haven't. Have you?"

The boy shook his head, his eyes those of a beaten puppy, then he looked at his mother.

"Henry, I'm sorry, darling, but as I've explained, we can't go."

"Why can't you?" Jack asked.

"I'm a widow in mourning. I can't go out and about."

"You seem to when it suits you. You went out this afternoon."

"Very discreetly, to visit my sister-in-law, who is also a widow. I wasn't gallivanting about."

"Let his nanny take him."

She arched a brow. "We can't have it both ways. Either there are dangers or there are not. Besides, Henry is in mourning as well. It wouldn't be appropriate."

"You like to follow the rules."

"Whether or not I like to is beside the point. I have certain expectations regarding behavior and I meet them."

"So if my expectations were that you'd behave badly, then you'd do all in your power to meet them?"

"Don't be silly. One doesn't strive to behave badly." She sighed. "I see no reason to prolong your presence at our dinner. What did you wish to discuss?"

"My bedchamber."

If she'd been eating, he had a feeling she would have choked. She came to her feet in a rush of black crepe that he was surprised didn't tip over the table, or at the very least, her chair. "May I see you in the hallway?"

"If you insist."

"I do."

In what he was coming to recognize as her self-righteous stride, she made her way around the table and headed for the door. He shifted around and watched her. He wondered what all she wore beneath those skirts. The ladies he'd been intimate with wore very little—when a man paid for services he didn't want to be bothered with having to work to get to what he'd paid for. He had a feeling bedding the duchess would be a great deal of bother—but a journey that might be well worth the trouble.

She stopped at the door and looked over her shoulder. "Mr. Dodger."

"Oh, right." He came to his feet, sauntered to the door, and opened it for her.

She stepped through and spun around to face him before he'd closed the door fully behind him.

"Discussing your bedchamber is hardly appropriate in front of a five-year-old, impressionable boy," she said.

"Does he not realize I sleep in a bedchamber?"

He actually heard the gnashing of her teeth. Her temper was so easily pricked. What sport Feagan's lads would have had with her.

"I assumed your sleeping arrangements were not what you wished to discuss, but rather mine, from last night," she said.

Leaning back against the wall, he crossed his arms over his chest and wondered what she found so offensive about bedchambers, what debauchery might have occurred in hers. "Actually, I wanted to discuss your husband's wardrobe. I need his clothes removed. Give them to the servants. I believe that's the usual practice, isn't it? Oh, and just so you know, I have the sort of memory that can remember the smallest of details. Be certain it's only the clothes that are removed."

"There are some personal items, some things a father might pass on to his son."

"If they're listed in your son's ledger, you have leave to take them."

"You can't possibly think Lovingdon listed every single item he possessed? Or that he truly meant for you to have everything within this residence. There are letters I wrote him, mementos I gave him. They mean nothing to you."

"True, but they mean something to you. Therefore they have value." He saw her temper flare, and before she could object, he said, "Consider their worth. We'll negotiate. Meanwhile, I'm going to my club, but I intend to take up official residence here tomorrow."

Her eyes widened slightly. "You're not planning to inhabit the bedchamber next to mine."

"It is the master bedchamber, is it not? And I am the master."

"I shall move myself to another room."

"Why go to the bother? I've told you I'll not seek out

your bed. Although I have no objections to your coming to mine. Is that what you fear? That with me so near you'll be unable to resist my charms?"

"I have no fear of you and find you not at all charming. Besides, I would never lie with a man to whom I was not married, and I'd certainly never marry you."

He shoved himself away from the wall. To her credit she stood her ground. "You think your tart tongue will hold me at bay, when all it does is cause me to wonder how it would feel against my skin."

Her lips parted slightly as a deep flush crept up her cheeks. The hell of it was, he'd meant the words to disarm her, but somehow they'd managed to undo him as well. He imagined her tongue gliding over his chest—

Before he lost control of the situation, of himself, he turned abruptly to walk away, then stopped and looked back, fighting to keep the sudden inexplicable tremors from his voice. "By the by, I prefer not to dine alone, so do be kind enough to join me for meals. Bring your son if you like."

With a jerk, she snapped from her haze. "It's proper for children to eat in the nursery."

"Have you not yet learned I don't give a fig about what is proper?"

"Have you not yet learned I do?"

He supposed she deserved a small victory. "Have it your way. We'll compromise. I'll have one meal with my ward: breakfast or dinner, you choose."

"Are you not listening? He shouldn't have any meals with you."

"Then how am I to educate him?"

"You hire tutors."

"They can't teach him what I know."

"I'm not certain he needs to learn what you know."

"One meal, Duchess. My word is final." He spun on his heel before she could voice another protest. She voiced it anyway, in the form of a screech and quite possibly a foot stomp, maybe even two. He didn't know why he was so insistent that they join him for a meal. Perhaps because when he'd walked in, they'd been smiling, and the smiles had disappeared with his entry.

The boy had eyed him warily, and Jack didn't like that level of distrust in a child. Something had caused it, and he didn't think it was anything he'd done. Maybe because this morning he'd promised the lad a dog and had yet to deliver it. He didn't have a clue where to find one. On the streets he supposed. He'd have to give it some thought. But not tonight. Tonight he had more pressing matters to deal with.

Olivia was unable to sleep. She couldn't quite rid herself of the image of her tongue playing over Jack Dodger's skin. How exactly would it feel—would it taste?

Although she was alone in her bed, alone in her room, she still felt self-conscious when she brought her hand up and licked the back of it. She did not think he would be so silky or taste so pure.

Would he lick her in return? She imagined that he would. That he would start at the tip of her toes and slowly slip along her flesh, perhaps stopping to detour around to the back of her knees, before journeying along the insides of her thighs—

She flung back the covers, desperate to relieve the heat.

But her thoughts wouldn't be cooled. She envisioned him at her hip, taking a leisurely sojourn toward her breasts. She clamped her hands over them as though that was all she needed to stop this maddening fantasy, but in her mind he merely gave her his devil-may-care smile and pushed her hands aside. His tongue circled and tormented until he finally nipped at her shoulder. But he wouldn't stop there. He tasted her throat, and having his fill of one side of her, he began the journey downward to experience the other.

Gasping, she sat up. Oh, God. She squeezed her legs together in an effort to quench the lovely ache throbbing between her thighs. She wanted to reach her hand down . . . Lord help her. She didn't know what she wanted. She was trembling with desire such as she'd never known.

It was Jack Dodger's fault. Speaking to her of intimate things. Making her crave an illicit touch. Just once for sweet release.

She scrambled out of bed, stumbled and almost fell, her knees were so weak. Righting herself, taking deep, gasping breaths, she glared at the door that led into the dressing room. Through it was the path to the master bedchamber, the room that held the bed where Jack Dodger would now sleep. He would remove his clothes . . . he would be so near.

She should transfer to another bedchamber, but it would be an admittance of cowardice and he'd lord it over her. If she was to have any hope at all of curtailing his influence over her son, she had to never retreat. She would stand her ground and curse him while doing it.

She needed to get some sleep so she'd be rested and better prepared for whatever tomorrow brought. Perhaps some warm milk would help. She considered ringing for her maid, but she was in the mood for wandering through the house when Dodger wasn't around. During those moments, she could pretend it was hers, pretend that Lovingdon had cared for her enough to notice how much she'd treasured the residence. But he'd noticed so very little. It left her with a deep sadness that they'd given almost nothing of themselves to each other. She blinked back the tears that threatened. How could she miss a man who, since she'd conceived, had been more a stranger than a husband?

But at least thinking of him allowed her thoughts to wander away from Jack Dodger. She drew on her night wrap and left her room.

She was halfway down the stairs when she heard the feminine laughter drifting up from the foyer, followed by a deep rumble that she recognized as Dodger's. After tossing and turning with unfulfilled desires for the past hour because of his innuendo, she wasn't in the mood to tolerate his flirting with the maids or taking advantage of his position over them. If she was to go unsatisfied this night, he could as well.

Quickening her pace, she arrived in the foyer just as Dodger was dismissing Brittles, who promptly took his leave. A woman stood with Dodger, her hair a vibrant red that diminished all the colors in her proximity. Olivia didn't know her, but she had no doubt regarding the type of woman he'd bring to the residence at such a late hour. She wouldn't tolerate this sort of behavior. She simply wouldn't. Especially in the bedchamber next to hers.

Dodger and the strumpet turned toward her. "Ah, Olivia, you're up rather late, aren't you?" he drawled.

She marched up to him. "I will not allow you to bring strange women into the house. You must take her elsewhere to sate your lust."

He narrowed his dark eyes, and she watched as a muscle jumped in his jaw. "It's *my* house, and she is here because I desire it. We're going to take care of our business in the library." He leaned toward her. "You're even welcome to watch if you'd like. I'm sure you'll find our exploits quite imaginative and entertaining."

Before Olivia could offer a solid retort, the woman slapped his arm. "Jack, what mischief are you about?"

"Stay out of this, Frannie," he growled, never taking his gaze from Olivia.

Olivia fought not to look away. An obvious familiarity existed between him and the woman, and she didn't want to consider that she might be more than a prostitute he'd picked up off the streets for an evening's entertainment, that she might be his mistress, someone who frequently warmed his bed. He possessed a magnetic virility her husband hadn't, and she suspected it took frequent beddings to keep his lust in check. With those thoughts, she could feel heat swarming to her cheeks, knew she was blushing, because satisfaction touched his eyes.

What was she thinking to confront him? Olivia was playing with the devil. A dangerous thing to do when she didn't know the rules of the game.

"You will apologize to my guest," he said.

"Jack—"

"Not now, Frannie."

"Jack."

The single word came out as a command and to Olivia's surprise, her nemesis obeyed it. He backed up, and while the taut muscles in his jaw didn't slacken, the heat in his eyes cooled somewhat. "She owes you an apology."

"She does not. What else is she to think when you bring a woman into the house this late at night?"

"She's not to think you're a whore."

"Well your behavior upon our arrival didn't help matters." She stepped in front of him and curtsied slightly. "Your Grace, I'm Frannie Darling. His book-keeper. He's asked me to take a look at the books."

"Frannie, your purpose here is not her concern."

"Perhaps not, but you're giving the impression I'm here for a very different and improper reason. I deserve better than that."

He cursed harshly beneath his breath. "You're right. I'm sorry."

His contriteness was sincere, and Olivia wondered if the woman meant more to him than he would ever acknowledge.

"However, I'm not the one who first insinuated you are anything other than what you are."

"No, but you did nothing to correct the misunder-standing," Miss Darling said, sounding quite hurt.

"I must apologize as well," Olivia began. "I assumed the worst. I'm sorry."

She smiled. "Most do where Jack is concerned. It's a reputation he's worked quite hard to shape."

"Frannie—" he ground out.

"Oh, do be civil, or I'll not look at your books." She

gave her attention back to Olivia. "As unlikely as it seems, considering his success, he's terrible with numbers."

"I'm not as bad as all that," he grumbled.

When Miss Darling gave him a pointed glare, he muttered, "But I'm not as good as you. Can we get to work now?"

"Of course," Miss Darling said. "It was a pleasure to meet you, Your Grace. And Jack is quite right. You're more than welcome to join us."

Olivia was suddenly very much aware she was in her nightclothes, hardly the proper attire for entertaining. "I shall have some refreshments prepared for you."

"That would be lovely, thank you," Miss Darling said.

Olivia watched as they walked down the hallway, Dodger seeming to be very careful to leave a discreet distance between him and Miss Darling. She realized Frannie Darling meant something special to him. She wondered what it would be like to have the attentions of a man as young, virile, and darkly dangerous as Jack Dodger.

Frannie Darling sat at the large mahogany desk in the grand library and studied the books and ledgers Jack had set before her with almost as much concentration as she studied him. He was lounging on a couch near the window, looking through a black ledger as though he were seeking an answer to a puzzle that baffled him.

She'd known Jack for a good many years. He'd always been as an older brother might be, looking out for her, making certain no one ever harmed her or hurt her feelings. It was one of the reasons she'd been so surprised this evening when he'd purposely led the duchess to believe something improper was afoot. It made her wonder why he cared what the duchess's opinion of him was and why he wanted it to be unflattering. While she'd never known him to be afraid of anything, she was well aware he studiously avoided any entanglements that might involve the heart.

He never spoke of his past, his origins, or his mother, but Feagan had once told her that Jack's mother had sold him. "Imagine how ye'd feel if someone ye loved put a value on ye," Feagan had said. Frannie couldn't imagine it.

She also believed that something horrible had happened to Jack when he was in prison with Luke. Before he spent time in prison, Jack had laughed often, and when he did, Feagan's children laughed with him. But when he returned to Feagan after his incarceration, his laughter had changed. It no longer contained even a sprinkling of joy.

She'd asked him about it once, but he'd refused to talk about what he called the dark times. Luke, too, was silent on the matter; but when the two of them looked at each other, Frannie knew that whatever had transpired affected them both, brought them together and separated them from everyone else.

Jack had erected walls, and in some ways, she thought he was still in prison—one of his own making, but a prison just the same.

She also wondered what his true feelings were regarding the duchess. He'd been sitting on the couch nonchalantly as though he hadn't a care in the world, but when a knock sounded on the door, he'd looked up, and she'd seen a trace of anticipation cross his face, revealed for only a heartbeat and quickly shuttered. He'd had less success disguising the disappointment that registered on his face when only a serving girl came in with biscuits and tea. Frannie had a feeling he'd been hoping the duchess had decided to join them. Not that he'd ever admit it. He gave nothing away that would make him seem vulnerable.

With a yawn, she stretched her arms and arched her back to ease the kinks out of it. She'd been scouring the books for more than two hours now.

As though accurately judging that she was calling it a night, Jack got up, walked to the desk, and sat on the corner. "What do you think?"

"Not too shabby. But you're right. The money isn't being invested as wisely as it might be."

"I suppose I could invest it in Dodger's."

"I don't think your widow would approve."

"She's not my widow."

She wasn't entirely convinced of that assessment. "You're not very nice to her."

"I'm as nice as she deserves."

"But wouldn't it be better to be nicer than she deserves? Then she might come to like you."

"I've never cared what anyone's opinion of me is. You're well aware of that."

Ah, the man did have a stubborn streak in him. "Her life has taken a drastic turn. I can't imagine the strength it would take to go on after losing one's husband."

He drummed his fingers on the desk as though he was losing patience with her. "I've tried to be cordial."

She stared at him in disbelief. "I pray that encounter in the entry hallway was not your being cordial."

"She finds fault with me at every turn and I take exception to her opinion."

"Jack—"

"Frannie." He held up his hand. "I will deal with the widow on my terms as I see fit."

"Fine. Be stubborn." She slammed the book closed. "I'm tired. I'll take this book with me. I want to study it a bit more closely."

He shifted off the desk and dropped into the chair across from her. "We'll have to purchase her a house."

"What's wrong with this one?"

"It's mine."

"You have no need of it. You've told me on numerous occasions you'll never marry or have children."

"That's beside the point."

"Why did you want her to think we were going to do something naughty in here?"

"She thinks the worst of me. Might as well meet her expectations."

"So you *do* care what she thinks."

"Don't be daft, Frannie. It doesn't suit you."

"You're most disagreeable."

He rubbed his brow. "I'm sorry. I'm tired. I've slept very little since last night, but it's a small price to pay. What do you think of the residence?"

"I think it's very lovely." She eased forward and propped her chin in her palms, her elbows on the desk. "Feagan always said you'd go farther than any of us."

Jack glanced around. "But I didn't bring myself to this, so it doesn't count as my achievement."

"Most would just take their good fortune and be glad of it."

"I don't trust good fortune that comes so easily. There is always a price to be paid, Frannie. Always." He gave her a cocky grin. "I want to know the price before I have to pay it."

"You've had a harsh life, Jack. Maybe it's simply your turn to have some good."

"If only life were that fair." He abruptly came to his feet. "Come on, then, let's get back to the club. For us the night is still young."

Chapter 9

The following morning, as unprecedented weariness settled over him, Jack realized he should have slept after he and Frannie returned to his club. Instead he'd dealt with a lord who had been accused of cheating at hazard and spent considerable time explaining to one of his girls that he couldn't kill a man because he'd grown tired of bringing her favors. Then he had a short conversation with the Earl of Chesney that might offer a solution to one of his problems. Swindler had stopped by to inform Jack that all he'd discovered about the cousins so far was that they led very private lives—and *that*, he believed, was cause for him to scrutinize them more closely. Swindler liked a good puzzle. Whatever the cousins were hiding, he'd discover it. But the majority of Jack's night had been spent studying plans to increase his profits.

As he'd told Frannie, he'd slept little since the reading of the will, so exhaustion claimed him when he walked into his residence and was greeted with chaos. He heard scrapings as though furniture was being moved around, and various voices were calling, "Henry! Your Grace! Young Master!"

The lad had no doubt created some sort of stir. Jack wouldn't have thought him capable of much more than sitting quietly and behaving. Good for him. It was natural for a boy to create mischief now and then.

Jack had just started up the stairs when he spied the duchess hurrying down them.

"Oh, thank God, you're here at last," she said on a rush.

He grinned at her. "Finally starting to appreciate me, are you?"

"No, you buffoon, Henry is gone."

Jack wanted his bed, not to play a child's game of hide and seek. "What do you mean he's gone?"

"He's disappeared. When his nanny woke up this morning, he wasn't in his bed. No one has seen him. We thought perhaps you'd taken him. Did you?" She spoke quickly as though desperate to make her point so he could provide the answer she sought. Now he could see that worry clouded her eyes.

"No."

"Then where is he? Has he been stolen, do you think? Is it as you suspected? He's in danger?"

He grabbed her shoulders. "Calm down, Olivia."

She broke free of his grasp and nearly tumbled down the stairs. "I don't want to calm down! I want to find my son! What if . . . what if he's been harmed?" she wailed.

"Who would harm him?"

"You seemed to think someone would."

He rubbed his chin. "Yes, yes, yes." He had thought the lad might be in some danger, but how could anyone have gotten the boy out from under the watchful eye of his nanny? Well, not so watchful, apparently. But still, he thought it unlikely that someone had crept into the house, taken Henry, and crept out. "Where have you looked?"

"Everywhere. Is this one of your sick pranks, one of the ways you think to bring me to heel?"

"I've not been here for hours. How could this be my doing?"

"I haven't the foggiest, but I have no doubt that you could be responsible."

He'd had enough of her suspicions. He started up the stairs.

"Where are you going?" she called after him. She was panting as though she'd been rushing around and was suddenly unable to catch a breath. She always seemed in control. It unnerved him to see her in a panic.

"To my chambers to splash a bit of water on my face and get my senses back so I can deal with this situation."

He recognized the echo of her rapid footsteps as she followed him. Amazing how much about her was beginning to become familiar. The sound of her steps, her fragrance.

"You didn't take him with you when you left?"

"Of course not." He reached the landing. "Maybe he headed to the Great Exhibition. He wanted to go, didn't he?"

"He wouldn't strike out on his own. He wouldn't even know where to go."

"He's a boy, Duchess. He doesn't need to know the path to adventure. He simply needs to recognize that it awaits."

He opened the door to his bedchamber.

"But what if he's been stolen?" she asked. It sounded as though she was skirting the edge of hysteria. He knew the only comfort she'd welcome involved the finding of her son.

"We'll send for Swindler. The man can follow clues blindfolded."

He walked into his room, surprised that she followed him inside. Obviously her panic took precedence over proper behavior. If apprehension hadn't been rolling off of her in waves, he might have teased her about it.

He was walking to the stand that held the porcelain basin when he heard a bump in the wardrobe that he passed. Had they looked everywhere? Or had they only looked where they'd expected the boy to be?

Jack jerked open the wardrobe door. The boy lunged out like a wild thing.

"N-no! I w-won't l-let you! I d-didn't m-mean t-to!"

Jack instinctively caught the boy, wrapping his arms around him, trying to still his ferocious thrashing. He was in his nightclothes, fighting like a tiger. Lost in intense fear, he was tenacious. "Hold on there, lad."

"Let him go. What have you done to him? Let him go!" the duchess screamed.

Jack ducked. What the devil was she hitting him with? He felt the skin split in his cheek. He cursed soundly, dodged another *whap!*, and released the boy, who promptly kicked his shin.

Wasn't this all just bloody wonderful.

Breathing heavily, he backed up yet another step to get beyond reach of the offending weapon—he could see now that she was holding a cast-iron poker—and her wrath. The boy was blubbering that he was sorry. With hate in her eyes directed at Jack, and the poker still at the ready, the duchess had one arm wrapped protectively around her son.

"What did you do to him?" she demanded to know.

Jack touched the back of his hand to his aching cheek, brought it away, and stared at the blood.

"I'm s-sorry," the boy cried, tears streaking his cheeks. "I-I w-won't do it again. I p-promise."

"What are you on about, boy?"

Jack heard a sound in the doorway. The nanny had arrived, concern clearly etched in her features, but he wasn't certain it was for the boy. He thought it more likely it was for herself, because she'd lost track of the lad. What was her name? Hazel? Harriet? Helen? Helen, that was it.

"I'll take him, Your Grace," she said, reaching for the boy.

"No, you won't," Jack said sharply, and everyone stared at him. At least they'd stopped their yelling. "Not until I understand what's going on here."

"It's obvious he's terrified of you," the duchess snapped.

"I can see he's frightened," Jack stated calmly, when he felt anything except calm. "What did you do wrong, lad?"

The boy vigorously shook his head.

"What do you think I'm going to do to you?"

The boy shook his head again.

"Leave him be," his mother stated, turning toward the door, her arms wrapped around the boy.

"No." The threat of some sort of retribution must

have been clear in his voice because she stopped and glanced back at him. "You seem to forget that I'm his guardian. I will have the answer to my questions if we have to stand here all day."

He remembered how Swindler had crouched before the duchess the day before and while it went against Jack's instincts to cower before anyone, he crouched, putting himself on eye level with the lad, trying to be as non-threatening as possible. "Are you afraid of me?"

The boy nodded.

"Why?"

The boy looked up at his mother, looked at his nanny.

"Don't look to them for the answer, boy, look to yourself. What do you think I'm going to do to you?"

The boy began to study his toes.

"Do you remember what I told you yesterday morning? That your father asked me to protect you? I didn't know your father well, Henry, but I know he cared for you very much and I do not take lightly the request he has made of me. I told you I'd never let anyone hurt you. So why are you afraid of me?"

He watched as the boy swallowed. His lower lip quivered. "You-you'll b-burn my th-thumb."

"Why would I do that?"

"B-because I f-forgot and-and sucked it w-when I-I was s-sleeping."

So he'd awakened, discovered his thumb in his mouth, and went into hiding. The picture was beginning to take shape. "Who told you I'd burn your thumb if you stuck it in your mouth?"

"My nanny," he whispered as though he were bearing the weight of a heavy secret.

With his gaze on the nanny, who looked as though all the blood had drained from her face, Jack slowly unfolded his body. "I'll not be used to terrorize children into behaving. You're let go. Pack your things and be gone within the hour."

"But, sir, I saw no other choice. He's the young duke now. He shouldn't suck his thumb."

"It's *his* thumb. I don't give a damn if he sucks it until he's a grown man. Pack your things."

Helen looked to the duchess. "Your Grace, have pity."

The duchess opened her mouth—

"Disagree with me on this and you can pack your bags as well," Jack stated in a firm voice that left no room for argument.

She looked at him, and for the first time, no anger or hatred was reflected in her eyes. Only horror and a deep sorrow at what they'd discovered. She turned back to the nanny. "He's right. What you did was monstrously wrong, unfair to Mr. Dodger, and unbearably cruel to my son. I can neither forgive you nor speak in your defense. I fear Mr. Dodger was too generous in giving you an hour. I want you gone in half that time."

The nanny released a hideous sob before turning and fleeing down the hallway.

Jack lowered his gaze to the boy. "I will *never* hurt you. Do you understand?"

The boy blinked, nodded.

"Good."

"You're bleeding," the duchess said.

"I've bled before. Now, I want a bath, so get the hell out."

"Mr. Dodg—"

"Get out," he ground out through clenched teeth, interrupting whatever the hell the duchess was going to say. "Because you, Duchess, I'm likely to hurt."

She ushered the boy out, reached back to grab the knob, and stilled. "I wasn't going to disagree with your decision to dismiss Helen—even before you threatened me."

Did she think that confession would ease his temper? Before he could think of an appropriate response, she quietly closed the door.

Jack tore at his cravat. It wasn't enough. He strode to a small table beside the couch in the sitting area. He picked up a vase and slammed it into the hearth, shattering it into a thousand pieces. It didn't make him feel any better.

He'd garnered the low opinion of men for years. Why was he so bothered that a silly duchess thought him capable of harming her son? Her opinion didn't matter. She was nothing to him. He didn't care what she thought. At every turn she expected the worst. What had her husband been thinking, to name Jack guardian?

Staring at the broken vase, he thought of the boys who worked for him, of the night he'd almost killed a man in his club because he'd touched one of the boys in a way that no man should ever touch a boy. Had Lovingdon been there that night? Did he know that protecting young boys was Jack's weakness?

"Could it be that simple?" he asked himself in a low whisper.

The door to the dressing room opened. For a second, Jack had expected to see the duchess coming from the room, and much to his chagrin, he'd felt a momentary surge of anticipation. But it was his manservant, Stiles. Jack had met him briefly the day before. He wasn't much taller than the duchess, and he was up in years. But he still stood proud.

"The duchess said you were in need of some attention and a bath," he said formally.

"Attention?"

He bowed his head slightly. "You're cut, sir."

Jack again touched his tender cheek. His fingers came away with barely a speck of blood. "It's fine."

"I could send for a physician—"

"I said it's fine. If you wish to stay in my employ, you won't make me repeat myself."

"Yes, sir. I have the maids bringing up the hot water now. The bath should be ready shortly."

"Good. I'll want one prepared every morning after I arrive and every evening before I leave."

"As you wish, sir."

"And when I take clothes off, I don't wear them again until they've been washed and pressed."

"Yes, sir."

Jack had never had a manservant. He wasn't certain he wanted one now. "I'm not a duke. I understand that your status might slip if you serve me. If you wish to leave, I'll provide a good reference."

The man tilted his head in acquiescence, a small smile playing at the corners of his mouth. "Thank you, sir, but I have served the duke from the time he was a young man. I'm comfortable in this household and change does not suit me. I prefer to stay if you have no objections."

"Fair enough. I packed some clothes. They're in the coach. Have a footman bring them up."

"Yes, sir. Will there be anything else?"

"After my clothes are brought up, lay out something for me, then leave. I plan to sleep for a bit and I can dress myself."

"Very good, sir."

"Tell me, Stiles, did you ever disagree with the duke?"

The wrinkles in his face shifted as he smiled. "On occasion, sir. He had an atrocious lack of good judgment when it came to coordinating colors. Sometimes he would look like a randy peacock."

"That won't be a problem in dressing me. Everything I wear is black or white, except for my waistcoats."

"Yes, sir. I did notice that you seemed to have quite the flair when it came to your waistcoats."

Jack heard no censure in his voice. He thought the two of them might get along. "You miss him?"

"Very much so, sir."

"Tell me, Stiles, did the other servants accept my becoming their master as well as you have?"

"I believe they're reserving judgment, sir."

"A pity the duchess couldn't have done the same," Jack mumbled. Then he waved Stiles off. "See to your business, while I see to my bath."

"Yes, sir."

Stiles quit the room. Jack went into the dressing room. His gaze immediately went to the other door, the door that led into Olivia's bedchamber. She wouldn't be there now; she'd be with Henry in the nursery. Maybe she'd even sleep in there now that he had no nanny.

Removing his jacket, he wondered if she'd bathed in that copper tub, imagined her lounging back, the heated water steaming her cheeks and throat, causing her hair to curl around her face. He imagined the water lapping at her breasts, her stomach, her hips, her thighs. He imagined her sitting with her knees serving as small islands in the middle of the tub.

He groaned with his body's reaction to the erotic images bombarding him. Damned good thing he'd instructed his manservant to leave. He didn't need to be parading about when his body was standing at full attention.

He removed the remainder of his clothes, stepped into the tub, and sank beneath the water. It was lovely. Absolutely bloody lovely.

Resting his head against the back of the tub, he closed his eyes. He wondered if he'd return to this house every morning to find some crisis afoot. He was going to have to find some time to spend with the boy. He supposed he should talk to Luke, find out what sorts of things a child of the nobility should know. Jack could teach him how to hide—

He chuckled with a mixture of pride and admiration. The boy had done a fairly good job of that himself. He was also more courageous than Jack had originally given him credit for—to hide so close to the lair of the one he feared. Yes, there was more to the boy than Jack had first realized. He still needed nurturing to become a man, but even with his stammering, he had a good start. If his mother would just give him leave to let go of her skirts.

His mother. Lord, when she was angry, she was something to behold. Jack slid down further in the tub. Not since he was a boy had he had anyone wash him, though he could certainly imagine her gliding the cloth over him. But as she wasn't here, he'd have to do it himself. Pity.

He released a long sigh. He seemed unable to stay angry with her for long. He admired her tenacity when it came to protecting her son. He thought she was probably a woman capable of great love. He'd be content if she'd simply give him the benefit of the doubt from time to time.

Olivia didn't want to think that at that very moment, Jack Dodger was in her dressing room . . . bathing. How would she climb into the tub and sink beneath the water knowing that his bare *person* had touched the same copper as hers? She should share a dressing room only with someone she knew well. While they wouldn't be in the tub at the same time, it still seemed rather intimate and decadent.

And thinking about Jack Dodger's bareness was not what she needed to be concentrating on. She needed to focus on finding Henry a new nanny.

Henry was nestled against her side as they sat on a settee beside the window in the day nursery. He'd tucked his thumb inside his hand and curled his fingers around it, as though determined not to suck on it. Yet if ever a time was right for sucking it, this morning seemed to be it.

She knew he needed to break his habit, but she could hardly fathom that Helen had used so cruel a means to try to stop him from slipping his thumb into his mouth. But as unsettled as she was by Helen's actions, she was even more amazed by Dodger's. Her opinion of him had shifted during those tense moments, shifted in his favor. She'd been on the receiving end of his blistering glare, but it had never burned as hotly as it had when he'd directed it at Helen. Olivia was surprised the young lady hadn't burst into flames.

Olivia had feared Dodger would be as cutting with Henry as he was with her. She'd expected him to give no care to her son's feelings. She'd expected him to be as harsh and unforgiving as he seemed to be with all things. He'd surprised her.

She'd judged Jack Dodger based on conversations she'd had with other ladies. They'd spoken of men coming home in the early hours reeking of drink and women—and Olivia had assumed Jack Dodger drank heavily and fornicated often. One lady had mentioned that her husband had sold her jewelry to acquire funds for his gambling habit—and Olivia had assumed Dodger spent an abundance of time at the gaming tables. He lounged while sitting, and she considered him slovenly. But he dressed impeccably and even now he was bathing.

She'd considered him mean-spirited, and yet he'd not fought back when she'd struck him with the poker. He'd simply moved beyond her reach, when she had little doubt he could have effectively wrestled her to the ground. As bluntly as he'd spoken to Henry to get to the root of the problem, he'd somehow managed to elicit the child's confidence, and he had confessed everything.

She'd considered him unlikable, but the woman last night—Frannie Darling—had teased and cajoled and even slapped his shoulder playfully. She'd chastised him and he'd not retaliated. He'd taken it as his due.

She'd considered him a man who would do anything for a coin. Her son's finances were now in his hands and he could surely divest him of everything—yet he'd indicated he wouldn't. A ploy perhaps, to cause her to lower her guard. If she trusted him, then he could get away with a good deal more. If she trusted him, might she find herself enjoying his presence? No, never. The only thing they had in common was her son, and they disagreed on every aspect concerning him.

Well, almost every aspect. She did agree with Dodger that Helen had to be dismissed. It was an appalling bit of behavior on her part to use Dodger to frighten her son into behaving. How had she missed that Helen was capable of doing such a thing? Had she made other veiled threats to Henry?

He was such a quiet, good boy. Shy, to be sure, but Olivia had always assumed his stammering was responsible because it embarrassed him. Lovingdon hadn't been concerned by it. "It's the Lovingdon curse. He'll grow out of it. I did."

So Olivia tried not to worry about it. He was like his father in so many ways. He had his blond hair, but her amber eyes. He had long limbs and she knew eventually he would grow into his father's height. But with Dodger as his guardian, she didn't see how he would acquire his father's dignity.

The door burst open, startling both her and Henry, and Dodger strode in with a confidence she didn't think even Lovingdon had possessed.

"Henry, let's go," he said.

Henry started to ease away from her, but she drew him back. "Where are you taking him?"

"As I'm his guardian, I don't have to explain my actions to you, but as you're his mother and no doubt concerned about his welfare, I shall tell you. I'm taking him for a ride in my brougham."

"I thought you were going to sleep." After hearing something shatter, she'd had a quick word with Stiles after he'd left Dodger's room to make certain everything was all right. He was going to have the remnants of a vase cleared away after Dodger awoke.

He narrowed his eyes at her. "I was, but I decided I needed to see to this matter instead."

"What matter is that?"

She heard a deep purr like that of a large cat contemplating its next victim. "Olivia, you do try my patience. Come on, boy."

Olivia could feel the tremor that went through Henry before he pulled away from her and got to his feet.

"I can't let you take him anywhere without me," she said as she rose. "I'll come with you."

"Shouldn't you be interviewing nannies?"

"I'm going to have one of the chambermaids assume the role until I can gather some recommendations."

He gave her an impatient glare. "I've had the brougham readied. I'm on a schedule today. I don't have time to wait for the coach, and as you so kindly pointed out, my vehicle is more suited to two."

"Henry can sit on my lap. I will fight you tooth and nail if need be, but I will not let you take him without me."

Something shifted in his eyes as though he'd welcome the challenge. She wasn't altogether certain it would end in fisticuffs, but the thought of them wrestling—

"All right, let's go, then. Be quick about it. I haven't all day."

Grabbing Henry's hand, Olivia wondered what she was getting herself into.

Henry sat on his mother's lap. He'd always liked riding in the brougham with his father because the front of it was a window that made it very easy to see everything. He could observe the world and it was all so fascinating.

Although the carriage did seem very small with Mr. Dodger sitting in it. He wondered if his mother had realized how much room Mr. Dodger would take up and how crowded they'd be. He could feel the tension in his mother. She was barely breathing. It was what Henry did when he got frightened at night—he lay in bed, barely breathing, as though somehow bad things couldn't find him if he didn't breathe.

He wondered if his mother was afraid of Mr. Dodger. He wondered if he should be afraid of him. Mr. Dodger had told him he wouldn't burn him, had told Miss Tuppin he didn't care if Henry sucked on his thumb. That had made Henry feel better, but it had also made him want to stop sucking on his thumb, so he was keeping it tucked tightly behind his fingers to prevent his putting it in his mouth.

Mr. Dodger didn't wear a top hat like Henry's father

had done. But he wore a nice black jacket. And his waistcoat was a dark green with gold buttons, not the purple one he'd worn yesterday.

He looked tired. Once he yawned without covering his mouth, which had made Henry's mother sniff. Even Henry knew a gentleman was supposed to put his hand over his mouth when he yawned. After his mother made her sound of displeasure, Mr. Dodger had winked at Henry as though they were sharing a secret. It made Henry think that Mr. Dodger knew the rule about yawning, too, but thought it would be more fun to make Henry's mother sniff. While he didn't think his mother liked Mr. Dodger, he thought maybe Mr. Dodger liked her.

The carriage pulled into a cobbled drive, and Henry could see a large residence looming before them.

"That's Lord Chesney's residence," his mother said. "It's far too early in the day for a social call."

"We're not here for a social call," Mr. Dodger said.

"Why are we here?" his mother asked.

"Because the young duke needs to see him."

"Whatever for?"

Mr. Dodger was looking forward, but it seemed to Henry that he was suddenly happy. He noticed just the smallest shift in the shape of his mouth as though he might have the tiniest of smiles.

"Because the earl's bitch recently had a litter of puppies."

Henry thought his heart was going to leap out of his chest. "Puppies?"

Mr. Dodger looked at him and winked again. "Promised you one, didn't I?"

Henry didn't see his hand move, but suddenly he was extending a card toward Henry. "Your calling card."

"That's the duke's," his mother said.

"Yes, I found them in a desk drawer. They rightfully belong to your son now, as he's the duke."

Henry's mother blinked several times, the way she did when she was trying not to cry.

The carriage came to a stop. The footman hopped down, opened the door, and unfolded the steps. Mr. Dodger climbed out. Henry scrambled out after him. Mr. Dodger looked back into the carriage and extended his hand. "Coming, Duchess?"

She looked at Mr. Dodger, then looked at Henry and gave him a sad smile. "I'm in mourning. It wouldn't be proper. Be a gentleman, Henry."

Henry nodded and looked up at Mr. Dodger. He was a little afraid and wanted to take Mr. Dodger's hand, but Mr. Dodger didn't look at all frightened. He patted Henry's shoulder, which was almost as comforting as taking his hand. "Come along, lad."

Henry followed Mr. Dodger up the steps and into the house. A butler approached.

"Show him your card," Mr. Dodger said.

Henry did as he was told. The butler put it on a silver plate and walked away. Henry fought very hard to stand perfectly still, as still as Mr. Dodger. He wanted to hop and jump around and clap his hands. He was getting a puppy.

It seemed forever before a fellow with a large, round belly appeared. "Ah, Your Grace. Mr. Dodger here informed me that you're in want of a puppy."

"Yes, s-sir."

He smiled. "I'm Chesney. Sorry about your father. Good man. Very good man."

Henry was sure he was supposed to say something—

"Thank you, Lord Chesney," Mr. Dodger said. "The duke appreciates your sentiments."

"But you're more interested in my dogs, aren't you, lad?"

Henry nodded quickly.

"Come on, then, I have a special room for my collies. I treat them royally . . ."

As he led them through the house, Lord Chesney continued to talk, telling Henry all about the dogs' history, but Henry barely paid attention. All he cared about was the fact that he was going to have a dog.

Finally, they came to a small room. In a corner on a mound of pillows and blankets was a large white-and-brown dog. Around her three puppies tumbled.

"Go ahead, Your Grace, play with them. See which one suits you."

Henry sat on the floor and the puppies bounded over to him. He laughed. Lord Chesney crouched beside him. "Which one do you want?"

Henry looked up at Mr. Dodger.

"Don't look to me, lad, look to yourself."

Henry studied the puppies. It was so difficult to decide. What if he made a mistake?

"There's no wrong answer, lad," Mr. Dodger said quietly.

Henry snatched up the first puppy that had landed in his lap and hugged him close. "This one!"

"That one, it is," Lord Chesney said with a laugh, standing up, his knees creaking as he went.

Henry glanced back at Mr. Dodger, who handed Lord Chesney a small pouch that jingled when it landed in his palm. As they were walking back to the carriage, holding his puppy close, Henry said, "He c-cost a lot."

"Not really. I suspect in the end he'll make me money."

"How?"

"Can you hold a confidence?"

Henry nodded even though he didn't know what a confidence was.

Mr. Dodger grinned broadly. "When his pockets are full, Lord Chesney plays very loosely at the gaming tables. Tonight he'll spend what I just gave him and then some, so it comes back into my coffers."

Henry wasn't exactly sure what Mr. Dodger was talking about. "Will he t-take the dog back then?"

"Hell no. The dog is yours."

"Thank you, sir."

"You're welcome, lad."

He knew his mother wouldn't agree, but Henry thought Mr. Dodger was a very good guardian.

Chapter 10

Olivia stood outside the library door waiting for her courage to return.

Henry adored his new puppy. He'd named it Pippin. She didn't know where he'd gotten the name. But he already loved the animal so much, that it was as though they'd been made for each other.

She had one of the chambermaids watching Henry while she offered an olive branch—or in her situation, a meal.

As soon as they'd returned home, Dodger had gone to the library, no doubt to study the books further. He'd asked for no refreshments nor called for any of the servants.

It was early afternoon. As she thought of his assortment of bottles, she tried not to wonder if he'd indulged, if no one had heard from him because he was lying on the floor in a drunken stupor. She seemed unable to think about him without expecting the worst, and to her shame, she had to acknowledge her low opinion of him was unfounded.

Regardless of her trepidation it was time to confront him, time to put matters to right. She nodded at the footman. He opened the door. Taking a deep breath, she walked in, carrying the tray. Her heart thudded with the closing of the door. She'd expected Dodger to make some scathing comment and was surprised to find he wasn't sitting at his desk but in a chair near the window.

Although sitting wasn't the correct word. He was fairly sprawled in it, with one leg stretched out, the open ledger in his lap, his head at an awkward angle, his eyes closed. Yet even in slumber, he didn't appear innocent.

As quietly as possible, she walked over the carpet and set the tray on the desk. Curiosity getting the better of her, she cautiously approached the man whom Lovingdon had deemed worthy of guarding his son. She was not yet ready to proclaim that he was the best selection, but she was willing to reluctantly admit he might not be the worst.

He really was in dire need of having his hair trimmed. She considered what it might be like to thread her fingers through his unruly curls. The disheveled strands should have given him the appearance of a child—but nothing about him reflected the innocence of youth. She suspected he hadn't been innocent even when he was born.

His face contained a cragginess that remained, even in sleep, as though the harshness of his life never left him at peace. She wanted to reach out and ease the furrow between his brows. A strange thing to desire.

She felt a trifle wicked standing there, watching him without his knowing.

His hand flicked, and she almost screeched. It was resting on an open page of his ledger. Curled slightly, it revealed that horrible burn. She'd not given any thought to how much it had to have hurt, but had focused on what it represented. She couldn't imagine him willingly holding out his hand to accept a brand. He would have fought. They would have had to hold him down. Her stomach roiled. Even if he'd stolen, did he deserve to be burned? Did anyone?

She lifted her gaze back to the welt on his cheek. It was red, inflamed. He hadn't deserved that, either. He hadn't deserved her wrath or mistrust.

What he did deserve, she decided, was undisturbed rest. She remembered how he'd expressed concern she'd wake up stiff if he'd left her in Henry's bed. He was going to do the same, but she certainly couldn't carry him to bed. Although she thought she could make him a bit more comfortable. If she just eased the ledger. . .

Iron clamped around her wrist, jerking her forward—

Releasing the tiniest of screeches, she halted her progress by shoving her hand against something hard—Jack Dodger's chest. Her face was uncomfortably close to his, and for a moment she knew sheer terror, because in his eyes she saw reflected a savagery that she suspected existed only on battlefields. His breathing was harsh, his chest moving up and down beneath her fingers. Her knees had hit the chair, and to her mortification, she realized she'd somehow become wedged between his thighs.

She was afraid to move, afraid not to. He was looking at her as though he'd never seen her before, as though he was trying to determine how every aspect of her features had been formed.

"What are you doing?" he rasped.

She swallowed the tight ball suddenly lodged in her throat. "You-you were sleeping. I thought to make you more comfortable."

He lowered his gaze to her mouth and she realized it had been so very long since she'd been this close to a man, so very, very long since her lips had been so near to being kissed. She recognized the passion flaring in his eyes. Her heart thudded, her knees weakened, and she thought she was in danger of finding herself sprawled in his lap. She fully expected him to draw her nearer, to place that perfectly shaped mouth, those full lips on hers—

Lifting his free hand, he cradled her cheek. His palm was much rougher than Lovingdon's had been. Rougher and larger. He skimmed his thumb over her lips, before lifting his gaze back to hers. "Careful, Duchess," he said in a gruff voice. "I'm not a man who settles for only a kiss."

Humiliation slammed into her, and she feared he saw in her eyes what she saw reflected in his. Desire. Desire that must go unsatisfied, that must be left to burn itself out, lest she find herself burning for all eternity. She had too much pride to admit he'd accurately guessed what she wanted and was too cowardly to reach for. To protect herself, she chose to be stern. "Unhand me, sir."

Abruptly he released her. Her balance was off. She started to fall and he grabbed her waist with both hands. With great difficulty in retaining her dignity, she righted herself and stepped back, brushing her hands over her skirt.

He cocked his head to the side. "What are you doing here, Olivia? Trying to steal my ledger?"

"I'm not the thief here, sir."

"No, you're not. So what did you want?"

She felt so terribly silly. "Brittles said you had yet to eat, so I brought you something."

He gave her a look that made her think he was considering devouring her. She spun on her heel and went to the desk, moving the tray closer to the chair on the other side. "It's lamb and potatoes. You really should eat."

"Should I?"

She cleared her throat. "I prepared the tray myself."

"I haven't servants to prepare trays?"

"You're making this so blasted difficult."

Jack studied her, tried not to think about how his hands had spanned her waist. He didn't want to remember how he'd awoken to find her hovering over him. How close her lips had been to his, how with the slightest of movements he could have known the taste of her. He was not in the habit of denying himself pleasures, but she was dangerous in ways he didn't care to examine.

"Are you trying to make amends?" he asked.

She looked over her shoulder at him. "I'm trying to be a bit more pleasant."

"Pleasant, is it?" He got out of the chair, went to the table in the corner, and lifted the top from a decanter. "Would you care to join me?"

"No, thank you. You do like your spirits, don't you?"

"Been drinking gin since I was eight. See no reason to stop now." He walked to the desk and removed the lid covering the plate. The delicious aromas hit him, and only then did he realize he was famished. He took his chair.

"Brittles said you didn't eat yesterday afternoon. Do you often work without taking the time to eat?" she asked.

"I can't stand hovering females. Either sit down or leave."

To his immense surprise and pleasure, she sat. "You didn't answer my question."

He cut off a bit of lamb and popped it into his mouth, savoring the flavor. "I work during most meals. Time not working is time spent not making money."

"You care a good deal about money."

"I care only about money."

"Is that the reason you agreed to the terms of the will?"

He chewed, swallowed. "Yes." He tapped the knife against the plate. "Why are you here?" He waved his hand over the plate. "Why this?"

Glancing down at her hands, balled in her lap, she shifted in her chair before lifting her gaze back to him. "I may have judged you unfairly. In every situation, I have thought the worst. I thought the inspector was here to arrest you. I thought your bookkeeper was a prostitute. I thought you'd done something to hurt Henry. I'm trying to apologize and I'm not very good at it."

"Don't apologize often?"

"I'm not often wrong."

In a heartbeat, she'd gone from contrite to haughty.

He preferred her that way, displaying her steel rather than her softness. But even with the steel, she possessed an uncommon beauty. It hadn't been entirely noticeable when he'd first met her. It was as though with each moment's passing, he noticed more things about her and those in turn enhanced her beauty. She had the faintest dusting of freckles across her cheeks, and he imagined her playing outside without benefit of a hat or parasol. He imagined her first Season and all the gentlemen who would have swarmed around her.

"Why did you marry him?" he asked.

She glanced at her hands again, as though she kept the answer hidden there. "My father wished it."

"Lovingdon was considerably older than you."

She nodded, lifting her gaze to his. "But he was my father's friend. He needed an heir for his respected title. And I was a dutiful daughter. I did as my father wanted. In my world, Mr. Dodger, daughters tend to obey their fathers."

"Were you a dutiful wife?" Before she could answer, he said, "My apologies. That question was uncalled for. Obviously when it comes to polite society, my conversational skills are lacking."

"Based upon your reputation with women, I'd have thought you'd have exceptional conversational skills."

"When I'm with women, my mouth is usually occupied with things other than talking."

She blushed profusely. He didn't know why he took pleasure in bringing the color to her cheeks. He'd like to do it with a great deal more than words. But she was an aristocratic lady, and he knew that simply touching one put a man in danger of having to take a trip down the aisle—a trip he had no plans to ever make. Besides, he wanted no claim on her. He wanted her married, so he could shuck off the responsibility of raising her son.

"You seemed very insistent you didn't want to marry Briarwood."

She looked down at her hands again. "If I should ever marry again, I would like very much for it to be my choice and my decision."

Unfortunately, that attitude was going to cause a problem for Jack. It indicated a delayed process and he wanted her married very soon. "So if you could choose to marry anyone, who would he be?"

She looked up, startled. "I'd not given it any thought."

"Oh, come now. Surely over the years, someone caught your fancy. At a dinner or during a ball. Perhaps you danced with him and thought you'd enjoy something more."

"I was married."

"I'm not suggesting you had an affair, because God knows you'd never do anything inappropriate, but thinking about it isn't wrong. Surely you thought about it."

"I did not, sir. Never."

To his utter amazement, he realized she was speaking the truth. Never to fantasize about the forbidden? He couldn't imagine it.

"All right, I'll give you that you probably never thought about getting close to any other man, but surely you liked someone, found someone else pleasant to be around. I could arrange for him to visit you here so you could come to know him better—"

"I'm in mourning."

"So you keep reminding me when it's not necessary, Olivia. Quite honestly, it's evident by your attire. You look ghastly in black, by the way. Have you anything in violet?"

She stammered out a few sounds. He raised his hand. "Never mind. We can address your clothing later. Here's the thing. You don't want me to be guardian of your son. I don't want to be guardian. The simplest solution to both our problems is for you to marry. And I'm willing to help in any way I can. I'll bring the suitors to you. Who do you fancy?"

"It would be entirely inappropriate for me to take male callers."

"Of course, it's inappropriate. That's the reason we'll do it discreetly."

"When a woman is in mourning, she's not to issue invitations."

"You won't. I will."

She stood up. "I'm not sure why I bothered to try to make matters right between us."

And he didn't know why he kept trying to make them un-right. "Sit down."

She hesitated.

"Please."

With a nod, she sat. "Henry likes his dog very much."

The change in topic startled but pleased him. "As well he should. Cost me a fortune."

"So he told me." She smiled, and again he was struck by how approachable it made her appear. If she were his, he thought he'd always seek to make her smile. "He wasn't quite certain how to go about holding a confidence since you didn't give him anything to actually *hold*."

"That must have been an interesting conversation."

"I daresay it was most enlightening."

He should have taken more care about explaining things to the lad, not that he was particularly bothered his mother knew the truth of the situation. He just didn't want it to get back to Chesney.

"How did you know?" she asked.

He finished chewing the remarkable lamb and swallowed. "Pardon?"

"Helen. Henry's nanny. You were suspicious of her from the start. Henry told me she kept a stick in her pocket and would whack him on the hand if he displeased her. Those aren't his precise words, of course, but they are the gist of what he confessed. How did you know she was frightening him?"

Something was shifting between them, something he wasn't quite comfortable with. But he was also weary of the bickering. Until he could get her married off, they'd be living in this house together. Might as well do it amicably. "When I was very young, for a short time, I lived with someone who hurt me. While I was frightened I stammered. I'm certain people stammer for all sorts of reasons, so perhaps one thing had nothing to do with the other. Plus he is a boy, and they are not by nature so terribly well behaved."

"What you said about Lovingdon earlier, about taking your task as guardian seriously—things between us might not have been quite so difficult had you voiced it to me sooner."

"Quite honestly, Duchess, I'm not certain I realized it myself until I spoke the words. I'm as baffled as you by your husband's choice of guardian, but I like this house and everything in it. I intend to keep them."

"As long as you're good to Henry, I shall strive to be more gracious."

He wasn't quite certain he wanted her gracious. He preferred her with a bit of fire in her. "You're the late Duke of Avendale's sister."

She seemed surprised he knew that information. "Yes. My father died a month after I was married. My brother inherited the title. He recently died, leaving the title to his son. I have no other immediate family. Do you?"

She'd uncharacteristically shared so much personal information with him in one go that it took him a moment to realize what she was asking of him, and when he did realize it, he laughed and lifted his glass in salute. "No. Not in the traditional sense anyway."

He downed the gin, laid the knife and fork on the plate, and covered the dish. "Thank you for bringing me the meal."

"I'm glad you enjoyed it." She rose. "I do hope you'll have a physician look at your cheek. I would hate for it to get infected."

"I suppose you're right. A scar would ruin my good looks."

"You're assuming you possess good looks in the first place."

"Are you implying I don't?"

"I'm implying it's conceited to state you're hand-some." She lowered her gaze again, then lifted it. "I'm sorry I hurt you. I thought—"

"That the boy was in danger. If a mistake is to be made, Duchess, I prefer it go the way it did this morning."

"You care about Henry."

"Not in the least. But he's my ward. If he's harmed, it's more trouble to me."

She leaned over his desk. Her lavender scent teased him and her lips were so tantalizing near. "I'm not quite sure I believe you, Mr. Dodger."

She lifted the tray and nearly hit his nose in doing it. His fault for not noticing he'd been moving toward her.

"Believe it, Duchess," he said, striving to regain the control slipping away from him.

"I don't believe I shall."

With that, she turned and strolled across the room, her backside swaying.

Something was happening, something very dangerous. He was beginning to let down his guard. And he couldn't afford to do that. It could spell disaster for him. He'd spent a lifetime erecting the walls around his heart. He wasn't going to let a lovely widow tear them down.

Chapter 11

With her back pressed against a mound of pillows and her arms wrapped around her drawn-up legs, Olivia sat in bed, stared at the ornate door leading into the dressing room, and strained to hear even a whisper of Jack settling in for the night. Every once in a while she'd grow dizzy and realize she'd been holding her breath.

Late that afternoon, he'd sent her a missive informing her he'd not be available for dinner and she was free to dine with Henry. She didn't like that he thought he was in charge of her schedule. She also found it interesting he'd chosen not to find her and tell her in person. Was he avoiding her? Could it be that he was not comfortable with their relationship shifting away from adversarial? She hardly knew what to make of the man, but she was certain of one thing: he'd not intrude on her here. In spite of everything the ladies had ever said about him, she was discovering he did have some semblance of a moral compass. One that was a bit skewed perhaps, but still on occasion it seemed capable of pointing in the correct direction. At least where Henry was concerned.

She was certain he'd honor his word and not seek out her bed. She struggled against the tinge of disappointment. Not that she wanted him to quietly open that door and walk serenely—

No, that had been Lovingdon's way. Jack Dodger would burst through, fervor in his stride, virility emanating from every pore. He would be demanding, his hands exploring greedily, his tongue eliciting pleasure—

With a low groan, she pressed her forehead against her knees. He would not come through that door. It was ludicrous to allow such carnal thoughts to run rampant through her mind. What did it matter if he was sleeping in that room? Two doors separated them. She'd not hear him breathing or tossing or turning. She'd not see his bare feet as he walked around in his nightshirt.

She raised her head, burrowed her chin into her knees. Would he even wear a nightshirt? Of course he would. All gentlemen did. But then Jack Dodger was no gentleman.

She couldn't envision him donning a nightshirt. Oh, she needed to stop thinking about him. Glancing at her clock, the time surprised her. It was past midnight. As he'd yet to arrive in his chamber, he'd probably gone to the club. How silly of her to think otherwise, to have spent precious time listening for an arrival that would never come.

She needed a distraction. She'd go to the library and find a book to read. Anything to take her mind off of Jack.

She slipped out of bed and drew her wrapper around her. Picking up the lamp from the bedside table, she made her way into the hallway. She descended the stairs and walked to the library. This time of night no footman was about. Opening the door, she was stunned to see Jack sitting at the desk, poring over ledgers. Why wasn't he at the club and how could she retreat? She realized with a mounting sense of dread that she couldn't, because she'd drawn his attention. "I thought you'd gone to your club."

Shaking his head, he leaned back and stretched his arms over his head. "I had some things to attend to here."

He came to his feet, perhaps finding his manners as an afterthought. "Why aren't you asleep?"

Because I can't stop thinking about you hardly seemed a prudent confession.

"I'm not sure. I thought finding a book to read might help to lull me to sleep."

"I've found that only works when it's a dull book."

She couldn't imagine him reading a book for pleasure. She assumed he took his pleasures from more carnal avenues. Feeling her cheeks warm with that thought, she eased closer to the desk. "When do *you* sleep?"

"A few hours here and there. I've never required much."

She glanced at the various ledgers strewn over the desk. "You certainly devote a lot of your time to your finances."

"Actually, it's *your* finances I'm studying."

Surprised by his words, she jerked her head up. "Why would you care about *my* finances?"

"I suppose it has to do with my humble beginnings."

She laughed. "I can't see anything about you being humble."

He didn't seem offended. Instead he indicated the couch near the window. "Have a seat and I'll explain to you what I'm thinking."

It was late, she was in her nightgown, and they were alone in the library. She could barely envision anything more improper—unless they were alone in his bed-chamber. Still she was hesitant to leave. She'd always been glad when Lovingdon spent a bit of time with her, but it was because his visits had offered a respite from loneliness. Jack was offering her nothing more, and she could no longer deny her curiosity regarding him. He was not at all as she'd originally envisioned. She had a desire to explore this newly discovered facet to him.

She strolled as nonchalantly as she could to the couch. Little tremors were dancing beneath her skin, and she hoped he couldn't discern that she was nervous. Sitting, she watched as he moved lithely to the table in the corner and proceeded to splash the contents of one of his bottles into two glasses. He carried both snifters between the fingers of one hand while carrying the de-canter in the other. After setting the decanter on a table beside the couch, he extended one of the snifters toward her. She hesitated—

"My finest brandy. Come on now, where's the harm? You'll not go to hell for a bit of indulging."

"Does God whisper in your ear, offering those truths?"

He offered her his tantalizing grin. "The devil, more like."

"That doesn't surprise me at all. I suspect you're good friends."

"The very best. Now, drink up. It'll help warm you."

"I'm not cold."

"You're shivering."

"Must you always be so observant?" She took the snifter from him and drank. The liquid burned her throat, her lungs, brought tears to her eyes.

He reached over and patted her back, the heat of his hand burning through the material of her clothing. What would it be like to have flesh upon flesh? She fought not to contemplate the possibilities.

"Careful now, brandy is meant to be savored, not gulped."

She took a deep breath as the warmth settled in the pit of her stomach. She thought it was from the liquor, but perhaps it was merely his nearness. His presence was almost overpowering, as though he were larger than life. From the first night, she'd noticed that he dominated any room—any conveyance—he occupied. It was part of the reason he unsettled her. He was not a man ever to be ignored.

"I'd not expected you to appreciate fine things." She fairly wheezed the words, which made him grin.

"I've long appreciated the finer things in life. Why do you think I've worked so hard to acquire them?"

He sat on the other end of the couch, stretching his legs out in front of him, laying one arm lazily along the back, his long fingers tantalizingly close to her shoulders, and suddenly the furniture seemed incredibly small, hardly suited for holding more than one person.

"When the ladies spoke of you, your penchant for hard work was never mentioned."

"The ladies?"

She took a sip of brandy. Inhaling the fumes burned her nostrils, yet she found pleasantness in the sensation. She wondered what pleasures the other bottles held. "During afternoon tea, you're often discussed."

He chuckled as though unexpectedly amused. "What would the ladies say about me?"

"That you're on familiar terms with the devil."

"That I am." He lifted his snifter in a salute and drank its contents.

She tried not to be mesmerized watching his throat work. He was not wearing his cravat, waistcoat, or jacket. He'd loosened the buttons at his neck. Considering that she had no desire to upset the camaraderie that was developing between them she decided not to complain about his slovenly dress, especially as he hardly looked slovenly. Even disheveled, he looked wickedly handsome.

"We were going to discuss my finances," she reminded him.

"Ah, yes. Your finances. You may recall that your late husband placed money into a trust that will provide you with two thousand per annum."

"Of course, I recall."

"With a bit of careful investing, I believe I can arrange it so you make five thousand."

"Per annum?" The words came out on a whisper of disbelief.

"Per annum."

"Why would you do that?"

"Because it'll make it easier to marry you off." Snatching the decanter off the table, he reached across the short space separating them and refilled her glass.

She took a sip, studying him over the rim. The flavor of brandy was growing on her. "You seem quite obsessed with the notion of marrying me off."

"It solves numerous problems for me."

"If you didn't want to be guardian, why did you agree to it?"

"Surely, in the short time you've known me, you've learned I consider nothing too unpleasant to undertake when it places more coins in my palm."

"After observing you with Henry today, I'd gotten the distinct impression that you liked him."

"I do. Charming lad. Doesn't mean I don't prefer my freedom."

She took another sip of brandy, then another. Feeling herself growing lethargic, she brought her feet up to the cushions. It was her guilty pleasure, sitting so unladylike in her bedchamber when she read before the fireplace. The brandy made it seem as though now was the time for guilty pleasures.

"Your freedom you can easily gain by simply getting out of our lives," she reminded him.

"I find it difficult to believe that *you*, who are so keen on being dutiful, would suggest I shirk my duties." He poured more brandy into her glass.

"Are you trying to get me foxed?"

He laughed, a deep raspy sound that made her skin tingle. "What do you know of the delights of spirits?"

"I know on more than one occasion my brother returned from your club barely able to walk. I think you would take great sport in bringing me to my knees and spreading rumors about my scandalous behavior."

His eyes darkened and his gaze was unflinching as he studied her. She was left with the impression she'd said something he found intriguing. He barely moved his arm, but it was enough to take her braid and as his hand skimmed over her shoulder, a shudder of pleasure rippled through her.

He toyed with the end of her braid, brushing his thumb over it. "In my business, Duchess, I have learned to be very discreet. I assure you nothing that happens within this residence will be whispered about beyond these walls. Unlike your ladies, I take no pleasure in gossip. So get roaring drunk and fall to your knees as often as you like."

She had no plans to get drunk or fall in any manner, but she didn't object when he poured her more brandy. Feeling more relaxed than she had in a good long while, she swirled the glass, watched the liquid spin. "So how would you do it?"

He seemed startled by her question. "Do what?"

She wondered what he'd been thinking about. "Increase my yearly income."

"Ah, yes, I'd forgotten that's what brought us here. I would increase your income by investing your money."

"In something improper I presume?"

She saw a measure of respect light his eyes, and she couldn't help but feel a bit thrilled that she'd guessed what he'd planned to do with her money.

"Let's just say, for the sake of propriety, you'd be investing in providing entertainment. I don't know that you'd need or want to know the specifics."

She shook her head. "It would make me a hypocrite."

"A wealthy hypocrite."

Smiling, she took another sip of brandy. It was tempting. Spirits she was deciding weren't nearly as awful as she'd originally thought. They were in fact quite delightful. And they made her feel very happy. More happy than she'd felt in a good long while.

"There is more to life than wealth," she told him.

"Those who make such reckless proclamations are usually wealthy."

"You're wealthy."

"Because I recognize it's the only thing that matters, and I put all my efforts into acquiring and holding onto it."

"That's sad. Terribly, terribly sad. Have you no one special?"

For a moment, the way he was looking at her, she thought he was going to tell her about someone he loved.

"Do you want me to invest your money or not?" he asked sharply.

It seemed inherently wrong to have her money invested in things of which she didn't approve, but the thought of five thousand per annum, a sum that would make her quite independent, was a temptation too great to resist. She downed the remainder of her brandy, able for some reason to tolerate it in larger quantities, and nodded.

"Splendid." He refilled her glass. "Now on to the next subject."

"And what would that be?"

"Your husband."

"Lovingdon?"

"No, your future husband." He reached for her feet, stretching out her legs and placing her bare feet on his lap.

"What are you doing?" she asked, alarmed by the intimacy, but lost enough in lethargy not to want to pull them back.

"Offering you a little more indulgence."

"I think you seek to corrupt me."

"With a bit of brandy and a foot rub? Oh, I am the devil."

Smiling at him over the rim of the glass, she said, "That's what I thought the first night. That the devil had come to call."

"And now?"

"I'm not quite sure what to make of you." Suddenly she felt very comfortable with him, as though all her inhibitions had floated away. She thought she might even be able to trust him with her deepest, darkest secrets.

Jack's large rough hands began to knead the soles of her feet. It was absolute heaven. Looking at him through a brandy haze, she decided he was quite charming.

"Since you won't tell me who you fancy, tell me what qualities you prefer in a man and I'll scout around, see what I can find," he said.

Olivia couldn't help it. She giggled. "You make it sound so simple."

"Isn't it?" He ran the pad of his thumb up the center of her sole, causing her toes to curl. "What qualities do you want in your next husband?"

She shook her head. She didn't want to discuss these things. She didn't want him to know—

"Come on, Olivia," he said in that soft, raspy voice that did strange things to her insides. "What is it you want from your next husband?"

Closing her eyes, she let more brandy slide down her throat. The heat of it seemed to rise through her head, urging her to confess. It made her feel daring, bold, and not so ashamed of what she wanted. Running her tongue over her lips, she gathered up the last remnants of brandy. She opened her eyes to discover that Jack had moved nearer, near enough that he could tuck behind her ear strands of hair that had escaped her braid.

"Tell me, Olivia."

"I don't want him to cast me aside once he has his heir." She held her snifter with both hands and looked into the glass as though it held images from the past. "Lovingdon did that. He never touched me again once he realized I was with child."

It took every ounce of courage she possessed to lift her gaze to his. She didn't expect sympathy from a man like Jack Dodger, and he didn't disappoint her in that regard. She wasn't quite sure what his thoughts were, but based on the hardness of his jaw, she suspected it might be a good thing that Lovingdon was dead.

"I thought it was because I was *with* child and he feared intimacy might cause me to lose it," she tried to explain. "I thought after Henry was born everything would return to the way it had been. But it didn't."

He trailed his finger along her cheek. "The man was a fool."

"I was the fool. I went to his bedchamber once, thinking to seduce him." She'd felt so silly then, had never thought to tell anyone, but tonight in the shadows with the brandy coursing through her veins, embarrassment was a distant memory. "He rebuffed me. He tried to be kind. He told me there was a girl in his youth, and when she left him his heart went with her. That he'd betrayed her and could not keep betraying her. I truly didn't know what he was talking about. I was so mortified, I didn't really listen."

He swept his thumb across the sensitive flesh of her throat. "Who was she?"

"I don't know. It's often that way among the aristocracy. Political alliances or financial gains hold more sway than matters of the heart." She shook her head. "I was married to Lovingdon for six years and I hardly knew him at all. It seems as though I should miss him more, that there should be a gaping hole. All I feel is a sense of emptiness, that something's missing, but I think it was missing long before he died."

The brandy made her daring. She eased toward him slightly and whispered, "I'm not even certain I've actually truly been kissed."

It was uncanny how still he suddenly became, still and tense, his gaze intensifying as it held hers. "I've told you before I'm not a man who settles for only a kiss."

He'd also warned her never to challenge him because it would only make him do it. She was five and twenty and she'd only ever received a kiss while standing at the altar. Lovingdon had not been cruel, but neither had he been passionate. He'd treated her with kindness, but he'd never stirred her emotions as Jack Dodger did. Jack infuriated her. He mesmerized her. He terrified her. He made her curious.

Licking her lips to steal the remnants of brandy, she saw his eyes darken. His reaction shored up her courage.

"I forbid you to *only* kiss me."

"I've warned you not to forbid me," he growled.

Before her next heartbeat, he'd slid his hand around her neck, holding her still, as he slashed his mouth across hers. He was not gentle or polite. He was almost savage with his desire to deliver what she'd requested. She relaxed into him, offered up no objections when his tongue urged her lips to part and slid smoothly into her mouth. Heat spiraled through her, melting her bones as though they were little more than tallow. He touched her with nothing except that one hand and his mouth, yet it seemed as though he caressed her everywhere, inside and out, shallow and deep. How could a kiss be this powerful, elicit such yearnings?

His hand clutched the back of her head as though he would hold her there forever while his mouth ravaged hers. She wondered if he tasted the brandy on her tongue that she tasted on his. It was suddenly a richer flavor, more intense, more enjoyable. She wanted to lap it up, become drunk on it.

She'd always been so good about exhibiting proper behavior, and suddenly she was relishing the forbidden, understanding its appeal. His bristly beard abraded her skin, but it only served to enhance her enjoyment. Intense pleasure swirled through her. Oh, she'd never felt anything like this before. She wanted to curl around him, hold him close. She scraped her fingers along his scalp, the thick tendrils of his hair soft against her skin.

She heard a low moan, barely realizing that it came from her. Her entire body seemed to be awakened, as though all these years she'd been unaware that it had been asleep. If at all possible, he deepened the kiss as though he couldn't have enough of her. As though he desired her.

The notorious Jack Dodger wanting her? It was a thought almost too heady to bear. Her husband had kissed her at the altar because duty required it. Even though she'd challenged Jack, she felt no sense of duty in his reaction to her. She felt only an overwhelming power, barely leashed. Her own reaction to his greedy demands shocked her. She didn't want him to stop. She never wanted him to—

Suddenly he broke away and heaved himself to his feet, leaving her bereft, reaching for him before she even realized what she was doing.

Breathing heavily, his back to her, he said, "I'll prepare a proposal for you, outlining what I intend to do with your money. You can discuss it with Beckwith in order to be assured your best interests will be served."

Gaping, she stared at him in stunned disbelief. The kiss that had left her trembling from head to toe meant nothing to him. He could play his mouth wildly over hers and then get up and calmly discuss her finances? What a fool she'd been to give in to temptation, only to have it thrown in her face. Tears stung her eyes as she fought desperately for composure and some hint as to how to make a graceful departure from his presence.

Abruptly he spun around and was leaning over her, his arms braced on the couch, hemming her in, his eyes smoldering with passion barely controlled. "I cautioned you that I was not a man who would settle for only a kiss, so be forewarned, I will collect what I am owed. I'll hold to my promise and not go to your bed, but by God, you will come to mine. I'll leave the choosing of the moment up to you, but choose a moment you will."

With a force that tipped the couch, he shoved away and headed for the door. "I'm going to my club," he threw out, as though she'd asked about his intentions.

But she hadn't the strength to form words. She could barely stay sitting upright. Her entire body felt weak. Tremors cascaded through her as she gasped for breath. All she'd wanted was a kiss and he'd delivered a great deal more.

She squeezed her eyes shut, his velvety threat echoing through her mind. Oh, the arrogance of the man. She'd never go to his bed. *Never.*

But even as she thought the words, she feared they were a lie.

Jack stormed into his club, a man with a purpose. He'd thought leaving the duchess would be enough to tamp his desire. He'd been wrong. Even now, it was roaring through him with an ungodly vengeance, refusing to be ignored.

For the first time in his life, he wanted more than he'd ever had. He wanted to hear a woman's cries as she gave herself over to pleasure. He wanted to be the one who brought the cries rising out of her throat. He wanted to touch her in ways that pleased her. He wanted to taste her. Start with her mouth and work his way down to her toes.

He made his way to the room where the girls worked. Standing in the doorway, he scanned the crowd until he caught sight of Prudence lounging on a man's lap.

He knew how intense his gaze could be, how he could force a person to feel it and gain his attention. Finally, she looked over at him. He jerked his head in the direction of the offices. She gave him a quick nod before turning back to her customer to smooth any feathers that might be ruffled by her unexpected departure.

Jack barreled through his establishment, ignoring those around him. Something in his face must have shown that he wanted them to disregard him as well, because no one approached or vied for his attention.

Jack shoved open the door that led to the offices, walked by Frannie's without peering in, and strode into his own, closing and locking the door in his wake. He went to the wall and took down an oil painting of a woman sitting beneath a tree. Removing a key from his waistcoat pocket, he inserted it into the lock and opened his safe. He gathered the required coins and dropped them into a velvet pouch. After closing the safe door, removing the key, and returning the painting to its place, he unlocked his office door.

Tossing the pouch onto a desk corner for easy reach, he sat, opened a drawer, removed a condom, and slipped it into his pocket. Tonight he just needed a quick romp. His desk would suffice. He'd have Pru back to her customer before she was truly missed. Reaching behind him, he grabbed a bottle of whiskey, poured some into a glass, and downed it in one long swallow.

He'd never felt the need this badly. It was almost barbaric. He couldn't seem to get the vision of Olivia out of his mind. The innocence in her request: *I forbid you to only kiss me.*

Yet there had been no innocence in her response.

What had possessed him to accept her challenge? It would have been far better to have rebuffed her, to have walked away, to have not tasted her, to have not known the sweet echo of her sighs and moans as pleasure took hold. It had required every ounce of willpower he possessed to go no further than a kiss. He'd desperately wanted to loosen her buttons and remove that hideous nightgown. He'd wanted to bare her skin to his hands and his mouth. He'd wanted to pull her beneath him, grind himself against her—

It was lust—just lust, and nothing more. But even as he thought the words, he feared they were a lie.

He stood, grabbed the pouch, and walked out into the hallway, to the door that led outside. They would go to his room, his bed, for a longer, more satisfying encounter. He'd bury himself so deeply within her—

The footsteps he heard were not the ones that of late caused his heart to pick up its tempo. He watched as Pru approached in her sensual attire. But she didn't entice him as Olivia did in her ghastly black dresses.

Pru slipped her arm through his and pressed her breast—much larger than Olivia's—suggestively against his arm. " 'ello, love. It's been a long while since ye called for me. Are we goin' to your room?"

He'd always felt nothing with her. With every woman he'd paid for, he'd always felt nothing beyond the physical. He'd always thought he was incapable of feeling more, that something inside him was broken and held his emotions imprisoned at a distance. But suddenly what she could give him was not enough.

"Jack?"

He touched her cheek with regret. "Sorry, Pru. It seems I'm not in the mood after all."

He handed her the pouch. "That's for the trouble."

"Jack, I can't take yer money for not doin' nothin'."

"You came to me. That was enough."

"Is everythin' all right? Ye don't seem yerself."

"Couldn't be better. Go see to your customers."

She gave a hapless shrug. "All right."

She wasn't devastated because he'd turned her away. Just as Prudence was business for Jack, so Jack was business for her. Nothing more.

His entire life had never involved anything more.

Chapter 12

Olivia rolled over in bed and shielded her eyes from the sunlight creeping in through a part in the draperies. She remembered how unhappy her brother would be when he finally tumbled out of bed after a night at Dodger's. Was this the curse of brandy? To leave her with an agonizing headache, a raw throat, and thoughts that swirled through her mind with the wispiness of fog?

With great effort, she turned her head to the side and looked at the clock ticking on her bedside table. The little cherubs decorating it greeted her as they always did each morning, causing her to smile. It was almost nine. She'd overslept. She was surprised Jack hadn't come knocking on her door seeking company during breakfast. Perhaps he'd not yet returned from his nightly prowling.

Jack. The memories of his mouth having its way with hers assailed her. How would she face him? But face him she would. Last night was an aberration, the brandy loosening her morals. She'd avoid spirits in the future, and she'd make it perfectly clear that she'd avoid his bed. He was owed nothing. He'd accepted the dare of receiving only a kiss, and he would just have to live with it. She was certain he'd have no trouble whatsoever finding solace elsewhere. Why did that thought cause an ache near her heart?

Would he go to Frannie? Would she welcome him with open arms, give to him what Olivia was afraid to offer? Would Frannie know the delight of greeting the morning nestled within his arms?

With a lethargic sigh at her stupidity for tormenting herself, Olivia eased out of bed. The floor felt cool against the soles of her feet. Perhaps today she wouldn't bother with shoes. She giggled at the thought of a duchess without shoes. Or she thought she giggled. She hadn't heard any sound. What was wrong with her?

She staggered toward the door that led to the dressing room. Someone had moved the blasted thing. It seemed so far away of a sudden. Halfway there, she realized she'd forgotten to pull the bell for her maid. How could she get ready for the day without Maggie? Perhaps she'd go back to bed, sleep a bit more, and start the day over.

Instead, she opened the door to the dressing room. Steamy warmth greeted and comforted her, even though she was hot.

And growing hotter with embarrassment, shame, and awareness.

Standing in front of the mirror, lather on a portion of his face and a razor in his hand, was a man. Images darted in and out of her mind: slender back, broad shoulders. His buttocks—pale and rounded and firm. Long legs. Solid thighs. She was fascinated, watching his muscles ripple with his movements just before he stilled. She'd never seen anything quite so exquisite before.

He was naked—completely naked. Droplets had gathered on his back as though he'd toweled off but been unable to reach those few. She had an insane urge to pick up a towel and glide it over his skin, absorb the remnants of his bath.

"You bathed *yesterday*," she rasped, the words sounding as though they came from a great distance.

Holding her gaze in the mirror, he said, "I bathe every morning."

Apparently the man had no shame. Why was she not surprised? With a challenge in those dark eyes and a come-hither grin, he turned to face her. She was familiar with the shape of a man's anatomy even though her husband had bedded her with propriety. He'd always worn a nightshirt. She'd felt, but never seen . . . and even if she'd seen, she didn't think her husband had been quite that . . . enticing. It was the only word she could think of to describe what Jack Dodger so proudly displayed. Every facet of his being was little more than an invitation to indulge in wickedness.

"Oh, my word," escaped from her mouth on a shaky breath.

Suddenly the room was spinning, black edges rushing toward the center of her vision, until she saw nothing at all.

"Damnation!"

His razor clattering in the bowl as he released it, Jack lunged for Olivia, somehow managing to grab her before she hit the floor. How was it that a woman once married could be so squeamish at the sight of a naked man?

But as he shifted her into his arms and her head lolled against his bare shoulder, he realized something else entirely might have been responsible for her swooning. "Good God, you're burning up."

Not weighted down by anything except her cotton nightgown, she was lighter than she'd been the first time he'd carried her.

He laid her on her bed. Reaching for the bellpull, he hesitated. How was he going to explain his lack of clothing if her maid responded quickly to the summons?

Grabbing a towel as he went through the dressing room and wiping the lather from his face, he hurried to his room. Jerking on his trousers and slipping into a shirt, he wondered if she'd been fighting an illness from the beginning. He didn't like thinking he might have made a sick woman's life miserable—or that he might even have been responsible for bringing on the illness. Last night she'd seemed fevered only by passion; surely he'd have noticed if she was ill.

Buttoned and tucked, he decided the rest could wait. He could explain being partially dressed much more easily than he could explain nakedness.

In long strides, he returned to her bedchamber and yanked on the bellpull. She was still dead to the world, but not dead. He patted her cheek. "Livy? Come on now, sweetheart."

"Sorry," she mumbled. "So sorry."

"As well you should be, barging in on me like that." For one glorious moment he'd thought she'd made the decision to come to his bed. His body, damn its weakness, had immediately responded.

His gentle pats weren't stirring Olivia. Was that a rattle in her chest? Lowering his ear to her bosom, he heard a rasping sound, but it didn't sound ominous. More disturbing was that through the thin material he was suddenly very much aware of the softness of her breasts against his cheek. The intimacy made his mouth go dry. Her breasts were smaller than Pru's, but damn if they didn't incite his desire into rebellion, nearly shattering his control.

The door opened, and Jack sprung back guiltily, shaping his features into a wall of uncaring.

The maid gasped. "What are you doing, Mr. Dodger?"

"She fainted. I've been trying to revive her. We need to send for my physician."

"She has her own." The maid rushed over and began tapping her fingers against Olivia's cheeks.

"I've tried that already," he told her.

"She's on fire." She looked up at him, and he realized until that moment she'd believed he'd done something to make her mistress faint. Or perhaps she was holding him responsible for her fever. He was blamed for so many things, what did one more matter?

"Stay with her." He began striding from the room. "I'll fetch a physician."

She might have her own, but he wouldn't send for him. Jack wanted someone he trusted. He didn't care to explore the sudden terror ripping through him at the thought of her possibly dying.

* * *

Olivia awoke to the sight of an angel hovering over her bed. His blond curling hair formed a halo around his face. In some distant part of her mind, she realized she should be frightened that a stranger was in her bedchamber, and yet his smile was so kind, so reassuring, that all she could do was offer a weak smile in return.

"Hello," he said softly.

"Who—"

"I'm Dr. Graves. Mr. Dodger sent for me. How do you feel?"

She remembered now, remembered what she'd seen. "He was naked."

"Was he?"

She heard a harsh sound—someone clearing his throat?

"I suspect you were probably dreaming," the doctor said.

She fought to shake her head. "No. I'd never dream him looking as magnificent as *that*."

She thought he looked as though struggling not to laugh.

"Yes, well, we have more pressing concerns. Do you hurt anywhere?"

"Everywhere. So tired."

"I suspect you are. How long have you been feeling unwell?"

"Forever. But not so hot."

"So mayhaps the fever just came upon you."

She nodded, or thought she nodded.

"Why don't you go back to sleep now?" he said.

Sighing, she closed her eyes. "Henry—"

"He's fine."

The man was wonderful. He knew the answers to the questions before she asked them. And his hands were incredibly gentle as he prodded here and there. So gentle.

Lovingdon had never really been tender. Bedding her had always been more about getting down to business. He'd spoken no sweet words before and whispered none in the dark afterward. Sometimes she'd had the impression that he was apologizing for inflicting himself on her. He'd always come into her room, slipped into bed, slipped into her, and then slipped out, leaving her with an aching loneliness. Always so lonely. . .

"Well," Jack snapped as soon as Graves finished his prodding.

"I suspect something akin to influenza."

Jack felt his stomach drop as the maid gasped. She was sitting in a nearby chair for the sake of propriety to provide witness that nothing untoward was happening. Originally, she'd objected to Jack's presence, but it had only taken reminding her that he now paid her salary to silence her. Ah, yes, with the dispensing of coins came power and a tendency for people to look the other way.

"Will she die?" Jack asked.

Graves looked at him. "She's young. I can't attest to her strength because she's so thin. Aristocratic women tend to eat little. They have the means to buy food and they don't take advantage of it. They think an appetite is vulgar."

"So we need to feed her?"

"I doubt she'll feel like eating, but yes, she does need nourishment when she awakens. I've given her some laudanum so she'll sleep for a while in comfort. I'll leave a poultice to help draw out the fever. Cool baths might also help, but then you have to take care that she doesn't get chilled."

"How can she not get chilled in a cool bath?"

"You see the dilemma. The best thing is probably just to let it run its course."

Jack felt the anger and frustration building. "I called for you because you're supposed to be so damned good at administering to the sick—and the best you can offer is, Let's see how it goes?"

"As much as I wish it were otherwise, no remedies exist for what we're dealing with here. I'm sorry."

"It's summer, for God's sake. I thought people got ill in winter."

"More people are usually sick in winter, but illness doesn't take a holiday. When conditions are ripe, people get ill. She's in mourning. Probably not eating, not sleeping. Grief takes a toll."

Only if love was involved. Did that mean she'd loved her husband, her husband who'd left her a mere two thousand pounds a year? Her husband who'd never properly kissed her? What caused people to love? How did that emotion come about? Jack had loved his mother, but he'd be hard-pressed to think of anyone he'd loved since. He had a tender regard for Frannie, but it was not love.

"I'll see to her needs," her maid said.

"You can't do it twenty-four hours a day," Jack snapped. "We'll hire a nurse."

"The good news is that it should pass rather quickly. The fever should break in two or three days," Graves said.

If it's going to break at all was left unsaid.

"I'll return to check on her tomorrow." Graves picked up his ominous black bag.

"Come back tonight," Jack ordered.

"I have a lot of patients—"

"I'm going to build you a damned hospital."

"Because you lost a wager. It doesn't make me owe you."

The hell of it was that Jack knew if Luke asked, Graves would not only come back, he'd never leave. Every one of Feagan's children was more loyal to Luke than to Jack. They'd been jealous of Jack's relationship with Feagan. He was the son Feagan had never had, the one he confided in if something needed confiding. They all worried that Jack knew their deepest, darkest secrets.

Unfortunately for them, he did. But he'd never lorded it over them, never threatened them with exposing what they wished to remain hidden. As much as he was tempted, he wouldn't use what he knew now, either. For the sake of the boy who had already lost his father, Jack swallowed his pride. "Please."

"I'll try. That's the best I can promise. But really, I can do little for her and so much more for others."

Jack nodded, studying Olivia's still form, preferring her marching around the residence, chastising him for one thing or another. "Do you ever feel like you're playing God, picking and choosing who gets your attention?"

"I won't dignify that question with an answer."

"I'm sorry. I know I'm being difficult."

"Most people are when someone they care about is ill."

Jack snapped his gaze to Graves. He was on the verge of denying the charge, but the man had a speculative gleam in his eye. It was as though he had the uncanny ability to see deeply into a person—without medical instruments of any kind.

"I barely know her," Jack grumbled.

"Doesn't mean you don't care." Graves held up his hand. "I know. I know. You care only about Jack Dodger. I'll find a way to come by this evening." Heading toward the door, he stopped beside Jack and whispered, low, "You might want to button your trousers."

With a groan, Jack strode to his bedchamber. He needed to finish getting dressed anyway. He wasn't certain the maid believed his story that he was dressing when he heard a loud thud coming from the duchess's room. He supposed it didn't really matter what anyone believed. All that mattered was that she got better.

Sitting at his desk in the library, Jack was quite content with the day's achievements. To keep his mind from wandering to Olivia, he'd undertaken a great many tasks. He hired a nurse, a lady named Colleen, to watch Olivia during the night. Her lady's maid insisted she would stand vigil during the day. While he interviewed nurses, he also interviewed nannies. The young lady he hired to watch over Henry was named Ida. She was short, the top of her head possibly reaching the middle of Jack's chest—and that was with shoes on. Her black hair was pulled back into a no-nonsense bun, but her blue eyes sparkled with merriment, even when she was answering Jack's tough questions regarding her attitude about punishment. She didn't believe in striking children.

"How will you make him behave?"

"With kindness."

Surely not a conventional approach, but then, Jack had never cared much for following conventional wisdom. At twenty, her experience was limited to watching over her younger brothers. But Jack recognized a gentleness in her eyes, and he liked the way she treated Henry and the manner in which he responded to her. Henry seemed comfortable with her, and the boy seemed to understand that if he was unhappy about anything, he was supposed to interrupt Jack at any time and tell him.

So with the nanny situation taken care of, Jack was able to focus on the financial matters, but suddenly nothing was adding up. He didn't think it had much to do with the numbers in the ledgers but the fact he was concerned about Olivia.

Near midnight, when he should have gone to the club to see to matters there, he went instead to Olivia's room. Ever aware of her devotion to proper behavior, he left the door open. The room was dark save for a lamp with a low flame sitting on the bedside table. The nurse came to her feet.

"How is she?" he asked.

"Still fevered. Mumbling a lot. But I think she's comfortable. I'll move over here to the corner if you'd like a moment of privacy."

He almost asked why he'd need a moment with Olivia. He had the information he required. He could leave now. But he found himself nodding before he'd really given it any thought. "Yes, thank you."

He took the velvet-covered bench near her vanity, set

it beside the bed, and sat. So great was his concern for
Olivia earlier he'd barely noticed the room, the room
she'd asked him not to enter. Glancing around quickly,
he couldn't see anything unusual, anything that might
embarrass her or that she might want to hold as a secret.
Perhaps it was no more than that this room was her
sanctuary and she didn't want the likes of Jack Dodger
invading it. She shouldn't have taken ill, then.

He considered taking her hand, but the action somehow seemed more intimate than the kiss. He didn't even
know why he was there. He could do little enough for
her—but he felt a need to do something. He hated feeling as though he had no control over the situation. It
didn't help that the infernal clocks were ticking—

He looked to the bedside table. A clock with winged
cherubs was marking the passing of time. But that
wasn't enough to set up such a ruckus. Twisting around,
he looked to the corner and discovered the clocks he'd
had removed from the library were resting on a small
lace-covered table. Why were they so precious to her?

He shifted back around and studied her. She seemed
to be resting comfortably. He slid his gaze over to the
nurse. She was sitting near the fireplace, her profile to
him, concentrating on her knitting. He suspected that
she'd notice if he did anything not of a gentlemanly
nature, but she was far enough away not to hear any
words whispered. Not that he wanted to whisper anything to the duchess.

There was a considerable amount that he wanted to
yell at her. She was really inconveniencing him. It was
damned irritating. She needed to get well, and quickly.
He didn't have time to waste looking in on her, and her

son was worried, so Jack had to take moments away from his work—moments he couldn't spare—to reassure Henry. He needed to take care of matters here and at his business. He didn't have the patience for this nonsense.

Still, he placed his elbows on his knees and leaned forward slightly. "No need to worry about your son," he said in a low voice. "He has a proper nanny now. The Countess of Claybourne helped me locate her."

That had been irritating as well: asking Catherine for help. Jack was accustomed to taking care of matters on his own, but he was not as familiar with this world as he was with his. He didn't want to disappoint Olivia by choosing poorly. That too was irritating: that he *cared* about pleasing her.

"You'll approve of her, the new nanny. Her name is Ida. Henry likes her well enough."

Olivia's eyes fluttered open. He could claim he hadn't meant to awaken her. After all, he was skilled at lying. But he had wanted her awake, had wanted to see for himself that life remained in those golden eyes. Had wanted to gaze into them again.

"How are you feeling?" he asked.

Her eyes closed briefly as though it took all her strength to respond. "Tired."

He thought about touching her forehead to test the extent of her fever, but he could see the flush in her cheeks, the dew on her skin. He had no doubt she was still fevered.

"Henry?" she croaked.

"He's fine. He's asleep now."

"Time?"

"A little after midnight. I can give you the precise time if you like. You've got all the damned clocks in here."

One corner of her mouth shifted up into a weak smile. "Gave them . . . to him."

"You gave Lovingdon all the clocks?"

She nodded slightly. No wonder she'd been upset that Jack had thought so little of the precious collection.

"He always said time was his enemy." Tears welled in her eyes. "Tried to make him see it wasn't. But he claimed there were things he needed to do. Things to set to right."

"What things?"

She shook her head slowly, closed her eyes, and opened them. "Wouldn't say. His secrets."

Jack couldn't help but wonder if any of those secrets concerned him. He looked around the room again. Nothing looked familiar, but it could have changed as much as London had. The man who'd taken him in had given him a room next to his, but Jack didn't think this was it.

"So sorry," she rasped.

He looked back at her, for the briefest of moments fearing she had the ability to read his mind, to know the dark roads down which his thoughts had traveled. So his tongue was a bit sharper than he'd intended when he finally spoke. "What do you keep apologizing for? What did you do that requires eternal apologies?"

"Lovingdon. I killed him."

Chapter 13

Jack stared at Olivia. She'd closed her eyes as soon as the words were spoken, as though her admission had taken all her remaining strength. Did she think she was dying, in need of a deathbed confession? Why had she said such a thing? Had she suddenly climbed out of bed, removed all her clothes, and run through the London streets stark naked, Jack wouldn't have been more surprised.

A sound startled him, and to his everlasting irritation, his body jerked. The nurse was standing at the foot of the bed. Did they all have to creep around? He was going to insist bells be sewn onto everyone's clothes so he was aware of them approaching.

"Was she awake?" she asked.

"For a minute."

"Did you give her anything to drink?"

"No."

Colleen scowled at him as though he'd revealed that he'd been more interested in undoing Olivia's buttons than seeing to her comfort. She moved around to the other side of the bed. She touched her fingers to Olivia's brow. Olivia mumbled incoherently.

"Dear Lord, she's on fire."

Which meant her confession was probably the result of delirium. It could have been spawned by a dream, a nightmare, a hidden wish for her older husband to die so she could marry a younger man.

He scoffed. The last was unlikely. She was in a position now to marry a younger man and she rebuffed Jack's attempts to match her up with one. Of course, the fact she didn't seem to want to marry didn't mean she didn't want to be free of her husband. But to kill him? She didn't seem the bloodthirsty type.

Colleen reached for the bellpull.

"What are you doing?" Jack asked.

"I'm going to have to put her in a cold bath. I've got to get the fever down."

He nodded. "Get it ready. I'll put her in the tub."

"That's not proper."

"Modesty be damned. She's not in any condition to walk on her own. You're not strong enough to carry her. And I'm certainly not going to let one of the male servants do it. I'm paying your wages, you'll do as I say. Get the bath ready."

"Yes, sir."

A few minutes later, a flurry of activity commenced as maids scurried around, bringing up water and ice under the careful eye of Brittles. Jack wondered if the butler slept in his clothes, as he always seemed ready to tend to any situation that arose. Perhaps it was only that they were all concerned about the duchess and keeping vigil in their respective parts of the residence.

Jack removed his jacket and turned to toss it on a nearby chair. It was then that he noticed the flash of blond curls at the doorway. Rolling up his sleeves as he went, he walked into the hallway. Young Henry was squatting beside the door, his back pressed to the wall, holding his puppy close, fear evident in his eyes.

He'd obviously heard the commotion and was expecting the worst. Jack assumed all the rushing about might have also occurred the night the duke died.

Jack crouched in front of the boy. "She's going to be all right, lad."

"C-can I see her?"

"It's best if you don't, not right now at least. She'd never forgive me if you got sick as well." Jack barely had a second to ponder why he was concerned with the notion that he might do something for which she wouldn't forgive him.

"What if she d-dies?"

"She won't, lad. I promise you that, and Jack Dodger is a man who keeps his promises. Ask anyone."

"Who?"

Jack grinned. "No one you know, fortunately." He patted the boy's shoulder. "Now go back to bed, so I can see to your mum."

With a nod, the boy got to his feet and started scuffling back to his room. His nanny was waiting for him at the door. She hugged Henry when he reached her, and Jack felt more confident that he'd selected the right woman for the boy. He unfolded his body and went back into the duchess's bedchamber.

"It's ready," Colleen said.

He quickly unbuttoned his waistcoat and tossed it onto the jacket. His cravat followed. He walked to the bed and threw back the covers. Olivia was modestly dressed, with her nightgown bunched around her knees. He lifted her into his arms and carried her into the dressing room. He hesitated. No welcoming steam rose from the water. Ice bobbed along its surface. He was familiar with the unpleasantness of a cold bath. It had been years since he'd been dunked in cold water at the prison and scrubbed unmercifully, but it wasn't an experience easily forgotten.

"Sir, it's for her own good," Colleen said quietly.

As though Jack were a man who cared about the comfort of others, which he surely was not.

"Right." He walked to the tub, took a deep breath as though he was the one being submerged, and lowered her into the water.

Olivia jerked awake with a start. She'd been surrounded by warmth, comfort, safety, and suddenly she was being lowered into freezing water. It was cold, so very cold. Chunks of ice clacked together. She screeched, thrashed, clawed, fought to get free, even as her body sank beneath the water and her drenched nightgown floated around her.

"Olivia."

Someone grabbed her wrists, held them in place with one hand as strong as iron, while the other hand grabbed the back of her head. "Olivia. Olivia! Do you want to frighten Henry?"

She stilled, staring at Jack. At that moment she hated him. "I-i-it's cold."

He released her wrists and cradled her face. His hand was warm, so warm. She wanted to curl her entire body into it.

"I know, but we've got to get your fever down, sweetheart," he said.

Shivering, she nodded. He dropped to the floor, sitting beside the tub as though being in the dressing room while she was in there was proper. It wasn't and she wanted him to leave, but more, she wanted him to stay.

"Think about something else," he ordered.

"L-like wh-what?"

"The clocks. Do you like clocks?"

She nodded, her teeth clattering.

"I'll buy you a clock for every minute you stay in the tub."

"I d-don't like them th-that much."

He laughed, a deep resonate sound.

"I'm glad s-someone's having fun," she stammered.

"I'm not."

She glanced around the room. The only other person was the nurse. What was her name? It danced at the edge of her mind.

The nurse lowered herself to the other side of the tub. "Only a couple of minutes, Your Grace."

Olivia nodded. She was miserable, so very miserable.

"Think about how lovely it'll be when you get out," Jack said.

Olivia jerked her head up and down. "Will you hold me again? You're so comfortable and warm." She released a half laugh. "Silly to want to be warm when that's what got me here in the first place."

"When you get out, you're going to have some warm soup," he said. "You don't eat enough."

"How w-would you know?"

"I've carried you three times now and you're a wisp of a woman."

She was certain he'd managed to insult her, but she really didn't care.

"It's h-hurting." She grabbed the edges of the tub.

"Here." He slipped his hand beneath hers. "Squeeze my hand."

"I m-might b-break b-bones."

"It's not like they won't mend. Come on, squeeze."

She did, squeezing his hand, squeezing her eyes shut, squeezing, squeezing, squeezing. "T-talk to me."

"About what?" he asked.

"Your childhood. T-tell me a story. Your thumb."

"Why is everyone so fascinated with my thumb?"

"W-hat did you s-steal?"

Tenderly he brushed some hair back from her face. "Nothing."

"You were innocent?"

"Of that particular crime, yes. But I was guilty enough of others that I took the punishment as my due."

"Here, Your Grace," the nurse said, pressing a rolled cloth to Olivia's mouth. "You need to clamp down on this, before you bite your tongue."

She did as told then ground out a muffled, "Talk."

He sighed as though he had no more patience for her, but then he said, "It was Claybourne. He tried to steal a block of cheese. You always want to steal something small that you can slip in your pocket or easily hand off to someone else without being seen. But he stupidly wanted the cheese. I went back and tried to break the grocer's hold on him, and all I managed to do was get myself caught. It was the only time I got caught, by the way."

He sounded so proud of that achievement. She nodded, urging him to go on. When he spoke, she could lose herself in his gravelly voice and almost forget the agony she was in.

"I was ten. We were sentenced to three months in prison. When we were released, we returned to our life on the street, a bit wiser and a bit more careful. Frannie was our little mother. She's younger than most of us, but she tended our scrapes. And I think you've had enough of this bath."

"Another minute," the nurse said.

Olivia hated her, hated Jack for hiring her.

"She's turning blue," he said. "She's had enough."

"No, sir."

"She's had enough," he said in that irritating voice that signaled he thought he was master. She hated it.

She loved it as one arm went beneath her knees, the other behind her shoulders, then he lifted her out with a grunt. Perhaps she wasn't so light after all.

He set her on a chair. "Grab the towels."

"I'll see to her, sir," the nurse said.

Jack stepped back and Olivia saw that his shirt was almost as soaked as she was.

"I'm going to my club," he said. "Send word if I'm needed."

Olivia almost reminded him that she needed him to hold her, to warm her, but the cloth was still in her mouth and she was afraid if she removed it, she'd bite off her tongue. The nurse was trying to help her out of her nightgown, and she was fairly certain she'd be warm again soon. But still she couldn't deny the disappointment that it wasn't Jack who was going to be warming her.

As Jack tore off his wet clothes, he was determined to leave the residence as quickly as possible. He'd not promised Olivia that he'd hold her, but he couldn't get her request out of his mind. He reminded himself that she was sick, delirious, possibly not even aware of what she was saying. The very last thing she probably wanted was to be held by him.

Jerking on his dry clothes, he could see her shivering in the tub. Forcing her to stay in the frigid water had been the hardest thing he'd ever done. Chill bumps had erupted over her skin. Her dark nipples had hardened. He knew they were dark because they'd been almost visible through her drenched nightgown. Thank God, she was too ill to notice he was well aware of every aspect of her soaked state.

As soon as she'd started thrashing, he'd wanted to take her back to bed. But he'd promised Henry she wouldn't die and if the nurse thought a cold soak was needed, a cold soak she'd get. He rubbed his brow. Whatever had possessed him to make such a promise?

He jerked open his door and stormed into the hallway—

"D-did she die?"

Jack swung around. Henry stood there in his nightshirt, appearing so small and afraid, his eyes huge.

"No, lad." He walked over and crouched in front of him. "She's going to get well. Where's your nanny?"

"Sleeping." Henry looked at the door, peered back at Jack.

"You can't see her yet, lad. Do you want to sit outside her room for a bit?"

He bobbed his head.

Jack sat on the floor with his back to the wall. Henry crawled onto his lap, pressing his face to Jack's chest. "She'll be all right, lad. She'll be all right."

They sat in silence for a moment before Jack said, "You can suck your thumb if you want."

Henry shook his head.

"Here." Jack reached in his jacket pocket, removed his locket, and handed it to Henry. "Hold it for good luck."

Henry's small hand fisted around it.

"Do you know Lord Claybourne?" Jack asked.

Henry glanced up at him. "No."

His voice was so soft, as though he feared disturbing his mother, that Jack almost didn't hear him. "Well, I suspect you will someday. I lived with the previous Lord Claybourne for a time. One day I was trying to decide if I wanted to run off. I was standing at the back gate, looking at my locket when your father approached."

Henry's golden eyes widened.

"This was years ago," Jack said. "Before you were born. He thought I'd stolen it, but I told him my mum had given it to me . . ."

Jack remembered that day as though it were yesterday.

"I'll give you a shilling to let me look at it," Lovingdon said.

"Why do you care?"

"A girl I once knew carried a locket that looked very much like that one."

Jack didn't like him. He didn't trust anyone with green eyes. They reminded him of the man who'd hurt him so long ago. But where was the harm in taking a coin? "A crown."

The man smiled. "You are a bargainer. But it's a deal."

He gave Jack the crown and as soon as he held it in his hand, he wanted to run. Take the coin and dash off. Instead, with a tightness in his throat that he thought might suffocate him, he handed over his precious possession.

The duke very slowly opened the locket and studied the miniature for what seemed an eternity. Then he closed it and handed it back to Jack. "It's a very pretty locket, but not the one I was remembering."

Jack tucked the locket away and gave him a cocky grin. "Thanks for the crown."

"Are you thinking of leaving?"

"I don't see it's any of yer business."

"The earl is offering you an opportunity here that few such as yourself are given. If you don't want to learn from him, perhaps you'd be willing to learn from me."

"Yer not offerin' nothin' I want. Besides, yer wrong. I wasn't plannin' to leave. My mates are 'ere. I'm stayin'."

"Good for you, lad. Good for you."

By the time Jack finished relating his story, Henry had fallen asleep. Jack carefully extricated the locket from his tiny grasp, opened it, and gazed on the miniature of his mother. She had dark hair and eyes—like his. He'd always thought her beautiful.

His thoughts kept coming back to the man who had bought him. Was it possible he had been Lovingdon? It might explain why the locket had looked familiar to him. The man who bought him had been standing nearby when Jack's mother had given it to Jack as she said good-bye.

No, Jack refused to believe Lovingdon was that man. He'd go insane with the thought of him touching Livy, of being Henry's father.

Another reason existed behind the will. But how in the hell was Jack going to determine what it was? And why did he have the feeling it was important to find out? He should just let it go, but he couldn't shake the suspicion all was not right and he was overlooking something terribly important.

Lovingdon had told Olivia he had something to set to right. Jack wondered if he'd inherited that task as well. He just didn't know what it was yet.

Time crawled by. Sometimes Olivia was cold, shivering, and other times she was so hot she thought she'd burn up.

Jack never returned to see after her welfare. She assumed he'd lost interest, once he realized she'd survive and be around to manage his household. She missed Henry dreadfully, but she knew it would frighten him to see her so weak.

Every morning and every evening the angelic physician came to see how she was doing. His arrivals allowed her to keep track of the passing of the days. It was on the third night that her fever finally broke and he seemed most pleased when he arrived in the morning and saw her sitting up in bed.

"You're not my normal physician," she said. She was exhausted but feeling much better. She was freshly bathed, wearing a clean nightdress. The bed linens had been changed. The windows were open, the sunlight streaming in, and the odor of illness was dissipating.

"No, I'm not. I'm a friend of Jack Dodger's," Dr. Graves said.

"You seem too respectable to be a friend of his."

Dr. Graves smiled. "I knew him when I was a lad."

"Did you grow up on the streets as well?"

"I did."

"How is it that you learned compassion?"

He narrowed his eyes at her. "Are you really asking, How is it that Mr. Dodger *didn't*?"

"You just seem an unlikely pair."

"Children are seldom given the luxury of choosing their childhoods, but I cannot fault the friendships formed in mine. They have stood me in good stead."

She plucked at a thread on the comforter. "It's just that he hasn't even bothered to see how I'm faring."

"Oh, he's bothered." He was grinning as though he was privy to some grand joke. "Each time I come to see you, afterward I'm put through a grueling interrogation regarding your health."

As though to discount the veracity of his words, she said, "He hasn't come to see me." She sounded mulish, not at all like herself.

"It wouldn't be proper, would it?"

As though what was proper had stopped him before. Hadn't stopped either of them, truth be told.

"I want you to stay in bed for two more days, regain some strength," Dr. Graves said.

"What about Henry?"

"He's fine. You can see him in two days."

"I'd rather see him now."

"Two days." His voice was succinct, allowed no room for argument.

"Are all of you street lads so bossy?"

"Indeed, we are." He picked up his black bag. "Now, I must go face the great inquisitor."

Olivia watched him leave the room. Then she looked over to where the nurse was sitting. "Do you suppose I could sit by the window for a while?"

"He said to stay in bed."

"But surely sitting calmly by the window will accomplish the same thing."

Colleen set her knitting aside. "I suppose it can't hurt too much."

It hurt more than Olivia had anticipated. Her muscles ached, her bones creaked. If she didn't know better, she'd have thought she had aged a hundred years. Leaning on Colleen, she was out of breath by the time she finally settled into the chair. "Oh, my word. I'm not sure I'll be able to get back to the bed."

"If not, we'll call for Mr. Dodger and have him carry you."

She felt the heat of embarrassment warm her cheeks, and although she'd complained about his not being there since the first night, she couldn't overlook the fact that he shouldn't have been in her room even then. She didn't need scandalous gossip running rampant. "He shouldn't have been in here. It was improper."

"He was every bit the gentleman."

Olivia thought she heard something in her voice, as though the nurse were offended on Jack's behalf. "How well do you know him?"

"Hardly at all. I've heard of him, of course, but never met him until I came to work for him. I have to admit to being surprised that I rather like him."

Olivia leaned back and looked out the window. She was too weary to spar, too weary to ask more questions. She wondered if Jack liked Colleen, if perhaps his being in Olivia's room had more to do with the nurse than with Olivia. Having kissed her, had he now grown tired of her? It was an odd thing to worry about, especially since she really didn't want Jack's attention.

She saw Dr. Graves walk to his carriage. It was a rather nice carriage. She hadn't expected that. She wondered how it had come about that he had such fancy things.

It was easier to eat sitting in a chair, so she had a bowl of stew. Not until she began eating did she realize how famished she was.

She didn't stay in the chair very long. Perhaps an hour. Then she gingerly made her way back to bed and promptly fell asleep. When next she woke, it was nighttime. The lamp beside her bed was burning low. At Colleen's urging she ate more stew. Then she collapsed into another deep sleep.

When she awoke again, the lamp was still burning but Colleen was curled on a cot, snoring softly. Olivia glanced over at her clock. It was almost nine. Henry would be asleep by now. She feared he'd had to go to bed without anyone reading to him all these many nights. He still didn't have a proper nanny.

She furrowed her brow. Had someone told her he *did* have a nanny? She had a faint recollection . . . surely not. She could only imagine the sort of woman Jack would approve. Dr. Graves wanted her to stay in bed for one more day, but she'd stayed as long as she could. She was desperate to see Henry. Now was the perfect time because he'd be asleep, and she didn't have to worry about him taxing her overmuch. Tomorrow she would spend some time with him and read to him. He so enjoyed being read to.

It exhausted her to move aside the covers. She wondered how long it would be before she was fully recovered and had her strength back. Her wrapper was resting at the foot of the bed. She drew it on. In bare feet, she crept toward the door, as though she were a child doing something she shouldn't. She was fairly certain that if Colleen awoke, she'd chastise Olivia and insist she return to bed. And she would, as soon as she saw that Henry was all right, that someone was watching over him.

Opening the door, she slipped into the hallway. It was as quiet as she expected. The door to the night nursery was open and as she neared, she heard a rumbling voice. She stopped at the doorway and peered inside. Surely she was still fevered and delirious, because sitting in a chair, his elbows on his thighs, a book in his hands, reading to her son was Jack Dodger.

She'd never seen Henry so entranced. He was sitting up in bed, an odd lump at his side beneath the covers.

She didn't want to contemplate that he was sleeping with his dog.

Jack got to a portion in the reading and Henry interrupted him to announce, "Dodger. That's your name."

Jack looked up from the book. "So it is."

Henry studied him for a moment, his small brow deeply pleated. "Are you the Artful Dodger?"

"What a silly assumption. There are lots of dodgers on the street, boy. Do you know what a dodger is?"

Henry shook his head. Olivia had never seen him so animated, so unafraid.

"A dodger is someone who is very skilled at dodging." Jack moved his body side to side, back, then forward. "When you take something and they reach for you, you dodge away. It's an honor to be called 'dodger.' I suspect Mr. Dickens knew that when he wrote the story."

"Were you good at dodging?"

"The very best."

Oh, the audacity, but Olivia held her tongue because she didn't want to make them aware of her presence. She was fascinated, watching them. Henry hadn't stammered once.

"Will you teach me?" Henry asked.

Jack seemed to consider that. "I don't think it's a skill that a lord would ever need, but I see no harm in it."

"Now?"

"No." Jack chuckled. "When your mother's strong enough to sit in the garden. You'd best go to sleep now. If your mum finds out that I've been letting you stay up this late, I'll never hear the end of it."

Henry laughed. Olivia couldn't remember the last time she'd heard so sweet a sound. He wiggled until he was lying down. The lump beside him wriggled and the puppy's nose because visible. It snuggled against Henry's side.

"Close your eyes and I'll read a bit more until you go to sleep," Jack said.

Henry obeyed, but then, he usually did. Still, there was something about the way he looked at Jack, the way he responded so quickly, the camaraderie that seemed to have developed . . . her son's reaction could almost be considered hero worship.

What had transpired while she'd been ill?

She heard Jack's voice carrying on with the story. She crept down the hallway to her room, grateful to have been undetected. She hardly knew what to make of all this.

In some ways, it seemed terribly wrong that Jack would usurp her position and give so much attention to Henry . . . and in other ways, it seemed so terribly right.

Chapter 14

The next morning, Olivia awoke to sounds coming from the dressing room. No doubt they were preparing a bath for Jack. An image jumped into her mind, an image that she'd been struggling not to remember. Jack Dodger stark naked. She couldn't have chosen a more opportune moment to swoon. Oddly, it left her with a bit of dignity. If she'd spun on her heel and left the room, Jack would have laughed at her retreat. And if she'd stayed, staring him down and trying to shame him into leaving, they'd probably still be standing there. Or worse, she might have invited herself into his bed.

The dressing room grew quiet, and she imagined Jack sitting in the copper tub, warm water lapping at his body. She had an unusual desire to go into the room, lather her hands with soap, and stroke them slowly over his chest and shoulders. Along his back and down his arms. He appealed to her in ways he shouldn't, made her desire uncivilized behavior. She'd always been good, and suddenly she found herself wondering what harm would come of her being bad.

"You're awake."

Olivia was startled from her misbegotten musings. She'd forgotten about the nurse.

Colleen smiled warmly and pressed her hand to Olivia's forehead. "The fever hasn't returned. As soon as Mr. Dodger is finished with his bath, I'll have one prepared for you."

Olivia could do little more than nod at the thought of crawling into the tub after Jack had used it.

"I don't think my services will be required any longer," Colleen said, reaching for the bellpull.

"I appreciate your seeing after me. It must take a great deal of courage to put your own health at risk, caring for others."

"I like to help. And I had the opportunity to meet Dr. Graves. Rumors are Mr. Dodger is building him a hospital. I'm hoping to work there."

Jack was building a hospital? The man was a source of constant discoveries. "I don't know if it'll have any influence, but I'll put in a good word."

Colleen curtsied. "Thank you, Your Grace. You're most kind."

Olivia didn't feel kind. She felt put upon waiting for Jack to finish with his bathing. But then he had so very much to bathe, she supposed it was understandable that it would take him a while. While he may have been equal in height to Lovingdon, he was considerably broader; yet, not an inch of him had gone to fat. He was taut and lean. She'd only ever seen the naked male form as a statue and even then modesty prevented her from allowing her gaze to linger overlong. She'd had a devil of a time tearing her gaze from Jack.

Her maid soon joined her. Colleen left. Olivia didn't

know how Maggie knew the dressing room was finally available. But at long last, his bath was dumped and hers was prepared. It was heaven to sit in warm water, to allow it to ease away the lingering aches in her muscles. She felt so weak, but she didn't think her strength would return by lounging about.

She felt a bit more like herself once she was dressed. She looked at the black dress in the mirror, and for the first time since she'd become a widow, she wished desperately that she could wear something with a little color. Black didn't warm her features. Jack was correct about that, but it hurt that he'd felt the necessity to bring it up.

"Shall I bring you a tray?" Maggie asked.

Olivia shook her head. "No. I shall go downstairs for breakfast. I'm quite famished. I fear you'd be bringing me trays all morning."

Besides, it was time to face the devil, and she hoped she could do it without imagining him without his clothes.

While her usual ritual included visiting with Henry first thing in the morning, she decided she needed to have nourishment first. His anticipated enthusiasm was likely to knock her over if she didn't have her strength back. Going down the stairs, she held firmly to the banister, each step seeming to steal her breath. By the time she reached the foyer, all she wanted was to return to bed. She took a moment to gather her strength, then straightened her shoulders and strolled to the breakfast dining room.

The sight that greeted her took the last of her strength. Jack sat at the head of the table, fully clothed, his vest a deep blue. He was, of course, studying his ledger, which seemed to be his preferred reading material. But that wasn't what caused her to freeze in mid-step.

It was the sight of her son sitting beside him. Henry also had a black ledger beside his plate, which seemed odd as he had yet to learn to read. Whenever Jack turned the page in his ledger, Henry would turn one in his. It was both charming and disconcerting. If her son was so willing and eager to mimic such an innocent act, would he do the same of one not quite so innocent? She wasn't even certain she could hold herself up as an example of proper behavior.

Every now and then, a thump sounded. Henry's legs were too short for his feet to touch the floor and he would swing his legs and kick the underside of the chair. Olivia was amazed that Jack seemed not to be bothered by the constant knocking—especially as he had found fault with her ticking clocks. She'd have thought him to be a man with little patience when it came to dealing with children, yet he seemed to have an abundance of it—at least where Henry was concerned.

She wasn't aware of making a sound, but suddenly Jack lifted his head and gave her the wicked smile she'd come to recognize as always preceding something certain to gain her ire.

He came to his feet. "Why, Olivia, what a pleasant surprise."

After sharing the intimacy of his kiss, not to mention seeing him in the altogether, she was surprised his greeting was so cavalier. Was he going to pretend nothing untoward had passed between them?

Before she could decide what to make of this unexpected turn, Henry hopped out of his chair. "Mummy!"

He raced across the dining room and flung his body against her legs. If he hadn't also wound his arms around her, she might have toppled. As it was, he managed to give her some support. She lowered herself to her knees and hugged him close. He smelled of a recent bath, and he felt so sturdy—or perhaps it was just that she was so unsteady. She drew him back and studied him. "My word, I think you've grown."

Not in inches so much as in confidence.

He held his thumb up. "I don't s-suck it anymore."

"You are a big boy, then, aren't you?"

He nodded.

"Come on, now. Your mum needs to eat, lots and lots."

She hadn't heard Jack approach, but his hand was suddenly beneath her elbow, guiding her back to her feet.

His dark eyes were scrutinizing her, and she wasn't certain he was pleased with what he saw. "Why don't you take your chair? I'll prepare you a plate."

"Sit by me," Henry said enthusiastically.

Before she could comment that her proper place was at the foot of the table, Jack said, "No one in this room cares."

Oh, but she cared. She cared what he thought. Did he still feel he was owed? Or in light of her illness had he decided to grant her a reprieve?

Henry took her hand and led her to the chair as though Jack's comment had settled the matter. Once they were seated, Henry said, "We were w-worried about you."

Henry perhaps, but she doubted Jack was. Still, she saw little point in crushing him with the truth. "Were you?"

He nodded. "We sat by your room for hours and hours. Even at night."

"We? You mean you and Mr. Dodger?"

He nodded again, smiled, and whispered, "It's our secret."

A plate appeared before Olivia, causing her to jump slightly.

"I obviously forgot to explain what a secret was," Jack said, low, near her ear, and she shivered in response. He walked away from her and resumed his place at the head of the table. "You should have told me you weren't feeling well before you collapsed."

It seemed he was going to behave as though the brandy, the kiss, and their encounter in the dressing room had not happened. She would do the same, because suddenly she was a jumble of emotions. Did she want his regard or did she not? She honestly didn't know. "I thought it was grief. I appreciate all the trouble you went to in order to ensure my survival."

"Purely selfish, I assure you."

"Because you need me to oversee your household?"

"Because I need you to marry. Men tend to frown at the notion of marrying someone who isn't breathing."

He sounded so overburdened, but at least since he still had plans to marry her off, she was reassured that he'd lost interest in luring her into his bed. She was torn between relief and disappointment. "As we've discussed previously, what you *need*, Mr. Dodger, is not necessarily what I want."

"Have I ever told you that I enjoy a challenge?"

She glanced over at him. His dark eyes held a warning gleam as he smoothly said, "Perhaps I shall work to convince you that what I *need* is precisely what you *want*."

Olivia felt a fissure of anticipation. He might not have lost interest after all.

Olivia sat on a chaise longue near the garden watching as Henry tried to teach his puppy to fetch a stick, although it was his nanny who was doing the fetching while the dog continually ignored Henry's pleas and simply rooted around in the grass. It was an unusually warm afternoon, and the sunlight felt lovely on Olivia's face.

Jack had left the residence earlier, and while she'd normally use the time to pretend the residence was hers, it wasn't quite as appealing as it had once been to imagine him out of their lives. Did he truly intend to still marry her off? Or was a good deal of what he said that seemed so uncaring designed to protect himself because he did care so much?

He was an enigma and she was beginning to think solving the puzzle of Jack Dodger could be quite an enjoyable challenge.

Henry ran over and plopped down beside her, his forehead pleated, his eyes serious. "He won't do it."

Brushing the blond curls back from his brow, she said, "He could be too young, Henry. He's really only a baby. Perhaps when he gets older he'll be more inclined to learn."

"Mr. Dodger could teach him. He can do everything."

"He's a very busy man. I don't expect he'll have time for your Pippin."

He nodded slowly, as though accepting the truth of her words. Then his eyes widened with joy and he jumped up. "You're back!"

Olivia glanced over her shoulder to see Jack striding toward them. He was carrying what looked to be three small wooden boxes.

"What have you got?" Henry asked.

"Henry, it's improper to make such an inquiry," Olivia scolded.

He took a few seconds to look contrite before his bright smile again lit up his face.

"I thought since your mother has recovered, we should celebrate," Jack said, crouching beside her.

She fought to tamp down her joy at his words and the pleasure she took at his nearness. She was acutely aware of his familiar, enticing fragrance, and balled her hands in her lap to stop herself from reaching out to comb her fingers through his curling locks, as disheveled as Henry's but not at all boyish. No, there was nothing remotely boyish about Jack Dodger.

He set the boxes on her lap and gave her a grin. "Do you mind?"

"No, of course not." She was pathetic to take such delight in the smallest of attentions he bestowed on her.

He called to the nanny and when she neared, he said, "You'll want to see this."

Ida settled on the ground as though she didn't care at all about any grass stains she might receive.

Olivia didn't want to contemplate that Jack might have taken an interest in Ida while Olivia was ill. He was probably accustomed to juggling women. Why did she want to mean more to him than she possibly could? Was it because he was beginning to mean something to her other than her son's guardian?

"Do you know what a kaleidoscope is?" Jack asked as he took the first wooden box.

"No, sir," Henry said, while Ida shook her head.

Jack arched a brow at Olivia. She nodded. "Although I've never actually seen one."

"Then you're in for a treat." He urged Henry to settle in front of him, with his back to him. But Henry was too curious and as soon as he was in place, he twisted around to see what was going on. With an amused chuckle, Jack opened the case and removed the cylinder. "Now this one is clear. You look through here"—he pointed to the eyepiece—"and as you turn the other end, whatever you're looking at becomes very different."

He guided Henry's hand, teaching him to hold it, turn it. Henry laughed with delight. He jumped up. "I want to go look at Pippin."

Chuckling with obvious satisfaction at Henry's enthusiasm, Jack handed a box to Ida. "For you."

She smiled with delight. "Well, thank you, sir. I'd best see to the young master." She got up and hurried after Henry, who, unable to get Pippin to sit still, had moved on to look at flowers.

"I approve of her," Olivia said quietly.

Jack turned his attention back to her, a sparkle in his eyes. "Damn. Means hell will be cold when I get there. I'm not fond of the cold."

"I assume you're hinting you thought that abominable place would freeze over before I ever agreed with you."

"I did."

"Do you worry about ending up there?"

"Worrying about things I can't change is a waste of my time."

"It's not too late, you know. If you were to be very, very good—"

He laughed, and she realized she was beginning to welcome the raspy sound of it, that it stirred something deep within her. "Being very, very good would bore me into an early grave." He winked at her, tapped the box. "Open yours."

Her excitement at the thought of a gift caused her hands to tremble slightly. She now knew how Henry had felt, unable to sit still. His joyous laughter echoed over the garden and she wondered what delights he'd found.

"Yours is a bit different," Jack said, his long finger trailing over the rich, dark wood of the cylinder. He turned the larger end toward her. "It has bits of colored glass in it, mostly red and purple. When you turn it, you get different images."

As she lifted it to look through it, he slipped one of his arms around her shoulders placing his hand over hers where it held the turning mechanism, as though she needed assistance for so simple a task. A week ago, she might have shoved him aside. Now she welcomed his nearness as she might a warm blanket on a snowy winter night.

His cheek was almost touching hers, as though he could see what she was viewing. "Do you like it?" he asked in a low voice.

She wasn't certain if he was referring to the kaleidoscope or the way he was almost holding her. In either case, the answer was the same. "Very much."

Turning her head, she realized that she'd placed her lips only a whisper's breath away from his. Considering the madness that had consumed them when they'd kissed before, she thought it prudent not to close the distance between them. "Did you want to have a look?"

His gaze dropped to her mouth, before he leaned ever so slightly toward the kaleidoscope, his hands over hers, guiding it toward his eye. "The colors remind me of you," he murmured. "Fiery, passionate. Each turn reveals a different facet."

"I'm not certain I'm that interesting."

He leaned back. "Then you don't recognize your own appeal. How are you feeling? Strong enough for a walk about the garden?"

"With you?"

Jack studied her, not certain if she'd welcome his company, but he had some questions he wanted answered and he thought the garden might be a better place for answering them. He'd hoped the toys he'd brought would cause her to lower her guard. "Yes, I promise to be on my best behavior."

"Your best could still be quite bad."

It could indeed. He'd felt badly that she'd gotten sick and had wondered at first if his actions the night before she'd collapsed—plying her with brandy and then a kiss, the memory of which still had the power to make his body respond—had any bearing on her health. He couldn't ask Graves without explaining what he'd done—not that he was ashamed, but he wasn't accustomed to sharing the personal intimacies of his life.

"Out of deference for your recent illness, my best will be good. I was thinking I should be there in case you faint again."

"I'm not likely to faint. Still, I would welcome your company."

Words he'd never expected her to say. He wasn't certain what to make of their newfound camaraderie. He just knew things had changed between them. Whether as a result of the kiss or her illness or simply an acceptance that, for now, they were part of each other's lives, he didn't know. He still wanted to marry her off, but he also still possessed an almost uncontrollable desire to have her in his bed.

While she put away the kaleidoscope, he unfolded his body. When she was ready, he helped her to her feet, immediately releasing his hold on her hand once she was steady. Taking her into his arms wouldn't gain him what he needed at that moment.

"Have you even seen all of your garden?" she asked.

It was the first time she'd referred to anything there as truly belonging to him. Somehow it gave credence to his possessing everything, and he was left to wonder if she'd finally accepted the conditions of the will.

"I have, actually," he said. "I'm rather fond of gardens."

"I'd have thought you'd find them frivolous."

He escorted her to the narrow cobblestone serpentine path that led away from where Henry and Ida were still exploring their new toys. The hedges and flowers were abundant here, forming a sense of seclusion. "I grew up in the rookeries. They're filthy, crowded, not prone to offering much in the way of green grass or vibrant colors or pleasant fragrances. So, yes, I tend to appreciate gardens. And my mother sold flowers, so being near them has a tendency to remind me of her."

"Strange, I'd never thought of you as having a mother."

"Unlikely as it is, even Satan's spawn must have a mother."

She jerked her head around to look at him. "Sometimes you have such a low of opinion of yourself that it takes me by surprise."

He grinned at her. "Why would you think I'd consider it a disadvantage to be a relation of the devil?"

She rolled her eyes. "I suppose you wouldn't. Bless your mother for putting up with you."

"She didn't, actually. Not for long, anyway. She sold me when I was five."

Sympathy and horror swam in her eyes, and he cursed himself for revealing that little tidbit of personal information. He didn't know what had possessed him to tell her. He'd only ever told Luke. And of course, Feagan had known. Feagan knew everything.

"Don't look so horrified, Olivia. It was a long time ago."

"Why would she do that?"

"I don't know. I did something to displease her, I'm sure."

"I can't imagine you could have done anything to cause her to so callously sell you."

"Yes, well, I suspect there's a good deal you can't imagine. It's a very different world in the rookeries."

"To whom did she sell you?"

"It no longer matters."

"Surely you misunderstood her intentions."

"It's a bit difficult to misunderstand anything when the coin purse passes in front of your eyes." He was beginning to sound defensive. "Let's move on to another subject, shall we?"

"Yes, of course. I didn't mean to intrude on your painful past."

Inwardly, he cursed again for sharing as much with her as he had. Whatever had possessed him to show such poor judgment?

"I understand you're building a hospital for Dr. Graves. You're far more charitable than I realized," she said.

"No, I'm not. I lost a wager."

Her eyes widened. "You wagered that you would build him a hospital?"

He shrugged.

"And what was he to build you?"

"A tavern."

She laughed. "Of course. What was the wager?"

"Luke—Claybourne—had always loved Frannie. I knew he intended to marry her. One night Graves mentioned he thought Luke would marry Lady Catherine Mabry. And I, always on the prowl for easy money, said, 'I'll take that wager.' Luke married Catherine three weeks later. Now I'm obligated to build this hospital."

"How did he know?"

Jack shrugged again. "Those of us raised under Feagan's tutelage are skilled at deducing. In this instance, Graves was more skilled than I."

"I'm sorry. Who is Feagan?"

"He was the kidsman who ran our band of child thieves."

"Claybourne was one of these children?" she asked.

He nodded. "And Graves and Swindler and Frannie."

"That first night, you said you respected only a few—"

"They are the few. In spite of the odds, they've done well for themselves."

"As have you."

"I've not done too shabbily."

They were circling a portion of the garden where roses climbed the wall and flourished. The abundance of roses made their fragrance almost overpowering, certainly served to make it so he could no longer enjoy Olivia's perfume. They were also clearly beyond the hearing of anyone inside or outside the residence.

As they strolled along, he watched her surreptitiously out of the corner of his eye, waited patiently as he observed her thoughts shifting away from him. The furrow in her brow eased. Her eyes took on a soft glow, her lips curled up slightly as she became lost in the marvels of the lilies that now greeted them at this turn.

"So tell me . . . why did you kill your husband?"

Olivia staggered to a stop and stared at him. She couldn't possibly have heard correctly.

He gave her an indulgent smile. "You mentioned it while you were fevered."

She suddenly felt nauseous. "Who heard?"

"Only me."

The garden was spinning around her. She wasn't moving but somehow she stumbled. He grabbed her elbow.

"Here. Sit down over there," he ordered, and led her to the wrought-iron bench that she'd put in this area of the garden because it normally brought her a measure of peace and contentment to sit there.

She sank onto the bench. It was small and, as insane as it might be, she wanted him to sit beside her and hold her. Instead he crouched in front of her just as Inspector Swindler had done, as though that particular position would somehow elicit a confession.

"Were you delirious when you said that?" he asked.

He was giving her an easy way to escape her predicament, and if the weight of it weren't still bearing down on her, she might have taken it. But she'd told no one, and it was so hard, so hard, to live with. Blinking back the tears burning her eyes, she shook her head.

"Tell me," he urged quietly.

"You'll think I'm awful."

He reached into his jacket, removed a handkerchief, and extended it toward her. "I'm many things, Livy. A hypocrite isn't one of them. I've done far worse things than you could ever do."

She took the handkerchief, dried her tears, and sniffled. "You called me that when I was ill."

"It seemed to suit."

She swallowed hard, sniffled again. "No one has ever called me anything other than Olivia—at least when using my name. They've called me 'Your Grace,' of course, and 'Duchess,' but never 'Livy.' I rather like it, and now I'm rambling."

His gaze was penetrating and she felt as though he could see straight into her heart.

"If it makes it any easier, I don't believe for a

moment you killed him, not with malice, anyway," he said.

"But I'm the reason he's dead."

"How so?"

She squeezed his handkerchief, pulled it taut. "We were going to a dinner. Henry had seemed particularly distressed that we were leaving, so I'd taken some extra time to reassure him. As a result we were running late. Lovingdon made some comment about how it was difficult to believe I'd let time get away from me when I had this obsession with purchasing clocks. It was so unlike him to say anything unkind. His words stung."

Even now thinking about them, they hurt again. The clocks had always been for him. He'd always smiled when she gave one to him and said, "Oh, now I have more time."

Only he hadn't. He hadn't had nearly enough.

"I can certainly understand why you killed him," Jack said.

She scowled at him. "You're making light of my pain."

He shifted. "Because it makes me uncomfortable. I don't like to see you hurting."

"Who'd have thought you'd care? I think there's a very different side of you that you share with only a few."

"I don't share it with anyone."

He clasped his hands in front of him. He was holding them tightly. She could see the skin stretched taut across his knuckles, and she wondered if he was fighting not to reach out and touch her. It seemed when the situation warranted, they could both be extremely strong.

At that moment she wanted nothing more than to fall into his arms, yet she kept her distance.

"So you were running late . . ." he prodded.

She nodded. "We were hurrying down the stairs, and I thought I heard Henry cry. I turned to go back to check on him, and Lovingdon grabbed me. Told me to let Henry be. That he was fine. But I was still upset over the silly clock comment—so I jerked free and when I did—"

Oh, God, she could see it all so clearly, each second seeming to last a minute. The startled look on his face. His arms windmilling. His foot going back, searching for the step he expected to find there, searching for balance—not finding either.

"—he fell backward. I reached for him, but he was already tumbling, and I heard this awful, awful sound, like a huge egg cracking . . . and then he just lay there."

Jack suddenly looked blurry, and she realized she was looking at him through a veil of tears. "So you see, it was my fault."

He worked his handkerchief free of her death grip and very tenderly—with more tenderness than she would have given him credit for possessing—wiped at her tears.

"No, it wasn't," he said quietly. "It was an accident."

"It was all so silly. He didn't even want to go to the dinner party, but it was with the queen. She and the prince were celebrating the success of the Great Exhibition. You probably are unaware, but you don't turn down an invitation from the queen."

Through her continuing tears, she saw a corner of his mouth hike up. "I suspect etiquette involving royalty is something I shall never need to know."

She released a small laugh, a hiccup. "Probably not." She hiccupped again. "Do you want to hear something ludicrous?"

"I could use a laugh."

Since he'd stopped wiping her tears, she snatched his handkerchief and gathered up those that remained. "It's silly now, but when the will was read, I thought you were my punishment. I thought maybe Lovingdon had somehow known I'd be responsible for his demise and so he left this ridiculous will to punish me."

"I'm sure it must have felt like it at the time."

"It was just so unexpected. I don't mean to sound ungrateful for what he did leave me, but I'd had high hopes he'd leave me the residence. I know it's much too large for a dower house, but when I moved in, it was so gloomy. He never let the light in. His staff was a quarter of the size it should have been. Much of the house went untended. I changed all that. To be honest, I felt betrayed that he'd given it to you, and then to name you—a known scoundrel—as guardian of our precious Henry . . . it was simply too much to bear. I fear I took all my disappointments and frustrations out on you. I'm sorry for that."

"You apologize far too much, Livy. You had every right to be angry. My reaction wasn't particularly charming either."

"I just don't know what he was thinking. I suppose we'll never know." She sighed. "I miss him, but not as much as I probably should. I was very lonely. Sometimes I wish I hadn't been the good daughter. I wish I'd rebelled and run off with someone of my choosing. The gardener perhaps."

"You were in love with the gardener?"

She laughed lightly, because he sounded so appalled. She'd never envisioned Jack being horrified by anything. "I was only giving a ridiculous example. There wasn't anyone else really." She clutched her hands, studied them. "You were correct, by the way. Lovingdon was concise in all matters. But I don't regret marrying him. When I look at Henry, I'm thankful. I just wish I hadn't killed him."

"You didn't. If anything he killed himself with his clumsiness."

She shook her head. "I'll always feel guilty. If I'd loved him more deeply or not coddled Henry so much . . . I know I coddle him. But I have to put my love somewhere."

"If it makes you feel any better, I suspect," he said quietly, "based upon what we now know of Helen that you did hear Henry cry out."

If he thought to make her feel better. . .

"You're trying to absolve me of my guilt, which I truly appreciate, but unfortunately it only serves to show I was not only a terrible wife but a horrible mother."

"You can't blame yourself for not knowing about Helen. People who take their pleasure in harming children are very skilled at hiding it."

"Did the person who hurt you hide it?"

"Yes, I believe he did."

She didn't press for more details, although she dearly wanted to know everything about him. She took a last swipe at her eyes before handing him back his handker-chief. "Are you going to tell your friend from Scotland Yard?"

"You didn't kill him, Livy. We can ask Swindler's opinion if you like, but he'll tell you the same thing I have."

She slowly rose. "They say confession is good for the soul. I actually do feel somewhat better. Thank you . . . Jack."

"My pleasure, Livy."

He made no move to return to the house. His gaze dropped to her lips, and she wondered if he was think-ing of other pleasures.

"The morning you came into the dressing room—" he began.

"I didn't realize you were in there," she interrupted, anxious to stop him before he said too much.

"I'd thought perhaps you were coming to pay me what I was owed."

"I don't believe I owe you anything." She was breath-less and feeling warm again. "You accepted the chal-lenge, and it came with limitations."

"Then we are once again at odds."

"It would seem that we are."

He gave her a seductive smile. "Strange that it doesn't seem that way."

Before she could counter his claim, he extended his arm. It was a truce of sorts, she realized.

As they walked back to the house, it occurred to her that the more time she spent in his company, the more dangerous to her heart he was becoming.

Chapter 15

He was by nature a patient man. He was also a cautious one, but of late he'd grown bored.

Being in the gaming hell when he knew he'd not be welcomed if his purpose was discovered was quite . . . thrilling.

The hazard tables did not interest him. Nor did the tables where various card games were played. The room that contained the women was boring. And he'd never taken any pleasure from spirits.

But the boys. They were another matter entirely.

No one noticed if a child went missing in the rookeries.

But here they might notice.

Especially if that damned inspector Swindler was nosing around.

The key was to take his time, to determine which was the right boy, and then to make his move.

Olivia knew she needed to get up and begin her day. Instead, she indulged herself and stayed where she was, listening as Jack took his morning bath. In the four days since her illness, she was very much aware of Jack watching her intently, as though trying to judge her readiness to face something. It made her a bit uneasy. Maybe he'd told Swindler about her confession and she was going to find herself carted off to Scotland Yard. Every morning Jack asked after her health, wanted to know how strong she felt, and put her through an inquisition somewhat similar to what she envisioned Graves had endured. She found herself sympathizing with the man. Anxious to determine why Jack was so concerned with her health, yesterday morning she'd answered, "I feel as healthy as I was before I took ill."

All he'd said was, "Glad to hear it."

Which made her wonder if she'd opened herself up to his attempts to lure her into his bed. He'd exhibited particularly good behavior since their walk in the garden. They enjoyed dinner together in the evenings. Their relationship had taken a definite turn toward the pleasant, and she was finding it difficult to recall why she'd ever objected to his being guardian.

When all grew quiet in the dressing room, she stayed where she was for a bit longer, trying not to imagine him dressing his enticing body. Of course, the more she tried not to imagine it, the more she did.

A sudden sharp rap on her door startled her. She'd barely sat up before the dressing room door burst open and Jack walked into her room. Gasping, she clutched the covers to her chest. "What are you doing here?"

"I've been putting this off until you were recovered enough to join us and the appropriate day rolled around. Henry wants to go to the Great Exhibition."

"I know he does, but—"

"We're going today. We'd like you to join us. It's shilling day, a day designed specifically for the lower classes, so the upper classes—snobs that they are and I forgive them this one instance because it works to our advantage—don't have to breathe the same air that the lower classes do. The people who will be in attendance today aren't ones you normally associate with, so you're not likely to be recognized." He tossed a bundle onto the bed. "To reassure you further, I brought you those clothes. They'll ensure that you don't stand out. We leave in half an hour."

Before she issued another objection, he closed the door. She reached for the bundle, loosened the knot in the string, and unfolded the scruffy-looking clothes: a jacket, a shirt, trousers, shoes, and a cap. Was he insinuating she should dress as a boy?

Snatching up the trousers, she scrambled out of bed and headed to the door to confront him. It was entirely inappropriate—

But not as inappropriate as kissing him.

Did one bit of bad behavior excuse another? She staggered to a stop and clutched the garment. It was clean, just a bit tattered. Jack, who bathed twice a day and— she'd heard from her laundress—had his clothes washed more often than a normal man should, had provided her with clean clothes. She held the trousers against her waist, letting the legs dangle down to her feet. They were long enough, appeared to be wide enough.

She didn't want to think about how closely he must have studied her to accurately judge the clothes that would fit her. She didn't know whether to be unsettled or flattered, to thank him or take him to task. She had little doubt he was expecting the latter, was possibly waiting on the other side of that door, his arguments at the ready.

Weighing her choices, she took a tentative step back. Truth be told, she wanted to see the Great Exhibition as much as Henry. But to dress like a boy. . .

A bubble of laughter escaped and she slapped her hand over her mouth. Just the thought made her feel carefree and young and adventuresome. Where was the harm? Who would know?

She ran the arguments through her mind. The problem would be her hair. It might work if she braided it tightly, pinned it up, put on the cap, and brought it down low.

"No, I can't," she whispered. "I can't."

"Why not?" a little voice that didn't quite sound like hers asked. It was deep inside her mind. Maybe she was going insane. It was bad enough to talk to herself, but then to answer back was total lunacy.

A rap sounded on the door leading into the dressing room. "You ready?" a deep voice asked.

"No."

"You decent?"

"No."

"Get decent. I'm coming in."

"No."

The blackguard opened the door, peered around it, and studied her. "Come on, Livy, you know you want to."

Feeling uncharacteristically vulnerable with him in her bedchamber, she put one bare foot on top of the other.

"Who will you hurt if you go?" Jack asked. He stepped out from behind the door, leaned against the wall, and crossed his arms over his chest as though offering her a challenge.

He wasn't dressed in his usual tailor-made clothes. The brown tweed coat wasn't fitted to him. It was a little large and made him look common. She'd never realized before how uncommon he appeared. It occurred to her now that if she hadn't been aware of his background, when he was properly dressed, she might have mistaken him for an aristocrat. He had that air of entitlement about him. It wasn't very well hidden with his drab clothing. It seemed odd not to see him with his splash of color.

"Who will it hurt if you *don't* go?" he asked, as though giving up on her answering his earlier question.

She looked at the clothes strewn on the bed.

"Years from now, Henry'll be talking about his memories of the Great Exhibition. Don't you want them to include you?" Jack asked.

"That's not fair. Besides, what if someone *does* recognize me?"

"No one looks in the faces of the poor. Wearing those clothes, you'll look like a pauper."

"Then how did I obtain coin for admittance?"

He sighed. "No one will ask. Come on, Livy, for once in your life, do something that you shouldn't."

She almost reminded him that she'd kissed him, but as he'd not alluded to the encounter once since their walk in the garden, she suspected that he either wanted to forget it or had decided it really meant nothing at all. She tried not to be disappointed with that conclusion.

He tempted her, made it seem so easy to slip off her pedestal of high moral standing. Yet what he was asking of her was not terribly awful. It would be so nice to leave the house and do something with Henry. "I suppose there are worse things I could do."

"With a man in your bedroom and you in your night-gown" —he winked— "what I'm suggesting isn't nearly wicked enough."

Before he'd kissed her, she might have thought he was being offensive, but now she thought he was merely teasing, trying to make her laugh, to see the silliness of her dilemma.

"If I go to hell for this—"

"I'll be there as well. I'll dance with you," he promised.

Something in his tone of voice, his gaze, made her think that this time he wasn't teasing, and she had an absurd desire to weep. It had to be the lingering effects of her illness, or perhaps it was simply that he recognized she feared being alone.

If she thought too much about what Jack was asking of her, she might take the coward's way. Instead, she jutted up her chin and waved her hand. "Go on with you now. I have to get ready."

He gave her a quick flash of a grin before disappearing behind the door and closing it. Oh, she wished he hadn't done that, given her that beam of pleasure. It brought such an unheralded thrill to her heart. It was a wondrous feeling to bring a man joy, to know he wanted to be with her.

Happiness. She was experiencing happiness beyond anything she'd ever known.

Reaching for the bellpull, she couldn't recall a single moment in her life when she'd ever been so excited.

The clothes were a mistake, a dreadful mistake, because Jack was forced to admire the lovely shape of her bottom as they stood in line waiting to enter the Crystal Palace. She must have had her maid bind her breasts, because she was as flat as a board in that shirt. Or maybe it was the way the jacket hung over it. The too-short jacket that let him see her trouser-clad bum.

They looked like three mates searching for adventure. Or at least she and Henry looked like lads. Jack looked more like their father. Felt like it too. He felt old and cynical. He'd never before minded his harsh outlook on life, except now it made him feel ancient, while she and Henry were filled with wonder, and they hadn't even gotten into the building yet.

He'd never seen her eyes filled with such merriment. Every now and then she'd bend down and talk to Henry, while pointing out something. As much as he knew he shouldn't, Jack wanted her to share it with him, to touch his arm, rise up on her toes, and whisper her delights in his ear.

Even when she was dressed in ill-fitting clothes, she was delectable. But she also still looked like someone from a higher station in life. He could put dirt on her cheeks and mud on the end of her cute little nose and she still wouldn't look as though she belonged in the quagmire that had been Jack's life. If someone bumped into her the way he'd just knocked into Jack, she'd either apologize or do that little sniff she did when she was displeased. She wouldn't shove—

Damnation.

Searching the pocket of his coat, he glanced around quickly. Not a thief in sight. "Bloody hell."

"'ere now, mate, watch yer language. Got a lady 'ere."

Jack jerked around to the man who'd spoken. He was considerably older, his wife unattractive—but blast it, he looked like he cared for her, that they really were a couple.

"What's wrong?" someone croaked.

He slowly turned his head to Olivia.

"What's wrong?" she repeated in a voice that he guessed she thought mimicked that of a lad, when in truth it didn't come anywhere close. If it weren't for the fact they were striving not to be noticed, he might have teased her about it.

"Got my pocket picked." A hell of a thing to have to confess.

"What was in it?" she asked, concern returning her voice to normal, which earned her an eyebrow raise from both the gent behind them and his lady fair.

"A locket that contained a picture of my mum."

"Why would you carry something that valuable—"

"I always carry it," he stated succinctly, not in the mood to have his foolishness pointed out. "I must have had it lifted half a dozen times over the years, but I was always quick enough to catch the blighter who was trying to snatch it." He wanted to curse again, but didn't want to get into a fight with the bloke behind him. The man might be older, but he had more bulk to him and a meaty fist that Jack knew could do some damage. If it was only him, he could dart away easily enough, but he had to worry that Olivia or the boy might take a blow intended for him.

"So someone with your skills lifted it," she said, more than asked.

He almost told her the truth, that skill had nothing to do with it, that he'd been distracted by her, not paying attention, which must have been obvious to whomever had identified him as an easy mark. But he decided that confession would make them both uncomfortable. "It's of no value to him. He'll have to fence it. I'll find it."

She stepped around Henry, who'd been standing between them, serving as an innocent buffer. She touched Jack's arm, and even though he was wearing a jacket and a shirt, he felt the warmth of her palm as though nothing separated them. If he didn't know better, he'd think she was fevered. Or maybe he was. He wanted to jerk away, he wanted to move closer.

"I'm sorry," she said softly, a whisper of comfort that had the power to penetrate his carefully built wall.

"Not your fault—my foolishness." His throat felt raw, his voice scratchy. What in the bloody hell had made him think that going on an outing with her was a good idea? *Had he completely lost his mind?* He wanted her more now than he had the night he'd kissed her. Her innocent lack of awareness regarding his desire for her tormented him.

"Do you have another picture of her?" she asked.

"No. It doesn't matter. It's not important." Although her hand wasn't moving, he felt as though it was, as though it was stroking his shoulders, his chest. He could imagine it, wanted it with a fierceness that was almost his undoing.

"Why aren't they opening the doors?" he asked irritably.

Her hand slipped away as she looked toward the glass building. He wanted to snatch it back, hold it tightly, and never release it. *He had lost his mind.* He no longer had any doubt.

"Looks like perhaps they are," she said. "I see some movement at the front."

She looked back at him, held his gaze, and for a horrified moment, he thought she could see the turmoil she caused within him. He suddenly wanted more than he could have—so much more. He wanted to bring her on a day when the elite came. He wanted to wear his tailored clothing and see her in a dress other than black. He wanted her hand on his arm, knowing he would be envied because she was at his side.

"Come on! Come on!" Henry shouted.

Jack realized the line had begun to move and he'd completely missed it. "We'd best start paying attention here."

She smiled gently as though she understood his struggles. Reaching out, she took Henry's hand. "Stay close."

Jack didn't know if she was speaking to her son or to him, if she recognized that he suddenly wanted to run away. But he stayed near, holding the firm conviction that nothing within that glass and metal building would fascinate him as much as the woman dressed as a boy who now walked beside him.

He became aware of the stares, the attention they were drawing, no doubt because Olivia was talking and acting like a mother, not like a young lad. As though she also became aware of the interest, she glanced around.

She looked at Jack and he could see the panic on her face that people were beginning to notice her, notice that she wasn't a boy. Before he could reassure her that it was of no consequence, she said, "Bloody hell," in that deep-throated gargle she seemed to think was the way a young man would talk.

"Bloody hell," Henry repeated.

Olivia couldn't have looked more horrified if Jack had lifted her up and planted a kiss on those parted lips. And then she began to giggle, covering her mouth, shaking her head.

"'ere, 'ere, yer language," the man behind them said.

The eyes of the woman behind them widened considerably. "I don't think that's a lad, Jonah. What's going on 'ere?"

Jack took Olivia's hand. "Come on."

She grabbed Henry's hand. Jack led them away from the line.

"We're going to lose our place in the line," Olivia said, but she didn't sound angry. He could still hear the trace of laughter in her voice.

"We're going to get a better one," Jack said, marching them toward the front.

"You're not thinking of stealing a place."

"I've told you I don't do that anymore." He glanced back at her and grinned. "Steal."

He didn't want the beginning of the line, because it would be too obvious. But he wanted them closer than they were. He spotted a man, a woman, and a young girl. With Olivia and Henry trailing behind him, Jack approached.

"How many in your group?" Jack asked the man.

"What concern is it of yers?"

"I'll pay you handsomely for your place here if you'll take your family to the back of the line," Jack told him.

"You're knockers. We've been 'ere since five in the morn—"

He looked at the money Jack had shoved into his hand. He lifted his gaze to Jack, then doffed his cap. "See ye, gov'ner." He turned to the woman and girl. "Let's go."

"I'm not—"

"Back of the line, now, love," he said, pushing the woman away from the crowd, before showing her what he held.

Her eyes widened before she tucked her hand in the crook of his arm and happily walked away.

"I thought we were going to work not to get noticed," Olivia said as Jack drew them into the line.

"We lost that opportunity when you tried to draw attention away from yourself."

"What was I supposed to do?"

"Exactly what you did. I should have done this earlier."

"We're almost there," Henry yelled excitedly, tugging on Jack's hand and jumping.

Yes, they were, and already Jack was wishing this day would never come to an end.

Olivia had never paid much attention to the masses. They weren't part of her world. Yet, walking among them, she couldn't help but notice that they didn't seem so very different. Jack blended in very well, but she knew it was because he was making a point to do so. She'd considered him as coming from the dregs of society, but that wasn't where he belonged. She thought he belonged exactly where he was.

It was improper for her to be so very much aware of another man and yet it seemed so natural. She knew when Jack would grin—before he grinned—because a bit of the devil would first appear in his eyes and then it would work its way into a slow smile. He didn't grin often, but when he did, it had the power to steal her breath. When he wasn't quite certain of himself or was thinking through a problem, he rubbed the underside of his jaw. His voice always sounded confident, but she was beginning to suspect there were times when he wasn't, and that small mannerism somehow shored up his self-assurance. She wasn't quite certain why she detected that vulnerability in him, but she did.

She was positively charmed, watching as he explained things to Henry, lifted him up so he could have a more advantageous view, and sat him on his shoulders when he grew tired of walking. She suspected none of that would have happened if they'd come on any other day. Henry would have been expected to behave in a manner befitting his station, his title. Or perhaps there would have been no difference. Jack might have taught him not to care what people thought.

Yes, that was more likely. If she didn't marry, if she had no husband to usurp Jack's role as guardian, she had no doubt Henry would grow up with little fear of expressing his opinion. She wasn't altogether certain that was a bad thing.

Of all the artwork, inventions, and wonders to explore at the Great Exhibition, Henry was most fascinated with the huge locomotive.

"Have you never traveled on the railway, lad?" Jack asked.

With eyes wide, Henry shook his head.

"Many of these folks—that's how they got here. Traveling on the railway. Before that, it would have taken them days and days to get into London. Imagine what they would have missed."

"Have you traveled on the railway?" Olivia asked. She kept meaning to speak in a deeper voice, but she'd get entranced by everything surrounding them and forget. People weren't paying attention to them anyway. Too many marvels drew their interest, and they paid no heed to the oddly dressed trio.

Jack shook his head. "I've never been outside London."

"Never?"

He rolled his shoulders into a careless shrug. "Why would I?"

"The country's very different. I daresay you're in for a treat when we travel to the estates."

He rubbed his jaw. "When we do, sure."

"You're not afraid—"

"'Course not," he interjected, cutting her off. "London suits me just fine. Never had a need to go elsewhere."

"How can you know if you've never been anywhere else?"

"I simply know."

"I don't see how you could."

"How do you know you wouldn't enjoy a bit of wick-edness?" he demanded hotly. At her silence, he arched a brow and that slow smile that started in his eyes eased down to his mouth.

She knew exactly what he was asking with that look. How could she question his judging what he'd never experienced when she was guilty of the same thing? She'd never sinned, and God help her, she was beginning to realize she'd never truly desired her husband. In the beginning, she'd thought of him before she went to sleep, missed him, felt the loneliness of his leaving her bed. She hadn't anticipated seeing him at breakfast in the morning. She hadn't thought the afternoons without him were too long and the evenings in his company too short.

She hadn't thought of him with yearning. She suspected if she wasn't very, very careful that, when it came to Jack, she could find herself yearning for more than a kiss—

She grabbed Henry's hand. "I think we've dawdled here long enough."

Henry glanced back. "Can we g-go on the rail-railway?"

"Someday, lad."

She heard in Jack's voice the promise.

The sun had disappeared by the time the coach pulled up in front of the residence. Henry—all of them—had eaten at the refreshment area, enjoying a variety of offerings. Olivia didn't think any of them would be in the mood for dinner, which was a good thing as Henry was already asleep.

With Henry clinging to him like a little monkey—his arms around his neck, his legs around his waist—Jack gracefully exited the coach. As they walked toward the manor, Olivia felt tears prick her eyes at the sight of the tall, strapping man beside her and the small boy who trusted him implicitly. She couldn't deny that what she was beginning to feel for Jack was wondrous in its scope, frightening in its intensity.

She wanted to be with him in ways she knew she should not. Scandalous ways, sinful ways. She had to shore up her resolve to resist what she knew would only lead to disaster. To abandon her upbringing for a night of passion in the bed of a man to whom she was not wed, a man who had plans to marry her off to another—it was a foolish, foolish woman who would contemplate traveling such a road.

Henry stirred not at all as they entered the house and began their ascent up the stairs. He was well and truly worn out. Olivia certainly understood that feeling. She would welcome a warm bath and an early night.

Ida greeted them in the nursery. "How is the young duke?"

"Dead to the world," Jack said as he laid Henry on his bed with a gentleness that surprised Olivia. After all this time, she was still astonished that where Henry was concerned, Jack showed such extreme consideration.

"I'll prepare him for bed," Ida whispered. "You see to yourselves."

Leaning down, Olivia kissed Henry's forehead. "Good night, sweetheart."

She followed Jack into the hallway. "I haven't the strength for dinner."

His eyes held concern when he looked at her. "Was today too much?"

"It was perfect. I'm just tired. If you don't mind, I'll use the dressing room first."

"I have to go out, and where I'm going my present appearance will serve me well."

"Where are you going?"

"I want to find my locket."

"Do you think you'll have any luck?"

"I know where it's likely to be pawned. I'll find it."

He had such confidence. Confidence in everything.

She placed her hand on his arm. "Thank you so much for today."

He splayed his fingers beneath her chin and they curled around her neck. Her breath hitched with thoughts of him drawing her near and giving her a scalding kiss before marching off to attend to his business.

His gaze took a leisurely journey from her toes back to her eyes. "I have to confess that I'd not expected you to look so delectable in trousers."

She felt a spurt of giddiness.

"Damn, if you don't make me wish I was a man who'd settle for only a kiss."

"I suppose I could forbid you."

Only one corner of his mouth lifted, as though he were faintly amused by her shameful wantonness.

"For now, where's the harm?" he asked in that smoky voice that did strange things to her insides. "It'll just add to your debt."

She didn't bother to correct him, to inform him that she'd never pay what he presumed she owed. She'd not go to his bed. As much as the notion was beginning to appeal to her, she would hold onto the moral high ground even as he lowered his mouth to hers, even as she rose up on her toes to meet it.

It was, after all, only a kiss.

But it felt like so much more. From the moment his lips touched hers, she became lost in the sensations of his mouth playing over hers. She sensed that he tempered his hunger, that he held himself in check as though he feared he'd not have the power this time to settle for anything less than having her beneath him.

But this kiss was as marvelous as the first. A distant part of her was aware of her boy's cap leaving her head. As she skimmed her hands up over his shoulders, she felt his arms come around her, holding her nearer, and then her hair tumbled around her. He was a man of nimble fingers and talented mouth. He could distract her so easily until all she cared about was him.

His bedroom was so near. If he was to lift her into his arms, she didn't know if she'd have the strength to resist. She might simply lean down and open the door for him.

No, no, she had to be stronger than that. She had to take this kiss that stirred her desire and be content with it. They both had to be content with it.

Suddenly changing the angle of his mouth, he deepened the kiss, his tongue leisurely exploring, enticing her to do the same. As he drew her nearer, held her close, she was not hampered by layers of petticoats or skirts. Quite frankly, there was little more than a few pieces of fabric separating her skin from his. His body responded with a fierceness that she needed no imagination to envision. She knew exactly what he looked like, images of him in the dressing room bombarding her, igniting a fire low in her belly.

She heard a harsh plea and feared it came from her.

Breathing heavily, he tore his mouth from hers. Only then did she realize she'd fairly wound herself around him. She immediately dropped her arms, stepped back.

"You do bewitch me," he rasped. "Fair warning, Duchess, I fear this is the last time I can settle for only a kiss."

With that, he spun on his heel and headed toward the stairs. Closing her eyes, she sank against the wall.

His warning wasn't at all fair. All it did was make her anticipate their next meeting.

Climbing out of his brougham, Jack inhaled the foul stench that had surrounded him for much of his youth. He didn't return to the rookeries often, but when he did, it was always with a sense of coming home.

What sort of sad commentary was that on his life when this filth was where he felt most comfortable? He snatched the burlap sack out of the carriage and slung it over his shoulder. He knew there'd be nothing left of his carriage if it remained. "Drive off, return here in an hour," he ordered the driver.

"Yes, sir."

Jack could see the clear relief on the driver's face right before he set the horses into motion. No one wanted to be here, not even those who lived in the dilapidated buildings. It was late evening, yet children were still scurrying around. When they got too curious, too close, he reached in his pocket and tossed a few coins into the dirt and filth to send them scrambling away from him.

He reached the dwelling he wanted. The door was a challenge to open because it wasn't secured to all its hinges. Inside was dark and dreary, the stench of decay even thicker. He started up the stairs, knowing which steps were broken, which squeaked, which to avoid. Nothing improved in this area of London. He discovered a new hole had formed in one of the steps when his foot went through it. Cursing, he worked his boot free and continued on up, albeit a bit more carefully. At the top of the stairs, he turned down the blackened hallway, treading carefully over what he couldn't see but knew was garbage.

Once he left this place, he'd burn the clothes he wore. It was the only way to ensure he brought back with him no disease or infestations. Lice, fleas, crawling things. He'd always hated the feel of tiny bugs.

When he reached the door at the end, he tapped three times, waited a second, tapped two times, waited, tapped thrice. He heard a shuffling movement on the other side of the door. It slowly creaked open. A grimy, wrinkled face appeared. What had once been vibrant hair, as red as Frannie's, was now pale, almost white. The long, scraggly beard was white as well. Rotting teeth formed a smile framed by cracked and bleeding lips.

"Well, if it's not me dodger." With bent and gnarled fingers, he urged Jack inside. "Come on in, boy. Let's see wot ye got for ol' Feagan."

Jack stepped into the squalor and he was transported back to a time when he'd slept on the floor like a dog, spooning around whoever slept beside him, offering and receiving warmth. He'd seldom gone to bed hungry.

Feagan had always been good about feeding his crew. A sickly child wasn't of much use to him.

"Wot ye got? Wot ye got?" Feagan asked, making his way to the rickety chair at the scarred table where a single burning candle standing upright in the mouth of a brown bottle provided the only light in the room.

Jack could see the milky-white film that now hampered Feagan's vision. He moved the sack off his shoulder, set it on the table, and unveiled four bottles: two each of whiskey and rum.

Feagan cackled again. "Oh, me dodger. Ye was always good to Feagan."

Jack's mentor had always been in the habit of referring to himself as though he were another person in the room. It was one of the reasons Jack had never been convinced Feagan was his real name—it was as though he was always having to remind himself, remind others who he was. It wasn't unusual for people in the rookeries—after they'd been arrested—to move to another section of London and change their names. Only once had Feagan reminisced about his past, and it was a story Jack intended to take to the grave.

Jack opened a bottle of whiskey and poured it into the dented tin cup Feagan extended with a shaking hand, a hand that had taught so many how to slip into tight places without being detected. "You should let me move you into a flat at Dodger's."

Feagan took a gulp, then his tongue darted around his lips, determined not to let any drops go to waste. "Wot good would that do Feagan, I ask ye?"

Jack took the chair across from him. "You'd have

food, warmth, company. I'd even give you a gambling allowance."

"Ye was always kinder than anybody give ye credit fer."

"Kindness has nothing to do with it. I don't like trudging through the filth to get to you when I need you."

"Yer the only one wot comes to see me." He leaned forward. " 'ow's me darlin' Frannie?"

"Doing well."

"Married?"

"No."

He shook his head sadly. "I shoulda taken better care of 'er."

"We all should have." She'd been forced into the white slave trade at the age of twelve. Luke had taken it upon himself to kill the man responsible. Olivia might consider him a murderer; Jack didn't. Some dogs needed to be put down.

"But she ain't the reason yer 'ere."

"No." He sighed heavily. "I had my locket picked."

Feagan guffawed, coughed, sounded like he was choking with merriment. "Ye? Ye was me sharpest."

"I was distracted."

Feagan gave him a crafty look. "That's not like ye. She must be a fancy piece."

Jack wasn't going to comment on Olivia. She was too fine a lady for him to even have thoughts of while he was in this cesspool. "I know you're not running boys anymore, but you know who is, and I suspect you still have your finger on the fence trade. I'll pay you a hundred pounds if you locate it for me."

It was an ungodly amount, but the locket was Jack's most precious possession, perhaps the only thing that mattered more to him than coins.

Feagan rubbed his hand over his mouth. "That's a lot of gin. I'll put the word out." He narrowed his eyes. "Anyone else I'd ask fer half up front."

Jack tapped a bottle. "I brought you something you value more."

"That ye did."

Shoving back his chair, Jack stood. "I'll be seeing you."

"That ye will, me dodger, that ye will."

Jack took one last look around the squalor, remembering a time when his goal in life had been to be a more successful kidsman than Feagan. It irked him not to know who his anonymous benefactor was. If not for him, even with the teachings of Luke's grandfather, Jack knew he would have returned to this foulness and lived a life only marginally better than Feagan's.

Chapter 16

Jack was teaching Henry to be slippery, nimble, quick . . . in essence, to be a dodger.

Sitting on the terrace and watching her son dash across the lawn, Olivia wasn't certain how she felt about that development. She supposed no harm would come of it, as long as Jack wasn't instructing Henry on the proper way to slip his hands into pockets without being detected.

In this particular game a ball was involved, but Olivia couldn't determine what the object was or how the game was played. She wasn't certain the players even knew. They were content to grab the ball, run with it, and avoid getting caught. It was a rather undignified game for grown men to be involved in, especially when one was an earl. The Devil Earl, to be precise.

Olivia had never met him before this afternoon. With his dark hair and silver eyes, he was almost as devilishly handsome as Jack.

"It must be something they played on the streets," Catherine, the Countess of Claybourne, said. Dressed in somber black, still mourning her father, she sat at the table with Olivia. She and her husband had arrived shortly after Jack had taken Henry outside for what was becoming a daily afternoon ritual. Within minutes Claybourne had followed Jack's example and discarded his jacket, cravat, and waistcoat; then he rolled up his sleeves in order to gallivant over the lawn unhindered and give chase to Henry, who would run from one end of the lawn to the other carrying the ball and avoiding capture.

Coming to a stop, he'd jump up and down, hold the ball high, and crow, "I won! I won!"

Then they'd start at it again. The puppy was also involved, following Henry, darting in and out, sometimes tripping up the men—who laughed. Olivia couldn't remember a single time that so much merriment had been exhibited in their garden.

"Do you think that's how they learned not to get caught when they stole something?" Olivia asked, imagining the ball symbolizing a loaf of bread or a melon.

"Possibly." The countess laughed lightly, then quieted. "Probably."

She didn't sound at all disturbed by the idea. Her voice carried a bit of wistfulness, as though she thought about her husband's earlier life and wished it had been different. A time existed when many of the aristocracy weren't convinced he was the true heir, but something had happened to change their minds, although Olivia was unsure as to the particulars. "I never doubted for a moment," Lovingdon had mentioned to Olivia in passing. "Resembles his father too much not to be."

"We came to visit several days ago, only to learn you were ill," Catherine said quietly now. "I'm glad you've recovered."

"Thank you. I'm feeling much better." She was acquainted with Catherine, although they'd never been dear friends, and she certainly wasn't going to confess that she was well enough to go to the Great Exhibition.

"I suppose some of your ill health may be attributed to the shock of learning Mr. Dodger was to serve as your son's guardian."

Olivia shifted her gaze over to Catherine. She saw no censure, only a need to reassure. Two weeks ago, Olivia might have welcomed the reassurance. Now, she hardly felt any need for it. Jack was proving his suitability as guardian quite admirably.

"If it's any consolation," Catherine continued, "he'll serve as guardian of our children as well."

Olivia felt her jaw drop. "Not your brother?" *Not the Duke of Greystone?*

Catherine shook her head. "Sterling was gone for some time. Since he's returned, he seems very different. I can't explain it. And Claybourne doesn't know him at all, so he's not comfortable with the notion of Sterling serving as guardian. Jack Dodger he trusts. Mr. Dodger saved his life on more than one occasion."

Olivia sipped her tea, wondering how all that had come about. Had it happened in prison? Why hadn't he shared that story? She'd not ask Catherine for an explanation. Strange how Olivia suddenly felt uncomfortable remembering all the afternoon teas and speculations the ladies had made regarding him, each one eager to share the latest bit of unsavory gossip that had come her way. They'd treated him as a curiosity, not a man. In retrospect, it had been quite rude.

Now, Olivia didn't want gossip. She wanted to know the truth of his life, from his own lips. They'd settled into an easier camaraderie of late. They had breakfast every morning with Henry. In the evening, she dined with Jack alone. He asked her questions about herself: what she enjoyed reading, her theater preferences, how her day had gone. He gave away very little of himself. It occurred to her one night that he was striving to create a mental portrait of her so that he could better determine whom she might marry.

"What's *your* opinion of Mr. Dodger?" Olivia asked.

Catherine turned her gaze back to the men and boy lumbering over the lawn. "Quite honestly, when I met him, I didn't like him. He was insolent and has an exceedingly low opinion of the nobility. But I trust Claybourne and his judgment. Of course, it could also be that I don't believe anyone will ever raise his children other than him, so I don't really worry about it. It seems when a person has such a rough life in his youth that his later life should be filled with nothing except pleasantries."

Catherine glowed with the radiance of a woman madly in love with her husband.

Olivia felt a spark of envy. She couldn't imagine anything more wonderful than being married to a man you loved—unless it was being married to a man who also loved you.

She watched Jack loping over the lawn. He possessed an athleticism she'd expected. She was quite mesmerized watching him, and hoped her company didn't notice how he garnered her attention.

He caught Henry and with a joyous laugh lifted him over his head. Henry guffawed with delight and Olivia smiled. She'd grown up in and married into a very staid household. She'd never questioned the quiet, the reserve, the constant proper behavior. Only now was she beginning to realize that laughter was as intoxicating as brandy.

She also realized she had an opportunity here to learn more about Jack without bombarding him with questions that he'd astutely avoid answering.

"I know this is entirely inappropriate, since I'm in mourning and shouldn't be issuing invitations" —she glanced, embarrassed, at Catherine— "but would you and Claybourne care to dine with us tonight?"

"As I'm in mourning as well, it would be entirely inappropriate for me to accept."

"Of course. I'm so—"

With a twinkle in her blue eyes, Catherine reached across and took her hand. "I would be absolutely delighted. To be quite honest, I find all our rules regarding mourning to be rubbish."

Olivia released a short burst of laughter. It seemed Claybourne had been as bad an influence on Catherine as Jack was on Olivia.

"I have an even more inappropriate notion. As we're all friends, and the dinner will be small and private, let's dispense with the mourning attire, shall we?" Catherine asked.

"Are you certain?"

"Who will know except us? And quite honestly, I'm so dreadfully tired of black."

Olivia smiled. "All right then."

* * *

Jack could hardly believe that Olivia had invited Luke and Catherine to dine with them.

"It's not as though I sent a gilded invitation," she said petulantly when he'd given her a questioning stare.

It seemed the little duchess wasn't opposed to dispensing with proper etiquette as long as it was her idea. Now that she was fully recovered, he'd work to convince her it was her notion to come to his bed. He was looking forward to the challenge, although his patience had been sorely tested as he waited for her to regain her strength. He should be considered for sainthood, considering the forbearance he'd shown.

"So what are you drinking?" Jack asked Luke.

He and Catherine had only just arrived. They'd returned home to prepare for the evening. Jack felt rather underdressed next to Luke in his dinner attire. He had never invested in formal evening clothes because he wasn't invited to balls or dinners, which suited him just fine. He was a curiosity, but one preferred from a distance.

Catherine wore an emerald green gown. Olivia was likely to go into a conniption when she walked in and saw Catherine out of her mourning clothes. He smiled at the thought of at last not being the only one on the receiving end of Livy's scathing rebukes.

"Whatever you're having," Luke said. "I know you serve only the finest."

Jack glanced at Catherine. "Countess?"

"None, thank you."

Luke reached for her hand and brought it to his mouth, placing a kiss on her fingers. The man looked so ridiculously besotted. Jack would never let a woman have a hold on him like that.

"Not everything is agreeable to her these days," Luke said.

Jack poured port into two goblets. "You might have Graves take a look at her, make certain she's not coming down with whatever Olivia had. Nasty stuff, that."

"Have you not told him?" Catherine asked.

"I knew you didn't want people to know, not yet, anyway."

"What? What have I missed here?" Jack asked.

"She's with child," Luke said, and Jack was surprised the buttons didn't pop off Luke's waistcoat.

"How can you know already? You've only just married . . . ah." That explained the quiet, hasty marriage taking place before she was out of mourning. He raised his glass. "My congratulations to you both."

"What are we celebrating?"

Jack turned toward Olivia and froze.

Gliding into the room, smiling shyly, she wore a violet gown, and just as he'd predicted, she looked ravishing. Her throat, shoulders, and the barest hint of her bosom were revealed. Her hair was pinned up in an elaborate style with ringlets bouncing on one side.

As though suddenly uncomfortable, she averted her gaze from his. "Don't look so shocked. Catherine and I thought for an evening amongst friends, there was no harm in our putting aside our mourning clothes."

"No" —Jack cleared his throat to make it so he didn't sound as though he were strangling— "no harm in it at all. You look lovely." The words were grossly inadequate. He didn't possess Luke's societal charms. The women Jack associated with didn't need fancy words, but dear God, Olivia deserved them. Every one that his feeble brain could dredge up.

She blushed becomingly. "Thank you. I remembered you'd asked me about violet. Anyway, it appears we're celebrating."

"Yes." Jack handed her his goblet and poured himself another one. He tipped his head toward Luke. "You do the honors."

Luke smiled with satisfaction. "Catherine is carrying my daughter."

"Your heir," Catherine corrected him.

"Whichever, I'm immensely pleased."

"Oh, how wonderful," Olivia said, and Jack could see the true joy in her eyes. Had she felt that delight when she'd discovered she was with child? If he married her off, would she be ecstatic when she learned she carried her new husband's child? Why did he suddenly want to smash something?

"I'm amazed you already know," Olivia continued.

"Dr. Graves confirmed it," Catherine said, and she was now the one to blush.

"Is he your physician as well?" Olivia asked. "He's wonderful. He saw to me when I was ill."

"I'm surprised he had time, now that he serves at the queen's pleasure," Luke said.

Olivia's eyes widened. "He's physician to the queen?"

"One of several." Jack poured himself more port. "According to Graves she's a hypochondriac."

"You mustn't speak of her that way." Olivia's voice held chastisement.

She'd forever be correcting his manners. For some reason, it truly bothered him tonight. Could she not accept him, imperfections and all?

"Not to worry. When next I have an audience with the queen, I won't mention it." Jack sounded surly, even to himself, but he was acutely aware that these three would be welcomed into Buckingham Palace, while he would not.

An awkward silence descended. He didn't want to ruin this dinner for Olivia, but he also wished Luke and Catherine would leave so he could have Olivia to himself.

"So, Luke, what do you think of Henry? He's quite the dodger, isn't he?" Jack asked, in order to get things going again.

"Indeed. I was very impressed. I didn't think I'd ever see anyone as skilled as you."

"I intend to teach him to have nimble fingers next."

"He's not going to become a pickpocket," Olivia said sternly.

"I wouldn't dream of that. But nimble fingers have other uses."

Before anything else could be said, Brittles walked in and announced, "Dinner is served."

As Jack offered his arm to Olivia, he leaned near and whispered, "With any luck, I may demonstrate those nimble uses before the night is done."

She gasped and Jack chuckled. "Don't look so shocked, Livy. Sooner or later you must pay the devil his due, and I'm of a mind to collect sooner."

*　*　*

It seemed her reprieve had come to an end. Olivia was surprised to discover she wasn't nearly as disappointed as she probably should have been.

The appreciation that had lit Jack's eyes when she walked into the library had flattered her no end. He'd given the impression he desperately wanted to cross the room, take her in his arms, and bestow upon her a kiss that was likely to lead her into his bedroom.

Even now, Jack rarely took his eyes off her. He was being an abominable host, ignoring their guests, not bothering to even attempt to carry on any sort of conversation. Having his undivided attention was thrilling, although she was concerned that she might not be able to hold him at bay when their guests left. More fearful was the realization that she wasn't certain she *wanted* to hold him at bay.

While no one seemed uncomfortable with the absence of discourse—in truth, Claybourne and Catherine seemed amused by it—Olivia was well aware that a good hostess didn't let silence reign.

"I met Frannie recently. She seemed lovely." Jack gave her a dark grin and she wished she hadn't traveled down this path.

"I like her as well," Catherine said, as though aware of the sudden tension. "She's built an orphanage, and hopes soon to open the doors."

"She's just waiting for the furniture," Claybourne added. "I suspect you'll lose all your boys then, Jack."

Olivia was aware of shock rippling through her. Had Frannie been his lover once? Did he have bastard children? She swallowed hard to force back the lump of unease that had formed in her throat. "What boys are those?"

Jack scowled at Claybourne as though he'd revealed some dark secret. "Just boys."

"Your sons?" Had she truly asked? The voice didn't sound like hers.

He gave her a wry smile. "No, I take great pains not to populate London any further. They're street urchins, orphans."

"You keep orphans at your establishment?" She didn't know whether to applaud him for his benevolence or be appalled that he'd allow children into those environs.

"I don't *keep* them, as though they're possessions. They earn their place. As you may recall, I strongly believe that a person must earn the roof over his head or the food in his belly. So I take them in and give them a job. It prevents them from being recruited by mobsters and ending up in gaol. It's nothing, really. I have chores that need doing and they're capable of doing them."

He spoke as though burdened by the need to explain, but she was grateful he had, because it helped her to see him yet again in another light. He was a continual kaleidoscope. And his actions weren't nothing. It was far more trouble than she went to for orphaned children. She felt quite humbled. She also thought his care of other boys helped to explain his rapport with Henry, had perhaps prepared him for his role as guardian.

"Is that where you got the clothes?" she asked.

He lifted his glass to toast her. "Indeed."

Olivia realized she was leaving her guests out of the conversation. What an atrocious hostess she'd become. "Jack brought some clothes for Henry to play in."

"You, as well," he said, seemingly very pleased with himself. He looked at his guests. "We went to the Great Exhibition, with Livy and Henry dressed as boys."

"Really?" Catherine didn't look at all appalled. "What was it like to wear trousers in public?"

"Quite . . . liberating, actually."

"I daresay, I think we wear far too many layers of clothes."

"I agree," both men said at once.

Olivia and Catherine giggled like young girls.

"You know," Claybourne said, lifting his wineglass and studying its dark red contents, "it's possible Lovingdon chose you to be guardian because of the protection you give the lads who work for you."

Olivia was surprised by his words, because the same thought had crossed her mind.

"I considered that, but it seems a flimsy reason. I'm not sure it really even matters anymore."

But Olivia couldn't help but wonder if it did. It was something to ponder later. For now, she was well aware that she had Jack's attention. He lifted his wineglass in a quiet salute and a promise that set her heart to racing.

As much as she'd thought she wanted company, as much as she thought she would welcome a distraction from her isolated mourning, suddenly she was more than anxious for her guests to leave. She wanted a little time alone with Jack before he left for the club—which he would inevitably do. He always went to the club.

Olivia felt wholly inadequate to entertain. In mourning, she'd been rather isolated and didn't even have any gossip to share. Although she enjoyed the company and it was nice to visit with others for a change.

She was more tired than she'd expected to be when Claybourne and Catherine took their leave. Jack was standing with her on the front steps, watching them drive away in their coach.

"I can hardly believe I had the Devil Earl to dinner," Olivia said, as Jack closed the door. He'd never been welcome in either her father's or her brother's homes.

"The next thing you know, you'll be inviting all of Feagan's brood to dinner."

She doubted that, but she wasn't going to be rude and admit it. After all, they were Jack's friends.

"None of you truly seems to give the impression you grew up on the streets."

"Claybourne's grandfather hired tutors for us. He was determined we wouldn't reflect our origins. It wouldn't do for us to embarrass his grandson."

"You've had a rather unique upbringing." They'd reached the stairs. She glanced upward, hesitant to retire.

"Come have a little brandy," Jack said quietly. "It'll help you sleep."

"The last time I had brandy I woke up ill."

"Then I'll pour you some whiskey."

Her breaths were becoming shallower as she anticipated that she might receive another kiss. She wanted it, wanted it desperately. She could do little more than nod.

They walked to the library without touching. As soon as the footman closed the door in their wake, Jack had her in his arms, holding her close, as his mouth swooped down to claim hers. She wanted to laugh from the joy of his eagerness. She'd never felt desired, and with him, it was as though he was hungry, hungry for her alone.

His mouth blazed a trail along her throat. "I was going mad sitting at that table making pleasant—and utterly boring—conversation, when all I could think about was how much I wanted to taste you instead of the chicken."

Perhaps not the most poetic of compliments, but she moaned and gave him easier access to her throat.

"Come to my bed, Livy."

"No."

"I'll kiss you from head to toe, I'll kiss you in places I doubt Lovingdon ever did."

Heat poured through her, melting her bones until she was surprised she was still able to stand. *Yes. Yes. Yes.* "No."

She shoved the word up from the depths of her soul, a soul that refused to be compromised. Pushing away from him, she shook her head, deciding she needed more than the word to convince them both. "No. I can't, Jack. I can't."

His gaze slowly traveled over her. "And I can't kiss you without wanting more."

"I'm sorry."

Reaching out, he touched her cheek. "Don't apologize, Livy. If I were a proper gentleman" —regret touched his eyes— "but I'm not. Will you at least take a walk about the garden with me?"

"That would be lovely." And just maybe she'd gather up the courage to forbid him once again to give her only a kiss.

Olivia stood still and silent on the terrace while Jack had a footman go through the garden lighting the lanterns that would mark the path. A part of her regretted that she'd turned him away in the library. She was so tempted to give in to her desires, but a lifetime of moral upbringing could not be so easily set aside. She had to set an example for Henry, and maybe in a way, she wanted to set one for Jack. He seemed to believe a person was entitled to everything he wanted. But she knew if she gave in she'd lose his respect. She suspected he was only toying with her, seeking to add her to his long list of conquests.

Not until the footman was finished and had retreated into the house did Jack extend his arm toward her. It was a lovely night. The fog had yet to arrive. She was not even bothered by the coolness of the air, because whenever Jack was near she always grew so incredibly warm, as though passion simmered just below the surface of her skin.

"Of late, you've been asking me a lot of questions regarding the type of man I'd want for a husband," she dared to begin.

"Have you finally decided what you want? Or even better, which lord you prefer?"

She fought back the disappointment that he still wished to be rid of her. Even though he claimed to want her in his bed, his words confirmed he was interested in nothing more than a dalliance.

"No, actually, but I was curious regarding what you want in a wife."

"I have no plans to ever marry."

"Never?"

"Why so shocked? Surely you of all people know the difficulty I'd have in finding a woman to take me as a husband."

"If you were to reform—"

His low, dark laughter cut off her words, shimmered through her, and seemed to blend in with the shadows hovering at the edges of the path.

"I have no interest in reforming."

"I can't even begin to comprehend why you would willingly choose a lonely life of decadence over one that offered marriage and a family."

"Then allow me to demonstrate."

His arm snaked around her, drawing her up against his body, even as he maneuvered her off the path. His mouth claimed hers with a hunger that startled her. If at all possible, this kiss was more intimate, more demanding, more persuasive than the previous one they'd shared. It was all-consuming, encompassing every aspect of her being, until she was aware of nothing existing beyond them. One of his large hands cupped the back of her neck, his fingers playing a seductive tune along her spine. Her knees immediately weakened and she clutched his shoulders, reflexively pressing her body against his for support. With a groan, his mouth never leaving hers, he urged her farther into the shadows, until the brick of the wall cooled her back. But it couldn't touch the fever rampaging through her.

She was mad with desire as she cradled his face. It wasn't enough. She wanted to feel more of his skin against her fingertips, but she couldn't bring herself to ask for more—or to take that which she so craved. Surely he felt the want shimmering through her, just as she felt his yearning in the tautness of his muscles as he wedged his knee between her thighs.

The pressure was heavenly even as it stoked the flames of passion. She'd never, never experienced such intense longing, had never felt the nerve endings whispering along her skin, begging for more, for something elusive, something she didn't quite comprehend—but she knew it was waiting, knew he had the skills, the knowledge to bring it cresting toward fulfillment.

She moaned as his mouth left hers to blaze a heated path along the underside of her chin. She tipped her head back in ecstasy, gave him leave to taste her.

"Come to my bed," he rasped.

"I can't." Her words carried her profound disappointment.

She'd expected him to stop then, to relieve her of this torment, but instead he took his mouth lower, his lips and tongue skimming along her collarbone, settling in the hollow at the base of her throat. How could so small a touch create such intense weakness in her limbs while ushering in such powerful pleasure?

As he eased the bodice of her gown down, his low groan of triumph filled her with unbridled satisfaction, so intense that she couldn't bring herself to chastise him for the liberties he was taking. Then his mouth closed over her breast, and suddenly his thigh pressing against her wasn't enough. She heard her mournful cry, was barely aware of her fingers slipping beneath his jacket to dig into his shoulders, and her hips squirming against him.

"Shh, shh. Easy, sweetheart. All in good time," he murmured.

Good? There was nothing good about this. It was decadent and wicked, but she'd never felt more like a woman in her entire life. She'd lost all semblance of control. Sanity was a distant concept.

She was vaguely aware of the rustling of her skirts a heartbeat before she felt his warm fingers gliding along her thighs. Whimpering, she cradled his jaw, urged his mouth back to hers, and thrust her tongue between his lips, muffling his dark chuckle. Was he feeling victorious over her? Or was he simply pleased beyond measure that she'd taken the initiative, that he'd stirred to life something over which she no longer had any control?

His nimble fingers worked their way through her clothing until they were lost in her curls, skillfully enticing her to respond to his urgings. He was a thief, stealing from her any power to resist. Her body tightened and thrummed. Pleasure such as she'd never experienced hovered, taunting her with the whispers of something more.

"Come to my bed," he growled.

"No." She nearly wept with wanting what she knew he could give her, cursed her own strong-willed purpose.

She was aware of movement at her hip, even as his fingers never stilled their dancing over her sensitive flesh. With his free hand, he threaded his fingers through hers, those digging into his shoulder and brought them down, down, wrapping them around his bulging and heated velvet shaft. Guiding her hand to touch him intimately, stroking him even as he stroked her, while her pleasure rioted beyond control.

He slid a finger into her, then two, his thumb pressing

against her swollen flesh, caressing intimately, creating incredibly sweet sensations—

As the cataclysm rocked her, he turned his face into her shoulder, his mouth pressed against her neck. His body bucked, his harsh growl echoing around him, his hot seed surging into and over her hand. Breathing harshly, he collapsed against her.

Tremors cascaded through her while she slowly became aware of her surroundings. Recognizing what had transpired here in the garden, shame swamped her. Shame for her lack of control. Anger at him for doing this to her. Fury at herself for letting him, for encouraging him, for pressing against him instead of moving away.

"Oh, God." Finally, at long last, she found the wherewithal to push him aside.

He staggered. "Livy—"

"No, no." Then she was running toward the house, tugging up her bodice, ignoring the remnants of the delicious release, swiping at the tears that threatened to blind her.

Grief nearly overwhelmed her. While married she'd never experienced anything closely resembling the heights of passion she'd just achieved. Jack Dodger had certainly earned his reputation. He was indeed the devil. Tonight he'd carried her to heaven.

Now she'd languish in hell.

Chapter 17

Sitting on the bench in the garden, Jack knew he should have gone after her. That she'd recovered enough to run, while he could barely stagger, had made an immediate pursuit impossible. He'd considered going to her when he was more in control, but what good would that do? He'd heard her sobs. Did she expect him to apologize? He had no regrets. If he was honest, that wasn't exactly true. It bothered him that she was upset. As for himself, he was bloody-well terrified.

He'd never reacted to a woman like that. He'd never wanted to bring one pleasure that exceeded his. And now he felt so damned vulnerable. He wanted to crawl into her bed, fold himself around her, and have her hold him.

What the hell was the matter with him?

His business was sex. It was all about satisfying physical urges and then moving on to the next source of pleasure.

But she wasn't his *business*, and God help him, what had transpired between them hadn't been only sex.

He should go to his club, return in the morning, and pretend tonight hadn't happened.

Or he could get drunk, go to bed, get up in the morning with a staggering headache, and pretend tonight never happened.

But it *had* happened, and he wasn't likely to ever forget it.

With her head buried beneath the pillow, Olivia awoke to gritty eyes, a stuffed nose, and a woozy head. If she didn't know better she'd think she was getting ill again. But she did know better. Just as she had when she was a little girl and her dog had died, she'd cried herself to sleep. How had she let Jack take those liberties with her? Although she was plagued by a more important question: How had she wanted him to? And she had. He'd effectively stolen her willpower. Now she was going to have to go down to breakfast and face him. How could she meet his gaze without remembering every wickedly wonderful thing he'd done to her body?

Rolling over, she screeched at the sight of Jack standing at the foot of the bed. Scrambling up, she pressed her back to the mound of pillows. "You promised never to come to my bed."

"I've kept my promise. I'm at least two inches away."

His voice held none of its usual teasing. He was completely dressed, yet he left her unsettled. Perhaps it was the way he held her gaze as though he had nothing of which to be ashamed, or the fact that he was familiar with not only her body but its reaction to his touch. She lowered her gaze and began tugging on a thread on the counterpane. "Why are you here?"

"Look at me, Livy."

It was so very hard, but she refused to be cowed. Defiantly she glared at him, surprised to discover his eyes held not a speck of triumph. She'd expected him to lord her shameful behavior over her. Instead, the arrogant, self-assured, confident Jack Dodger appeared—dare she even think it—remorseful.

"I'm not in the habit of losing control when I'm with a woman." She lowered her gaze to that wondrous mouth he'd pressed to her throat, his hot breath heating her skin as he—

"I want you, Livy. I want you as I've never wanted any woman, and that's not an easy thing for me to admit. I'm certain my behavior is not what you're accustomed to."

She thought that could possibly be the understatement of the century.

"But I won't apologize for it," he continued. "I can promise you that it won't happen again."

With that he spun on his heel and left the room. She wasn't quite sure it was a promise she wanted him to keep.

They studiously avoided each other for the next two days—or perhaps it was only Olivia who was finding so many excuses to be in other portions of the residence whenever she thought Jack was on the prowl. Breakfast was not too terribly thorny because Henry was always there, serving as a buffer. Olivia would sit at the foot of the table and surreptitiously watch Jack as he patiently answered the thousands of questions that Henry seemed to have—all of which began with *why*.

Dinner was a bit more challenging. The night before, they'd actually discussed the weather, which had almost made Olivia weep. They'd become such polite strangers. He no longer teased her or challenged her or flirted with her.

And she missed him terribly.

Standing in the window in one of the upstairs bedchambers, she watched as Jack darted over the lawn, trying to catch Henry in their regular afternoon game. Henry was doing his usual crowing and Jack was laughing. It was amazing how well they got along. It was almost like watching two boys at play—

But Jack was not a boy. While she suspected life was more carefree for him now than it had been when he'd grown up on the streets, she also thought he carried a good deal more responsibility.

She knew him only from his life here. But he had another one that was very different. She wanted to see it.

Jack had his carriage brought around earlier than usual. He could hardly stand to be in the house any longer. Dinners shared with Livy had turned unbearably awkward.

She'd taken to once again studying him as though he should be on display somewhere. They discussed the perfection of the food they were eating—if they spoke at all. Most of the time, he avoided looking at her because he didn't want her to see how very much he yearned to have her.

After dinner, she retreated to her room and he went to the library. He was at his desk drowning his desires in whiskey when Brittles came into the room.

"Your carriage is ready, sir."

He nodded and finished off his whiskey. As he passed the stairs, he considered going up them, going to Livy's room, and breaking his promise not to go to her bed. But when he gave his word, he meant it. It was the only honorable trait to which he could still lay claim.

A footman opened the door. Jack strode on, determined to do whatever was required to get her off his mind. Use Pru if necessary, even though the option left him with a hollow ache. Hurrying down the steps, he ignored the light mist falling. It suited his mood.

A footman opened the carriage door. "Sir."

Jack acknowledged him with a nod, placed his foot on the step, vaulted up, became aware of a familiar scent—

"Going to your club?"

At the unexpected feminine voice, one that haunted him, he jerked upward and banged his head. "Dammit!"

He swung inside and dropped onto the bench. "What the devil are you doing here?"

Olivia had not expected to take him so completely by surprise. Served him right, though, for that first night when he'd given her such a fright. "I want to go with you."

"Don't be silly. The only women allowed in my club are those willing to provide services to men. Is that what you're entertaining? If so I can accommodate you here."

She should have known he'd not make this easy, but she'd not be dissuaded.

"As you're the owner, surely you can make an exception."

He settled back into the corner of the carriage. She could feel his intense gaze on her. "Why?"

"I know you're a fair guardian to Henry. I know you're very astute when it comes to acquiring money. I'd like to see your business firsthand."

In the shadows, she didn't see his hand move, but suddenly she was aware of his hand slipping beneath her veil and felt his thumb caress her cheek.

"Why, Livy?"

"I don't want secrets between us, Jack."

"And if you don't like what you see?"

Her feelings toward him might dissipate like the fog in late morning. "You said you weren't ashamed of your affairs."

He came nearer to her, his mouth against her cheek. "What does it matter, Livy?"

She swallowed hard. "I care for you far more than I should. I spend countless hours thinking of going to your bed. And I can't. I just can't, not without a clearer understanding of the man you are." She placed her hand on his chest, felt the hard beating of his heart beneath her fingers. "Your business is a good part of your life. All it has ever been to mine is gossip. I want to know the truth of it."

"I've told you the truth of it."

"I want to see it. I assume it's a shadowy place. I'm in black. My hat has a black veil. I should think it would take a very discerning eye to figure out who I am, and if all your customers indulge in spirits as much as my brother did, I think it unlikely they'll remember seeing me anyway."

She heard his sigh. "I can't take you in through the

front door. You'd be too much of a curiosity, and your reputation would be destroyed if someone did recognize you."

"I assume you have a back one."

He studied her for a moment. "You can't share the things you witness at Dodger's with your ladies during tea. You can't ever reveal the name of anyone you see in Dodger's."

"I won't tell a soul."

"I'm deadly serious, Livy. My customers pay exceedingly well to have their secrets kept, and that trust is vital to my success."

"I swear to you I won't breathe a word to anyone."

"I shall no doubt regret this," he muttered, even as he signaled for his driver to be off.

Olivia could hardly give credence to the thrill of adventure that shot through her. She was going against her upbringing to do something that was absolutely and irrevocably wrong, while holding onto her belief that she needed to thoroughly know a man before she succumbed to temptation. It was a ludicrous rationale, but she couldn't deny that he stirred within her breast intense feelings such as she'd never experienced.

They rode in absolute silence, although even in the darkness she could sense his unwavering gaze as it homed in on her.

"There," he finally said, and she peered out the window to catch the first look at his gentlemen's club.

It didn't look seedy, as she'd expected. It was well maintained. The white columns and liveried footmen opening the door gave it an air of luxury she'd not anticipated.

"Is that Greystone going in?"

"No."

"It certainly looked—"

"You didn't see anyone going in. That's the game we play, Livy. You see nothing. You hear nothing. And by damn, you speak nothing."

"The lords must trust you a great deal."

"They trust me with a good many of their secrets. I may not be as respectable as Beckwith, but I know how to hold a confidence. Besides, they pay me an extraordinary amount, and I in turn pay my employees, to ensure their skeletons stay in the cupboard."

The carriage went around to the back. After Jack disembarked, he reached inside for Olivia. "Are you certain you want to do this?"

"Absolutely."

He chuckled softly. "You're like a child being offered a sweet."

When she stepped out, he drew her near and tucked her up against his side. "Stay near until we're inside."

She could hear people singing off-key. *Drunks*, she thought. And there were the sounds of people walking quickly through the alleyway. Her heart sped up. A lantern hung above the back door. Jack inserted a key into the lock and was soon ushering her inside.

The first thing that struck her was that the hallway smelled clean. The doors to several rooms were closed, the door to one open.

"These are the offices." He nodded toward the open doorway. "Frannie works there."

"Is she there now?"

"Probably."

"I should stop in and say hello."

"This isn't like your morning calls."

"It would be rude."

He rolled his eyes. "Fine."

He led her to the doorway. Once again she was surprised. While the furniture appeared to be of good stock, it was sparse. Frannie was making notations in a ledger. She glanced up and her green eyes widened. "Well, hello. This is a surprise."

"She wanted to see a gaming hell," Jack groused.

"And you brought her? This is an interesting development." She rose.

Olivia flapped her hand self-consciously. "I don't mean to disturb you. I just wanted to have a look around. I will admit to being surprised that everything is so clean. You run a tight ship."

"That's Jack's doing. He can't stand anything not being tidy. I think probably because he was so filthy as a child."

She thought of the baths he took, the way he insisted on never putting on anything that wasn't cleaned and pressed first.

"I'm just going to give her a quick look around," Jack said, taking Olivia's arm.

After saying good-bye to Frannie, she allowed Jack to lead her up some stairs that he said were restricted to employees only. "Does she have a suitor?"

"Good God, no. She has little interest in men."

"Surely she wishes to marry."

"I don't think so, and that's all I'll say on the matter. Frannie's secrets are her own."

At the top of the stairs, he led her down a narrow hallway. Then he parted some curtains and they stepped out onto a shadowy balcony. Olivia was absolutely stunned by how elegant everything appeared. The hunter green walls were framed by intricate woodwork. But it was the activity on the floor that mesmerized her. Gaming tables, too many to count, filled the room. Some men were playing with cards, others with dice. A couple of the gents had ladies sitting on their laps, but even they were nicely dressed.

Cigar smoke created a haze. She could see all the glasses filled with various shades of amber, from light to dark, or clear liquid that she was certain wasn't water. Boys dressed in purple livery confidently carried items for the gentlemen. It wasn't as rowdy as she'd expected. In some cases, it was disturbingly quiet.

She recognized a good many of the lords. Why weren't they home with their wives?

"I would have expected there to be more . . . girls," she finally said.

"There's another room where most of them stay. You can peer in from over there."

He took her farther back into the hallway and then once again through a curtain onto a secluded balcony. She'd hesitated, not certain she wanted to see the debauchery, but her curiosity got the better of her. She was slightly disappointed. It appeared most were simply talking. She could see some kissing and a little teasing, but it wasn't the orgy she was expecting.

"You look crestfallen," he said near her ear.

"No, I . . . yes. I thought they'd be more naughty."

He chuckled darkly. "They are. But those rooms you can't peer into, except by invitation."

"Invitation?"

He shrugged. "Some of the men like to be watched, so we have a viewing room."

"Why would they want to be watched?"

"I suppose they think they have something to show off."

"Oh." She shook her head. "I told myself I would come here and not judge, but I don't like that you use girls, that you make them—"

"I don't make them do anything they don't want to do. I pay them to keep gents company with a bit of conversation, a dance, maybe a kiss. What they do in the back rooms, that's their business and their coin."

"But you condone the activity."

"They're going to do it, Livy. In an alley, in a room that is neither clean nor safe. Here, at least, neither the gents nor the girls have any worries."

"But why have them at all?"

"Because gents get lonely. And a happy gent spends more money in my establishment. Seen enough?"

She could see that she wasn't going to win this argument for now, but maybe in time. . .

She nodded. "I think so."

It wasn't until they were back in the carriage headed home that Olivia asked, "How did you ever afford to open a business?"

"When I was nineteen, Beckwith came to see me. I had an anonymous benefactor who gave me ten thousand pounds. I used it to purchase the building."

"Who was he?"

"I don't know. He was anonymous."

"But you must have some idea. Could he have been that Feagan fellow?"

"No, running pickpockets doesn't make one wealthy."

"Who else might it have been?"

"I always assumed he was Luke's grandfather. We didn't get along very well, and I thought he saw it as an expeditious way to get rid of me. An investment well worth making."

"I expect you were too headstrong for him."

"I did think my way was the best." He chuckled, then quieted. "For an instant, the night the will was read, I had an insane notion that it was Lovingdon. But I asked Beckwith and he spouted some nonsense about holding my benefactor's secret."

"Why would Lovingdon do that?"

"Why would he leave me his non-entailed properties?"

"If it was Lovingdon, I should think you'd find the information in his record books."

"What record books?"

"They've kept records on everything. Every cow purchased, every horse bred, every servant hired, every salary paid. Lovingdon was obsessed with those books. I suppose in retrospect, he was scouring them in order to determine what was entailed and what was not—I can show you if you like."

"Seems unlikely that I'd find anything, but I don't suppose it would hurt to look."

His business beginnings and record books. She was carrying on conversations about things that had no importance while her scent wafted toward him.

"What's your opinion on Dodger's?" he asked.

Silence stretched between them while the carriage wheels rattled over the street.

Finally, she said, "It wasn't as decadent as I expected it to be."

He wrapped his hand around her neck, slipped his thumb beneath her veil, and skimmed it over her jaw. "You sound disappointed."

"What? No." Then she released a self-conscious laugh. "A little, I suppose. If you want the truth, I was expecting orgies and lewd behavior and barbarism. It was all disenchantingly civilized."

"Gents just enjoying themselves."

"It's a shame there's not something similar for women."

"What would you do? Serve various types of tea, discuss the merits of each?"

"We could play cards," she said tartly, and he knew he'd offended her. "Have handsome men serving us, giving us the attention our husbands do not."

He stilled his thumb. "You have someone here willing to give you the attention your husband didn't, yet you constantly retreat."

With a sweep of his hand, he lifted the veil over her head, lowered his mouth to hers, and cursed his weakness. He'd sworn that he'd not settle for a kiss. But suddenly it was torturous to go so long without even a taste of her. It pleased him immeasurably that she returned the kiss with fervor equal to his. He knew she wanted him. Where did she find the restraint to continually say no?

Chipping away at years of proper behavior required

a man who possessed a good deal more patience than Jack had. He wanted what he desired as soon as he realized he wanted it. He supposed she found him equally frustrating, with his years of improper behavior that she wanted to correct.

Perhaps she was having some influence over him after all. Aware that she'd enter the house and some servants would still be about, he didn't take down her hair or unbutton her bodice. He didn't take liberties that would leave her panting and short of breath.

He dragged his mouth to the sensitive spot near her ear, felt the thrumming of her pulse beneath his tongue. "You see, I can be civilized. Tell me you don't want me to be."

"I don't know anymore. I can't think when you do that."

"That says it all, doesn't it? You belong" —he startled to a stop, the words *with me* dangling on his tongue— "in my bed."

Desire fled, replaced by an almost overwhelming need to run.

Chapter 18

J ack stood at the window in his bedchamber, gazing out on the night. Whatever was the matter with him? When had he begun to think of Livy as *his*?

He could never marry her. He could never make her respectable. Marriage alone to him would be enough to lower her in the eyes of Society. He could have her for perhaps two years, while she was in mourning. And then he'd have to let her go. Her and Henry. He'd obtain the last item, of "immeasurable worth," and in time, he'd no longer think about them.

But for now she was all he thought about.

When the door leading into the dressing room opened, his heartbeat kicked up a notch and he slowly turned. She stood in her nightgown, her hair unbound, her small feet bare, her toes curling into the carpet, her hands folded primly in front of her, trepidation clearly visible on her face.

"I'm not quite sure how to do this," she said quietly. "I'm not sure how to go about seducing you."

"Seducing me?" He released a bark of laughter, saw the hurt flash over her features, and closed the distance separating them in four long strides. He took her soft face between his roughened hands. "Livy, you've been seducing me since that first night."

He kissed her forehead. "I find your defiance exciting."

He kissed her temple. "I find your temper thrilling."

He kissed her cheek. "I find your love for Henry humbling."

He pressed his lips to the tip of her nose. "I find your laughter enchanting."

He kissed the corner of her mouth. "Your eyes mesmerize me and your kisses have the power to bring me to my knees."

He watched as the doubt in her golden eyes turned to certainty. She gave him an impish smile. "I forbid you to make love to me."

His mouth went dry at her words. He'd never made love to a woman. He'd bedded many. The sex had been satisfying. But to make love, he hardly knew where to begin, but it was a gift she deserved. It was what he wanted to give to her. She was unlike any woman he'd ever known. She'd come to him with no expectation of receiving coins. What she was offering to him was far more valuable than anything he could ever give to her.

"I've warned you, sweetheart, to never forbid me. You'll only make me do it."

And with that, he took her mouth as tenderly as he was able, but tenderness was foreign to him. With the first taste of her, the hunger he'd been holding at bay broke free with a fierceness that astounded him. He wanted to clearly see what clothing and shadows had kept from him.

Without tearing his mouth from hers, he lifted her into his arms, carried her to the bed, and set her on her feet beside it. She swayed, and he drew her near, allowing her to take strength from him.

Olivia had felt the power of his passion in the garden. Still it astounded her that it could be so forceful, could weaken her so easily. She grew so hot that it was almost as though she were taking ill again. And her legs were quivering. If his arms weren't around her, she thought she might simply melt into the floor.

She wrapped her arms around his shoulders, skimmed her fingers up into his thick hair, hair that suddenly didn't seem too long. She wanted to bury her face in it, and she thought that perhaps before the night was over she might.

Jack withdrew from the kiss, trailing his mouth along her jaw as though he were reluctant to leave her lips, didn't want his mouth far from hers. She lifted her chin, giving him easier access to her throat, and a small whimper escaped. His velvety touch teased and cajoled. "Ah, Livy, Livy." His voice was low, seductive, and she knew she would follow it to whatever sins it led her.

She felt his mouth brushing over her shoulders and only then did she remember that he had a pickpocket's fingers and light touch. He'd worked her buttons free from throat to stomach and she'd not even noticed. And now the gown was sliding off her shoulders, gliding to the floor.

She had a second to consider that she should feel a need to cover herself and then she was considering nothing at all except for the wondrous sensations of his mouth playing over her breasts: tasting, licking, suckling. All the while, he murmured that she was "beautiful. So beautiful."

Without warning, he swept her up into his arms and laid her on the bed. As soon as his arms were no longer around her, he was tearing at his clothing, hastily discarding each piece until they were nothing more than a crumpled bundle on the floor.

She barely had time to appreciate the magnificence of him before he was placing a knee on the bed and coming for her, like some large predatory cat, with intent and the knowledge that the prey could not escape.

She didn't want to escape. She opened her arms to him, touching what she'd only seen that long-ago morning in the dressing room. He was a young man and his body reflected the strength of youth. Firm muscles, taut skin. And flexibility.

He'd stretched out beside her, the hand bearing the brand wrapping over her hip, almost with significance, as he twisted his body and laid a kiss on her stomach. He nibbled his way up to her breasts, kissing the inside of one, then the other, giving equal attention to each. She thought she should have been prepared for the pleasures rippling through her.

Was it the forbidden that heightened the pleasure? Was it the taste of sin that made her so much more aware of her body's awakening? Or was it simply that he had the devil's own touch, that he had the power and the knowledge to bring forth carnal delights?

She dug her fingers into his shoulders, his back. She held him close while he ravished her breasts. His bristled jaw prickled, adding to the sensations. Her hips turned toward him of their own accord.

He skimmed his hand down her hip, her thigh, and brought it around to rest heavily between her legs, his fingers gliding intimately—

She gasped as the pleasure spiked.

He lifted his head, studying her. He glided his finger over her, eliciting another cry, her legs squeezing together as though to hold him there or perhaps to urge him on.

"I want to watch you, Livy," he whispered roughly. "I want to see what the darkness of the garden kept from me. Let go, Livy. Let go."

She shook her head fiercely, but he gave her no respite. He returned his mouth to her breasts while his fingers worked their magic. When she was close, so very close, he stopped to ease up, roll between her thighs, and take her mouth as though he owned it. His tongue probed and explored as though he didn't know every intimate corner, while she returned the favor with more boldness than she ever had. She loved his flavor, loved the scent of him heated by their passion. His skin was hot and velvety beneath her fingers, dampened by a light coating of dew.

He rose above her and she might have been frightened by what she saw in his eyes if she didn't know him as well as she did. It was almost animalistic, barbaric.

She felt him testing her readiness, and she immediately tensed.

"Shh, shh, gentle now," he whispered near her ear, and she wasn't certain if the words were for her or himself.

He glided his hand down her side, over her hip,

around her thigh, and he urged her to open herself more fully.

Then she felt him pushing into her, inch by delicious inch, the fullness of him stretching her further, increasing the pleasure tightening low in her belly. When she thought she could take no more, he lifted her hips slightly, shifted his weight, and buried himself completely into her, bowing her back with the exquisite sensation of feeling his weight pressing against her.

"Oh, God," she whispered.

Threading his fingers through hers, he moved her hands so they rested on either side of her head while he rode her unmercifully, mercifully. Her body sang to his tune, pleasures rippling through her, increasing in intensity as his powerful thrusts moved not only her, but the bed.

His groans echoed around her, harsh, yet satisfying, and she heard her answering moans. The pleasure became almost unbearable. She wanted to close her eyes, but he was so beautiful, so magnificent to watch, his jaw clenched, his smoldering gaze locked onto hers. She'd never before felt this connection with anyone— that wherever they went they went together.

He was a devil, tempting her, demanding with every stroke of his body against hers that she surrender. And surrender she did, not only her body, but her heart and her soul.

He cried out, his thrusts going deeper, so deep that she wondered how she'd survive—

Then the cataclysm hit, her body tightening around him even as she arched beneath him, catapulting her into never-imagined pleasure. She had no choice except to close her eyes as the sensations rocked her. Her last thought as she shot into oblivion was that she'd vastly underestimated the benefits of being with a man whose life was devoted to carnal intrigue.

Raised up on an elbow, stretched out alongside Livy, Jack fought not to think about what had just happened. He'd never in his life experienced anything so intense, so gratifying. Even their encounter in the garden, for all its splendor, paled when compared to the reality of taking her in his bed. Watching her as she peaked, with lamplight flickering, had served to enhance his own pleasure.

He didn't fool himself regarding what had transpired here. She might want him for a bit of sport, but she was nobility, while he was gutter trash. They would never have more than this. And with that thought came an unexpected sharp pain in the center of his chest.

Never before had he felt so much a part of some-thing, of someone. It terrified him to feel this closeness, he who'd always worked so hard to maintain his dis-tance. She'd effectively knocked down his walls. If he thought about it too hard or too long, he'd gather up his clothes and leave, never to return.

If he cared for her as much as he suspected he did, that's exactly what he'd do. Leave, now that he'd had a taste of her, and do all in his power to find her a proper husband. Instead he recklessly trailed his finger between her small breasts, gathering up the dew that lingered there, and said, "You're not going to sleep, are you?"

Slowly she rolled her head from side to side where it rested on the pillow. "You're very good at this."

He laughed softly, taking his fingers across her shoulders from one side to the other. He thought he'd never get enough of just touching her. "It appears, based on your body's responses, I invested my money wisely."

She furrowed her brow. "You pay for it?"

"Always." He shrugged. "Except for tonight."

"Why?"

"Why I did before? Or why I didn't tonight?"

"Before."

How to explain without sounding callous. "Because I wanted no emotional entanglements. It was always business. Some business ventures are more enjoyable than others." And some rewards were intangible.

"Have you been in this bed before?" He didn't know why he asked or why the answer mattered.

"Only once, when you brought me." With her hand, she cradled his cheek. Covering her hand with his, he turned his face into her palm and kissed it.

She rolled into him. Reaching down, he whipped back the sheet gathered at her waist. She kicked it down farther, until nothing separated them, until their naked bodies were pressed together.

"I'm sure it's in bad form to talk of another man, but I want—I need—you to know that it was never like this with him."

He didn't know what to say to that, so he simply kissed her palm again, then her fingers.

"It was so very impersonal, which always struck me as odd for such a personal act. And I never, I never realized that I should actually enjoy it. You are really quite remarkable, Jack Dodger."

Again, he was left with nothing to say. He dipped his head and took her mouth as he intended to take her body, with a bit more patience this time, a more leisurely pursuit of pleasure.

Her hand stroked his chest, almost tentatively, as though she thought he might break. He drew back and studied her. The wonder was still there, a wonder he'd never known because it had been stripped of him at an early age.

"As tonight appears to be a rather new experience for you, you should know that I will not break and that there is no part of me that you are not welcome to explore."

Her gaze traveled the length of his body, her cheeks turning a rosy hue. Her hand glided down, wrapped around him, and he couldn't stop the low moan of satisfaction.

He kissed her, rolling onto his back as he did so, giving her easier access to learn the various textures of his body.

With each passing moment, her hands became less tentative as her confidence grew. She touched, she stroked. She broke off the kiss to rain smaller kisses over his chest. She flicked her tongue over his hardened nipple, and his body jerked. He rammed his hands through her hair, holding her close, encouraging her with sweet words and low moans.

When he could stand it no more, he eased her over him until she was straddling his hips, her hair forming a curtain around her shoulders.

"Don't look so shocked," he said.

"I don't think this is proper."

"Sweetheart, nothing we've done tonight is proper." While he'd meant to tease, he regretted his words as soon as they were spoken, because he saw in her eyes the hint of shame. "Don't, Livy."

She raised her gaze to his.

"Don't regret any of this."

She shook her head, but he could see the damage was done. He threaded his fingers through her hair and brought her down to his chest, holding her close.

"You'll never tell anyone, will you?" she whispered after a time.

"No."

She lifted her head, digging her chin into his chest. "I don't regret what passed between us, but I suppose a small part of me knows it was wrong."

With his fingers, he combed back her hair. "How can it be wrong when it's what two people want?"

"But there will never be more than this between us."

"Quite honestly, I don't see how there can be, but that doesn't mean that *this* can't be very, very good while we have it."

With his hand buried in her hair, he turned her head and latched his mouth onto hers, kissing her deeply, wondering how in the hell he was ever going to let her go when the time came.

Chapter 19

"**T**his is probably an exercise in futility," Livy said.

They were in the study, a small room where Lovingdon had stored all manner of ledgers, record books, journals. Livy had told Jack that Lovingdon had often sequestered himself inside for hours. "They go back for years and years."

Jack looked up from a book whose dates corresponded with the year Beckwith had first come to see him. Livy was sitting on a sofa by the window, the sunlight casting a halo around her. He'd never been one to believe in angels, but he couldn't deny that she appeared very angelic sitting there. Not at all like a woman who'd been ravished that morning before calling for her maid.

"Even if we find nothing, I'm fascinated by all this information. To see the fluctuation in the number of servants hired, the salaries paid, the income brought in from various estates. Even the investments that have been made. I have the present-day information, of course, but it's advisable to examine past practices."

She made a funny face and shuddered. "You're not going to look through everything are you?"

"I may."

She gazed around at all the books housed on shelves, stacked on the floor. "There's almost a haphazardness to the way things are arranged. I wonder what he was looking for in here."

"Maybe it was those who came before him who left the mess and he was simply trying to tidy it up."

"Perhaps. I suppose all this really belongs to Henry."

He leaned back in his chair. "How do you figure that, Duchess?"

She gave him a pointed stare. "Because most of these records involve ducal properties."

"But they're in my residence. Consider their worth. We'll negotiate."

"You can't be serious."

He got up, walked over to her, and placed his hands on the back of the couch, effectively hemming her in. "Deadly. That book you're holding, I'd say, is worth a kiss."

He cut off her laughter, his mouth plundering hers, no doubt giving the book she was holding far more value than it was worth. She returned the kiss with equal fervor, turning into him, the heavy book sliding off her lap and onto his foot.

"Damn," he muttered, breaking free of the kiss, wiggling his throbbing toe, grateful it didn't seem to be broken. He bent to pick up the book that had fallen open and froze—his gaze arrested by words precisely written in an elegant script.

Very slowly he lifted the book as he sat beside her.

"Jack? What's wrong? You look as though you've seen a ghost."

He placed his finger beneath the words, and Livy leaned in for a closer look. "Emily Dawkins? June 15, 1815. Hired as a scullery maid at the age of twelve. Five guineas. What of her?"

"That was my mother's name."

Olivia helped Jack scour through the books. He was almost obsessive. Not that she could blame him, but it also worried her to see him so consumed.

"Jack, it might not be her. Neither 'Emily' nor 'Dawkins' is an unusual name."

He snapped the book shut. "I can't find any notations to indicate when she left. Someone must know something."

"It's been thirty-six years. Most of the servants are no longer here, and the few who are . . . they're not likely to remember a scullery maid." She placed her hand over his. "Why did you change your name?"

"Because I didn't want the man to whom she'd sold me to ever find me." He gave a caustic laugh. "I changed my name several times before I settled on 'Dodger.' "

"I still have a difficult time believing she sold you. You told me in the garden that you did something to lose her love. What did you do?"

"I don't know. When she gave me the locket, she said, 'Never forget I loved you, Jack.' Loved." He shook his head. "She loved me once, but no longer."

"I'm not convinced that's it."

"I know what I heard, Livy."

"You were a child, Jack." He opened his mouth and she pressed her fingers against his lips. A mistake, because he began kissing them. "Hear me out."

He nodded, still nibbling on her fingers.

"If you'd sent me away, I'd have said to Henry, 'Don't forget I *love* you.' Because I would have been sending him my love from wherever you sent me. And I'd expect to see him again. But if I thought I'd never see him again, I might say 'loved.' Was it possible your mother was ill? Perhaps even, heaven forbid, dying?"

He stilled, her fingers pressed against his lips. "I remember she had a cough." Still holding her hand, he dropped his to his lap. "Good God, Livy, all these years I thought she was trying to get rid of me, that I'd disappointed her somehow."

Releasing her hand, he got up and walked to the desk. "She seemed to know that man—"

"Could it have been a servant in the Lovingdon household?"

"No, he was no servant. And it was a grand house."

"You may never know, Jack."

"Swindler likes a good puzzle. I think I'll take some of these books to him tonight."

Olivia was helping Henry put together a wooden puzzle while Ida was downstairs having a spot of tea. When the door to the nursery opened, Jack didn't come into the room. He simply stood in the doorway, leaning nonchalantly against it, with arms folded across a chest that she'd kissed every inch of the night before. She wondered if his heart beat as rapidly as hers.

He'd gone to his club in the early hours of the morning and had not returned in time for breakfast.

"Did you have any luck with the books?"

He shook his head. "Frannie and Swindler are taking a closer look."

"Do you want me to help you search some more?"

"Maybe later."

"Then what is your purpose in coming here? Did you come to check on your ward's progress?" Olivia asked.

"Not exactly," Jack said lazily.

"Did you wish to see me?"

His smile was a flash of white that promised forbidden things. "Not exactly," he repeated.

"Am I to guess your reason in being here?"

He unfolded his arms, sauntered into the room, reached down, and moved the last puzzle piece into place. "Now that's done, how would you like to go on an outing?"

She gave him a look and before she could speak, he'd rasped his finger beneath her chin as though he might tickle her.

"I know you're in mourning," he said, "but there is very little chance you'll be spotted where I intend to take us."

"And where would that be?"

"On the railway."

Henry's eyes widened. "With a locomotive?"

"Naturally."

Olivia scowled at Jack. Honestly, how could she convince the man he could not speak in front of Henry until he'd confirmed with her that she agreed to the matter? Now Henry would be disappointed. Or Olivia would be forced once again to don her boy's clothes.

"Hundreds of people travel on the railway," she pointed out.

"Ah, yes, but I now have a private car, and the only ones who will be in there are you, Henry, Ida, and me. So you'll be separated from the masses."

"You purchased a private railway car?"

"In a manner of speaking."

She narrowed her eyes at him.

He sighed as though his patience with her was dwindling. "One of my customers owed me a great deal of money. I took the car as payment—which was a very good arrangement for him as the car is worth less than what he owed me."

"I'd have thought you a better bargainer than that."

"I thought the enjoyment we might have would make it worth it."

"But we must get to the railway car," she pointed out.

"We'll move quickly. Besides, those who know you seldom take the railway."

"Where are we going?"

"Brighton. We'll go there, dip our toes in the sea, and head back."

"You're going to leave London?" she asked.

He shrugged. "Can't imagine I'll like anything I'll see, but I'm a bit curious."

"Please, Mummy," Henry said. He looked so hopeful.

She'd never traveled on the railway, was almost as excited by the prospect as Henry was, but more, she wanted to be with Jack when he first left London, when he first saw the world beyond this city. She took a deep breath. "Very well."

Seeing the satisfaction in his eyes, she had a feeling she was agreeing to more than he'd revealed.

He was as good as his word, getting them to the private car quickly. His footman brought in a large basket of food so they could either eat on the journey or picnic at the seaside. Olivia removed her veiled hat and glanced around at what appeared to be finer than some people's homes.

"Who was the gentleman who originally owned the car?" she asked.

"I don't remember."

She gave him a hard look, while he gave her one to remind her that he had secrets to keep. She graciously let the matter rest.

The private car was well appointed with a red couch in the center, but it was unlike any couch Olivia had ever seen. It had a curving back with a seating area on either side of it. She supposed it made sense. It saved turning the couch around if a more pleasant view was visible in another direction.

Two plush chairs were set on either side of the window, on both sides of the car. While they waited at the station, the curtains were drawn. Olivia took one chair, while Jack—wearing a red waistcoat that matched the décor of the car—sat in the other with Henry in his lap. Ida sat at the other window.

Jack looked so handsome, but then he always did. She was struck by how natural it seemed for Henry to be in his lap. Her son had no reservations whatsoever concerning his guardian. Jack had effectively earned his trust—but then he'd also earned hers. With him, at that moment, she felt more like a family than she'd ever felt with Lovingdon.

Jack lifted the edge of the curtain and peered out. "Pockets ripe for pilfering. People are in a hurry, not paying attention, more interested in the railway and securing a seat. Ah, the pockets I could have picked if the railway expansion had taken place when I was a lad."

"Of course you no longer pick pockets because you realized it was the wrong thing to do," Olivia pointed out.

"No, I don't—"

She cleared her throat. His brows drawn together, he looked at her, then down at Henry, who was watching him with rapt attention. Jack cleared his throat. "You're quite right. I realized it was wrong."

"Will you teach me?" Henry asked.

Olivia was amazed by how greatly reduced Henry's stammering problem was of late. She didn't know whether to attribute it to the dog or Jack. Maybe a little of both.

"No, lad. As your mum said, it's wrong. However, I can teach you to have nimble fingers. Never know when they might come in handy."

Before Olivia could respond, the train whistle blew and the car was being pulled over the tracks. Jack returned his attention to the world beyond the window. It wasn't long before he pulled the curtain back, and Olivia could see that the platform was no longer in sight. The train was chugging along.

Henry scrambled up, sitting on his knees on Jack's thighs, his nose pressed to the window. He'd made several journeys in the coach to the family estate. He hadn't taken much interest in the scenery then. Something about the train fascinated him.

"It's a different view of London," Jack said.

"I can't believe you've never left the city," Olivia told him.

"I know London. I'm comfortable there. Never saw any reason to leave."

"Why now?"

"Thought Henry might like to drive a train."

Henry gasped and shifted around to face Jack. "I can drive it?"

"During one of the stops I'll take you down to the locomotive. The engineer, I think he's called, is expecting you."

"Isn't he a bit young for this?" Olivia asked.

"He'll be fine. Ida will be with him, and the engineer will keep his hands steady."

"I can't believe he'd allow a child—"

He winked at her. "Livy, there's nothing a few well placed coins can't buy."

"And where will you be?"

"I'm going to come back and watch the scenery with you."

Jack couldn't help but think it was strange to look out the window and see nothing except green countryside. No houses, no buildings, no black, no grime. He hadn't expected to find it pleasing. A part of him had even been anxious about leaving behind what he knew. Not that he was willing to admit that to anyone except himself. He'd not known what awaited them on this journey. He'd only known he wanted to take it.

The whistle blew and the train began to slow.

"I can see the next platform coming up," Livy said.

"All right, then," Jack said. He stood up with Henry holding on like some sort of clinging ivy. "I'll be back. Come on, Ida."

"Are you sure this is safe?" Livy asked.

"Perfectly."

Rising, she pressed a kiss to Henry's cheek, bringing her sweet scent closer to Jack. "Be a good boy, Henry."

"I will."

Jack stepped onto the platform, holding the door for Ida. They walked past the open car where the poorest traveled for a penny a mile, exposed to the elements. Farther up, servants were scurrying out of the second-class cars to see to the needs of those they served, who were sitting in the first-class cars.

"It's generous of you to allow me to travel in your car, sir," Ida said.

"Nonsense, I don't believe in treating those who work for me as less than me."

"I have to say, sir, the servants are often saying they've never worked for anyone finer."

"Well, we'll see what you have to say after you've ridden in the locomotive."

"I'm actually lookin' forward to it, sir. Can't wait to tell me brothers."

Jack spotted the engineer waiting for them beside the locomotive. The man skimmed his fingers over his dark mustache as though to make certain he was tidy.

"Mr. Gurney, this is the Duke of Lovingdon."

The man bowed slightly. "Your Grace, are you ready to drive my train?"

"Yes, sir."

"His nanny, Ida, will be staying with him."

He tipped his hat. "Miss."

"Sir."

Jack didn't think he'd ever seen Ida blush. "I'll come back for the lad at the next station."

"Very good, sir," Mr. Gurney said.

Jack stepped onto the locomotive, carrying Henry on board and watching his eyes widen. The expense of the railway car and paying for this extra privilege had seemed frivolous at the time, but now Jack thought it was well worth it.

As he walked back to his private railway car, he slipped a crown into a pocket here and there. Yes, nimble fingers had their uses. His only regret was that he wouldn't be near to see the delight on the faces when the people discovered the unexpected coin.

He opened the door to his car, stepped in, and grinned at the sight of Olivia sitting on the couch. "That's exactly where I pictured you when I took possession of the car."

He tossed his jacket onto the chair, began unbuttoning his waistcoat.

"What are you doing?" Livy asked.

"Taking advantage of the time we'll have alone before the next stop."

"You can't be serious."

"I've never been more serious in my life." He tossed the cravat onto the chair, barely noticing when it slid to the carpeted floor.

The whistle sounded, and the train began to rock over the tracks.

"I suppose a kiss or two—" she began.

"I've told you before, Livy, I'm not a man who settles for only a kiss."

"But to . . . here?"

"No one can see in. No one will hear us. It's our own little room. It's just on a railway track."

"But it's all bumpy."

"Which might make it all the more fun." Chuckling, he moved in and began to nibble on her ear. "I don't know why you're arguing. You know you want to do it."

"I do," she sighed. "I do, but my clothing—"

His two favorite words in all the world. "No one will know."

He couldn't believe he'd actually decided that first night that she had too many buttons to bother with. Considering the delectable body those buttons hid, they were well worth the trouble, and his nimble fingers were quick to get them all undone. He didn't plan to remove all her clothes, because he didn't think they had time for that. But there was time to loosen various ribbons so he could fill his hand with her breast, scraping his thumb over the dark nipple. He placed his mouth over hers, delighted by the eagerness with which her lips parted and her tongue parried with his.

As he urged her down on the couch, it occurred to him that her fingers had become almost as nimble as his. He'd not noticed his buttons coming undone until she was shoving his shirt back off his shoulders.

"We don't have time for everything to go, sweetheart," he murmured, before sipping at her mouth once again. Easing his hand down, he worked up her skirt until it was bunched around her hips. He skimmed his fingers along her thigh, relishing the velvety feel. He took his hand higher, to where the warmth waited for him.

Moaning, she writhed beneath him. He unbuttoned his trousers, freed himself with a groan, and eased himself closer to heaven.

His clothes were less of a deterrent for her, and he felt her hands skimming along his skin. No woman had ever touched him as she did—as though she appreciated every inch of him. One night she'd kissed him from his big, ugly feet to a scar on his cheek— the faint remnant of the morning she'd attacked him with a poker. No matter where she began kissing him, she always stopped there, and he wondered if it would always be her final destination, a reminder of a time when trust between them hadn't come easily—when he'd even discouraged it.

He couldn't remember now why he'd been so re- luctant to encourage anything between them. In some ways, it seemed years ago, in others only a few hours ago. With all her ticking clocks, time should have been the one thing between them that remained steady, but everything seemed to want to change.

His opinion of her, his desire for her.

He wasn't normally an impatient man. He'd learned on the streets that more and greater rewards came with patience, but he'd hardly been able to wait until he could take Henry and Ida to the locomotive. Now he was with Livy, alone, and again the time was ticking away.

She was begging him to take her. His modest Livy, his proper Livy, was urging him toward completion.

There was barely room on this couch. He had to wrap her legs around his waist, place one foot on the floor to give himself leverage so he could get the angle he needed, then he was plunging inside her, feeling the hot, silky wetness of her surrounding him.

He rode her hard, the motion of the train whispering at the back of his mind, giving him a cadence that he matched. For some reason, he thought of the people in the open railway car. He covered Livy's mouth, absorbing her scream as her body tightened, pulsed, and throbbed around him. It was all he needed. His body bucked, the pleasure intense, almost painful. It was always more with her, more than he'd ever had, ever known.

Everything with her was different. Everything was better.

As he buried his face in the curve of her neck and shoulder, he heard the train whistle signaling they'd soon be arriving at the next stop. "Damn."

Livy's hand rested against his cheek, limp as though all energy had been drained from her. "I'm not certain if this was a very good or a very bad idea."

He lifted himself up, then dipped down to buss a quick kiss over her lips. "A good idea."

Olivia sat on a blanket, watching as Henry—barefoot—darted into the sea up to his ankles and darted out again, with Ida keeping a close watch on him.

"We should have brought Pippin," she said.

"We will next time," Jack said. He was stretched out on his side, raised up on an elbow, enjoying a glass of wine. They'd finished their picnic earlier and he was determined they not take any wine back home. "Why didn't you want him to have a dog?"

She picked at the blanket. "When I was a young girl, about ten, I had a puppy. I loved it so much. One morning I woke up and it was dead. I was inconsolable. I always suspected my brother had poisoned it."

"Avendale?"

"Yes. Of course, he wasn't Avendale then. He was a bit of a bully, though. I can't say I was particularly sad when he died. Still I cried. I don't do well when things die." She glanced over at him. "Since we're asking personal questions, why do you care so much for money?"

"Asking about your dog didn't seem as personal."

"Money is everything to you," she insisted.

"Not everything, otherwise, I wouldn't have the private car so we could get away for a bit."

"But very, very important."

"Absolutely. For those of us who grew up without it, it is very important indeed. It allows you to protect yourself from those who would do you harm."

"Who would harm you?"

He swirled the wine in his glass. "No one anymore." He glanced toward the sea where Henry was now trying to splash water on Ida, who merely laughed. "Did his father give him much attention?"

"Not really. Oh, he thanked me on the day he was born, for giving him an heir, but now I realize he was probably thanking me because he'd no longer have to come to my bed."

He jerked his head around. "You don't mean that."

"I think I do, yes. In retrospect, I can see that he was a very sad man."

"I thought the same thing the first time I met him."

She perked up at that bit of news. "At your club?"

Reaching out, he took her hand, pressed a kiss to her fingers. "No, years ago. I met him in the Earl of Claybourne's garden. I think they were friends and he was visiting."

"I think he knew all the lords."

"That's not uncommon, is it?"

"No, not really. What did you talk about?"

"I was thinking of leaving Claybourne's, striking out on my own. He convinced me not to."

"Why were you thinking of leaving?"

"The old gent, Luke's grandfather, demanded perfection. He was a hard taskmaster, harder than Feagan ever was. I didn't appreciate what he was teaching me at the time. And I suspect Henry will not appreciate what I'm teaching him."

She glanced toward her son. "To frolic and play?"

"To take from life what you can, while you can."

She looked back at Jack and brushed the hair off his brow. "I think that's an admirable philosophy."

"Now you find something about me admirable? I daresay hell will be naught but ice by the time I get there."

She leaned toward him and whispered, "Will Henry be driving the train on the way back?"

He gave her a slow, sensual smile. "I imagine something can be arranged."

Chapter 20

"I like this gown," Jack said, nibbling on Livy's ear in the library. "Can hardly wait to divest you of it."

As soon as they finished dinner, he would. It had been nearly a week since they'd traveled on the railway, and while she wore black during the day, each evening before dinner she surprised him with a different gown. While he always awaited her arrival with anticipation, he took additional pleasure in seeing her dressed in something other than mourning clothes. Tonight it was red. She was breathtaking in red. He was convinced that in the future, she should purchase clothing only in that shade. He trailed his mouth along the side of her throat. She moaned, a lingering sound that threatened to weaken his resolve to allow her to wear the gown at least through dinner.

"I think the servants are beginning to talk," she murmured.

"I pay them enough that they won't utter a single word, not even to each other." He'd have never before considered paying to keep wagging tongues silent, but a proper perception was so important to her. Amazing how what was important to her was becoming increasingly important to him.

She leaned back. "We've not been very discreet."

"I beg to differ. All they know is that in the evenings you don't parade around in black. I haven't been chasing you around the residence, though God knows that idea has merit. Maybe I won't go to the club tonight, and after the servants are asleep—"

She slapped his shoulder. "I'm serious, Jack. What began as one night of indiscretion has grown into something that consumes me. I'm hardly acting the widow."

"In public you do. In private, it's no one's damned business."

She glided her fingers lovingly over the faint scar on his cheek. "I suppose I just worry that Lovingdon deserves better from me in death."

"And you deserved better from him in life. The man failed to appreciate you." He ran his mouth along her bare shoulder. "You must admit that is not one of my failings."

Her soft whimper urged him on. There was no hope for it. He couldn't last until after dinner. Lifting her, he sat her on the desk.

"What are you doing?" she asked breathily, her arms wrapped around his shoulders. "We'll be called in to dinner soon."

"I have a hunger for something else," he growled. "I think I'll inform Brittles we're not dining this evening. We shall eat in bed later. How does that sound?"

"Lovely. Absolutely—"

A rap sounded on the door. She released a tiny screech, shoved him so hard while sliding off the desk that he nearly stumbled over his feet to land on his backside. He grabbed her waist to steady them both.

"Relax," he ordered.

"Who can it be? It's too early for dinner."

"I haven't a clue." He released her, watching in amusement as she righted herself, but even righted she looked like a woman who had been in the midst of being ravished. He decided for her comfort not to mention that. How things had changed since that first night when he'd taken delight in unsettling her.

She licked her lips and angled her chin. "All right."

Jack turned to the door. "Come in."

Brittles opened the door. "Lord Briarwood—"

"I've been made to wait long enough," the man roared as he barged into the room before Brittles could make the proper announcement.

Brittles appeared alarmed. Jack waved him off. With a nod, Brittles retreated, closing the door behind him.

Briarwood sneered at Olivia. "I should have known he'd turn you into his whore."

Jack's fist landed on Briarwood's jaw with a satisfying thud that sent the man sprawling over the carpet. "I'd watch my tongue if I were you."

Rubbing his jaw, Briarwood glared up at him. "Yes, I'm well aware of your reputation for guarding those who work for you."

"You say that as though it's a fault," Olivia snapped.

"He is a scoundrel, his morals questionable." He staggered to his feet and barreled around Jack until he was standing directly in front of Olivia. "He seeks to bring everyone down to his level. Look at you. You are in mourning, and you look as though you should be walking the streets."

"You will stop those accusations now," Jack demanded. "Or you'll feel the power of my fist again."

"That's the way of it with you, isn't it?" Briarwood didn't attempt to hide his scorn. "Barbaric. You don't know the first thing about being civilized."

"I believe the fact you still have your teeth is an indication that I do," Jack ground out.

Briarwood turned back to Olivia. "Are you aware he keeps boys at his gaming club?"

"As a matter of fact I am. He provides them with employment and a safe haven. An admirable undertaking."

"It's not natural for a man to have such interest in boys."

"What are you saying?" Olivia asked.

"I'm concerned for Henry's welfare. Rumors abound that Dodger molests them."

"Rumors, I have no doubt that can be laid at your door," Jack said. "You should leave—"

"He's never harmed Henry," Olivia cut in.

"Would you know if he did?"

She looked at Jack, and he felt the weight of doubt in her gaze, knew she was remembering how she'd not known that Helen had harmed her son.

She nodded jerkily. "Yes, I would know if he hurt him, and I know he would not."

The conviction in her words eased the tightness around Jack's chest.

"You'll not turn her against me, Briarwood. Whatever you hope to accomplish with these false accusations—"

"The boy is not safe here. Stanford agrees with me."

"Rupert Stanford?" Olivia asked.

"Yes. My cousin and I are appalled we're being investigated by Scotland Yard. The inspector will find nothing untoward regarding either of us. The same cannot be said of you, sir. The duchess here is proof." He turned back to Olivia. "Look at what he has done to you."

Jack grabbed Briarwood's arm. "You're leaving."

Olivia held up her hand. "Wait. Let him have his say."

"He has nothing of any importance—"

"Then let me hear it."

Briarwood jerked free, straightened his jacket, while Jack struggled between insisting he leave and giving Livy an opportunity to prove . . . what? That she believed him over Briarwood? On the other hand, he needed to know what he was fighting.

"He has caused you to forget your place," Briarwood said. "You are in mourning, yet you wear red. You are not married to him, yet I can see where his roughened jaw has abraded your skin. If he can turn you, a woman of such high morals, to his sinful ways, imagine what he'll do to an impressionable lad. All I care about is your son, that he be raised to be a proper lord. I can achieve that end for you. And if you will not support me in this endeavor, I will go to the courts, I will go to Parliament. By God, I will go to the queen. But I cannot in all good conscience stand by and allow this devil—"

"I don't think you have a choice," Jack stated calmly.

Both Livy and Briarwood jerked their heads around to look at him.

"You can spout all the good intentions in the world and all your concerns for Henry's righteous upbringing that you want, Briarwood, but you and I both know at the heart of the matter rests finances. I will not be blackmailed."

Briarwood straightened his shoulders. "I assure you, sir, I care only for the welfare of my cousin's son. You will see your good name ruined—"

"As you've pointed out on several occasions I have no good name. The name I have means less to me than my money. Make all the threats you want, I'll not pay you."

Briarwood was losing his composure and Jack had little doubt he'd accurately guessed the man's reason in coming here.

"I shall go see Beckwith in the morning. If you should change your mind—"

"I won't," Jack said.

Briarwood looked at Olivia. "Think on it. Together we can put matters to right."

Without a further word, he lumbered out of the room.

"Is this blackmail? Is that what he's doing?" Olivia asked quietly.

Jack turned back to her. "Yes."

"Why not pay him to stop these vicious rumors?"

"His accusations are false. If I pay him, I give credence to them, and then he'll only come back for more. It'll become a circle and we'll be left with no way out."

"But what if he adds my indiscretions to his rumors?"

"We gain nothing by paying him."

"We gain his silence."

"I will not be blackmailed."

"Briarwood thought you'd blackmailed Lovingdon. He thought that was the reason you were named guardian."

"It seems Briarwood has an uncanny ability to be wrong."

"You don't like him."

"Not particularly."

She studied him a moment before saying, "I know you'd never hurt Henry."

"Good." He moved toward her and she skirted around him. It seemed she'd been paying more attention than he realized when he'd been teaching Henry how to dodge.

"But. . ." she began and stopped.

"But?"

She turned to face him. "But regarding me: I am loath to admit it, but Briarwood is correct. My behavior has been abominable."

"Livy—"

"No. I know you have the wherewithal to convince me otherwise. If you but touch me, kiss me, I will follow you wherever you lead. Look at me." She spread her arms wide. "I'm barely a month into mourning and here I am wearing red. Lying in bed with a man to whom I'm not married. For God's sake—look what we did when traveling on a railway!"

"Livy, this is exactly what he wanted, to give you

doubts, to make you question me. It only serves to strengthen his standing."

"Did you seduce me to strengthen yours?"

He spun on his heel, went to his table, and poured whiskey into a glass. "I'll not dignify that question with an answer."

"Do I mean anything to you other than a bit of sport?"

"You're playing right into his hands."

"I've played right into yours often enough, haven't I? What are we doing here, you and I?"

Did she really expect an answer to that question? Did she truly think he knew? Yes, she was a bit of sport, but she was more, and he didn't know how to define their relationship. He couldn't imagine his life without her in it. But neither could he imagine telling her that.

"Do you still intend to try to marry me off?"

Did he? The thought of another man touching her was enough to send riotous fury rushing through him. He'd never before had a problem sharing women. Why her? Why could he not stand the thought of her going to any other man?

"What then?" she asked, as though growing tired of waiting for him to form some sort of comprehendible answer to what should have been such a simple question. "Your mistress? I think not. I fear Briarwood was correct. I have forgotten myself." He heard her swallow. "Jack, tomorrow I'd like to take Henry to the country," she said quietly.

"No."

"Please don't insist I go alone."

Alone. She was leaving him, with or without Henry.

God, that she would want to be rid of him badly enough to go without Henry said everything. He looked over his shoulder at her. The sadness in her eyes almost brought him to his knees. The sadness and the regret. He'd taught her the enjoyment of immediate pleasures, encouraged her to taste them without giving thought to the hard price to be paid later. She was now paying a dearer price than he ever would.

"I'm going to the club." He strode past her, stopped. "I want you and Henry gone before I return late tomorrow morning. And take the damn dog with you."

He was almost to the door when he heard her first sob. It took every ounce of strength he possessed to continue on.

Henry wasn't nearly as excited at the prospect of going to the country as Olivia expected him to be. It was because Jack wasn't going with them. Henry adored the man.

Not that she could blame him. He could be charming when he wanted to be, and he certainly seemed to have a way with Henry. Was it because of all the boys at his club?

Sitting in a chair beside his bed, she read to Henry, her words flat, his interest flagging. Not because he was tired. She could see that he wasn't. Each creak of the residence had his gaze darting to the door as though he was expecting—hoping—Jack would come through it and tell him that he wouldn't be going to the country.

Had Henry loved his father even half as much as he seemed to love Jack?

Olivia closed the book. Henry gave her a guilty look.

She thought it unlikely that he was going to fall asleep anytime soon, which would make him grumpy in the morning when they began the journey.

"I'm thinking of going for a walk in the garden," she said. It was dark but not terribly late. She wasn't in the mood for bed either, or for being alone. "Would you like to go with me?"

He nodded. "Can I take Pippin?"

She couldn't remember the last time he'd stammered. "Of course." She turned to Ida. "Henry and I are going for a walk in the garden."

"I'll get him ready for you, Your Grace."

It was only a few minutes before she and Henry were strolling through the garden, the occasional lantern providing a shadowy path.

"I think Pippin will like the country, don't you?" Olivia asked.

She could see Henry nodding.

"Why isn't Jack coming?"

"He has business to see to here." She crouched before him, turned him to face her. "Henry, you have to understand—"

A shadow stepped out of the darkness.

Chapter 21

Damn her. What did she want him to do? Profess undying love? Ask for her hand in marriage? She was a duchess, for God's sake. She acted as though he'd forgotten what she was, what he was. He hadn't. All the money in the world wouldn't cleanse his origins from him, wouldn't make it acceptable for him to marry her.

Not that he'd ever consider marriage.

Still, he couldn't imagine his house without her in it. Couldn't imagine not hearing the echo of her sharp steps as she strode through the hallways to confront him about one matter or another. Couldn't imagine the scent of her perfume not wafting from her bedchamber into his via the dressing room, couldn't imagine it not being on the pillow next to his. Couldn't imagine silence at meals, laughter unheard, smiles unseen.

He, who had always longed for the next coin, now yearned for something more. A woman. He thought he'd give up every coin he possessed if she would bestow upon him just one more smile.

The knock on his office door made him glower. He didn't want company, but before he could tell whoever it was that he wasn't at home—what a silly bit of nonsense that was—the door opened and Swindler stepped in.

"Frannie said I'd find you here."

No doubt after he'd spent considerable time talking with her. Jack didn't know why the man didn't just profess his love for her, ask for her hand in marriage, and be done with it.

On the other hand, maybe he should ask the same of himself regarding Olivia. What was the worst that would happen? She'd say no and he'd send her to the country.

"You all right?" Swindler asked.

"Of course." Jack reached back and grabbed a glass. He filled it with whiskey, set it in front of Swindler as he took his seat, and then refilled his own glass. "You're a bit late in informing me that Briarwood is spreading rumors about me."

"I'm sorry, but I've had several things I've been investigating of late, and you're not the one who pays my salary."

"Quit your job and come work for me exclusively. I'll pay you more than Scotland Yard does."

"I like my job, thank you very much."

Jack shrugged. "So what do you have? Did you find out anything about my mother?"

"I'm not hopeful there of ever finding anything. But the other matter you asked me about—Lovingdon engaging in any perversions . . ."

A hint of something in Swindler's voice had Jack sitting up straighter. "Yes?"

"I found nothing where he was concerned, but his cousin gives me pause."

"Briarwood?"

"Rupert Stanford. He's very much a recluse. According to his maid-of-all-work, the only servant he had until he let her go two days ago, he nearly worked her into the ground keeping everything clean. She was with him for nearly twenty years. He took in maybe a dozen boys during that time. One at a time. Apparently with the intent of finding each boy a proper home. One day she would come into work and find the boy no longer there. She always assumed he'd carried through on his promise, found them someplace else to live."

"Which he might have," Jack said, but he wasn't feeling good about this.

"He well might have. I have nothing conclusive, but I find it troubling in light of your earlier concerns."

"Perhaps we should visit him."

The house was not particularly grand, but it was vaguely familiar. Could this be the dwelling he'd been searching for when he aimlessly walked the streets? He remembered the man's house as being larger, but then to a child of the rookeries—the child that Jack had been—a residence such as this would have taken on the mystique of a palace. Swindler banged the knocker.

"Doesn't appear anyone's home," Swindler said.

"I want to see inside."

The light from a nearby streetlamp cast a faint glow over Swindler's face as he arched a brow and gave Jack a stare. Jack stared back until Swindler sighed. "Did you want to do the honors, or shall I?"

Jack felt the slightest of tremors in his hand. "You."

"Your coachman and footman—"

"Are discreet."

"They'd better be."

Swindler reached into his pocket for his tools. Jack angled his body to form some cover for the illegal action. He heard the click and the door swung open with an ominous creak.

He walked in and was greeted with the fragrance of too much soap and furniture wax. A match flared to life. Swindler located an oil lamp and lit it.

"What exactly are we looking for?" Swindler asked.

"A bedchamber." His voice rasped along his nerve endings.

"Upstairs, I'd say."

With a nod, Jack bounded up the stairs. Swindler followed. The lamp Swindler carried cast an eerie glow, chasing back shadows, revealing things bit by bit. Nothing looked particularly familiar.

Then they reached the upstairs hallway. There were only four doors. Jack opened the second on the right.

And he was five years old again. Missing his mother, but excited at the prospect of having a bed to sleep in. It was winter. There was a fire in the hearth and it was so nice and toasty. His mother had begun to talk a lot about going to a place called heaven. He decided this had to be it.

"Let's take a bath, shall we?"

Jack squeezed his eyes closed against the memories. Had Stanford met his mother when she was a servant in the Lovingdon household? He fought to remember—

"Miss Dawkins?"

She was holding Jack's hand, late at night in the rookeries—

She turned, curtsied. "Mr. Stanford."

"What have you here?"

"My son, Jack."

"Jack? Jack? Are you all right?"

Jack opened his eyes at Swindler's urging and walked farther into the room. "They talked. I couldn't hear the words. We went to a tavern, ate this wonderful pie with meat in it. They kept talking. All the while he held her hand."

"What are you talking about?" Swindler asked.

Jack shook his head. He couldn't explain the unexplainable, but he remembered that when they left, Stanford gave Jack's mother the coin purse and she'd given Jack the locket. Then Stanford had brought him here.

Jack walked to the fireplace, bent down, and looked up the flue that had served as his escape tunnel. He'd worked to get the coals off the hearth, burned his feet and hands going up. That had been his first lesson in what a person would do if he wanted something badly enough. He'd been willing to suffer anything to get out.

He spun around and looked back at the bed with the four posts decorated with elaborate vines carved into them. His stomach roiled with memories of what had happened there.

Walking back to Swindler, Jack took the lamp from him and tossed it onto the bed. Flames erupted over the counterpane.

"Good God, have you gone mad?" Swindler asked.

Jack was already on his way through the door. "We have to find Stanford."

They returned to the club—not as quickly as Jack would have preferred since Swindler insisted on alerting the fire brigade so they had an opportunity to prevent the flames from spreading beyond Stanford's residence. Jack took some comfort in knowing at least the bed was destroyed.

"You do realize that I can't arrest him," Swindler said now as they sat in Jack's office.

"Sodomy is against the law."

"But I have no one to testify."

"I'll testify."

Swindler looked away as though suddenly very uncomfortable. Jack supposed it was one thing to have suspicions, another to have confirmation.

"We should probably just handle it ourselves," Swindler said quietly. "It's not as though we haven't done that before. I'm sure there's someone scheduled for a hanging who doesn't deserve it."

"You'd switch prisoners? You don't think anyone would notice?"

"You could beat him until he was unrecognizable. I'm certain you'd find some satisfaction in that."

Jack nodded. "I would indeed."

The door suddenly opened and Thomas Lark, one of the older boys who helped out in the gaming room, rushed in.

"Thomas, you're supposed to knock," Jack said.

"Yes, sir, I know, but this was just delivered by a gent who said it was of the utmost importance."

Jack snatched the envelope Thomas extended. Inside he found a message that caused his heart to thunder.

Mr. Dodger,

Please return to the residence immediately. A dire situation has arisen and you're desperately needed.

> *Your faithful servant,*
> *Brittles*

"Thank God you've arrived sir," Brittles said in a rush as soon as Jack walked into the residence, Swindler at his side.

"What's the trouble, man?"

"It's the duchess, sir. She's gone missing."

"Is that all? She was going to take Henry to the country. I'm assuming she couldn't wait until the morning to be rid of me—"

"No, sir, Henry's here."

Everything in Jack stilled. "She'd not leave Henry."

"Exactly, sir. She and her son were walking in the garden when someone apparently came out of the shadows, according to the young duke. He escaped, but by the time we realized what he was trying to tell us—he was stammering something fierce, sir—the duchess was gone."

"Where's Henry now?"

"In the day nursery, sir."

Jack bounded up the stairs, aware of Swindler and Brittles following behind him. For the first time, Brittles's steps were not silent. Jack took no comfort in that.

He barged into the day nursery. Ida was sitting in a rocker, Henry in her lap holding his dog. Henry scrambled out of Ida's lap, Pippin leaping to the floor. Before Jack could react, Henry had rushed across the short distance separating them and wound his arms tightly around Jack's legs.

"I d-did wh-what you t-taught me, sir. I d-dodged away," Henry said, his words muffled, his face pressed against Jack's thigh.

Jack crouched, hugging Henry tightly. "You were a good boy, Henry."

"I think h-he t-took Mummy." Henry leaned back, tears coursing down his cheeks. "You should have t-taught Mummy how to dodge."

"Yes, I should have. Do you know who took her?"

Henry bobbed his head quickly. "Cousin Rupert. Father told me t-to n-never go any-anywhere with Cousin R-Rupert."

Had Lovingdon known what Jack now did? Was Rupert Stanford the one Jack was supposed to protect Henry against? It all made sense, if Lovingdon had seen how Jack protected the boys who worked for him. Couldn't he have left a bloody message?

"Did he hurt you?" Jack asked.

Henry shook his head emphatically. "But when I ran off, I heard Mummy scream. I think he might have hit her. I shouldn't have r-run."

"No, you did the right thing, because now I only have to worry about your mum and not you."

"You'll save her?"

"Absolutely." Although he hadn't a bloody clue where to start. Thank goodness, Swindler was there.

"Sir, I don't mean to interrupt," Brittles said, holding out an envelope with Jack's name on it. "This was delivered a short while ago."

Jack snatched it from him and tore into the envelope. The missive was short and to the point.

I have the duchess. Bring me one hundred thousand pounds by dawn or she dies. We'll be waiting at the top floor, far corner.

Jack knew the address written at the bottom of the note. It was in the rookeries.

"Where are we?" Olivia asked.

She was sitting on the floor in a shadowed corner, her hands tied behind her. She was fighting not to be terrified. She'd taken a blow to the head and woken up here. Her mouth tasted of laudanum and her thoughts were fuzzy. She wanted to go to sleep but she knew there was a reason she shouldn't.

"The rookeries." The hoarse whisper came from another dark corner, near the window, the man's silhouette swallowed by the gloom. A solitary lantern was no help against it. It served to illuminate her more than him. "It's easier to handle improper things here. I've instructed Mr. Dodger to bring me a hundred thousand pounds or you'll die."

Olivia heard in his voice that he was deadly serious. A fissure of dread threatened to overwhelm her.

"If he doesn't deliver, I'll carry out my promise, then I'll return for your son."

"Not Henry." She remembered Henry had been with her. "Where is he?"

"The little bugger eluded me."

Relief swamped her. She had a vague recollection of him darting away. Jack wouldn't part with his precious money for Olivia, but she had no doubt that he would protect Henry.

"Dodger won't come," she said.

"He'll come."

She released a bitter laugh, fighting to control it so she didn't sound hysterical. "You've asked him for money. It's the one thing with which he will not part."

"Then that will be most unfortunate for you."

Suddenly he moved quickly, crouching before her. She felt something eerily cold against the underside of her chin. "Is that a pistol?" she whispered.

"It is indeed, and I'm very accurate. I've given him until dawn."

Then, to her astonishment, she recognized him. "Stanford? Rupert Stanford?"

"I'm surprised you remember me. Your husband did not welcome me in his home very often."

"Why are you doing this?"

"Because your son's guardian has been making inquiries about me and things are coming to light that I wished to remain in the dark. I need to make a hasty departure and I haven't the funds needed to do so."

"So you kidnapped me?"

"I saw the way he looked at you when he brought you to Dodger's. You see, I, too, was in the shadows. He has some lovely boys working for him, but he and his staff watch them as though they were the Crown Jewels. And they all have so much confidence that they aren't easily swayed. But I'm certain wherever I go that I can find what I need."

"Dear God, you're a monster."

"Yes, yes, I am."

He moved away. She swung out her legs as best she could, hoping to trip him up but he easily sidestepped. "Careful, Duchess. I'm not in the habit of hurting ladies, but I can always make an exception."

Jack knew the rookeries like the back of his hand. A lot of evil men lived there. A lot of good men too. With the satchel filled with a hundred thousand pounds gripped tightly in one hand, a lantern in the other, he walked among the detritus of society, fearing no evil because he carried a knife in his boot, a pistol in his pocket, and—in the hand holding the satchel—a walking stick that came apart to reveal a sword.

The abductor had said to come alone. He'd said nothing about coming unarmed—which made Jack think Rupert Stanford was only marginally familiar with the rookeries. Obviously he knew it well enough to identify a meeting place, but not well enough to know that many of the people there were armed. Or maybe he knew little of Jack, thought he wouldn't have a clue regarding the destination to which he was walking.

Jack wasn't a fool. He thought it unlikely Stanford would let Olivia or Jack live once he had his money.

There was just enough light that Jack could see the shadows keeping pace with him if he turned his head just so. Shadows had always served as his friends.

Tonight was no exception.

They effectively hid Luke and Swindler as they followed at a discreet distance. Graves and Frannie walked in the open, giving the impression they were a couple looking for a place for an illicit rendezvous. When Jack desperately needed them, Feagan's brood had come through for him.

He reached the abandoned building, which looked as though a strong wind might blow it down. In foul weather people would take refuge here, but on a clear night it wasn't worth the risk. It would be very difficult to go up to the third floor without being heard. He supposed that was the point.

He made his way carefully inside, the rats scurrying away. He knew they'd return. They always returned. Holding the lantern high, he glanced around. Even though he'd never been here before, everything was familiar. Little difference existed between one building and another there.

He started up the stairs. They creaked beneath his weight. No point in treading lightly. He hurried up them, his heart pounding.

"Livy!"

He heard nothing. She could be gagged, she could be dead, she—

"Jack!"

He staggered, the relief so great his legs nearly gave out on him when at the same time a surge of energy shot through him. He rushed up the stairs, barely stopping at the landing, simply charging down the hallway. He could see pale light easing out of one room. It could be a trick, so he slowed his step, angling the lantern to give him the best light.

"Livy!"

"We're here!"

She and Rupert Stanford. He could barely stand the thought of that bastard touching her, but he fought back the fury because he had to keep a clear head.

Jack walked slowly, cautiously. He peered into the room—

Livy was standing beside Stanford in the corner, near the window, and Jack wondered if he'd been looking out, watching for his approach. It didn't matter. He'd have not seen anything.

As Jack stepped into the room he was hit with an odor. Anyone else probably would have considered it a fragrance. It was a rich scent, undoubtedly masculine, but it caused his stomach to roil as memories assaulted him. That scent crawling into bed with him when he was a boy, offering comfort before it hurt him.

He raised the lantern higher and saw the unholy gleam in the eyes that glittered at him—like those of a rat coming up out of the sewer. Everything in Jack went cold. He thought he'd prepared himself for this encounter, but suddenly he was five years old again, terrified, hurting, ashamed.

He fought to focus on the here and now. "Rupert Stanford."

"You say that as though I know you."

"We've met before. My mother was Emily Dawkins."

"You're Jack Dawkins?" Stanford released a bark of laughter. "It is a small world. You changed your name . . . how clever. I'll do the same, now that my meddling cousin and your suspicious inspector have been uncovering my business."

"*Business*? Taking advantage of young boys?"

He heard Livy's sharp intake of breath at the revelation.

"My cousin has told me all about you, about the boys you keep. I think we're very much alike—"

"I'm nothing like you," Jack ground out. "I protect them."

"As I did you. Your mother was dying, poor thing. I gave her a few coins to ease the way and took you in so she wasn't burdened with worry. But then you had the audacity to escape. The only one ever to escape."

Something in the man's voice . . . Jack knew the longer he kept him talking the greater his advantage. He needed to give the others time to position themselves.

"The only one? Do the boys still live with you?" He'd seen no evidence of it.

"In my garden," Stanford said wistfully.

"You killed them?"

"I'd love to stay and chat, but I really must be off."

"You're not taking Livy with you."

"She's my insurance. Set the satchel down and move across the room."

Jack took two steps and released a shrill whistle. A crash sounded as the window was smashed.

Stanford glanced back, giving Jack the narrow space he was looking for, just enough that he could shoulder his way in, shove Livy aside, and take Stanford to the floor. He fought to wrench the pistol free of Stanford's grasp, but the man, while older, was surprisingly strong and agile. They struggled, rolling over the floor. Jack tried to leverage himself—

An explosion rent the night as the pistol went off, and Jack felt the fire of its report burning his chest as warm blood seeped through his favorite red waistcoat.

Olivia had barely hit the floor before the pistol thundered and both men went completely still.

"Oh, God, oh, God. Jack."

Suddenly someone came in through the window. Before she could scream, she heard, "It's all right, it's Swindler."

The thud of heavy footsteps sounded outside in the hallway and two more large shadows burst into the room, followed by a smaller one. Frannie crossed over and took Olivia in her arms. "Are you all right?"

Olivia nodded and whispered. "Jack?"

Frannie began working on the knots in the rope securing Olivia's hands.

"Jack," Swindler said sternly.

Olivia watched as a man rose up. She recognized the form, would forever recognize that shape. "Jack?"

"I'm all right," he said, his voice hard as he crouched beside her husband's cousin.

She heard harsh breathing, a gurgling sound—

"Jack, I need to see to him," Dr. Graves said, and Olivia realized he was one of the men who'd come inside. The other was Claybourne.

"No," Jack said.

Stanford coughed and gagged.

"The boys? How many were there?" Jack demanded.

"You . . . the first."

"And after me? How many, damn you?"

"Don't . . . know."

"You killed them? Buried them in your garden? Is that what you were saying with all your cryptic words?"

But Rupert Stanford made no sound.

"Answer me, you bastard."

"He's dead," Dr. Graves said somberly.

Jack slowly unfolded his body. Suddenly his arms were around Olivia, holding her tightly until she could barely breathe. "I didn't think you'd come."

"Of course I'd come," he growled.

"He said he was asking for a hundred thousand pounds."

"I'd have given him everything, Livy. Everything to have you back safely."

Jack and Olivia returned home immediately while Swindler and the others saw to the matter of Rupert Stanford and reporting tonight's incident to Scotland Yard. The first thing Olivia did was dash up the stairs to the nursery and hold Henry close.

"I knew he'd save you," Henry said.

It humbled her that Henry had possessed so much unquestionable faith in Jack, while she'd had so little. Never again would she make that mistake. Tonight she'd made many, and she intended to correct them all.

She considered how to go about that while she took a wonderful hot bath to get the grime of the rookeries off her. After that night's experiences, she thought she'd probably take a full bath every day in the future. She'd hoped Jack would join her that night, would come in to see how she was doing, but when he didn't, she put on her nightgown and went in search of him.

She found him in the library, sitting in a chair, his elbows on his thighs, his hands wrapped around a glass, the bottle nearby waiting to do its duty, to numb what had been a traumatizing night.

She padded across the carpet, knelt before him and wrapped a hand around each of his wrists. "I can't imagine what you're feeling."

"No, you probably can't. Before tonight I had no name for the man who took me, but he was Stanford. I don't know if I never knew his name or simply forgot it. It's been nearly thirty years. I think he must have known my mother. She knew him, trusted him. They must have met when she worked here. She gave me into his keeping, thinking I'd be safe. The first night" —she heard him swallow hard— "he bathed me, put me to bed, then he crawled in with me. He touched me in ways a man shouldn't touch a boy . . . he did things that not only ravaged my body but my soul."

"Dear God, Jack." She touched his cheek, tried to offer him comfort, but he wasn't looking at her. He was peering into his past.

"He wept afterward, promised to never do it again. The next night, I learned he was a liar. The third night I ran away."

Scalding tears welled in her eyes. "You can't blame yourself for any of that. You were an innocent child. I'm glad he's dead."

He shook his head. "There's more, Livy. I told you that Luke and I were arrested. When you're convicted, you serve your time in a boys' prison. But before that, before your trial, you're kept in gaol with men. There were three, a nasty lot. They set their sights on Luke, but he fought them. God, he was only eight, but he wouldn't stop fighting. His face was a bloodied mess. I thought they were going to kill him. I knew what they wanted, had survived it before."

Dear God, no, she thought. *Please no*.

"I offered myself to them." The words came out on a strangle.

"Oh, Jack." She squeezed his hands, pressed her lips to them while the tears coursed down her face and pooled at the corner of her mouth.

"It was worse than I remembered. Or maybe they were just meaner. They broke something in me that night, Livy. I stopped caring about anything except for surviving, and I became convinced that if I had enough money I would always be safe. But inside, I stayed broken. Until you.

"You made me start to feel again. You and Henry. You brought joy into my life. Laughter and smiles. But there is pain in that, too. Caring for someone makes you vulnerable. What I was feeling whenever I was with you terrified the bloody hell out of me, Livy. I didn't want it. I fought it with everything I could, but tonight I realized if something happened to you, if you died, I'd break again and this time I would remain broken. It's a safer way to live, but it's also a life not worth living.

"I love you, Livy. I know I'm not worthy of any affection you might hold for me—"

"Not worthy? I know of no man more worthy."

"I live in the gutter."

"You live in St. James. You may have begun your life in the gutter, but I know of no other man who has achieved what you've achieved. You are a man of means, who owes nothing to anyone. You have a generous heart. I know you don't want to hear that, but it's true. Henry adores you. And damn it, so do I.

"I love you, Jack, with all my heart and soul. I was wrong to listen to Briarwood. I realized it as I was waiting in that dwelling, or whatever it was. I thought of all the moments I had with you, and with Henry. And I prayed I would have a thousand more."

"You're wrong there, Livy. Briarwood was right."

"No—"

He put his finger to her lips. "Shh. He was right. I have corrupted you. Did you not hear what you just said? You used profanity."

She gave a brittle laugh. "And the roof didn't fall in on me."

He cradled her cheek. "I told you that first night there isn't anything a person won't do if he wants something badly enough." He released a deep, painful moan. "I want you—and Henry—to be mine for all eternity. Marry me, Livy."

"Oh." She wasn't expecting that. She was prepared to live the remainder of her life as his mistress, but as his wife? "Oh."

"Is that a yes or a no?"

She laughed from the joy of it. "I think you're supposed to be on your knees and I'm supposed to be sitting."

"You and your damned etiquette," he said, shaking his head as a teasing smile formed on his lips.

She placed her hands on either side of his face. "Yes, I'll gladly marry you."

"We'll mark the calendar. One day after your mourning period ends—"

"Don't be silly. I'll marry you tomorrow."

"You think the London ladies will forgive you for that breach of etiquette?"

"Of course. I shall have firsthand accounts to share over tea, so they'll promptly forgive me because they'll want to know everything I know about the deliciously wicked Jack Dodger."

"Deliciously wicked?"

"It was how we referred to you."

"I don't know that I'm in the mood to be deliciously wicked tonight, but I would like very much to sleep with you in my arms."

As she lay with Jack that night, she didn't know if it had been Lovingdon's intent, but in his passing, he'd given her in death what he'd been unable to grant her in life: joy, passion, and love.

Chapter 22

"**B**riarwood."

"Good God, I said I was not at home. Do you not know what that means?"

Jack walked farther into the man's study, having ignored the butler's attempt to stop him from coming in. The room reeked of cheap liquor and stale sweat. Sprawled on a couch, Briarwood was slovenly, his shirt stained, his jacket, waistcoat, and neck cloth discarded.

"I wanted to know if you'd ever heard of Emily Dawkins," Jack said.

Briarwood rolled his eyes. "No."

Jack persisted. Since Stanford had known her . . . "She worked in the Lovingdon household, thirty-six years ago."

He stared at Jack. "I was ten years old, man. What did I care of servants?"

"Stanford knew her."

"He was twelve years my senior. Maybe he had an interest in her." He groaned. "Although that seems unlikely. Apparently, he preferred boys. Scotland Yard was here this morning. They've found bones in his garden, for Christ's sake. Small bones. Children's bones. Hundreds of bones. The family is ruined."

And what of the families of the children?

Jack could see the despair clearly outlined in Briarwood's face, a man who always put his own interests first.

"Beckwith was here as well. I've inherited a house that someone tried to burn down. Stanford had no money to speak of and as I have none, what good does a burned-out house do me, I ask you?"

"I'll purchase it," Jack said, before he even thought through all the ramifications. He could totally destroy the residence and build a hospital for Graves there. A memorial hospital for those boys he'd not been able to save.

Briarwood sat up. "How much?"

"Get yourself sobered up and we'll discuss the particulars—including gaining control of your gambling habit."

"I don't like you, Dodger."

"I don't like you either."

Briarwood nodded. "As long as we're clear on that."

"I could also do without the rumors—"

"Consider them squashed. Not that I have any choice. Rupert Stanford is sure to be the name on everyone's tongue in the coming days. I can hardly blame my cousin for naming you guardian. As disreputable as you are, I'm beginning to see you are far better than either Stanford or I."

Jack accepted the praise graciously and said only, "We'll talk" before taking his leave.

* * *

The ceremony was to be small, private, with invitations issued to only a select few.

Jack, Olivia—wearing a modest ivory gown—and Henry arrived at the chapel to discover their guests waiting for them near the front steps.

"We're so glad you came," Livy said, greeting each in turn: Luke and Catherine, Graves, Swindler, and darling Frannie.

"This is an event I had to witness for myself," Luke said. "The notorious Jack Dodger taking a wife. It's bound to be the talk of London once word gets out."

"We hope to keep it quiet for a bit," Jack said. "After all, Livy is in mourning."

"As though you've ever cared about proper etiquette," Graves said.

"You're right. I've never been one for rules." He winked at Henry, who was going to stand with Jack at the altar. The ring was nestled in the boy's pocket.

"I'm so happy for you, Jack," Frannie said as she kissed Jack on the cheek. He could see the truth of her words sparkling in her green eyes.

"We should probably go inside so we can get the ceremony taken care of," Livy said.

As he offered her his arm, he asked, "Nervous?"

"No, not at all. I'm too incredibly happy to be nervous."

It was as they were going up the steps that a movement to the side of the building caught Jack's attention. "I forgot something. I'll catch up with you in a bit. If you don't mind, go on and see that things are ready."

"Is everything all right?"

"Yes. Just a small matter I need to attend to." He gave her a quick buss on her lips. "I'll be right in."

When the door closed behind them all, Jack went back down the steps and walked around the corner of the church.

"Hey, me dodger. I've got a present for ye," his old mentor cackled. Leaning on his cane, Feagan held out his gnarled hand and there in his palm rested Jack's locket.

With a tightening in his chest, Jack took the precious offering, opened it, and studied his mother's portrait. How young she looked, much younger than Olivia was now, he suspected. A girl really. Still, it would be as though she were with him during the ceremony. "Thank you, Feagan. But I don't have the money I owe you with me."

He waved his hand in the air. "Awk. Don't worry 'bout it. Next time yer in the rookeries, bring me a bottle of gin."

"How did you know I'd be here today?"

"I pick up things along the way."

"You should come inside."

"Nah, me and God, we never got along once 'e took the love of me life. Wouldn't want 'im thinkin' I've fer-given 'im, 'cuz I 'avn't."

"Frannie told me once she thought you were her father."

"Wot'd ye tell her?"

"Nothing."

"Ye was always me best at keepin' secrets."

"Because I learned from the best."

Feagan cackled. "That ye did, me boy, that ye did. Best wishes to ye and the new mizzus." He turned to go.

Jack called out to him. "Feagan, at least let me have my carriage take you back to the rookeries."

"Nah, I loikes to walk." Feagan winked. "Never know wot useful things I'll pick up along the way."

Jack watched him ambling off, crooked and bent, a man who'd been a father to him in many ways.

Jack could only hope he'd do as well by Henry.

The wedding had not been as grand as Olivia's first one, but as she brushed her hair at her vanity, she found no fault with it. Henry had stood beside Jack as his best man. Following the ceremony, the sight of the two of them, heads bent, conspiring about something, had brought tears to her eyes. Jack gave Henry far more attention than Lovingdon ever did.

A small part of her couldn't help but mourn what she and Lovingdon had never had. She wasn't certain why, but she thought he'd be happy for her, would approve her marrying Jack. Since he'd named Jack guardian and given him so much, he obviously thought well of the man. She thought it might have gone better all the way around, though, if Lovingdon had shared with her the weaknesses his cousins possessed.

She realized it was sometimes impossible to know everything about a person, but she had faith Jack would not keep harmful secrets from her and that their marriage would be very different from her first.

As she stood up, she couldn't help but smile at her gossamer nightgown. It left very little to the imagination. She walked across her bedchamber, opened the dressing room door, and screeched at the sight of Jack standing there.

"I was coming to get you," he said. "I'd grown tired of waiting." He angled his head. "But I can see now it was worth the wait."

He lifted her into his arms, and she laughed joyously. She wondered if these walls had ever heard so much laughter. "I'm perfectly capable of walking."

"I prefer to carry you, so I can judge your weight."

"How romantic."

"You need more weight on you. It'll keep you healthier, and I want you to be healthy for a very long time."

"I'll have to purchase new gowns."

"You'll need to do that anyway. I finally found your clothes in my ledger."

She laughed again. "You did not."

"I did. I'm taking them away from you so you'll have to be naked all the time."

"Have you forgotten that we have servants and a child in the residence?"

"Damn."

She burrowed her face into his neck. "But I promise to be completely nude when it's only the two of us."

"I suppose I can live with that."

He laid her on the bed. She scrambled up to her knees and began unfastening the buttons on his shirt. "And what about you?" she asked. "Are you going to make me work for what I so enjoy gazing on?"

With all the buttons undone, he pulled his shirt over his head. "No. I promise to be naked as well."

He was out of his clothes in short order. Then he took a few moments to appreciate her nightgown before working quickly to add it to the pile of clothes. She didn't know why she'd bothered to try to be enticing, but she found joy in knowing he was so eager to get her undressed.

"Let's dispense with the two bedchambers," he said as his mouth took a slow journey across her shoulders. "We have plenty of room in here for your vanity and anything else you want. Rearrange the whole blasted house."

"All right." He could have asked anything of her at that moment and she would have granted it. She rubbed his shoulders, stroked his back. She thought she'd never grow tired of this, of being with him. She couldn't imagine being without him, without this if she got with child.

"You'll never leave me, will you?" she asked.

He lifted his head, gazed down on her, and she could see the barely banked passion. She did that to him, made him want her as much as she did him.

"Whatever brought that question on?" he asked.

"If I get with child—"

His hot mouth cut off whatever she'd planned to say. His hands came around, holding her head in place, while he devoured her mouth, tasted deeply, urged her to do the same. When he tore away from the kiss, she might have been left bereft if not for the hunger she saw remaining in his eyes. "Whether you are with child or not, you shall spend every night in my bed, in my arms. There are ways, sweetheart, ways around all things."

In his smile, she saw wickedness and a dark teasing. Easing himself between her thighs, he lowered his mouth to her breasts, kissing one and then the other. She'd expected him to move up then, to slide into her, but he began moving down, his hands bracketing her ribs as he kissed above her stomach, before he moved lower and lower and lower.

"Oh, my God," she said breathily. "What are you—"

"Shh." It was so simple a sound, but within it she heard the promise of ecstasy.

He parted her thighs further and lowered his mouth to the nesting of curls. The first stroke of his tongue almost had her coming off the bed. Lifting her arms, she grabbed either side of the pillow, but it wasn't enough as he carried her into sinful pleasures.

She jerked, dug her fingers into his hair, knowing she should push him away, and instead realizing she was holding him closer. It was an intimacy she could share only with a man she loved. And she did love him.

She was fairly certain what he was doing to her was unlawful—and if not, it should be. Because it was deliciously wicked. He knew so many wondrous ways to be wicked, and she had a lifetime with him now to learn them all and to discover more ways to pleasure him.

She stuffed the pillow into her mouth to stifle her cries. He reached up and pulled it free.

"I want to hear you," he rasped.

And hear her, she was certain he did. Writhing beneath him, she heard her cries echo low and breathless, hardly aware they were coming from her. She held him close, dancing at the edge of intense pleasure. He knew when to stroke, when to suckle, when to pause, when to thrust with his tongue. He tempted and teased. He of the nimble fingers had a more nimble mouth. It stole her strength, her resistance.

Then she was screaming out his name and before the last of the shudders had wracked her body he was buried deep within her, his gaze holding hers as he rocked his hips against hers, his powerful thrusts causing the sensations to begin building again. She skimmed her hands down his back, cupped them around his buttocks, urging him on.

He sipped at her mouth, then drank greedily, and this time when she cried out, he captured the sound, his rough growl quickly following as he reached his own release. He collapsed over her, resting on his elbows, keeping some of his weight off her. She ran her soles along his calves, ran her hands over his back.

"Oh, you are the devil, and I am glad of it," she whispered lethargically.

He chuckled with satisfaction. "You're everything I could possibly desire, and I'm glad of that."

Jack awoke to the incredible sensation of his wife nibbling on his ear. *His wife*, a term he'd never thought to associate with himself. He was discovering she was insatiable, and he thought a wife could have no finer quality.

With a growl, he pounced on her, which caused her to shriek and giggle at the same time.

"I didn't think you'd ever wake up," she said.

He kissed her nose, her forehead, her chin. "I don't know if I've ever slept so well in my entire life. You fairly wore me out last night."

"I have no inhibitions left. You've chased them all away."

"How fortunate for me." He glided his hand down her side, cradled her hip, and urged her nearer, relishing the feel of her bare body against his. He thought flesh against flesh was the most remarkable of sensations, and nudity had the advantage of revealing everything a man might treasure. If he were king, he thought he might dispense with the practice of wearing clothes—well, except for brightly colored waistcoats.

"We need to get up," she murmured as he kissed the sensitive spot beneath her ear.

He playfully ground himself against her thigh. "Have you not noticed? I am up."

Her laughter echoed around them, shimmied through him. He wanted to be inside her when she did that.

"I did notice, but—" She pushed out from beneath him and scrambled out of the bed, not bothering to grab sheet or counterpane. She'd become quite the exhibitionist. Again, what a fortunate man he was.

"Come back here. Everything else can wait a bit longer," he said. "I've already told Henry he's having breakfast served in his bed this morning, and so are we."

"Is that what you two were conspiring about yesterday?"

"I thought I should start teaching him that when a gentleman has a lady, he should give her private attention as much as possible."

"Very nice. Unfortunately, yesterday I sent a missive

'round to Mr. Beckwith about our marriage. He replied that he'll come by this morning to bring you the final item. I don't want him to find us still abed."

Lunging for her, he grabbed her wrist and tugged until she tumbled back into his arms, tucking her up beneath him. "I don't care in the least about the final item. He can keep it."

"Have you no curiosity at all?"

"What does it matter what it is? Nothing Lovingdon can give me now is more valuable than you. He could take it all back and as long as I have you, it wouldn't matter."

Tears welled in her eyes. Tears of sorrow he hoped she'd seldom have, but tears of joy sparkled differently and those he enjoyed bringing her.

"You are not one to often say lovely things, Jack, but when you do, you have no idea how deeply I am touched."

"I don't believe in romance, Livy, but for you I will try to the best of my ability—as sadly lacking as that may be."

"I love you so much."

He wondered if those words would always slam into his heart and give him such an overwhelming sense of satisfaction. Taking her hand, he pressed a kiss to her palm, her wrist, her elbow . . .

With a sigh of surrender she murmured, "I have not the strength to resist you. I forbid you to make love to me before Beckwith arrives."

Chuckling at the challenge, he proceeded to show her, once again, that he was not a man who could be ordered about.

Chapter 23

Jack had told Livy true. He no longer cared about the final item. At this point it was little more than a bother, because it meant they couldn't spend the entire morning in bed engaged in making mad, passionate love.

Beckwith strode into the library with his leather satchel and bowed slightly. "Lady Olivia, Mr. Dodger, congratulations on your recent marriage."

Jack had known that by marrying him, Livy was giving up the title of duchess. Still, it was a surprise to hear her addressed as "Lady," an honor that came to her through her father. But she'd told him she was content with her new station in life. He intended to do all in his power to see she never regretted it.

"Thank you, Mr. Beckwith," Livy said, squeezing Jack's hand as though she thought he needed reassurance.

"We appreciate your making time for us in your busy schedule, Beckwith," Jack said. "As we're also quite busy, let's get this matter taken care of as quickly as possible, shall we?"

"Of course. If I may?" Beckwith indicated the desk.

"Absolutely. Whatever hastens your visit."

Olivia slapped his arm. Jack scowled at her. "What?"

"You're being inhospitable. Mr. Beckwith, would you care for some tea?"

Beckwith gave her a faint smile. "No, thank you. This matter won't take long."

He went to the desk and began arranging things to his satisfaction, removing items from his satchel. Jack and Olivia took the chairs they'd sat in the night Beckwith had read the will. The only difference was that now they held hands. Jack brought hers to his lips and kissed her fingers. As soon as Beckwith left, Jack was taking her back to bed. Or perhaps to the desk and then to the bed. Livy would no doubt be scandalized to know that Jack had placed the servants on notice: they were never to enter any room without knocking and receiving permission.

Jack could hardly fathom all that had happened in so short a time. He'd always wanted to be in charge of his life, but he couldn't deny others were somehow influencing its course. If Lovingdon hadn't named Jack guardian, he'd have never met Livy. For that alone, Jack owed Lovingdon his eternal gratitude.

Beckwith laid out several documents and a small velvet pouch. He folded his hands on top of the papers and cleared his throat. "The conditions of the will as originally stated have been satisfied with your recent marriage. Therefore, I shall read the portion of the will that has been kept from you." He picked up a sheaf of paper and once again cleared his throat.

"To Jack Dodger, christened Jack Dawkins, beloved

son of Emily Dawkins, I leave my most treasured possession, my gold pocket watch—handed to me by my father, who received it from his."

Jack stared in stunned silence as Beckwith opened the velvet pouch, removed its contents—a gold watch and heavy gold chain—and set them very carefully at the edge of the desk in front of Jack. Even from this distance, Jack could see the fine craftsmanship, could hear the quiet ticking away of time.

Jack tightened his fingers around Olivia's and with his free hand he reached for the timepiece—

And stopped within inches of grasping it. Shaking his head, he lounged back in the chair and held Beckwith's gaze. "He should not have left it to me. He should have left the watch to his son."

"I believe he did, Mr. Dodger."

Jack heard Livy's sharp intake of breath, felt as though his chest were collapsing on itself, as though all the air had been sucked from the room. He was aware of Olivia's fingers squeezing his almost painfully, her gaze on him, but he couldn't look at her, not yet.

He worked his hand free of her grasp. In spite of his best effort to control the tremors, his hand was shaking when he took the watch. Hesitantly he opened it. Nestled inside, opposite the clock face, was a familiar miniature. In disbelief, he looked at Beckwith, then at Olivia, whose brow was furrowed in concern. "It's my mother."

His voice was hoarse, as hoarse and rough as it had been when he'd screamed for her not to leave him.

Beckwith stood to indicate his job there was done. "The duke trusted me with all his secrets." He darted a quick glance at Olivia before looking back at Jack. "I hope you understand you may do the same. Had I realized you were going to marry, I would have brought this matter to your attention sooner. But whatever you decide, what has been learned today will go no farther unless you wish it so." He picked up an envelope and extended it toward Jack. "*This* I have not read, but it is addressed to you."

Jack took the offered envelope.

"Mr. Beckwith, out of curiosity, I would very much like to know who Lovingdon named in the second will," Olivia said.

For the first time, Beckwith seemed uncomfortable. "I fear there was no second will. The duke insisted I say one existed. Perhaps he knew his son better than one might think."

"He went to a lot of trouble for something that might have never come to pass," Jack growled, not at all surprised by the anger he heard seething in his voice. The icy shock of what he'd just learned was beginning to thaw and in its place was a savage fury.

"He knew it would come to pass, sooner than he wished," Beckwith said solemnly. "The duke was dying—a cancer for which there was no hope of a cure. If you will not think me callous, the fall gave him a quick death, which quite honestly, I think he preferred. At least he maintained a bit of dignity that his illness was certain to have stripped from him."

"He never said anything," Olivia murmured, and Jack heard the regret in her voice that Lovingdon had chosen to endure his pain alone.

"He didn't wish to trouble you," Beckwith responded.

"But I was his wife."

"I truly believe he meant to spare you of any worry. As he told me on numerous occasions, he was quite fond of you."

But fondness was not love. Silence permeated the air. Jack could only imagine what Olivia was feeling. His rage at Lovingdon was increasing with each tick of the timepiece. Lovingdon had not appreciated what he'd possessed. Jack reached out and squeezed her hand, hoping she understood with that simple touch that their marriage would hold no secrets, that every aspect of their lives would be shared.

"If you have no further need of me, I bid you both good day." With a quick bow, Beckwith took his leave.

The silence did not dissipate. If anything it grew heavier, thicker. Finally Olivia turned her palm over and threaded her fingers through Jack's. "I feel as though I've been hit by a carriage. I can hardly imagine what you must be feeling. You had no idea he was your father?" she asked quietly.

"No." He roamed his gaze over her beloved face, certain he knew the answer before he asked. "Did you?"

She slowly shook her head. "I hadn't a clue. I was married to him for six years and I knew him not at all. I want to be angry and lash out at him for not telling me all this. He was dying and I had no idea. But that was so typical of our relationship. He never truly shared anything with me. I may as well have been a broodmare."

"Don't say that, Livy. The man was a fool not to have recognized what he had in you."

She smiled softly. "Here you are comforting me when you must be more than devastated by this news." She indicated the envelope. "Are you going to read it?"

He swallowed hard and nodded. "But not here. I need to be alone. I will share it later—"

Reaching out, she cradled his cheek, touched her thumb to his lips. "You don't have to explain yourself to me, Jack Dodger."

He stood, bent down, and kissed the top of her head. "I love you, Livy," he whispered.

He strode from the library, down the hallway, to the door that led outside. He enjoyed the gardens because he always felt closest to his mother there. He made his way to the bench nestled among the roses and sat. Very slowly, he opened the envelope and removed the letter.

My dear son,

I always had grand expectations where you were concerned. The fact that you are now reading this letter is proof I judged your character correctly. You took after your mother in that regard. She possessed all the fine attributes I lacked.

Your sweet mother was a servant in this household when I fell in love with her. She was only fifteen when she discovered she was with child, my child. While I was seventeen, young and foolish. And weak, so incredibly weak. I did not have the courage to go against my parents' wishes, and perhaps far more unforgivable, I did not have the courage to stand beside my precious Emily as she faced society's censure with her head held high in order to bring you into the world. To protect my name, she never told anyone who fathered her child. Such was her admirable strength. She was turned out of the household, to make her way as best she could—and I did nothing to stop the injustice of it all.

The day I met you at Claybourne's I could hardly believe my fortune, that fate had brought you back to me. I was older then, wiser. I couldn't let such an opportunity pass. From afar, I watched your impatience with Claybourne's teachings, and I knew you would not remain with him for long, that you were far too independent and would quickly strike out on your own, and so I became your anonymous benefactor—anonymous because I still lacked the courage to face you and the sins of my past.

It was my greatest desire to embrace you as my son. On a few occasions I went to your club with that purpose in mind. But in the end, fearing the deserved disgust for my abhorrent behavior that I might see reflected in your eyes, I remained true to my character, I remained a coward.

I have no doubt that under your guardianship my second son will learn to harbor the strength his father lacked.

I do not expect you to think well of me. I do not expect you to think of me at all, but should I pass through your mind from time to time, I hope it is with the realization that I lived my life with nothing except regret—and perhaps that was punishment enough. It is my fervent hope, that

*God, in his infinite mercy, will grant me in death
what my cowardice denied me in life: a place at
your mother's side. It is not what I deserve, but
then that is the beauty of mercy. It allows even
the worst of sinners to be forgiven.*

                                    Respectfully yours,
                                        Lovingdon

It didn't escape Jack's notice that even now, he hadn't signed it "Father." But then Jack recognized it wasn't a title Lovingdon had earned, and tried to grasp some consolation in the fact he had not made a mockery of the term.

"I can see the resemblance now," Olivia said quietly.

Jack looked up at her.

"I think it's more difficult to notice because you are so dark and he was so fair. But sometimes when I walked into a room and saw you, for the briefest of moments I thought I saw him."

He didn't know what to say to that. He wasn't quite ready to talk about all this, didn't know if he ever would be.

"Are you all right?" Olivia asked. "You've been sitting out here for the better part of an hour."

It hadn't seemed that long to Jack. It seemed as though no time at all had passed. "I suppose I should have brought one of your clocks."

"Or your father's watch."

Jack shook his head. "He was not my father." He shook his head again, trying to deny the truth. "My mother was only fifteen when she gave birth to me. All my life, I thought she was a whore. He did that to her. His cowardice, his lack of strength."

He flung his arm toward the residence. "Do you know what Beckwith was talking about in there?" He didn't wait for her to answer. "The law does not allow a man to marry his father's widow."

She paled. "I'd not even considered that."

"The fortunate part is I have no desire to claim him as my father. I think he was more a bastard than I am." He leaned forward, burrowed his elbows into his thighs, and buried his face in his hands, crumpling the letter against his jaw. "Beckwith indicated he would hold our secret, but what if someone finds out? Our marriage could be declared illegitimate, our children will be bastards. Is there no end to the damage Lovingdon has wrought?"

She knelt before him, wrapped her hands around his, and pulled them away from his face. "Look at me," she demanded.

It was so hard to meet her gaze. It had been so much easier when he'd thought his father was a stranger, a man who had paid for the privilege to be intimate with his mother.

"I don't care," Livy stated emphatically. "I don't care if our marriage is nullified. As for our children, they will be loved and they will be taught to laugh at society's rules when they don't suit them. They will have your strength of conviction, Jack, and your mother's strength of purpose. We will all honor her. She was a remarkable woman. I wish I'd had an opportunity to know her. She gave me something very precious.

"I love you, Jack Dodger. I love you with all my heart and soul. If I must live with you without benefit of marriage, so be it. I shall do it with no regrets and with an amazing amount of pride that you've chosen me to stand at your side. And when I go to hell, I shall gladly dance with you."

Reaching out, he bracketed her waist and drew her up and onto his lap. He blanketed her mouth with his own, drinking deeply of her sweet nectar. How was it that this remarkable woman could love him, could want him, could look beyond his past—a bastard, an urchin, a thief—and appreciate him for the man he'd become?

Drawing back, he held her gaze. "You're all that matters, Livy. You and Henry." He dropped his head back. "Good God, he's my brother." He released a brittle laugh. "That's the reason Lovingdon named me guardian."

"I think our family tree will be more a maze than anything." She wrapped her arms around him, laid her head against his shoulder. "It all seems so wrong."

"The only thing of importance is that I love you. And I love Henry. From the moment I met him, I recognized something in him that touched something in me."

She lifted her head. "I'd rather not tell him until he's older. I think he's too young to understand all the ramifications."

Jack nodded, agreeing with her. Besides, Henry was young enough he might even lose the memories of his father.

"It's probably an awful thing to say, because you've had such a hard life, but it's shaped you into the man I love. And if Lovingdon had acknowledged you sooner, marrying you would not have been possible."

Jack smiled. "We'd have found a way, Livy. The wicked always do."

Epilogue

From the Journal of Jack Dodger

I was born Jack Dawkins, beloved son to Emily Dawkins, bastard son of Sidney Augustus Stanford, Duke of Lovingdon, Marquess of Ashleigh, and Earl of Wyndmere—a man who cared more for the pristine lineage of his titles than he did for either my mother or me.

I've yet to forgive him for allowing my mum to be turned out, and I doubt I shall ever hold him in high esteem. I consider it a blessing not to have been raised under his tutelage. He was never a father to me. That honor was held by another.

Feagan was a criminal destined for the gallows. That he managed to escape and live to a ripe old age was his good fortune and mine. He taught me to steal without getting caught. He taught me to survive and to harm others as little as possible while doing it. He gave me a family and he made me feel safe. In all ways that are important, he was my father.

When I was five, my mum gave me into an-

other man's keeping. I vaguely remember the last winter we were together, the winter that changed my life. She developed a deep, rattling cough that kept us both awake. She bloodied her handkerchiefs and ate little. I think she must have known she was dying, and she sought to provide for me as best she could—and she thought my father's cousin was the way to go. She died before spring and was buried in a pauper's grave, hopefully without ever learning the truth about the devil who'd taken me in.

It took a bit of work, but Feagan's brood is very skilled at ferreting out information. We discovered where my mum was buried, and Graves—a graverobber in his youth—saw to the matter.

My mum is now where she should have been all along, resting beside the man she loved. I cannot help but believe she loved him, because buried with her Graves found a locket similar to the one she'd given me. Inside was a miniature of the duke.

Because the Lovingdon crypt is at the family estate—which rightfully belongs to my young half-brother and stepson—I don't visit often. But I pay the gardener to deliver flowers to my mother every day. I built him a greenhouse so she has blossoms even in winter.

I remember my mum telling me once she sold flowers because it was the only way to have them in her life for a bit, and as sad as it was to have them taken from her, the joy they brought her while they were near was worth it.

No doubt I'm arrogant, but I like to think this could also be said of me: that while I was with her, I was a joy and not a burden.

In going through the duke's things, Livy found a journal. She says it chronicles the duke's love for a young servant—a love so deep it made it difficult for him to have another woman in his life. She thinks if I read it I will gain a better understanding regarding the strength and sacrifice required of the aristocracy, and that I will come to respect my father for his loyalty to duty and his desire to meet the expectations others had for him.

Perhaps she is right, but I am not yet ready. I believe a man must first look to himself to find the path he must walk, and that every man—from the poorest to the wealthiest—has difficult choices to make. I have known poverty, and I have known excess. Each brings its own troubles; each brings its own rewards. The men I respect are not influenced by their station in life or the amount of coin in their pockets. They remain true to themselves and those around them, regardless of how well— or poorly—life treats them. I am not altogether certain the duke could have survived the streets. We are all shaped by our pasts. I believe I am a better man because of mine. My children will no doubt live more grandly than I did, but I will see to it they look into the faces of the poor.

I suspect Henry will not become a typical lord—after all, he has me for a guardian. I have put the pocket watch away, to be given to Henry *on the day he reaches his majority. It seems only fitting. After all, he has fond memories of his father, which I do not possess.*

Livy no longer believes I was the worst choice. She is content, more than content I would say, with the knowledge that her son—all her children—will always be loved and protected by me. If I have any good trait at all, it is this: I'm fiercely protective of what is mine.

I suspect I shall never publicly claim Lovingdon as my father. To do so may result in the legitimacy of my marriage to Livy being brought into question. And I will not give her up. Not for any man's name or any man's fortune.

I remember a time when I hungered for the next coin, when I would do anything—anything at all—to possess it. Now, all I long for are moments spent with my Livy. She is the true gold of my life. The one who owns my heart and my soul—and for all eternity, my love.

At Avon Books, we know your passion for romance—once you finish one of our novels, you find yourself wanting more.

May we tempt you with . . .

- **Excerpts** from our upcoming releases.

- Entertaining **extras**, including authors' personal photo albums and book lists.

- Behind-the-scenes **scoop** on your favorite characters and series.

- **Sweepstakes** for the chance to win free books, romantic getaways, and other fun prizes.

- Writing **tips** from our authors and editors.

- **Blog** with our authors and find out why they love to write romance.

- **Exclusive content** that's not contained within the pages of our novels.

Join us at
www.avonbooks.com